Praise for *Come Back to Me*

"As a time-travel writer and a fan of Hedlund's work, I was eager to get my hands on this book. What a complete delight! I needed a 'break read,' and this fit the bill perfectly. There's a well-paced romance to make a reader Feel All the Feelings, an edge of science to bring on the intrigue, and suspense to keep the pages turning. I'll be first in line to get ahold of the second book in this duology."

Lisa T. Bergren, bestselling, award-winning author of *Waterfall*

"If you read time-travel romance—or even if you don't—this is a book you won't want to miss. Filled with intriguing possibilities and fascinating details of the Middle Ages, it's a story that will linger in your memory long after the last page is turned. I couldn't put it down and stayed up way too late one night because I simply had to see what happened to Marian and Will."

Amanda Cabot, bestselling author of *Dreams Rekindled*

"Brimming with wonder, *Come Back to Me* will keep you riveted until the last page, captivated by the possibilities. Readers who enjoy the whispers of an *Outlander* adventure and stories inspired by history and faith will love every moment of this perilous, romantic journey across time."

Melanie Dobson, award-winning author of *Catching the Wind* and *The Curator's Daughter*

"Fans of time-travel romance will be captivated by this sweeping tale full of suspense and intrigue and eager for the second book in Hedlund's Waters of Time series."

Booklist

"*Come Back to Me* by Jody Hedlund is one of the most engaging time-travel books I have ever read. It was addictive from the beginning to end."

Urban Lit Magazine

"Hedlund uses time travel, biblical knowledge, and history to create a thriller that will appeal to fans of Dan Brown's *The Da Vinci Code*."

Library Journal

Books by Jody Hedlund

The Preacher's Bride
The Doctor's Lady
Unending Devotion
A Noble Groom
Rebellious Heart
Captured by Love

BEACONS OF HOPE

Out of the Storm: A Beacons of Hope Novella
Love Unexpected
Hearts Made Whole
Undaunted Hope

ORPHAN TRAIN

An Awakened Heart: An Orphan Train Novella
With You Always
Together Forever
Searching for You

THE BRIDE SHIPS

A Reluctant Bride
The Runaway Bride
A Bride of Convenience
Almost a Bride

COLORADO COWBOYS

A Cowboy for Keeps
The Heart of a Cowboy

WATERS OF TIME

Come Back to Me
Never Leave Me

WATERS OF TIME #2

never leave me

JODY HEDLUND

Revell

a division of Baker Publishing Group
Grand Rapids, Michigan

IF
Hedlund

Published by Revell
a division of Baker Publishing Group
PO Box 6287, Grand Rapids, MI 49516-6287
www.revellbooks.com

Printed in the United States of America

Library of Congress Cataloging-in-Publication Data
Names: Hedlund, Jody, author.
Title: Never leave me / Jody Hedlund.
Description: Grand Rapids, MI : Revell, a division of Baker Publishing Group,
    [2022] | Series: Waters of time ; 2
Identifiers: LCCN 2021020290 | ISBN 9780800741129 (casebound) | ISBN
    9780800738440 (paperback) | ISBN 9781493434220 (ebook)
Subjects: GSAFD: Romantic suspense fiction.
Classification: LCC PS3608.E333 N48 2022 | DDC 813/.6—dc23
LC record available at https://lccn.loc.gov/2021020290

Baker Publishing Group publications use paper produced from sustainable forestry practices and post-consumer waste whenever possible.

22   23   24   25   26   27   28   7   6   5   4   3   2   1

To my editor, Rachel McRae.
Thank you for getting excited about this series with me,
for loving the stories and characters, and for being
willing to help me share them with the world.
I have appreciated your enthusiasm as well as your
encouragement in making this story the best it could be.

"I'M DYING, AND WE CAN'T CHANGE THAT." Even though Ellen Creighton spoke as softly and gently as possible, she could do nothing to soften the harshness of the truth.

In his wheelchair next to the garden bench where she reclined, Harrison Burlington's shoulders deflated. With his elbows propped against his knees, he jammed his fingers into his dark hair.

The May sun slid behind clouds as if to object to her pronouncement, and shadows crept out to cover the gardens surrounding Chesterfield Park, Harrison's enormous estate that had been in his family for generations.

Without the warm rays pouring over her, Ellen shivered. Her cashmere sweater over her silk blouse couldn't hold the chill at bay.

Oh, how she hated hurting Harrison.

She lifted her face, needing a dose of peace, letting the words of the Serenity Prayer whisper through her: *God, grant me the serenity to accept the things I cannot change; courage to change the things I can; and wisdom to know the difference. Living one day at a time; enjoying one moment at a time; accepting hardships as the pathway to peace.*

Focusing on the prayer had always kept her from veering down a dark tunnel and helped her accept the path she was on, no matter how short it might be. But lately, the darkness seemed to be creeping closer no matter how much she tried to avoid it.

She shifted her attention to the dangling wisteria forming an arch over the garden path. The purple hues were stunning against the vibrant green shrubs. She drank in the beauty and breathed in their sweet fragrance. The *chip chip chooee* of chaffinches serenaded her along with a garden warbler with a mellow song like a low, poignant violin melody.

Harrison released a deep, shuddering sigh.

"I'm sorry." She laid a hand on his arm.

His fingers wrapped around hers, warm and secure. Just like him. He'd been a constant presence in her life over the past year since her dad and sister Marian had died, and since her genetic disease, VHL, Von Hippel–Lindau syndrome, had stormed back into her body like a marauding army taking siege.

In her twenty-seven years of life, she'd never imagined she'd live longer than the rest of her family. Not after inheriting the deadly VHL from her mom. But she had outlasted everyone. By almost a year.

Now the end loomed within sight. And she was exhausted from fighting against the disease's invasion. She wanted to lift the white flag, surrender, and cease the battle. Then she could spend her remaining days without the stress of endless doctors' visits, grueling radiation, and painful surgeries.

"Please, Ellen." Harrison lifted his head. His green eyes were intense behind his thick glasses, and his features were strained. "Let's try one more round of radiation."

His plea was so desperate, how could she say no? So far, she hadn't been able to deny any of his requests. Not once in the past months as she'd battled renal cell carcinoma brought on by VHL.

She hadn't resisted when he'd suggested moving to Canterbury after the cancer had forced her to resign from her nursing job at the orphanage in Haiti. She hadn't resisted when he'd insisted she live at Chesterfield Park after surgeries had failed to keep the cancer from spreading. She hadn't resisted when he'd pushed for immunotherapy as well as new experimental treatments.

But just this morning, the doctors had received the results of a recent MRI, showing tumors on her spinal cord that were inoperable, and they'd suggested hospice care. She'd easily accepted what she'd known for years—she was dying, and nothing could save her.

All she could do was live each remaining day to the fullest and enjoy the time she had left—her philosophy since watching her mom waste away so thoroughly and painfully, especially the last year battling the disease. Mom's death had awakened Ellen to the fact that the disease was chasing her too and would one day catch up. Now it finally had.

She squeezed Harrison's hand and smiled at him. "You know what I'd really like?" In addition to more oxycodone to stave off the burning in her lower back.

Harrison leaned forward as though to soak in her smile and words. "Anything. Whatever you fancy, you'll have it."

Harrison had been a young scientist at Mercer when her dad had transferred from the Connecticut Pharmaceutical Research Center to the one in Canterbury. Harrison and her dad formed a friendship, and Harrison had been present in her life ever since.

He'd been at her graduation from Sevenoaks, the private boarding school in Kent she'd attended after Mom died. He'd flown with Dad to Columbia when she'd graduated with her pediatric nursing degree. And he'd spent every holiday and birthday with her family over the passing years. Truthfully, he'd been more present in her life than Dad, who'd always been distracted and busy with trying to find a cure for her disease.

At thirty-nine, Harrison was twelve years her senior. When she was younger, he'd seemed so much older and wiser, almost like a second dad. But in recent years, somehow the age gap had grown smaller and less significant, and he'd become more of a brother than a father figure.

"Your wish is my command, love." He situated her hand carefully within his, as though she might break if he put even the slightest pressure against her.

She could admit she'd grown frail and much too thin in recent weeks. The pain in her tailbone and back worsened every day. Her once-tanned skin was now pale, her healthy glow gone. She was thankful at least she still had her hair, even if the long blond waves were no longer lustrous. "I want a big juicy cheeseburger, salty French fries, and a chocolate shake." It was the kind of unhealthy meal she rarely ate. But what was the point of avoiding artery-clogging, cholesterol-inducing food now?

He sat back in his wheelchair, his mouth slightly agape. His hair, usually slicked back into neat submission, was lumpy from where he'd stuck his fingers. His bow tie was askew and his waistcoat uncharacteristically unbuttoned.

She couldn't remember a time she'd seen Harrison in anything other than a suit coat, waistcoat, and bow tie. He always dressed flawlessly, looking the part of the aristocratic nobleman he was. Now at the sight of him rumpled and ruffled, her smile widened.

He didn't smile in return. Instead, his brow furrowed, causing his glasses to slide down his nose, revealing even more clearly the anguish swirling in his eyes. "So, you're planning to give up? Just like that?"

"Harrison, please try to understand."

"I understand well enough. You'd rather sit back and die than fight to stay alive."

"I have tried to stay alive."

"Well, try harder!" He'd never shouted at her before, but his tone was decidedly loud. For the passing of several heartbeats, she could only stare at the frustration and helplessness etched into the lines of his face.

He'd already lost Dad and Marian, had watched them lie in comas and die before his eyes. Now she was all he had left.

Yes, he had a few distant cousins. But he rarely spoke to them. Yes, he had colleagues and childhood friends. But they were nothing more than acquaintances now—no one he was particularly close to. In fact, Ellen guessed he was closer to his butler, Drake, than anyone else.

She grazed the pearl necklace she wore most of the time, the one Marian had given her when she'd lain dying, the same one Mom had given Marian upon her deathbed. Stroking the glossy beads made her feel connected to Marian in a way she couldn't explain. Even so, Marian's death had left an empty place, one she hadn't been able to fill even though she'd tried hard over the past year by keeping busy with her new charity, Serenity House.

"I regret having to leave you behind." She reached for Harrison's hand again, and heat pricked the back of her eyes.

He yanked away at the same time he hit the power switch on his wheelchair. His chair hummed as it rolled backward. "If you regret it, then you'll hang on and keep fighting."

"I'm ready to die, Harrison."

His face blanched, and his lips thinned.

She despised that she had to state her feelings so starkly. But he was giving her no other choice.

"I won't let you die!" His whisper was harsh. Then he jerked his wheelchair around and whirred away.

She peered after him, wishing he wouldn't leave but knowing she had to let him go so he could finally accept what he couldn't change no matter how hard he tried, no matter how much of his vast fortune he spent, no matter the best treatments he could find.

• ● •

Harrison rolled down the marble pathway toward the side entrance, fuming and embarrassed at the same time. This was one of those times when he wished he'd been able to stomp off for effect, slapping his feet with each heavy stride, looking strong and purposeful. Instead, he bounced along at his wheelchair's top speed—five miles per hour.

If he glanced back, he'd find Ellen's bright blue eyes upon him, full of pity.

His chest tightened. He didn't want her pity. He wanted her admiration. Wanted her to see him as capable, not lost and alone in the world once she died.

Of course, he *would* be dreadfully lost and alone without her—more so than she'd ever be able to understand and in a way he mustn't reveal to her.

To be fair, Ellen never paid attention to his disability. At times, he even wondered if she realized he was in a wheelchair and couldn't walk. She had always been the one person who made him feel whole and strong.

But at this moment as he directed his wheelchair up the ramp, the pity in her eyes trailed him, and he loathed himself, loathed his wheelchair, and loathed his weakness.

"Lord Burlington." Drake opened the side door and held it wide as Harrison steered into the passageway that led to the kitchen. His butler bowed his graying head in deference, his stooped shoulders and thin frame belying his strength and stamina.

Drake had been his personal attendant for ages and knew Harrison better than anyone. Even now, the older man shifted his sights toward Ellen, anticipating Harrison's request. "Have no fear, my lord. I'll carry her back inside when she's ready."

"Many thanks." Harrison wheeled to the lift, pressed the arrow that would take him up to the ground floor, then expelled a weary breath.

"You should tell her, eh?" Drake's statement contained a gentle rebuke.

Harrison stared directly ahead at the lift doors. He considered pretending he didn't know what Drake was referring to. But the older man would see past his playacting. Nevertheless, he couldn't make himself acknowledge the bold truth. "I have nothing to tell her, Drake."

Nothing except that he desperately loved her—and not merely as a friend the way she thought he did. No, he loved her fully and completely as a man loves a woman. He had for years. He'd never spoken of his love to anyone—not even to Drake, but he wasn't surprised his attendant had sorted it out.

Behind him, Drake refrained from saying anything more, stepped outside and closed the door, leaving him alone. Harrison swallowed hard, but the lump in his throat remained. Only when he was safely ensconced in the privacy of the lift did he bury his face into his hands. He wanted to give way to the need to weep, except he wasn't a man who easily allowed himself to express emotions, even privately. His display of frustration in the garden with Ellen was more than enough. And now he regretted even that.

He was, after all, a scientist, a logical, rational thinker. He examined everything from each angle, analyzed the data, and drew solid empirical conclusions. He didn't let feelings cloud his judgment.

As the lift dinged and came to a halt, Harrison schooled himself into his usual composed demeanor. The doors opened to the front hall, which was a room unto itself. The floor was inlaid with white marble and the walls lined with dark oak paneling carved with exquisite detail. Two dozen tall columns supported a center dome decorated with colorful stained glass circles. A massive fireplace graced one wall, surrounded by the same white marble as the floors.

Marian had informed him the room in the Middle Ages had been a grand hall with trestle tables against the walls and a larger fireplace. She'd also maintained that the closet at the far end had housed an office used by the master.

Harrison had been fascinated by her detailed description of the original manor and had sketched out the floor plan the way she described it. He'd even excavated a vault underneath the hall closet. How could she have known it was there if she hadn't crossed over to the past and witnessed it firsthand?

Shoving aside the doubts that had assailed him more often of late, he powered his wheelchair toward the eastern wing he'd reconstructed over the past two decades to make more handicap accessible—doors and hallways widened, rails and grips strategically positioned, windows lowered and enlarged. He'd even had an extensive laboratory built so he could work from home as frequently as he wanted, which in recent months had been nearly all the time.

He pressed the button on the wall next to his lab and waited as the automated door opened. The waft of sulfur and the scents of other chemicals greeted him.

He wheeled inside, heedless of the untidiness of cylinders, spreadsheets, empty bottles, bags, and plastic tubing scattered about—his fruitless attempts to find a cure for VHL. Stifling a yawn, he stretched his arms over his head. He'd had too many sleepless nights of late. But the desperation pressed hard against his chest and wouldn't let him rest.

"Hospice?" The word echoed in the room, and it contained every trace of bitterness in his soul. He'd wanted to tear off the physician's head when he'd suggested it at the appointment. All the way back to Chesterfield, he'd ranted about the dreadful suggestion.

Now look what it had done. Given Ellen permission to stop trying.

"Rubbish, I say. The doctor's advice was all rubbish." He rolled over to his desk and peered down at the latest beta cell regeneration study he'd focused on last night. Should he work out the figures again?

What choice did he have? He was running out of time and absolutely had to discover a cure.

If only he could find Arthur Creighton's ultimate cure.

His attention shifted to the enormous world map he'd pinned above his desk, to the various red and blue pins scattered all over the continents. The blue dots represented places where miraculous healings had supposedly happened throughout history, many of them related to holy water or holy oil. Of course, Canterbury and Walsingham in England had the most documented miracles.

Arthur had concluded such miracles could be traced to the Tree of Life in the garden of Eden, specifically seeds that had been preserved from the Tree of Life and brought to Canterbury and Walsingham for safekeeping. Eventually the seeds had affected the groundwater in those locations, so that those who drank of it were cured of their diseases. Monks had bottled and sold the holy water to pilgrims in flasks known as ampullae. In Canterbury, such flasks were called St. Thomas ampullae and contained engravings of Thomas Becket, a murdered archbishop who'd been named a saint.

While Arthur's theory about the seeds from the Tree of Life was only speculation, historical records attested to the miracles that had taken place at both Canterbury and Walsingham in the Middle Ages. The very stained-glass windows within Canterbury Cathedral proclaimed the healing power of the holy water.

Over the past year, Harrison had researched other sites throughout Europe. If seeds from the original Tree of Life had arrived in England for protection from the invasion of the barbarians during the Roman Empire, then perhaps guardians of the seeds had taken remnants to other parts of Europe as well.

In fact, he'd recently inspected the Sanctuary of Our Lady in Lourdes, France. In the 1860s, a young woman named Bernadette claimed to have visions while washing in a spring. After her miraculous visions, more than seven thousand cures were reported as a result of the spring. Scientists at that time investigated the cures and analyzed the water. While they'd found it high in mineral content, they discovered nothing else that might contribute to the healings. Now nothing remained in the spring except normal, natural water. Harrison had gone there himself and tested it.

He'd also made a quick trip to Sienna, Italy, where over two thousand miracles were reported during the 1400s and associated with St. Bernardino. Unfortunately, no amount of investigating had uncovered any springs or other remnants of the holy water that had supposedly contributed to the cures.

The red dots on the world map over his desk represented every museum, every lead he'd pursued in his attempt to find more St. Thomas ampullae, which held the only known holy water left in the world.

Historians and museum curators knew of only three original St. Thomas ampullae to survive from the Middle Ages. One had been a part of a collection in England along with other relics passing from church to church as part of an exhibit. Arthur had stolen that ampulla when the relics came to Canterbury. Apparently the other two had disappeared over recent years from the museums where they'd once been displayed. And no one knew where they were.

Harrison's private antiquarians were looking for the second and third ampullae day and night. But so far, they hadn't discovered anything, anywhere. When he'd phoned up each of the fellows a short while ago, he'd told them to redouble their efforts, to branch out beyond museums, churches, and abbeys.

The men indicated they weren't the only antiquarians hunting for the St. Thomas ampullae, which meant Lionel Inc. also had people searching for them. Harrison could only pray his antiquarians would come across them first.

He pulled his mobile out of his inner waistcoat pocket, checking again as he already had a dozen times for a voice mail from the antiquarians. But there was nothing new.

Shoulders deflating, he stuffed his mobile away. What if there was *nothing* to Arthur's ultimate cure? What if the holy water didn't have any power after all—not to cause movement through time or to heal?

Ellen hadn't believed any of Marian's tales about crossing to the Middle Ages. Instead, she'd attributed her sister's experiences to the realistic and sometimes odd dreams that coma patients could have. In the end, Ellen blamed the holy water for poisoning both her dad and sister.

She wanted nothing more to do with her dad's theories and research, which was one of the reasons why Harrison hadn't told her about his efforts to track down the last of the ampullae. She'd specifically asked him not to look for any more holy water, had shed tears while begging him to abandon the dangerous pursuit.

Although he wanted to honor her request, he hadn't been able to stop the search. At times he felt guilty for his deceit, especially when he'd received permission from Canterbury's Archaeological Trust to excavate under St. George's Church tower on St. George's

Street. He'd spent thousands of pounds to pay a crew to drill underground and locate a wellspring rumored to have once been there and thought to be the original source of the miracle holy water.

Of course, he hadn't disclosed his true motive to any of the workers—that he hoped the wellspring contained curative residue from the Tree of Life, the same water that had been used to fill the St. Thomas ampullae. But after digging as deep as the equipment could go, the excavation team had come up dry. If there had ever been a wellspring in that spot, it was long gone.

After the failed attempt, more doubts had crowded in. Was Ellen right? Was he crazy for believing holy water could cure the ill or allow a healthy person to cross over time? Was the water poisonous after all?

Harrison reversed from his desk and steered to the window. He drew his wheelchair up at an angle that allowed him to look outside without being seen. He easily found the spot where Ellen was still sitting, her legs curled up underneath her, her arms crossed, her hair fluttering in the breeze. Even from a distance, her beauty made his heart ache.

In spite of the weight loss, she was willowy and graceful, tall with endless long legs. With her blue eyes framed by thick lashes, she had the power to knock the breath from his lungs with one glance.

She had that power over most fellows and could have had any number of suitors. Men were always agog over her. And even though he'd tried not to be jealous watching her interact with other fellows over the years, he'd had to swallow his frustration too many times to count.

Thankfully, she'd never grown serious with anyone. He wasn't sure how his heart could have handled seeing her in another man's arms.

Lately, he'd begun to suspect that with her VHL and reoccurring cancer, she'd purposefully thwarted relationships because she didn't want to burden a man with her problems.

Yet didn't she realize the right man wouldn't care about her VHL? The right man would love her regardless and would want to spend every moment of her remaining time together.

She lifted her face to the sunshine. The strand of pearls she always wore glistened, drawing his attention to her slender neck and tightening the longing deep within him.

He shouldn't have had a row with her, should have stayed in the garden and enjoyed being with her. While he wouldn't budge from his endeavors to save her, he had to make more effort to relish the time together.

He had to go out there straightaway, apologize, and sit with her, taking in every detail and moment with her. He'd ride with her to Serenity House for the afternoon and spend time with her there. He loved watching her interact with the families and children who stayed at her dad's remodeled home as a place of respite.

Regardless of how ill she'd been and still was, she continued to pour her heart out into the Serenity Foundation, a charity she'd started last year to assist children struggling with terminal genetic diseases. Not only did she provide the house with a loving staff, but she also granted wishes to each of the children who were a part of the program, giving them an experience she hoped would improve the quality of their lives.

He was proud of her. She'd taken the vast inheritance left to her by her father, along with Marian's share, and invested it in not only the Serenity Foundation but also a VHL research fund and had established an ongoing endowment for the Haitian orphanage where she'd once worked.

The truth was that he needed to do better at keeping his worries and frustrations to himself. In fact, he ought to plan a trip for them, take her somewhere glamorous where they wouldn't have to think about her disease for a few days.

A rush of adrenaline pumped through him. Yes, that was precisely what they needed. He powered his wheelchair so quickly he bumped against the wall and knocked into the coat of arms hanging next to the window. Half-hidden behind the thick curtains he rarely closed, the large shield wobbled.

He stuck out a hand to keep it from falling. At the same moment, the drapes shifted, giving him full view of the family coat of arms. Although long out of use and now nothing more than a symbol of bygone eras, it was still part of his family's heritage.

The golden stag took up the center of a crimson background with an azure outer edge. The stag bore enormous antlers upon its head, a flowing beard down its chest, and a simple strand of pearls around its neck. It stood in the statant position, a regal creature with all four legs firmly planted on the ground.

He straightened the shield, then froze. Pearls?

The emblem had always been that way. He hadn't thought anything of it previously. But with the vision of Marian's pearls gracing Ellen's neck just moments ago, his thoughts tumbled together. The larger teardrop pearl at the front of Marian's necklace was the same size as the larger teardrop pearl on the strand around the stag's neck.

He ventured more than one such style of pearl necklace existed. But how could it be a coincidence that Marian's and the stag's were the same?

He'd always thought the pearls a strange part of the family heraldry. But what if it wasn't so strange after all?

2

HARRISON TOOK OFF his spectacles and rubbed his eyes with his palms. He slipped his glasses back on, but his fingers were shaking so much he could hardly position them.

When he'd researched his family crest long ago, he hadn't found heraldry belonging to other families containing strands of pearls. Crowns and coronets used pearls interwoven with leaves to distinguish marquises from earls and barons. But the Burlington arms had remained unique with its entire pearl strand around the stag's neck.

What if the emblem was a message from the past? From Marian?

His mind spun for another logical explanation. Anything. But as he grasped for some rationalization, his heartbeat sped with excitement. Had she lived on in the past? Surely this was a sign.

He shook his head. Was he mad to continue to entertain the possibility that Marian had crossed the time and space continuum?

The more he'd studied the physics behind the structure of time, the more he'd realized time worked much differently than it appeared. Its operation was a great mystery that brilliant scientists were still attempting to understand. Most agreed time wasn't linear but instead fluctuated within a quantum dynamic.

If the *here* and *there* could coexist at the same time, wasn't it possible *then* and *now* could also coexist? Based on a logical way of thinking, people had once believed the earth was flat and that the sun revolved around the earth. Both theories were proven wrong, which demonstrated that reality was often different than what was perceived.

He suspected the perception of time to a finite man was also different than reality. Even so, he couldn't prove Marian had crossed to another era and was living *then* instead of *now*. Or maybe he could prove it . . .

He released the curtain, noticing that the drape fell back over the shield, half-concealing the emblem. He hadn't had any reason to examine it in recent months, since before all that had happened with Marian and Arthur. Now with the knowledge of Arthur's research and the possibility of crossing time, he shifted the curtain again and studied the coat of arms with fresh eyes, trying to recall everything he'd once learned.

A stag. In heraldry it stood for wisdom. And long life.

The hair on his arms prickled. Long life? That wasn't a coincidence, was it?

What did the antlers represent?

He plucked his mobile from his pocket and typed in a search. As the results popped up, he sat back in his chair, genuinely staggered.

Branch-like antlers were said to represent the Tree of Life and were also a symbol of healing.

And the pearls? What symbolism did they contain?

His fingers couldn't fly fast enough over his mobile's keyboard.

He pulled up the first search result. "Pearls are symbolic of wisdom and are born of water. People used to believe that pearls dissolved in wine could bring about immortality."

Wisdom and water and immortality.

He let his mobile fall into his lap, his thoughts zinging with anticipation and hope that he hadn't allowed himself to feel in months.

"Marian, did you do this to communicate with us?" he whispered.

If she had lived and amended the family heraldry, the effort would have taken quite a lot of trouble. She would have had to gain permission from the head of the house, the man she supposedly married. If her husband had been in agreement, then they would have had to petition officials, commission the design, and wait for the artist to complete the work, which would have entailed redoing all the crests around the manor as well as on the weaponry and other equipment used in battle.

If indeed Marian had made the change, why would she do it? Why go to so much effort?

Was she attempting to assure them she'd lived a good and full life?

He angled his head and studied the shield again thoroughly. With all the symbolism, she had to be telling him not to give up on Arthur's research into the Tree of Life and the miracles associated with the holy water.

Harrison picked up his mobile and texted Drake. Within minutes, his butler opened the door and poked his head inside.

"Would you like me to lay up tea and biscuits, my lord?"

Harrison nodded in the direction of the shield. "Have a look at the family crest and tell me what you think."

Drake stepped into the room, stood next to Harrison, and stared at the shield. "Is something amiss, my lord?" Drake asked tentatively, as though somehow Harrison was testing him.

"Think on it, Drake. What do you see?"

Drake studied the picture. "Well . . . honestly, nothing new."

"Look more carefully. Anything stand out?"

The older man examined the shield again, as though searching for the answer to a riddle. After a moment, he shifted nervously. "I'm flummoxed."

Harrison bit back a sigh. Was he wanting so badly to see a message in the coat of arms that he was letting his imagination get away from him?

Drake was quiet for several heartbeats before snapping his fingers. "The pearls, eh? Those look like Miss Ellen's pearls."

"Precisely." Harrison allowed himself a deep breath. "Not only do they look like them, I predict they are one and the same. Marian purposefully had the pearls painted in the crest."

Drake furrowed his brows.

"Do you know what this means?" Harrison didn't allow Drake a chance to answer before continuing. "It must mean Marian survived the time crossing and is alive in the past."

Harrison knew he sounded insane. But fortunately, Drake was accustomed to his idiosyncrasies from the previous year, when Harrison first learned of Arthur's speculations about breaching the space-time continuum. Drake had helped Marian and Harrison find the ampullae hidden in the crypt of Canterbury Cathedral. The faithful butler had protected them and gone along with Harrison's wild conjectures without any questions.

If Marian was trying to encourage him not to abandon the research, then that meant . . .

Harrison sat forward, renewed energy coursing through him. "We need to check the vault and crypt. Both of them. Right away."

Drake's brows furrowed. "Right away?"

Harrison understood Drake's skepticism. They'd searched the vault from top to bottom numerous times following the excavation. Harrison had even paid a specialist to come in and exhume further. But they'd found nothing of any consequence—a few historical artifacts and some jewels. But mostly everything of value had been removed when the vault had been filled in. Over the ensuing months, Harrison had no reason to go back to either the vault or the cathedral crypt, especially since at the mere mention of either one, Ellen got worked up.

Of course, with his assumption that Marian had died in the past as well as the present, he'd had no reason to look for more holy water in those places. But if he was analyzing the symbolism in the family emblem correctly, then he'd given up on her too soon.

If she'd lived, it was still possible for her to pass along holy water. He'd learned from the previous exchanges of ampullae that something in the molecular makeup of the holy water allowed it to defy constraints, the particles moving at planck, maybe even chronon, time—the smallest wavelengths possible. On some quantum level, the holy water itself was timeless, making it possible to transmit from one era to another.

In other words, just because the holy water hadn't been in the usual hiding places when he'd first checked, didn't mean it wouldn't be there now, not if Marian had located more for them.

"It certainly won't hurt us to check again, will it, Drake?" He pressed the switch on the control panel of his wheelchair and started for the door, his heart whirring as fast as his chair.

Only one other person wanted to save Ellen as much as he did. Marian. She would even do something as crazy as adjust the family heraldry and fill it with clues to get his attention.

"Very well, my lord." Drake moved ahead of him and swung the door open. "Where to first?"

"The vault. Marian would only use the crypt as a last resort." Marian knew the danger they'd encountered underneath Canterbury Cathedral when they'd previously gone there to retrieve ampullae, and she would spare them trouble if possible.

Not that they would encounter trouble. From what Harrison could tell, Lionel Inc., Mercer Pharmaceutical's biggest rival, had given up the pursuit of Arthur Creighton's ultimate cure after Arthur's and Marian's deaths. A new drug that led to comas and then death wasn't anything worth stealing. At the very least, Lionel's hired thugs hadn't harassed them further. Even so, Harrison kept in regular contact with his private investigator, Sybil Huxham, who had been helpful last year in tracking his kidnapper.

Drake led the way to the front hallway room and to the closet at the far end, where he readied the lift. During the excavation, Harrison had installed an automated lift not only to allow him access to the vault but also to enable the excavation team to more easily remove the stones and bricks and dirt that had been used to fill in the underground room.

Now as he wheeled himself onto the metal grate and started down, cool, damp air met his descent along with the darkness of the cavern. The lift landed with a jolt that reverberated through Harrison's wheelchair into his bones as though to ground him in reality. He had to keep from getting his hopes too high. He didn't know how he could endure more disappointment. But what else could the symbolism in the family emblem mean?

Harrison waited as Drake used his torch from his mobile to locate the electrical switch. Although the vault hadn't ever had electricity, Harrison had done up simple wiring to provide enough light for the excavation team. As two bulbs overhead flickered to life, Harrison wheeled through the layer of dirt that remained on the floor.

The walls contained a dozen or more recesses. His gaze skimmed over the ledges that had likely once been lined with priceless treasures but now contained only cobwebs and dust.

Drake followed behind him. "Where to start, my lord?"

"You start high." Harrison steered toward one of the hiding spots. "And I'll search low."

Harrison didn't bother to shine his torch into the first recess. He stuck his hand in and stretched it back as far as it would go. His fingers brushed the grit of stone and dust and rat droppings but nothing more.

He moved to the next nook.

"Harrison?" Ellen called from above the lift.

Harrison froze at the same time as Drake. Their eyes connected, and the guilt flashing across Drake's face surely mirrored the guilt on his.

"Are you down there? I'm getting ready to go to Serenity House."

Maybe he should have waited to search until she was in bed later. He shoved aside his trepidation and wheeled toward the lift. "I'll be back up in a jiffy, love."

"What are you doing?" Her voice contained an accusatory note.

He couldn't tell her he'd just realized Marian had lived and subsequently redesigned the family emblem with clues that communicated to them from the past. Ellen wouldn't believe him, would only get upset at him for bringing up the time crossing again. The last thing he wanted was for her to worry or stress.

Maybe if he kept things vague. "Nothing's amiss. We're making a study of something."

"A study of what?"

"I was keen to have a look. That's all."

"I'm coming down. I want to see what you're doing."

He exchanged another glance with Drake, who shook his head as if to confirm that she wasn't buying his pitiful act, and now it was impossible to budge her. "It's of no consequence. Really."

"Then you won't mind my coming down."

"It's too damp down here for you, love." He chucked out the last excuse he could find.

"Please, Harrison?" Her tone turned soft and pleading, one

he couldn't resist. In all honesty, there was nothing about her he could resist.

With a sigh, he pressed the lift button, sending it up.

A minute later, the clanking signaled her descent. When the steel grate touched the dirt floor, she stepped off, clutching her sweater closer about her shoulders. Her knuckles were white and her face especially pale under the sallow glow of the bulbs. Her blue eyes swept around the vault as though she expected to catch him in the act of doing something he shouldn't be.

She took a step forward but then stopped and reached for the wall to support herself, clearly too weak to be walking around on her own.

Harrison swiveled toward her and wrapped a hand around her wrist, pulling her onto his lap. She didn't protest but instead sank down, almost as if she was relieved not to be standing anymore.

He situated her closer than he needed to but couldn't help it. "You should have waited for Drake to carry you inside."

"My nurse assisted me." She rested her head on his shoulder, her long hair brushing against his cheek and bringing with it her lemony, lavender scent, and he fought the urge to bend in and nuzzle his nose against her neck.

He'd pulled her onto his lap several times over the past couple of weeks as she'd gradually weakened. Although he detested her weakness and all it represented, he couldn't deny he was taking advantage of having this excuse to hold her.

The first time he'd tugged her down they'd been in the gardens. She'd squirmed just a little, enough for him to know she was embarrassed. She tried to push herself back up, claiming she was too heavy for him, that she would hurt him, that together they'd break his wheelchair. He only laughed off her concerns and proceeded to wheel around the garden paths.

Ever since, she'd allowed him to capture her without resisting.

In fact, she stayed longer in his embrace each time he did it. He wanted to think she liked being near him just as he did with her. But he ventured her willingness to ride on with him in his wheelchair had more to do with her increasing debility.

He'd attempted to keep a modicum of propriety in his hold in every instance. But even now, his fingers twitched with the need to caress her.

Only the Lord knew how many times he'd tried to get her out of his system. But something about her sent his hormones raging like an adolescent rather than a full-grown man.

He'd been reacting that way ever since she completed her first year of college and had returned to Canterbury to live with Arthur. Before that, Harrison had seen her as nothing more than a child. But that summer, everything changed. She'd turned into a woman—one who dazzled him with just one look, one word, one smile.

Of course, he felt terrible for having such a reaction to her, especially because of the difference in their ages. She was so young and busy with her friends and education, and he was advancing with his career.

As much as he denied the attraction, it only grew with each passing year. By the time she graduated from Columbia, he'd known he wouldn't ever feel the same way about any other woman as he did about Ellen.

Even so, he made himself date occasionally, never at want for women who longed to be with him. With his title, family history, wealth, and power, he realized he was considered a prized match.

The trouble was, he couldn't muster any enthusiasm for anyone else, not even when Ellen was halfway around the world having her own adventures.

When she graduated, he considered the possibility of pursuing her. But he'd been embarrassed by the reality of his situation, that with his type of spinal cord injury, he might never be able to share normal marriage intimacies with a wife, and producing a baby would be complicated, if not impossible.

He finally concluded he wasn't meant to marry Ellen, maybe never meant to marry anyone. Besides, Ellen hadn't ever shown any interest in him beyond that of a friend. She never seemed ready to settle down, wanted to make a difference in children's lives, loved working at the Haitian orphanage. He guessed she'd never intended to leave Haiti and probably wouldn't have, if not for her worsening VHL.

The truth was, he'd lost the slight chance he might have had with her long ago. And now he simply wanted to take care of her and make her happy for as long as she had.

"The day has been really tedious for you." He attempted but failed to keep the huskiness out of his voice. "Let's get you up into bed for a rest."

"I'm okay now." She raised her head and smiled at him, the kind of smile that turned his already half-melted insides into complete liquid.

"But you're worn out, I'd say."

"I wanted to make sure you weren't angry with me." Her arms wrapped around his neck, bringing their faces much too close for his own good, especially when she lifted her long lashes in that slow, mesmerizing way she had and then peered at him with her innocent eyes.

"I could never be angry at you." Never. Didn't she know that by now?

Drake gave a small cough, one that told him he needed to get on with confessing the truth about how he felt.

"Then you're not frustrated?" Her fingers at the back of his neck grazed his hair, making him nearly forget her question.

"Only for a second."

"So, tell me the truth. What are you doing down here?"

Drake turned his back and stuck his arm deep into another recess, leaving Harrison to fend off Ellen's query by himself. What kind of excuse could he give her that wouldn't disturb her?

"They're here!" Drake shoved his arm farther into the hole in the wall.

At the excitement in Drake's voice, Harrison's pulse jumped.

"Two of them, my lord." Drake was stretching into the crevice as far as he could reach.

"Two what?" Ellen sat up.

Harrison shot Drake a warning look, hoping his butler wouldn't reveal anything more, not until he had time to prepare Ellen.

But Drake was focused entirely on the recess and responded before Harrison could stop him. "There are two ampullae tucked away back in here."

"Ampullae?" Ellen's eyes widened.

Harrison stumbled for an answer. "I can explain—"

"You know how I feel about the ampullae." She pushed off his lap.

He wanted to stop her, but if Drake had genuinely found ampullae, then he and Ellen were headed for a battle—a battle he intended to win.

Drake removed his arm from the recess and beamed as he held up two ancient containers.

The rectangular-shaped flasks tapered to spouts and were flanked on each side by arm-like handles. Even in the dim light, he could see the engraved picture of St. Thomas Becket with a fleur-de-lis pattern decorating the edges.

"Absolutely tremendous." A chill raced over Harrison. "Original St. Thomas ampullae."

Drake shook them. "Aye, and they both still contain the holy water."

"No!" Ellen's cry echoed in the cavern. "They contain nothing but poison."

Harrison wheeled toward Drake and took one of the flasks, unable to keep his fingers from wavering. He rubbed the dull metallic container, marveling at the faded but distinct depiction of the saint with one side showing angels flying over Becket and the other showing him being attacked by the knights who'd murdered him.

After all the months of searching, of hiring the antiquarians, of spending countless exhausting hours making phone calls and following leads, this was almost too good to be true.

"You've been looking all along, haven't you?" Ellen hugged her arms to her chest as though to protect herself from his answer.

He wanted to deny her accusation, but what was the point now? "I had to."

"After it killed Dad and Marian?" Tears glistened in her eyes, magnifying the pain there.

"But that's just it, love. Marian has to be alive in the past—"

"Please, Harrison. Don't say anything more. Please."

"How else would these ampullae appear?"

"Maybe they were here all along, and you missed them the other times you searched."

"I hired a special archaeologist. You know that." During the last hours of Marian's life, he'd scrambled to find an ampulla with the hope of being able to keep Marian from dying. "He had special equipment and detectors. How could he overlook these when Drake found them in only minutes?"

"Seconds, my lord." Drake cupped the ampulla reverently.

Ellen shook her head and swiped a stray tear from her cheek. "I don't care how the ampullae got here, the liquid inside is deadly, and we can't take any chances."

"You're already dying." Harrison's statement came out much more impassioned than he meant it to.

"So, you want me to fall into a coma?" Her tone rose a notch too. "Is that how you want to squander your last days with me? By my bedside, watching me on life support?"

"No—"

"I don't want to waste my time either. I want to spend my final weeks—days—relishing every second of every minute, not lying in a bed unable to be with you or with the children staying at Serenity House."

"I understand that. But to be fair, what if your father was right? What if the water has the power to heal the sick?"

"Marian tried, Harrison. And look where it got her."

Marian had consumed one of the flasks they'd located in the cathedral crypt and had fallen into a coma. She'd left them instructions to check the crypt once a week for the ampullae she planned to hide there.

Even though it had taken over two weeks, an ampulla had finally shown up in the crypt of Canterbury Cathedral—one that Marian had hidden there for them while she crossed over to the Middle Ages in the 1380s.

After they'd given her the holy water, she'd revived from her coma. Only then had they sorted out the fact that her 1380s body had fallen into a coma since a body could only be conscious in one era at a time. Belatedly, they'd realized that due to the lack of medical technology, Marian wouldn't be able to survive a coma in 1381. Once she died there, she would also die in the present. Unless she drank a second dose of the holy water.

Of course, Harrison hadn't been able to track down more, even after excavating the vault. But it was now clear she'd gotten sufficient doses of holy water to save her 1380s body. Since the holy water was more plentiful in the Middle Ages, it made sense that Marian's husband had found some and saved her.

Ironically, Harrison still had no idea if the holy water was truly the cure Arthur had believed it to be, the cure he'd risked everything—including his life—to find. While they'd learned it had the capability to allow time crossing, they'd yet to see any proof the holy water could heal.

"You know my dad was crazy." Ellen was watching him, likely reading his thoughts. "Both his and Marian's deaths prove just how crazy his theory was."

Harrison fingered the cork in the top of the flask. It was pushed in deeply and tightly to keep the liquid safe. "Please have a go at it, Ellen." He met her gaze only to find she was wiping more tears from her cheeks.

She shook her head. "Don't you want to spend as much time with me as possible before I die?"

"Naturally, I do." She had no comprehension just how much he ached to be with her.

"And what about Josie? I need to finish making her wish come true."

Josie Ansley was an adorable girl of only six with a rare case of Batten disease, currently staying at Serenity House with her parents. A bright, energetic girl only a couple of years ago, she'd deteriorated quickly both physically and mentally. Ellen was doing everything she could for Josie and her family to give them a restful vacation in Serenity House. She spared no expense, had an excellent staff, and spoiled every family who came.

While Batten disease was fatal and had no known cure, the family had heard of an extremely rare experimental gene therapy drug for Batten. Josie's parents were now raising money for the treatment with the hope of giving it to their daughter soon. Of course, Ellen and the Serenity Foundation were helping not only with the funding but also in attempting to speed the drug's process through MHRA regulators.

"But what if this water has the power to heal you?" he asked.

"And what if it doesn't?"

Harrison wanted her to take the risk. If she didn't, she'd most definitely die. But if she drank it, there was a possibility it could heal her.

"Please, Ellen." His voice rose with the earnest passion that burned within him. "Won't you at least consider it?"

A sob escaped from her lips. She clamped her palm over her mouth, spun toward the lift, and stepped onto the metal grate.

"Please, love." He didn't care that he was begging. He worked his fingers around the cork, loosening it. Pieces crumbled away until the flask was open, ready, beckoning.

With her back facing him, she shook her head.

Desperation crept into his chest and began to constrict his airways. He had the feeling he could plead with her the rest of the day, but every scenario ended with her refusing. He understood her fears about falling into a coma and losing the little time she had left. He didn't want to miss a single second of a single minute of her life. But what if the water could save her?

"Do this for me, Ellen." He spoke quietly, but an embarrassing amount of hoarseness crept into his voice.

She spun, her expression fierce, her fists balled at her sides. "Harrison, please. You're making me feel guilty for how I want to spend my remaining days."

He wished he could march over to her, sweep her off her feet . . .

His thoughts silenced, and he stared at the open spout of the flask. What if he proved the holy water could cure? If she saw firsthand the results, how could she deny his request any longer?

His pulse gave an extra kick as though urging him to prove it now before he thought of all the reasons why he shouldn't.

He sloshed the flask, feeling the liquid move inside. Then he looked up at Ellen.

Her litany about having so much yet to do for not only Josie and her parents but the families yet to visit Serenity House came to a halt. As though sensing what he was about to do, her eyes widened with panic, and she began to shake her head.

With one movement, Harrison lifted the container and tipped the contents into his mouth. The liquid poured over his tongue and down his throat, tasteless, odorless, and without texture. It was a scarce amount, no more than a tablespoon.

"No!" Her protest came out constricted, her face turning ashen.

He wasn't doing this for himself. He was doing it for her and only her. Because he loved her. Before he could speak the words, his mind went black. He felt himself falling, falling, falling, and then finally floating in oblivion.

3

ELLEN CLUTCHED HARRISON'S LIMP HAND. Drake had wheeled him from the vault to his bedroom on the second floor, several doors down from the room where she'd been staying. Now Harrison was on his bed, alive but unresponsive.

Drake had phoned Harrison's private physician, the one who had been coming almost daily to check on Ellen. Drake's thin face had been pale and creased with anxiety, surely a reflection of her own worry.

She wanted to shout at Drake and ask him why he'd gone along with the foolishness, why he hadn't tried harder to stop Harrison, why he'd looked for those stupid ampullae. But the regret on Drake's face spoke loudly enough. He hadn't expected Harrison to drink the poison any more than she had.

Hopefully the doctor would arrive quickly, and they could perform gastric lavage before the poison had the chance to seep into his bloodstream. Even now, Drake was downstairs, waiting to admit the doctor.

From her perch on the edge of the bed, she lifted her fingers to the carotid artery in his neck and checked his pulse. As with the other times she'd counted, the rhythms were normal. His breathing was steady and his color healthy. Although he was unconscious, he didn't seem to be in a coma. Yet.

She pressed a stethoscope to his chest and listened to first his lungs, then his heart. Nothing was out of the ordinary. In fact, the sounds were perfect. Even so, she glanced anxiously to the open door, waiting for Drake's return. "Come on. Hurry up, please."

Her mind churned. Maybe she needed to call an ambulance and have Harrison transported immediately to the nearest emergency room. However, if he was falling into a coma like her dad and Marian, he would want to be at home.

Of course, she hadn't been present, had still been in Haiti at the orphanage, when her dad and Marian ingested the holy water and became comatose. So she didn't know exactly how long Harrison had before the onset of the coma.

She rose to her feet, pressing her pockets in search of her phone but feeling only emptiness. A wave of dizziness hit her, and she dropped back down to the bed, breathless and weak. She was over-exerting herself.

"Harrison." She brushed a hand across his forehead, checking his temperature and smoothing his rumpled hair. "You need to wake up. Now."

Since the moment he'd passed out in the vault, she'd gone into nursing mode, had thought of nothing but every medical procedure he needed. Even so, her chest burned with the urge to weep. Why had he done this? He was a perfectly healthy man with a long life ahead of him. He would have outlived her by decades.

Now she would most likely bury another person she cared

about. She leaned in, letting her hand rest against his smooth cheek. "You can't fall into a coma. I won't let you."

His eyelids flickered just slightly.

Her heartbeat stilled. Was he responding to her voice? Could he hear her? Maybe if she continued to talk to him, he'd work harder at clinging to consciousness.

"You know I need you, don't you?" She bent low and pressed a kiss against his cheek, catching a whiff of his sandalwood aftershave. She loved his familiar scent as well as the smoothness of his jaw, the sleekness that came from having an old-fashioned shave every morning with a real razor blade and thickly lathered shaving cream.

She clasped his hand, and his fingers twitched against hers.

She sat up. He *could* hear her and was communicating as best he could. She had to keep him with her until the doctor arrived. Her mind scurried to remember all the information she'd reviewed about comas while Marian had been in one.

Physical touch. Yes, stroking gently was another technique that could work to communicate with coma patients.

She slipped off his glasses and then brushed his hair back from his forehead.

He didn't react.

"Please never leave me." Leaning across him, she kissed his other cheek.

This time, his breathing quickened against her neck. Though his eyes remained closed, she sensed her touch was getting through to him. She had to keep going, keep him reacting.

Maybe her method was unprofessional. But since it seemed to be working, she wasn't about to give up. No one else was around to see her unconventional treatment. Besides, when he awoke, he wouldn't remember anything she'd done. At most, he'd only have a vague recollection.

"Harrison, wake up." She skimmed her fingers down his arm to his hand. The moment her palm pressed against his, he squeezed. Her breath caught, and she examined his face, waiting for some other sign that he was reviving. She didn't see any change in his expression, but hope began to twirl a slow waltz inside.

"Don't give up." She didn't want him to die and leave her.

Was that how he felt about her? Was that why he'd been upset with her in the garden earlier? Because he wasn't ready to let her go?

She understood now. With tears heating her eyes, she threaded her fingers through his. "I'm sorry, Harrison. I should have tried to understand your perspective and how difficult all this has been."

She brushed a soft kiss across his lips. The move was platonic, wasn't it? Just like the kisses to his cheeks were.

He pressed back so slightly she wasn't sure she'd felt him.

She let her lips linger a fraction longer only to feel the movement again.

Her hope began to quickstep to a faster tempo. He was regaining consciousness. She could sense it. Before she could rationalize her actions, she let her mouth fuse with his more firmly.

She hadn't kissed anyone since the summer vacation at the beach after her freshman year of high school, when her boyfriend had taken her for a walk along the ocean's edge and told her she was beautiful. That was the last summer before Mom had taken a turn for the worse. Watching her mom's suffering over the following months had forced Ellen to grasp the reality of the genetic disease she'd inherited. Ever since, she hadn't allowed herself to get into a serious relationship, even though she'd had opportunities to do so.

After all, she'd seen no reason to give a man hope when there wasn't any. She had no future to offer, even with the mature men who'd claimed her disease didn't matter. They didn't realize she'd end up a burden, holding them back from having a full life and eventually causing them grief.

Right here, now, none of that mattered. Nothing mattered except drawing Harrison out of oblivion and back to reality. If kissing him was the key to opening the door, she would use it to her advantage.

Besides, they were just friends. In fact, he was one of her best friends, especially after the past year of experiencing so much tragedy together.

But even as friends, she wasn't immune to what a handsome man he was. She also wasn't immune to the fact that he was one of the most eligible bachelors in England. He'd dated occasionally, but over the past year, he'd fended off advances from women, too busy and consumed with her care to make time for himself.

A part of her felt guilty for taking up so much of his life and leaving him no room for anyone else. But another part of her rationalized she would have done the same thing for him if their roles had been reversed.

And now, as a friend, she was obligated to do what she could to help him . . .

She moved slowly, delicately, drawing him further out of his unconsciousness. But with each tender stroke, she felt sweet warmth stealing through her, awakening her body to needs and desires she'd always refused to acknowledge.

Only when he released a soft groan did she grasp that he was kissing her in return and had lifted his hands to her back. His grip exuded an utterly irresistible strength, so that when he angled his mouth against hers, she felt like she was getting a taste of bliss.

He's awake. Her brain registered the fact, but her overwhelmed senses didn't process it, not until his hands slid to her hips. The caress sent a shudder of pleasure through her, enough to make her more fully aware that somehow the kissing had gone too far.

She froze and her eyes flew open. At the same moment, his dark lashes lifted, revealing his green eyes, half-lidded and filled with desire.

Did Harrison desire her?

Alarms went off in her head, and she dragged her lips away from his. For the duration of several ragged breaths, she hovered above him, his gasps coming in soft bursts.

His attention was riveted to her mouth. His fingers trailed up her spine to her hair, and she sensed he planned to kiss her again. Surely, he didn't know where he was, or what was happening, or even that he was awake from his near encounter with a coma. He probably thought he was dreaming. Once he realized he was kissing her and with such ardor, he'd be mortified.

Somehow, she had to extricate herself and put a stop to the intimacy, now, before they embarrassed themselves any further.

* ◉ *

Harrison's blood pumped at triple—no, quadruple—the speed. And he couldn't seem to catch his breath.

He'd felt her feathery-light kisses on his cheeks. Then, the next thing he'd known her lips had touched his. He wasn't sure what had motivated her to make the change. He didn't care. All he knew was that he needed to kiss her again and again, that he didn't want to let her go.

His fingers glided through her silky hair to the back of her head. With gentle pressure, he tried to guide her down, desperate for another taste of her mouth. But she resisted, and splotches of pink stole into her cheeks.

Maybe he could pretend he didn't sense her discomfort. Maybe he could pretend he was still half-asleep and didn't know what he was doing.

"You're awake." She averted her eyes. "I didn't realize you'd regained consciousness . . . or I wouldn't have . . . I mean, I didn't know . . ."

"It's all right." His voice came out groggy.

"I didn't mean to do it." She broke away from him and scooted onto the bedside chair. "It's just that you responded to my touch. You moved when I kissed your cheek. So I thought I could wake you up . . ."

Disappointment punched him in the gut. He should have known her kisses hadn't meant anything beyond her effort to help him. He should have known the merest touch wouldn't affect her the same way it did him. He should have known he'd read much more into her overtures than she intended.

He'd made an absolute fool of himself, and now he had to work out something to say to put her at ease. But what?

She pressed her hands to her cheeks. "I shouldn't have done it."

He was glad she had. Couldn't he say that?

"I'm sorry." She stood abruptly, looking everywhere but at him.

He had to be honest with her that he wasn't sorry. That he'd loved every single second. That he'd do it over in a heartbeat. But at her keen discomfort over their moment of passion, he could do nothing less than be a gentleman. "You mustn't fret, love."

"You're sure?" She still avoided his gaze.

"Absolutely. I was a bit befuddled and didn't know what I was doing."

Maybe he'd been a little befuddled to begin with. But he'd quickly found himself kissing her back, hungrily taking advantage of the situation.

She twisted her hands together. "The doctor's on his way. But

I thought in the meantime, I'd do what I could to keep you from falling into a coma."

"I venture to say, your efforts worked wonders." He tried for a smile, wanting to put her at ease.

"Ugh." She released a tense breath. "I didn't intend to get so carried away."

His heart dropped a notch, and his smile fell. "Neither did I. I only hope you'll work it out to forgive me."

"As long as you'll do the same."

"Done."

"Then we can forget it ever happened."

"Absolutely." Never. He'd never forget his stolen moment with her as long as he lived. In fact, at the merest thought of the taste of her lips against his, the longing for her swelled against his chest painfully.

"Good." She managed a shy smile.

"Yes, good." He forced a benevolent tone in return.

"At least you're not in a coma. I was so worried when you passed out, and thought you'd end up like Dad and Marian." She reached out a hand toward his neck but then pulled back abruptly. "Your pulse. I was going to check your pulse."

If she so much as laid a finger on him, he wouldn't be able to resist pulling her down and wrapping her in his arms. "Many thanks, love. But I think I can look after myself now." He pushed himself up to his elbows and tested his strength.

She clasped her hands in front of her. "Of course. I'll wait to see what the doctor says when he arrives."

He hefted himself a little higher, a strange energy coursing the length of his body. "How long have I been laid out?"

"Not long." She glanced at her watch. "Ten minutes or so. How are you feeling?"

"I'll be fine in two shakes." Marian had always been sleepy

almost to the point of exhaustion whenever she'd ingested even the smallest residue of holy water. But he felt more awake by the second.

Ellen retrieved his spectacles from the bedside table and handed them to him. "I guess I'll go see where the doctor is."

Harrison froze with his spectacles halfway to his face and then glanced around the chamber, a combination of modern and historical. Every piece of dark antique furniture was in sharp focus—the toes on the claw-footed armoire, the elegant line of scrollwork on the settee, and even the carvings on the eighteenth-century Italian candlesticks on the fireplace mantel. Not only could he see the minuscule details, but everything was clearer than he'd ever seen.

For seconds, he could only sit in stunned disbelief, taking in the tiny, golden fleur-de-lis on the blue tapestries hanging in the window. With his terrible myopia, how was it possible he could see so clearly?

As soon as the question sifted through him, the answer followed on its heels along with a jolt of anticipation so immense, he could hardly breathe. He pushed himself to the edge of the bed, swinging his legs off with an ease that startled him.

"Even if you don't think you need a doctor," Ellen was saying as she crossed slowly to the door, "I'd still like him to check you over. You ingested poison, Harrison. Poison. And maybe it didn't put you into a coma, but we need to be sure it didn't affect you in any other ways."

Harrison glanced at his legs. They'd been useless for thirty-five years, since he was a boy of four and had been in a car accident. Although his parents sustained only minor injuries, he suffered a ruptured disk that bruised his spinal cord. While a surgeon successfully decompressed his spine, the paralysis in his lower extremities, including his legs and feet, hadn't gone away, and he hadn't been able to walk ever since.

His parents had done all they could. And while they blamed themselves for the accident, he didn't blame them in the least. He'd been content to hide away at home, spend hours in the library with his best friends—books—and stay aloof from people and their prying questions and pitying stares.

His parents had all but forced him to attend the best schools and helped him to see his natural aptitude for science. If not for their encouragement, he wouldn't have gone to graduate school, wouldn't have worked at Mercer Pharmaceuticals, and wouldn't have met Arthur Creighton and his two beautiful daughters. Having the Creightons as family after his parents had passed on had been a blessing.

Although he'd never needed the income from his position with Mercer Pharmaceuticals Canterbury Research and Development Headquarters, he'd enjoyed the stimulation and challenge the work had provided.

Of course, he'd had physical therapy throughout his life to maintain the little movement and muscular ability that had remained. He'd learned to adjust and had adapted so that he was fairly independent.

In spite of everything, he led a gilded life. He could keep up appearances by wearing expensive, tailored suits and smart, shiny shoes. He could act the part of an aristocrat. He could wield his power and money with abandon. But underneath the polished veneer, a thin layer of insecurity had always remained.

With a shaky, nervous exhale, he wiggled his toes on first one foot, then the other. The movement rippled up the length of his legs with an odd sensation he reckoned was normal but was one he couldn't remember ever having.

Part of his mind urged caution, not to get too excited, that the sensations and movement might not mean anything. His rational side told him to bend his legs, to test them first, to analyze his situation. But as he lifted his gaze to Ellen's retreating frame, to her long legs carrying her away from the room, her hair swishing in time with her hips, he threw caution aside, as he had in the vault, and he pushed himself up from the bed.

In one fluid, easy movement he was standing. Standing. His feet planted firmly on the floor. His legs supporting him. His knees bearing his weight. His muscles holding him in place.

4

HARRISON SWAYED, blood rushing from his head, leaving vertigo in its wake. He was going to fall, was still weak.

With a lurch, he groped for the bedside table and braced himself. He'd been too hasty and needed his wheelchair. If only it was beside the bed instead of at the end.

Slowly, he shifted, needing to somehow maneuver himself into bed without collapsing. But as he straightened, the dizziness evaporated. A strange serenity enveloped him.

He glanced down at his legs and could feel the solid pressure of the floor radiating up through his feet. He patted a hand against one thigh then the other, feeling the imprint of his hand.

A sizzle of excitement zipped along his nerves. The numbness of his flesh was gone. The dead, detached part of his body was humming with life.

He lifted one foot and took a step. Then he lifted the other and took another step. The movement was strange but easy. And smooth.

He took several more steps. In two ticks, he expected to buckle to the floor, where he'd end up in a heap, his atrophied muscles quivering in protest. But he halted in the center of the room and stood straight and tall without tottering.

Lord in heaven above. Was this really happening, or had he finally gone mad?

Ellen was already out the door, her footsteps shuffling down the hallway, uneven and tired. She needed to preserve her strength.

"Ellen."

"I'll be right back."

Did he dare chase after her? Could he make his legs work that fast?

Go. Keep moving. He started walking again, this time without any effort. His legs functioned as if they had a mind of their own and had been strong and healthy his entire life. He wanted to believe so badly this was real. But he was afraid he was in a coma and had only imagined himself walking.

Faster. His stride lengthened until he was out the door. Ellen was halfway down the hallway.

Run. Catch her. His legs obeyed his mind. As he closed the distance between them, a thrill shot through him. He *was* doing this. He was moving. On his own. Without a wheelchair.

He easily reached her, grabbed her arm, and pulled her to a stop.

She swung around with startled, anxious eyes, certainly not expecting him and likely wondering who would dare to touch her in the middle of the hallway. As her expression registered recognition, her eyes widened and then dropped to scan the length of him.

She sucked in a sharp breath and took a rapid step back.

He released her arm, wanting to prove he didn't need her help to stand, that he was strong enough on his own.

Again she drew in a breath and glanced from his face to his legs and back. Amidst the confusion, her eyes radiated a thousand questions.

Only one needed answering. He nodded. Yes, he was walking by himself.

"No way." Tears filled her eyes, and a sob slipped from her lips before she captured it into her cupped palm.

"Yes way." He couldn't contain a smile even as heat formed at the back of his eyes. He pivoted in a slow circle, needing to convince himself and her that he wasn't fabricating anything.

When he faced her again, this time the tears spilled over and ran down her cheeks. She was still covering her mouth as though she didn't trust herself to speak. And she shook her head in disbelief.

This was real. The holy water had healed him. He would demonstrate it to her—to them both.

He started forward, striding past her down the hallway toward the wide, winding staircase. His feet picked up pace until he was jogging. When he reached the top of the steps, he paused. How many times had he sat in his wheelchair at either the top or bottom of the stairs and watched guests and servants effortlessly climb up and down before sighing with resignation and rolling away to use the lift?

Never again.

With adrenaline pulsing through every vein, he stepped down tentatively, making sure both feet were firmly planted before moving to the next step. He took the first three stairs slowly, deliberately. The fourth he touched with only one foot, moving to the next and the next until, before he knew it, he was standing at the bottom looking up.

Ellen stood at the top watching him, the tears still trailing down her cheeks, her hand remaining over her mouth.

He wanted to jump up and let out a whoop. But aristocratic men like him didn't give way to such exuberant displays. Instead, he grinned with the crazy pleasure of his accomplishment.

"Can you believe it?" He hopped to the bottom step, his face upturned toward her. He could hop. The thought sent such a rush through him that he hopped to the next step, and before he could stop himself, he was charging back up. By the time he reached the top, he was laughing with the joy of being able to move in a way he'd only dreamed about.

Ellen dropped her hand and smiled in response, her lips tremulous, her cheeks wet.

He had the sudden overpowering urge to bound down the steps again. He spun and this time ran. His heart pounded in tempo with his feet. His feet. He relished the clomp of his footsteps muted by the runner. When he reached the bottom, she was laughing through her tears.

"Have a look at this!" He started up the stairs, taking them two at a time. When he slid to a stop in front of her, his chest was pounding hard, and his breath came in a burst. He was sure his grin was as wide as the universe. "Isn't it splendid?"

Ellen's eyes welled with tears again, tears of joy. "Oh Harrison." Before he realized what was happening, she wrapped her arms around him and buried herself against his chest.

He could do nothing less than slide his arms around her in return and hold her tight. He felt the length of her long, supple body in a way he'd never experienced before, her legs brushing his, her knees, her hips, her waist. The contact was electric, even more overwhelming than her kisses had been.

Her body shook with silent sobs. He could sense her relief and amazement in each shudder.

For a moment, he held her, his eyes stinging too. The miracle was massive beyond anything he could have anticipated. It was too good to be true.

"Pinch me," he whispered against the side of her head, her hair glorious and soft against his face.

"What?" Her voice wobbled.

"Pinch me so I know I'm not dreaming."

She squeezed, tightening her arms around him. "If you're dreaming, then so am I."

His throat ached with happiness. He lifted a silent prayer of thankfulness heavenward. He'd experienced a miracle. The holy water had fixed what was broken or damaged in his body, not only healing his paralysis but strengthening his muscles, rejuvenating his eyesight, and giving him fresh vitality. It was impossible to work it out any other way. He now understood why the stained-glass windows in the Trinity Chapel of Canterbury Cathedral had gained the name "Miracle Windows."

Arthur had tested the holy water in the lab and so had Marian. Harrison had reviewed their tests and studied their conclusions. They hadn't found anything within the molecular structure of the water that could be broken apart and examined—other than the compound of the water itself. The only explanation was that the life-giving residue wasn't of this world. It was of God and heaven. God had wrought the miracle.

"You know what this means, don't you, love?" Harrison closed his eyes and again relished every exquisite sensation of holding Ellen.

Ellen shook her head, not lessening her hold.

"It means you now need to drink the other flask of holy water."

At his proclamation, she jerked back. "I can't."

"What do you mean you can't?" Surely she knew he'd only ever been consumed with finding a cure for her, not himself. Of course, he couldn't deny he'd sometimes entertained the fantasy that he could do what he was doing at that moment, hold her as a healthy and strong man. But her healing was more important than anything. In fact, he'd give up his life for hers if he could.

He held her chin and gently tipped up her head so she had no choice but to meet his gaze. "I did this for you. I drank the holy water to convince you to take it."

"There are so many others who need it." Her lips trembled as she spoke. "So many sick children. Like Josie."

He shook his head and fought against his rising frustration. "The second ampulla is for you, Ellen. Only you."

"But how can I drink it when there are others worse than me?"

"Who's worse? The doctors told us this morning they can no longer operate. You only have months—if not weeks—left."

She nibbled at her lip, uncertainty bending her delicate brows together.

He pressed his hands on either side of her shoulders, marveling that he stood above her in height and for once was peering down at her and not the other way around. "Look, love. Your father and sister sacrificed themselves so they could give you this cure. You have to realize that's why they did everything." He couldn't stop himself from brushing a strand of hair behind her ear. "We can't let them down, can we?"

She hesitated.

"If you won't do it for them, do it for me." His words were a whispered plea. He didn't care if he was begging her or if she realized how desperate he was not to lose her.

She finally nodded.

He expelled a tense breath. "Let's go find Drake and get the other ampulla."

Thankfully, she didn't resist as he led her down the stairs and across the hallway room. When he walked into the entryway where Drake was anxiously waiting for the doctor's arrival, the older man took one look at Harrison, crumpled to his knees, and began to weep silent tears.

Drake's reaction brought Ellen to tears again and moisture to Harrison's eyes. After they composed themselves, they returned upstairs. Ellen lay down on her bed. Then Harrison uncorked the flask and tipped it to her lips.

"What if it doesn't work on me?" She pushed his hand away.

"We have nothing to lose for trying, do we?" He stood above her, his legs straight and strong. He shifted just to be sure, luxuriating in the solidness of muscle that radiated underneath his trousers.

Her gaze held his, the fear, worry, and anticipation turning the blue of her eyes stormy. "Please don't be disappointed if I'm not healed."

"I'll be absolutely devastated."

"I know. I understand now."

There was no way she could begin to understand. But he nodded anyway.

She studied his face for several seconds, as though attempting to memorize his features.

He tilted the container again. "Ready?"

She nodded. And this time, when he touched the ampulla to her lips, she didn't resist. He poured every precious drop into her mouth and then prayed.

* ● *

Ellen fought against the darkness that held her captive.

She wasn't sure how long she'd been passed out. But she had the vague awareness she'd been asleep for a while, much longer than Harrison had been. Did that mean the holy water hadn't worked to heal her in the same way? For whatever reason, maybe it had put her into a coma.

Voices beside the bed drew her into further wakefulness. Was Harrison speaking to the home health care nurse? Or the nurse's aide he'd hired to monitor her at night?

"The ampullae are gone," said a woman.

"That is what you wanted," a man replied. "Now we can do nothing more."

"But what if someone else took them before Ellen could?"

Ellen startled at the sound of her name. She tried to sit up, but her arms and legs felt as though they'd been chained to the bed beneath her. She struggled to open her eyes. Marian? Was Marian here?

"We have to put more holy water in the vault, just in case." The woman's voice was louder and most definitely Marian's.

"Impossible." The man spoke tersely.

Ellen's eyes flew open to a dark room lit by a stubby candle on the bedside table, except that it was a strange table and a strange bed canopy above her. There, only feet away, stood her sister, her long hair shimmering a rich auburn in the candlelight. It hung in curly waves down her back almost to her waist over what appeared to be a simple white nightgown.

But that made no sense. Marian was dead. Was this an apparition? With Marian's back turned to the bed, Ellen couldn't see her sister's face, but she knew without a doubt it was her.

"Please, Will." Marian pressed a fist into her lower back.

"You can either get back in bed on your own or I shall put you there myself." The man spoke from somewhere else in the room, but Ellen only had eyes for Marian.

Marian sighed and then turned. Her hand splayed across her white nightgown, pressing down and revealing a very rounded stomach. Was Marian pregnant?

Ellen gasped. The noise caught Marian's attention. Surprised brown eyes caught with Ellen's for just a fraction of a second before disappearing.

"Ellen, what is it, love?" Harrison's voice came from nearby.

"Marian?" Ellen searched the room, but the beautiful young woman with flowing red hair and brown eyes was nowhere in sight. Instead, Ellen's gaze landed upon Harrison sitting in a chair beside her bed.

She almost didn't recognize his face without his thick glasses. He seemed younger, his cheeks and jaw more defined, his eyes more intense. "Did you see Marian?" His expression was completely serious, as though seeing dead people was a normal, everyday occurrence.

Ellen glanced around again. But the room she'd been occupying for the past weeks was unchanged with its mahogany furniture, thick tapestries, bed curtains, and elegant decorations. Along with an array of medical equipment including the CPAP machine, oxygen tank, and monitors.

Even now she could feel the oxygen tube in her nose, the IV in her arm, the electrodes of the Holter monitor on her chest, and the thick, firm mattress of the hospital bed beneath her.

"What did you see?" Harrison squeezed her fingers, and only then did she become aware he was holding her hand tightly.

"I thought I heard and saw Marian." Her voice was raspy.

"What was she doing?" Harrison's brow rose in anticipation of her answer, his attention riveted to her.

She stared at the spot where she'd seen Marian—or thought she had. "She was talking with a man about the ampullae in the vault being gone."

"Then she knows we found what she left for us."

"I don't think she's certain." How was it possible she was having this strange conversation with Harrison? It was a good thing no one else was in the room to hear her rambling. "She mentioned trying to put more holy water there, just in case."

"That sounds like her." This time Harrison sat back and smiled.

Ellen tried to picture Marian again, the flowing nightdress, her slender frame, and her unbound hair. What if the image was nothing more than a dream she'd had while regaining her consciousness? Throughout her nurse's training, she'd studied the brain often enough to know it was capable of incredible feats.

"I think she might be pregnant." Once the words were out, Ellen wished she could pull them back. Who was the crazy one now? She'd always believed her dad was addled and that Marian had gone off the deep end last year. Was that what the holy water did to people? Make them slightly insane?

"Pregnant?" Harrison's voice held a note of amazement. "Can you imagine?"

"No. It was just a realistic hallucination. That's all." She hadn't just seen Marian. She couldn't have.

"It's possible you had a time overlap. Marian had a few brief occurrences. And after making a study, I've concluded the overlaps are a phenomenon of a quantum concept known as *entanglement.*"

"Entanglement?" Harrison hadn't spoken of any of his speculations for months, had been sensitive to her wish not to discuss any of her dad's research. But now? Her curiosity was growing by the minute.

"Entanglement is a theory proposing that different quantum particles can share an existence, even though physically separated. A quantum system interacts with other quantum systems, existing concurrently, so that the wave systems don't collapse but split into alternate versions which are equally real."

"You're speaking a foreign language, Harrison. I have no idea what you're saying."

"Basically, I'm saying physics supports the possibility of the same body existing in different places."

"It doesn't make sense. Since we both drank the holy water, why didn't you interact with the past? Why just me?"

Harrison dark brows came together in a puzzled scowl. "I'd previously come to the conclusion that the holy water would provide healing before a body could cross time. But it's possible if Marian was in this room, then your wave systems collided for a brief instant."

It was all too much to comprehend. Ellen stretched her legs. "How long was I passed out?" The lights on the clock on the bedside table glowed a bluish 9:00 p.m. The darkness outside the window confirmed the day was over.

"You've been out for eight hours." Harrison's fingers caressed hers, making her conscious again of his hold and the fact that he'd likely been worried sick about her during that whole time. After all, she'd been nearly frantic when he'd passed out for less than ten minutes. She could only imagine what he'd endured all afternoon and into the evening.

"How are you feeling?" His eyes practically begged her to tell him she was better and felt like a new woman.

She shook her head, sadness settling around her. Her eyelids were heavy, and the lethargy crashed over her again. "I don't feel any different. I guess the holy water didn't work on me."

"We don't know yet." His voice remained upbeat. "I'm still waiting for the test results to come back from the lab."

"But your healing happened so quickly."

"In reading about the miracles from the past, some took place immediately while others needed more time. Genetic inheritance can affect how a person responds to a drug's efficacy or toxicity. The same could be true of the holy water."

She could understand his desire to cling to hope, but she didn't need the test results to know she didn't feel any better. If anything, she felt weaker and more tired. The fact was, she was too near death's door for anything to help her.

"And how about you? How are you feeling?" She didn't want to look at his legs, didn't want to make him self-conscious, but her gaze slid there of its own volition.

He jumped to his feet and stood straight, tall, and proud. "I'm tremendous. Really. Feeling stronger and healthier than ever."

A thrill shot through her, the same thrill she'd had earlier when she watched him walk up and down the stairway on his own. "What did the doctor say when he saw you?"

"I actually decided it was better if no one knew what we've got up to. At least not yet. I sat back in my wheelchair and had the physician look at you and not me."

"Good idea." After his abduction last year by Lionel, he was wise to use extra caution. Even if no one was pestering him anymore about Dad's ultimate cure, the drug companies would certainly start up again once news of his healing became public.

How would he explain his miraculous recovery to everyone? Would he attribute it to the holy water or come up with some other explanation? What other explanation was there?

Harrison's gaze probed hers, asking her the same question. After what had happened to him, how could she doubt the validity of the ultimate cure and her dad's theories regarding the Tree of Life? After having the vision of Marian, how could she doubt the holy water's ability to enable a time entanglement—or at the very least let a person envision the past?

Exhaustion pulsed through her, and the questions were suddenly too overwhelming to consider. She stifled a yawn. "I'm so tired."

"Have a rest, love." Harrison clung to her hand. "But please don't give up yet."

Ellen sank back into the bed and gave way to the oblivion of sleep.

5

DELICIOUS WARMTH PULSED throughout Ellen's body. She stretched and opened her eyes to the darkness of the room, broken by the low light of her bedside lamp and the faint glint of dawn beginning to show through the half-open draperies. Had she slept all night? After sleeping for eight hours yesterday, how was that possible?

Was her cancer worsening? She did a rapid assessment, checking her breathing, pulse, and the pain. From what she could tell, her vitals were all normal, which wasn't unusual. The only thing different was the absence of the throbbing in her right side.

She probed her stomach near her kidneys, expecting the sharp jab that came whenever she touched her side, no matter how much pain medicine was in her system. But there was nothing.

With a jolt of strange anticipation, she sat straight up and pressed her fingers into her lower backbone, another spot that had been hurting. She waited to feel something, anything. But the compression against the rigid lumbar vertebra resulted in nothing more than a slight indentation.

She patted her arms and chest. Where was her oxygen tube, her IV, her heart monitor? The home health care nurse must have come again while she was sleeping and taken them off.

The chair next to the bed was empty. Having the aide was another one of the things Harrison had insisted upon, especially at night. But now, she was nowhere in sight.

Ellen threw off the covers and jumped out of bed, her body suddenly keyed with an alertness that usually came only after drinking a cup of coffee. She bent over at the waist, something that had caused her excruciating pain and had been unbearable yesterday morning.

Her fingers grazed her ankles, then her bare toes. The only feeling in her back was a tightening in the erector spinal muscles along her vertebrae. She straightened and then stretched her arms above her head, expecting a burning pinch, but felt nothing more than an ordinary contracting of muscles.

Was she healed?

A giddy, surreal sensation started to waft through her, but she shook her head. No. Impossible. Surely what had happened to Harrison couldn't be repeated. Two healings in less than twenty-four hours was too much to expect.

But even as denial barraged her mind, her heart tapped with the staccato of a drum playing faster.

The tests. Harrison had been waiting for the lab results. Where were they?

She scanned the room, then sat down abruptly.

Every single piece of medical equipment was gone. Not only was she free of the tubes and needles and wires and electrodes, but her room was free too.

Again, that giddy feeling rose inside her. She wanted to allow it to burst free, to believe a miracle had truly happened. But she'd been disappointed other times in her short life with promises of remission of the cancers that plagued her. She couldn't allow her hope to break free, not yet.

She grabbed her bathrobe from the end of the bed, slipped it on, and then exited her room. She didn't want to wake Harrison at this early hour, but she had to see him and find out the outcomes of the tests. As she stepped into the long, dark hallway, the faint sound of music beckoned to her. It was a low, sweet melody that came from the direction of Harrison's rooms.

When she stood in front of the closed door to his chambers, she knocked lightly and then stood back to listen. He was playing his violin, Vivaldi's *Four Seasons*, Concerto No. 2, "Summer." After listening for a moment, she tried the doorknob to find it was unlocked. She opened the door and slipped soundlessly inside.

He wasn't in the main bedroom, which was dark with the bed untouched. Instead, light cascaded from the side chamber he used when he tinkered with the various gadgets and instruments he collected.

She tiptoed across the room and peeked inside to find he was standing in front of his laptop. Standing.

Amazement and joy welled up inside her, as it had earlier. He was strong enough to hold himself upright on legs he hadn't used in decades.

If anyone deserved to find happiness, Harrison Burlington did. He was a good, kind, and giving man. In fact, none of her other friends had been as devoted to her during her battle with cancer. Yes, she still had plenty of wonderful friends from college and work, but no one had gone to the lengths Harrison had to make sure she was cared for and comfortable in her last days.

His violin was braced between his chin and shoulder, his fingers flying expertly over the strings, his other hand guiding the bow, tilting and angling in a perfect dance. He'd added harmonics so that the music was layered and complex and heart-wrenchingly beautiful. For several moments, he conducted the unseen orchestra until he halted abruptly and spun.

The music faded, and the silence was startling.

At the sight of her, the stiffness in his shoulders visibly relaxed, and he offered her a sheepish grin. "You gave me a fright."

She was struck again as she had been yesterday at how much more youthful he appeared without his glasses. He'd shed his suit coat and vest. His bow tie was gone and the top three buttons of his dress shirt unbuttoned—a decidedly wrinkled and untucked dress shirt.

"Did my noise wake you?"

"It wasn't noise." She stepped farther into his gadget room. The walls were lined with speakers, wires, monitors, and an assortment of electronic equipment she couldn't name. "It was lovely music."

He lowered his violin to a case and popped out the amp cord. "I've always wanted to have a go at playing from a standing position."

She understood what he wasn't saying, that tonight had been all about doing the things he'd never been able to. At the thought of him embracing each new activity with the same gusto he'd used when skipping the stairs two at a time, hot tears formed in her eyes. She fought them back with a smile. "So, I take it you haven't had any sleep?"

"Not a wink." The excitement on his face was like that of a little boy at Christmas.

"You need to rest, Harrison, or you'll make yourself sick."

"I'll rest soon enough. First, I'm keen to check another item off my 'Always Wanted To Do List.'"

"And what's that?"

He bent over his laptop and pressed a few buttons, and a waltz began to pour from the speakers on the wall, likely one he'd recorded himself. Then he faced her again and gave a formal bow before holding out his hand. "Would you give me this dance?"

"Dance? Here? Now?"

He glanced around the crowded room with the cords crisscrossing the cluttered floor. "You're quite right. This won't do." He beckoned her with his fingers, giving her little choice but to place her hand in his. As his fingers closed around hers, warmth pulsed down her arm, making her all too conscious of his presence, so tall and lean and alive.

He led her out into the spacious bedchamber. "This is more like it." He tugged her toward him.

A motherly voice at the back of her head warned her that what she was doing was improper, dancing in a man's bedroom in the dark. But how could she say no to Harrison? After all, he'd never been able to dance before, and if he wanted to waltz right here and now, then he deserved to do it.

In fact, he deserved to waltz and so much more. He placed one hand on her hip and began to move with surprising skill. She'd had dance lessons when she'd attended Sevenoaks, but she hadn't expected that he'd know how.

"You had no idea I could dance, did you?" he asked with a rakish grin.

"None."

He laughed lightly. "My mother was very old-school and insisted I have dance lessons. She hired a private instructor who specialized in giving lessons to people in wheelchairs. Whenever I protested, she always said, 'I've never known a nobleman who doesn't know how to dance, and I'm not about to start now.'"

"I wish I could have known her."

He spun her and then returned his hand to her hip. Harrison's parents had been much older when they'd had their only child. They'd died before Ellen had moved to the UK, within ten years of each other, his father to a heart attack and his mother to breast cancer.

"I wish she could see me now." He looked off to a place above Ellen's head. "I'm afraid I wasn't the easiest child. I was rather stubborn and full of self-pity."

"I can't imagine that." Ellen allowed her fingers to unravel at his waist, suddenly conscious of the solidness of his torso. "You must have yourself mistaken for someone else. I'm sure you were the perfect child."

He laughed and twirled her in a circle, catching her against him a little closer. "Are you saying I'm incapable of being naughty?" His voice rumbled near her ear, and although she was sure his question was innocent, a tingling heat spread through her middle, nonetheless. It brought back the remembrance of kissing him, of the entirely too pleasurable sensations of their lips melding together in their own kind of dance.

The heat in her middle widened to encompass her chest. And she suddenly couldn't look at his face for fear she'd gaze directly at his lips so that he'd realize she was thinking about them kissing. She didn't want him to know she was dwelling on it, not when she'd insisted they forget it ever happened.

"What else is on your 'Always Wanted To Do List'?" She had to focus on their friendship. Harrison was her friend. Nothing more. And she needed to keep it that way.

"Something I'm planning to do in a few hours." His hand slid from her hip to the small of her back.

Just the slight pressure somehow ignited her skin and made her want to arch against him. "What are you planning?"

"It's a surprise for you."

"For me?" She could hardly think of anything past the sensuousness of his fingers at the dip of her spine. She needed to pull away. She wasn't sure why he was affecting her this way. But she guessed the kissing had something to do with it. Had she ruined their friendship by instigating those kisses?

"I've planned a marvelous surprise for you." He swayed to the music, drawing her along, his presence enveloping her.

She extricated herself from his hold and took several steps away from the strange feelings. "You didn't need to plan anything for me." She clasped her bathrobe tighter even though she was entirely too warm.

"Of course I do." His voice wavered with a new kind of excitement. "It's not every day blood tests come back completely clean."

At his statement, her gaze snapped to his. There in the depths of his shining eyes she saw the news she'd come searching for. The cancer was gone from her body.

For a second, she couldn't register his words, couldn't make herself believe them. After living with the knowledge that with VHL, her body would always have cancer, how could she accept that she was cancer free?

"The CBC?" She couldn't keep the tremble from her voice.

"The complete blood count of both red and white blood cells is within the normal range."

Her throat constricted. She couldn't remember a time when she'd been normal in any sense of the word.

"I had the doctor run a battery of tests including the BTA and cancer marker tests."

"And?" The one word was breathless.

His grin widened. "And not one of them picked up a single abnormality."

"The BTA didn't show any problems?"

"None."

The BTA was a computerized device that measured blood, saliva, and urine for the amount of electrons present, pH balance, and minerals in the fluids. It showed the health of cells, whether the cellular environment was too acidic, if there were too few electrons to combat free radicals, or if there were too few minerals to buffer the acids. Surely if she still had cancer, the BTA would indicate it.

Harrison watched her face expectantly.

"Did the doctor do a dark-field microscopy or DR-70?"

"Yes. Both. And there's no sign of cancer, love. The TK-1 and antigen tests were clear too."

With so many tests showing her free of cancer, how could she doubt the news? The giddiness she'd felt earlier pushed for release. Could she set it free?

"Maybe I should have PET and CT scans just to make sure."

"The doctor said they weren't necessary. But if it would prove to you that you're healed, then we can do them this morning before we leave."

"And what about VHL?"

"We won't have the results of the genetic tests for a few more days, perhaps a week. But I think we can safely assume it's gone too."

She stood silently in the middle of the bedroom still shadowed by darkness. Out the window, the sky was turning a light blue tinted by faint hues of pink, orange, and yellow, reminding her of the tulips that blossomed in the gardens on the front lawn.

Did it matter if the cancer or VHL was completely gone? Hadn't she decided long ago to live each day as if it were her last, to enjoy every moment, to revel in the beauty of life as long as she could?

Whether the cancer or VHL was gone or simply in remission, she had to rejoice in every victory, big or small. She grabbed Harrison's hand and tugged him toward the door. "Come with me."

He allowed her to drag him along, out the door and down the hallway. "What are we doing?"

"We're doing another thing on the 'Always Wanted To Do List.'"

"And what might that be?"

She smiled at him over her shoulder. "You'll see."

The excitement in his eyes warmed her blood, making her steps feel lighter and her heart full. She led him to the old tower, a part of the original structure of the manor. They raced up the narrow steps and made their way out onto the open roof. With her hair streaming behind her and the cool morning air hitting her face, she marveled at the vitality pulsing through her body in a way she couldn't remember feeling in a long time—if ever.

Was this how Harrison had felt when he'd been healed?

She hadn't released his hand during the climb to the top of the tower, and he hadn't made a move to do so either. And even though she guessed she ought to let go now, she couldn't make herself, couldn't think of anyone else she'd rather experience this with than him.

They crossed to the battlement so they could see over the decorative edge to the sprawling yard below. The brilliant colors of the tulip bed formed a crescent adjacent to the winding driveway, and the dew-kissed grass sparkled like it was studded with diamonds.

She drew in a breath that was laced with the soft honey-musk aroma of all the many flowers growing in the gardens surrounding the manor. Then she tilted her head to observe the sky as an invisible painter brushed brighter strokes of color across the canvas.

Harrison lifted his face to the sky too and watched it wordlessly, the awe in his expression confirming that he appreciated the beauty every bit as much as she did. After a moment, his fingers shifted, slipping through hers more intimately. The caress was gentle but sent a powerful tremor through her.

She not only loved the handsome angular lines of his profile but the maturity and wisdom etched into his features, maturity and wisdom many men never gained. Perhaps the years of having a disability had been filled with many hardships and deprivation, but those difficulties had shaped Harrison into the man he was now, a man chiseled with a depth of strength and character that few others possessed.

He slanted a look at her before returning his gaze heavenward. "Penny for your thoughts."

She shifted her sights to the sky. Ugh. He'd caught her staring, admiring him. What was wrong with her? And what could she say about these new and confusing feelings that wouldn't jeopardize the closeness they had?

Her thoughts pinged all over the place and landed on the first safe thing. "You're a good friend, Harrison."

He didn't respond, only continued to look at the colors swirl in the sky.

Good friend? Why had she said that? It was a completely inadequate way to define their relationship. In fact, it didn't even come close to putting into words what he really meant to her. But how could she describe their relationship to him when she couldn't begin to explain it to herself?

She rested her head against his arm. "I think you're my best friend. The best friend I've ever had."

The description still wasn't adequate, but it seemed to be good enough for him. He leaned his head against hers. "You're my best friend too."

She released a breath and focused again on the sky and the sunrise. She'd never forget this moment together, no matter what the future brought.

* * *

Kneeling, Ellen hugged Josie and pressed a kiss against the little girl's blond curls. "I won't be gone long."

Josie's frail arms tightened around her. "Do you promise?"

"I promise." Ellen glanced to Mr. and Mrs. Ansley standing behind Josie in the hallway of Serenity House, both of their faces etched with gratitude. And a restfulness that hadn't been there when they'd arrived last week, frazzled and exhausted. Even though Josie was a precious, beautiful girl, the caregiving was exhausting for the couple, as it was for many parents who had children with terminal illnesses.

Not only had Batten disease weakened Josie's eyesight, but it also wracked her with spasms. With upward of thirty seizures a day, Josie needed constant supervision. In addition to the seizures, Josie's legs gave out when she walked, causing numerous falls and bruises.

All it had taken was one week of pampering and help watching Josie for her parents to look like a new couple. With a full-time cook, health aides, nurse, and activity coordinator, Serenity House was the perfect getaway for overwhelmed families. Josie, too, seemed happier and more rested. Though the little girl's memory resembled that of someone with dementia, she'd taken a quick liking to Ellen and became excited every day when Ellen visited.

Ellen attempted to release the little girl, but Josie clung to her. "Will you read me another story before you go?"

"I've run out of time, sweetheart." Harrison had texted her to let her know he was waiting outside in the car after running errands with Drake. Since she still had a closetful of clothing at Serenity House, she'd used the visit to pack as well as spend a few moments with Josie. Harrison instructed her to bring fancy clothing along with everything she'd need for warm weather, including her swimsuit. She suspected he was taking her to the south of France or even Italy or Greece for a long weekend, but he'd remained silent about where they were headed.

She'd hesitated in going, not wanting to leave Serenity House or Josie. But Harrison had promised her the trip was only a few days. With how excited he was, she couldn't deny him the experience of a lifetime. Besides, maybe by the time they returned, Dr. Li, who was heading up Josie's clinical trials, would finally have permission to administer the promising gene therapy, a onetime shot, into the spinal fluid. Dr. Li offered no guarantees the drug would work, but the Ansleys were willing to try something rather than nothing at all.

Ellen pulled back from the petite girl, running her fingers through the delicate curls and smoothing a hand over the child's cheek. Josie's cloudy blue eyes attempted to focus on Ellen.

"You're going to do all kinds of fun things while I'm gone." Ellen stood. "And when I return, I'll want to hear all about it."

"Will you bring me another strawberry shake?"

"Absolutely." The strawberry shake was one of the few things the little girl would eat without coercing.

"What about riding a unicorn?" Josie's features brightened with eagerness.

Ellen laughed and tousled the girl's hair. "You'll have to wait and see." She exchanged a look with the girl's parents. Josie's wish to ride a unicorn had proven more difficult to fulfill than some of the wishes Ellen had received from other children who'd come to Serenity House. But the Serenity Foundation manager had finally found an animal therapy centre in Scotland that had realistic unicorn costumes, and they were driving a horse and costume down next week.

With more hugs and kisses, Ellen tore herself away to the black Bentley parked out front. As she climbed into the back next to Harrison and waited for Drake to stow her bags, she stared at the four-storied terraced home her dad had purchased when he'd moved to Canterbury. At the time, the white brick Regency house with seven bedrooms had seemed extravagant for one man with daughters who no longer lived with him. Even if being in the home reminded Ellen of how much she missed her dad and sister, she was grateful now for the rare piece of real estate in the old part of the city that she could utilize for families like Josie's.

"You're quiet." Harrison spoke after they started toward the airport.

Ellen pressed a hand against her chest to ward off a swell of emotions. On the one hand, her heart hadn't stopped racing with joy and thankfulness for the health coursing through her body. She'd alternated between ecstatic and disbelieving for the past few hours since watching the sunrise with Harrison.

But another emotion had needled her since she'd awoken. Guilt. Why her? She didn't deserve to be healed more than anyone else. Now, after visiting Josie, the guilt prickled her more painfully.

Josie was so young and innocent and didn't deserve to experience the suffering. Neither did her parents.

Harrison's fingers covered hers on the leather seat between them. She clasped his in return, his warmth and solidness like an anchor amidst the confusion.

"I wish Josie could have the ultimate cure," she said.

"I wish so too."

If only they had more holy water. "Do you think we could communicate with Marian somehow? And tell her to put more in the vault?" Ellen could no longer deny the possibility that Marian was alive in the past. The vision she'd had of her sister had been too realistic to dismiss as a mere hallucination. And the appearance of the two vials had been too miraculous.

"You could try ingesting any droplets left in the ampullae." Harrison rubbed a thumb over her knuckles as though to soothe her, but all it did was make her insides tighten with strange longing. "In order to overlap, you'd both need to be in the same location at the same point of time."

"Night would likely be the best."

"We could give it a go when we get back from our holiday."

Ellen relaxed into the seat, watching as the historic section of Canterbury changed into the suburbs. "If we've been given renewed health, it's too good not to share. Don't you agree, Harrison?"

"You're quite right."

"Wouldn't it be wonderful if Marian could supply us with holy water on a regular basis? Water we could use for all the children who come to Serenity House?"

"Yes." Harrison hesitated, but then rubbed her knuckles again. "Maybe that's what your father planned to do all along. Supply Marian with holy water in the crypt for as long as he could."

"If so, now the job of carrying on his work to provide the ultimate cure belongs to us." Excitement coursed through Ellen at the prospect of delivering the cure to Josie and others like her. Was this how her dad had felt?

"When we return, we'll put our thoughts in order and get on with the work." Harrison squeezed her hand. "For now, promise no worries about anything but enjoying the gift we've been given?" His eyes implored her.

"Of course. Let's celebrate." For the weekend, she would lock away any traces of guilt and instead bask in the present and the new chance at life.

6

"WHEN ARE YOU GOING TO TELL ME where we're going?" Ellen peered out the jet's window.

"We're almost there." Harrison reclined in the plush seat, relishing something as simple as being able to sit directly across from her. Even though he'd always used his family's private jet for traveling, he'd never sat in the seats, had always preferred his wheelchair, which allowed him to maintain some mobility but kept him at a distance from other passengers.

He stretched his legs, tempted to jump up and walk around, just because he could. Instead, he glanced out the window to the glistening green-blue water and the white sandy beaches of the secluded island below.

He forced himself to continue looking out the window so he wouldn't be tempted to stare at Ellen again. In a daisy-yellow sundress, with her hair pulled up on the top of her head in a ponytail, she looked like she was a supermodel on her way to a photo shoot. Even though she was casually attired, she was more beautiful than should be permissible for any one woman.

Yes, she was too thin and had grown pale over the past months of living in Canterbury during her treatments. But this weekend trip would hopefully change that. She would be surrounded by food too delicious to resist, and she'd be able to bask in the warm sunshine. Although this trip was a dream holiday filled with all sorts of activities he'd never been able to do, he'd planned it for her, to help her regain her strength.

As she crossed her legs and kicked her top sandaled foot with unconcealed eagerness, his attention shifted to her again, and he couldn't keep from admiring the stretch of slender flesh and her shapely knees.

Lord help him. He closed his eyes to block out the sight and to block out the same disappointment he'd felt that morning while watching the sunrise, when she'd made clear she only considered him a friend.

Although his feelings went much deeper, he wasn't about to spurn the friendship they had. He'd already had plenty of practice in the past masking his attraction, and he could continue doing so . . .

Except he wasn't sure he wanted to keep up the charade. Maybe he'd had excuses to hide behind before when he'd been paralyzed. But what legitimate reasons did he have for not speaking up and telling her the truth now?

With the passing of so many years, was he too old for her now? Did she deserve someone younger?

She touched his knee. His eyes flew open, and she was leaning toward him, her forehead wrinkled with concern. "You're tired, Harrison. You should have slept more during the flight."

He'd rested for a couple of hours. It wasn't much, but his body was still too excited over everything that had happened.

He laid his hand over hers, knowing he was taking advantage of touching her every chance he had but unable to stop. "I'm fine, love. Don't fret over me." The last thing he wanted was for her to think he was an old bore who couldn't keep up with her.

"Only if you'll promise to stop worrying about me."

He hesitated.

She squeezed his hand. "You don't have to watch over me anymore. I truly feel like a new person. I promise."

Watch over? More like ogle her because he couldn't take his eyes from her. But thankfully she couldn't tell the difference. "I'll try to do better. But to be fair, old habits die hard."

"You've taken good care of me, Harrison. But I don't want you to put your life on hold for me any longer."

"I haven't put it on hold."

"Yes, you have. To oversee my health care."

"I wanted to. Helping you get better was the only thing that has mattered."

"And now that I'm better, you can get back to everything else—your work, Parliament, all the charities you oversee—"

"Being with you has been more important." Embarrassed heat speared him at his admission, and he tore his attention away from her to stare unseeingly out the window.

Had he been temporarily insane to plan a trip like this with her? Spending endless hours with her on an island paradise would likely push him past the point of endurance. He'd need the virtue and holiness of a saint if he hoped to resist his desire for her.

Nevertheless, what was done was done. They were here. And he intended to make sure she enjoyed every minute.

She'd been handed a second chance at life. Last night, when the results of her blood work and other tests had come back one by one, he'd nearly wept with the relief of seeing the results.

The doctor had been just as flabbergasted by seeing Ellen's tests, since he'd watched her deterioration over the past weeks. When the last tests confirmed that her blood was healthy without a trace of cancer, the doctor packed his bags and equipment and left, shaking his head in bewilderment and wonder.

Of course, Harrison hadn't said anything about the holy water. If he mentioned the ultimate cure to the medical community, he'd have a lot of explaining to do. In addition, he'd draw unwanted attention again from anyone else seeking the cure.

Instead, he'd allowed the doctor to believe the miracle had happened out of thin air. Harrison had asked him not to say anything just yet, to keep the matter private. When the medical specialists learned of Ellen's miraculous healing from cancer, they'd want her to come in for more testing. Physicians and researchers would vie to examine her and try to understand what had happened.

Cancer in remission? Cancer gone? As rare as it was, the phenomenon had happened in certain cases.

However, a paralyzed man regaining mobility overnight? Harrison couldn't recall a single incident of that ever happening—except, of course, the miracles recorded in the Bible as well as other historical records attesting to the power of the holy water.

So far, he'd managed to conceal his healing from everyone except Drake, his driver, Bojing, and a couple of his most trustworthy maids. The pilot also knew, but he was an old family friend who wouldn't think of gossiping. This trip would give him a chance to sort out how to tell everyone else.

Did he dare announce to the world that Arthur Creighton had discovered the ultimate cure? The original holy water? That it had the capability of vibrating energy particles that were billions of times smaller than a nucleus, and that the frequency and wavelength of the vibrations could heal and rejuvenate a body?

He and Ellen were living proof. When they returned, he couldn't deny Ellen her request to attempt to get more holy water from Marian to give to the children who came to Serenity House. They might be able to keep their own healings fairly private, but if they were able to help heal the children, how would they explain it? And what kind of danger would they bring upon themselves from competitors like Lionel?

Harrison pushed down the growing unease. For now, he intended to do as he'd requested of Ellen—not think of anything else and enjoy the time together.

When his jet landed a few minutes later and they disembarked at Hewanorra International Airport on Saint Lucia, he led Ellen to the helicopter he'd chartered to take them to Opal Mountain. When he'd phoned hotels last night after learning of her test results, he hadn't really expected to be able to get into the world-renowned exotic resort at the last minute. But it was still early May, not the peak tourist season. Thankfully, honeymooners had just canceled their reservation, so a room had become available.

Of course, it had also helped that his parents had holidayed there long ago. Sometimes inheriting his father's title of Lord Burlington had its perks.

As the chopper lifted into the air above the beaches into the more mountainous terrain, Ellen chattered with excitement through the headsets they'd been given. Instead of an hour of winding and bumpy roads in the back of a shuttle, they arrived within minutes at the landing pad behind the resort and were met by the hotel staff, who took their luggage and directed them to their room—one of only thirty private rooms.

Ellen peeked inside the door of their suite and then gasped. The elegance was more than even he'd expected, especially with the white lace curtains blowing in the breeze that came from the enormous open fourth wall that had a panoramic view of the Piton Mountains and Piton Bay.

She rushed across the room, past the raised whirlpool and the private infinity pool built half in the room and half outside, to the stone balcony complete with leather lounge chairs, towering potted ferns, and vases of white orchids.

"The view is gorgeous, Harrison!" She stood at the deck rail that overlooked the lush foliage of the rain forest. The twin volcanic peaks of Gros Piton and Petit Piton rose majestically, their cone shapes covered in dense green.

Even though the sight was every bit as stunning as Ellen claimed, even more stunning was the view of her standing against the backdrop.

"Come see!" Her eyes were as wide and bright blue as the bay that spread out before them. She leaned forward into the railing, the late afternoon sunshine turning her hair into golden silk.

He could hardly breathe, much less move, but somehow he managed to walk until he stood beside her, fighting the urge to slip his arm around her. For a moment, they stood silently side by side, taking in the magnificence. He had no doubt she was too awed to speak, while his silence had more to do with his inability to form coherent thoughts around her.

"This is the perfect place." She smiled, her eyes shining, her cheeks already taking on a healthy flush.

"I'm glad you like it, love." He returned her smile, forcing himself into the friend role he'd always played. "I thought this place would give us ample opportunity to tackle the 'Always Wanted To Do List.'"

"What are we going to do first?"

"Whatever you wish."

"What do *you* want to do?"

He didn't dare tell her that all he wanted to do was hold her, even though that was the truth. "What don't I want to do? Where to start? With a swim in our pool? With snorkeling? Or kayaking and paddleboarding? Maybe bike riding or a walk on the beach barefoot? I'm most definitely hiking Gros Piton all the way to the top of the volcano."

At his enthusiastic list, she laughed and reached for both his hands. "Let's do it all."

"I agree." He let his fingers intertwine with hers.

She glanced at the pristine water of their infinity pool, the blue tile making it as bright as the bay. "I say we try out our pool first, and then the hot tub, and then a bite of everything on that tray." She nodded inside the room toward the platter of fruits, cheese, and pastries on the coffee table in front of a low sofa.

He watched the delight ripple across her elegant face. He didn't need to do anything else for the entire trip, and he'd end it satisfied. He'd made her happy. And that was all that mattered.

* ● *

Harrison led Ellen up the stone path to the flat roof of the resort. Even though the sun had already begun its descent, the evening was still warm.

As they climbed, he held his fingers lightly at the small of her back and tried to keep his gaze from straying to her form-fitting red dress that didn't reach her knees and showed off her legs. A strap wrapped around one shoulder, but the other shoulder was bare. She'd gone with an understated elegance by wearing Marian's pearl necklace and matching pearl earrings. Her hair was pulled up into a twisted French knot, revealing the smooth beauty of her neck.

"Are you sure this is where we need to go?" she asked again.

"Trust me, love. This is what the concierge recommended."

They'd spent the remaining hours of the afternoon alternating between swimming in the pool and lying on the deck chairs and napping. Although his physical therapist had often used a pool for conditioning and muscle strengthening, he'd never been able to swim with such effortlessness.

In England it was past midnight, but they hadn't wanted to

turn in. So they'd dressed for the late dinner—which was on the sky deck and included stargazing.

As they ascended the last step, Ellen gave a low murmur of appreciation at the sight of the vista that opened before them. The rooftop view of the bay and mountains in the fading light was postcard perfect, surely a reflection of heaven on earth. The two dozen or so tables were lit by elegant glowing centerpieces as well as white lights strung from the trellises surrounding the rooftop. A small band played in one corner while servers mingled around the tables, pouring wine and carrying hors d'oeuvres.

A butler approached and escorted them to their table for two, introducing them to the couple at the table closest to theirs. Harrison pulled out the chair for Ellen, helped her sit, and then situated himself. Although he knew he should pretend interest in the scenery, he couldn't tear his gaze from her wide-eyed amazement.

As though sensing his attention, she shifted to face him. Her face alight with an adoration he loved, she reached across the table for his hand. "Have I thanked you yet?"

He had the urge to bend in further and claim a kiss. After working all day to keep his thoughts under control, he wanted to throw away caution and go with his impulse—just this once.

But suddenly, he was conscious of the couple at the table next to theirs watching them. He tore his sights from Ellen and nodded at them again, an older couple who looked to be in their sixties, both slender and tanned and smiling widely.

Their accent was American, and the butler had introduced them as Dr. and Mrs. Fletcher. Mrs. Fletcher had carefully curled auburn hair and had likely come directly from the salon. The artificial color contrasted with her husband's full head of silver hair. They both exuded an air of worldly wisdom, as though they made a regular habit of traveling to exotic locations.

"Young love is so precious." Mrs. Fletcher's gaze bounced between him and Ellen.

Young love? What was she talking about?

"I remember when we were madly in love." The older woman pressed a jeweled hand over her heart.

Her husband cocked a brow at her good-naturedly. "Remember when? Aren't we still madly in love?"

Mrs. Fletcher laughed, then leaned across the table, cupped her husband's cheek, and planted a kiss full on his lips. As she pulled away, he beamed, as though he'd been rewarded a million pounds.

Harrison was tempted to give them a polite smile and end the conversation, but his mother's training to be a gentleman in every circumstance held him in good stead. "I imagine you've had many happy years together."

"Oh no, honey," Mrs. Fletcher said with a breathy laugh. "We've only been married for three years. A second marriage for both of us." She launched into the story of how they'd lost their spouses around the same time and then met on a cruise six months later.

"Neither of us was looking for a relationship," Mrs. Fletcher finished. "But when second chances come, you have to grab them up while you can. Don't you agree, dear?"

"I agree 110 percent," Dr. Fletcher responded. "Don't let second chances pass you by."

Harrison wanted to echo their sentiments, wanted to explain that both he and Ellen had been given second chances too—not in love, but in life. But he realized how crazy he would sound if he told them that yesterday morning he'd been wheelchair bound but that after drinking holy water he'd been healed.

They spoke off and on with the Fletchers during the elegant three-course meal of sushi, broiled lobster tail, chocolate-covered fruit, and scrumptious cheesecake. Finally, after their servers had cleared away the last of the dishes, Dr. and Mrs. Fletcher stood.

"You're not going already?" Ellen reclined in her chair, her features relaxed and her eyes bright. "They're just about to dim the lights for the stargazing."

"We're not as young as the two of you." Mrs. Fletcher stifled a yawn. "Besides, I'm sure you didn't come all this way to spend time with a couple of old fogies like us."

Ellen waved off her concern. "We don't mind in the least. It's been a pleasure getting to know you."

Harrison didn't quite agree, but he refrained from voicing his contradiction.

"You're too sweet." Mrs. Fletcher linked her arm into her husband's. "But I can tell that handsome husband of yours is dying to pull you into his arms and have you to himself."

Brilliant. Just what he needed. Complete strangers informing Ellen of the feelings he'd tried to conceal from her for years. Before he could say anything to correct their wrong assumption, the lights went dim and the couple hustled away.

Once he and Ellen were alone, she sat stiffly in her chair. "What should we do?"

He crossed his arms behind his head and leaned back so he could view the sky. The expanse of stars that met his gaze was incredible. Thousands of light specks dotted the dark canopy of the universe. "Tilt back like this. It's a perfect view."

"No, not about the stargazing." Her tone was soft, almost shy.

"Then about what?" He knew what she was referring to, but he couldn't face her. If he did, she'd surely see the stark longing in his eyes.

"Their room is just down the hall from ours, and they were checking into their room at the same time we were." She twisted at the teardrop pearl in the middle of her necklace. "Now, apparently, they assume we're a couple. Perhaps everyone here assumes it."

"I'm sorry, love. We're staying in the largest room, the one reserved for honeymooners."

"So, people think we're here on our honeymoon?" Her voice contained a note of panic.

"We're not wearing wedding bands, so maybe not."

"That's true. Even so, maybe we should try to switch, perhaps get separate rooms."

"The honeymoon suite is the only one available at such short notice."

"And I'm not complaining. I love the suite. I love this place. But I do feel bad for allowing everyone to believe we're married—and sleeping together."

Of course, he'd never had any intention of sleeping with Ellen on the trip, but just the mention of it heated his blood several degrees. "We'll never see these people again, so why worry about what they think? However, if it makes you feel better, we'll work it out tomorrow and inform the Fletchers we're just friends."

She finally sat back and tilted her head up to the sky. "Good idea."

Just friends. The words grated him, as they had earlier. But he knew it was what she needed to hear whether he liked it or not.

Ellen twisted the teardrop pearl at the hollow of her neck. "Do you really think Marian is alive in the past?"

"As mad as it may seem, yes, I do." There was no other explanation for the two ampullae he and Drake had discovered. And Ellen's overlap into the past seemed to confirm it.

Ellen released the pearl. "If so, I hope she's as happy as we are."

"I hope so too."

Several beats of silence passed, and her expression grew wistful. "Let's pray she can help us get more holy water. We shouldn't be the only ones to experience this kind of healing and this kind of happiness."

He nodded. He wanted to agree with her. But if they were able to get a supply of holy water from Marian, it certainly wouldn't be limitless. They wouldn't have enough to match the demand. So how would they decide who was most deserving? Of course, Ellen wanted the holy water to help the children in her program. But what about others who were dying? Were they any less worthy?

The questions had been taunting him since their conversation before the flight. The even bigger question still nagging him was how he was going to explain what had happened to him. He couldn't hide away forever.

He tilted back and focused on the sky. "Now, let's put all that from our minds. Remember, we're here to enjoy the gift we've been given."

He wished he could simply enjoy the time and relish the healing of their bodies. But was it possible that the grass wasn't always greener on the other side? That whether sick or well, troubles would always abound?

7

ELLEN'S TOES SANK into the warm sand. A short distance away, the clear turquoise waves lapped the shore.

"I'll race you to the water." She dropped her beach bag and towel, kicked off her sandals, and began to shed her swimsuit cover-up.

"How long of a head start should I give you?" Harrison's teasing voice was muffled beneath his new Saint Lucia T-shirt as he slid it up over his head, revealing his well-defined chest. His upper body was much stronger than she'd realized before this trip, his muscles sculpted from long years of having to rely upon his arms to do things.

"I don't need a head start."

As he tossed his shirt off, she jerked her attention to the beckoning water so he wouldn't catch her staring like he had the time or two they'd used their private pool.

They'd kept busy doing all the things from his bucket list, and at night when they returned to their suite, they were both so tired that they fell asleep—she on the bed and he on the couch—the moment the lights went out, especially last night after they'd spent the day hiking Gros Piton.

The tour guide had led them up a heavily wooded path to the volcanic crater at the peak. The trek took over two hours, and they hiked the steep climb without a single problem or complaint. When they stood on the top and looked out over Saint Lucia, the view was so breathtaking they weren't able to do anything but stand in awed silence.

Although Harrison hadn't said so, she sensed his profound gratefulness to God. She felt it too. A week ago, she'd hardly been able to move, at least not without heavy doses of pain medication. Now here she was in Saint Lucia, doing the impossible. As if climbing the volcano yesterday wasn't enough, today she'd spent hours kayaking and windsurfing and diving and snorkeling.

Even now, when she should have been tired from the activity of the past two days, she wanted to run and splash in the water. The only thing casting a cloud over her happiness was the lingering guilt that she was so alive and well when Josie and all the other precious children in the Serenity House were dying.

She'd tried to do as Harrison had asked and not think about anything else. But with each new activity she accomplished, her determination to help Josie only grew, as did her desire to connect with Marian again and come up with a plan to transfer holy water.

"Ready?" She eyed the waves.

He stood beside her, twisting his torso in a stretch. "Whenever you are."

"Never been more ready. I doubt you can catch me!"

"Watch me!"

With a squeal, she sprinted toward the ocean's edge, the warm equatorial breeze tangling in her hair.

Behind her, Harrison counted to five. When he stopped, a quick glance over her shoulder told her the chase was on. He'd started after her.

Her heart leapt with delighted anticipation. As her feet splashed through the water, she kept going, running to meet the waves.

She could hear Harrison crash into the ocean on her heels. A second later, his hand grazed her shoulder. "Got you!"

She squealed again and dove out of his reach. But a wave swept into her and knocked her off her feet. She laughed as it tossed her directly into Harrison.

"No fair." She wiped the water from her face.

"Absolutely fair, love." His thick arms slipped under her knees and back so that he was carrying her.

Another wave splashed against them, and they laughed and sputtered, the salty water drenching them thoroughly.

She didn't resist as he held her, cradling her against his chest and taking the brunt of the splashes. In fact, she curled her arms around his neck and relaxed in the comfort and strength of his hold as she'd done over the past months whenever he'd pulled her down into his wheelchair.

Another wave pressed her, and she turned her face into his chest. His bare chest. His slick wet flesh surrounded her, so solid and strong and handsome. She leaned back enough to take him in. As though sensing her perusal, his sights shifted to her face. His dark eyes rounded with questions: Was she all right? Was she tired? Was she in pain?

He was always thinking about how she was doing, always more concerned about her than himself.

She lifted a hand to his wet cheek and smiled her reassurance. She was fine. She was always fine.

As her fingers caressed his jaw and the scruff he hadn't bothered to shave that morning, something changed in his gaze, a smoldering that loosened warmth inside her belly.

"Ah, you two lovebirds!" a voice called from the beach behind them.

Harrison lowered her to her feet and at the same time turned so that they were facing Dr. and Mrs. Fletcher, who were standing a dozen paces away, hand in hand, grinning at them.

"We missed you at dinner last night." Mrs. Fletcher gave them a smug, knowing look. "But we completely understand, don't we, dear?"

"That's right. We sure do."

Ellen felt her entire body flush at the older couple's insinuation. "We climbed Gros Piton yesterday, so after being gone all day, we were ready for an early bedtime."

"Of course you were." Mrs. Fletcher exchanged an amused look with her husband.

Embarrassed heat pulsed into Ellen's cheeks. "We were exhausted."

"From the hike." Harrison reached for her hand as if to reassure her he was there to help get them out of this predicament.

They still needed to clarify the status of their relationship and let the older couple know that they weren't there as honeymooners.

Harrison cleared his throat, apparently thinking the same thing.

Before he could speak, Dr. Fletcher's expression turned somber. "I was just telling my wife that seeing the two of you so obviously in love reminds me of my son and his wife."

Obviously in love? Ellen opened her mouth to respond but halted at the sight of the tears in Dr. Fletcher's eyes.

"He passed away last year after battling prostate cancer."

Mrs. Fletcher slipped an arm around her husband's waist and patted his chest with her other hand, her bracelets jangling.

"We're so sorry to hear about your loss, Dr. Fletcher." Harrison spoke with the grace and smooth charm that always seemed to come so easily for him. "It's bound to be painful for you to think on him."

The older man nodded. "It is. But as strange as it sounds, watching you two together also reminds me of how lucky he was to have experienced love for the short time he had here on earth."

Harrison slanted Ellen a sideways glance that said not to worry, that he'd fix the misunderstanding.

With a shake of her head, she leaned into him and squeezed his hand. They couldn't say anything, not now, not after this revelation from Dr. Fletcher about his son. What harm would come from allowing the couple to go on believing they were together?

Harrison peered down at her in confusion. He'd promised to talk to the Fletchers and clear up the misunderstanding from the other night. Didn't she want him to do that? The question radiated from his eyes.

"Not yet," she mouthed.

He nodded briefly and continued the conversation with Dr. Fletcher without the slightest hint that the man was mistaken in his insinuations about them.

"We can pretend for their sake, can't we?" Ellen asked once the couple had ambled off to the winding path that would take them back to the resort. "We only have tonight and tomorrow left." They were scheduled to fly out early on Monday. Surely they could keep up the charade until then.

Harrison crossed his arms over his chest and watched the couple's retreat. His damp dark hair was mussed, with several strands plastered to his forehead. After the hours of swimming and being in the water, he was gaining a healthy tan that only added to his appeal.

"Pretend?" His brow cocked. "What do you mean?"

"At the very least, let's not make a big deal about correcting their wrong assumption." Without waiting to see his reaction, she started up the beach toward where she'd left their towels. Only when she began to dry off did she glance at him. He stood up to his ankles in the ebb and flow of waves, and he was staring at her. Something in his gaze told her he'd watched her walk away and had enjoyed every second of it.

He shifted his attention from her at the same time she ducked for her cover-up. Harrison had been noticing how she looked? Warm pleasure bubbled inside.

Harrison approached, reached for his towel, and began drying off. "Look, love. Acting like we're a couple, married or otherwise, in front of the Fletchers isn't such a good idea."

"Someone very wise told me recently that we'll never see these people again, so why worry about what they think?"

"That was very wise. But I count myself a man of integrity. And I would loathe myself if I took advantage of you or the situation in any way."

"I know you well enough to say with confidence that you won't take advantage of me." She smiled at his sweetness and consideration.

"I'm a man, Ellen. Not a monk." He smiled back, but that same something burned in his eyes, reminding her of the new awareness they had of one another.

Perhaps he was right. She hesitated but only for a second. "We probably won't see them much anyway. So, let's not worry about it."

* ● *

Harrison had to bite back a groan as Ellen touched his arm. Again.

Her laughter tinkled in the air, laughter at something Mrs. Fletcher had said. He hadn't heard half the conversation, had been too enamored by Ellen. Fortunately, he had enough training in manners to at least give the appearance of participating in the formal dinner, even if he could focus on nothing but the vivacious woman by his side, which was only more difficult whenever she inadvertently brushed against him.

She was attired in a strapless light blue gown with a form-fitting silver-and-blue sequined bodice and a skirt that flowed in sleek lines around her legs. The diamond studs in her earlobes only drew his attention to the graceful expanse of neck beneath her ears.

The blue of her dress highlighted the blue of her eyes, as did her new tan, so that whenever she looked at him, his insides turned into liquid fuel. He feared that the smallest spark would enflame him, that he'd do something really stupid and move too fast before she was ready. Even if she'd insisted they were merely friends, he'd sensed a subtle shift in how she was beginning to view him. At least he hoped she was shifting . . . but he couldn't push her for fear that he'd end up pushing her out of his life altogether.

The low lighting, elegant table settings, and romantic atmosphere of the dining room weren't helping to keep his thoughts in check. The Fletchers' talk about marriage and romance wasn't helping either.

He should have known the moment Ellen predicted they wouldn't see the couple much that they'd end up sitting together after dinner as they waited for the dancing to begin.

"What do you think, Harrison?" Ellen's fingers still rested on his arm. Even through his tuxedo sleeve, her touch seared him.

"Anything you want, love." He shifted just slightly so that he met her gaze.

Her eyes were full of light and laughter. "You haven't been listening, have you?"

"Of course I have. You were talking about having a go at sailing on the bay."

"What about the sailing?" Her smile turned impish with challenge.

He had no idea, so he made an educated conjecture. "You're keen to try it tomorrow."

His answer brought a round of laughter from the other three, the sign he'd answered incorrectly.

"The opposite." Ellen squeezed his arm. "Since we can go sailing anywhere, I said I'd rather take the aerial tram tour above the rainforest."

"Sounds tremendous. Perfect, really." Doing anything with her was perfect.

Dr. Fletcher finished taking a sip of wine, eyeing Harrison over the rim of his glass. "Lord Burlington, it's quite obvious you have only one thing on your mind tonight."

"And what might that be?" The question came out before he realized he shouldn't have proffered it. He certainly didn't want to hear Dr. Fletcher's interpretation of his mood.

"Ever since you've stepped into the dining room, it's been clear you've wanted to pull Ellen into your arms and kiss her."

He stiffened. The last thing he needed was for Dr. Fletcher to broadcast his desires, which the fellow seemed inclined to do every time they were together. He didn't dare make eye contact with Ellen now.

"Go ahead, children." Mrs. Fletcher smiled at him and then Ellen. "We won't mind a little kissing."

He forced what he hoped was a lighthearted-sounding laugh. "I assure you, we're quite all right."

"Come, now," Dr. Fletcher insisted. "It's easy to diagnose your fever. Kissing her will keep the heat from rising too high."

While Mrs. Fletcher congratulated her husband on his witty comment, Harrison tossed Ellen a panicked glance. What had they got up to?

She gave him one of her "don't worry, let's live in the moment" kind of looks, which only ramped up the panic another notch.

He should have corrected the older couple's mistake about him and Ellen right away.

Now look at the trouble he was in.

"Go on, now." Mrs. Fletcher waved at them. "If a kiss is what the doctor prescribes, then you must do it. Doctor's orders."

Harrison had no choice. He had to put an end to this now before it got further out of hand. He started to open his mouth, but under the table, Ellen's fingers intertwined with his, halting all words and thoughts. All it took was one glance at her face, at her silent request not to say anything to the Fletchers, and he pressed his lips together.

"You've been dying to kiss her." Dr. Fletcher's voice rose louder, drawing the attention of the guests at a nearby table. "Look at it as a life-saving procedure like CPR."

Mrs. Fletcher clapped her hands and giggled at her husband's ongoing medical analogies.

Harrison was tempted to roll his eyes. When would they give it a rest?

"I didn't realize you'd been dying to kiss me." The teasing glint in Ellen's eyes mingled with something else. What was it? Desire?

Harrison shook his head and started to push back from the table. Now he was the one imagining things. He had to leave the room before he followed through with this crazy charade and kissed her.

Ellen didn't release her grip on his fingers and instead tugged him toward her, leaning into him so that they were suddenly face-to-face. She hesitated only a second before pressing her mouth onto his.

For a second, he froze. What was she doing? Her warm but firm lips caressed softly, tentatively, ultimately waiting for him to respond.

Pretending. That's what she was doing.

He had to give her a brief kiss in response, otherwise he'd hurt her feelings.

He returned the pressure gently, then pulled back.

Ellen's cheeks began to flush, and she folded her hands in her lap.

"That was hardly a life-saving kiss." Dr. Fletcher chortled. "You're going to have to do better than that."

Little did Dr. Fletcher know just how much he wanted to do better, to sweep Ellen into his arms and kiss her properly. He reached for his glass of ice water, in need of a cooldown. He took a big gulp.

"What else do you think you should prescribe for the newlyweds?" Mrs. Fletcher winked in their direction.

The sip of water stuck in his throat, making him choke. Coughing and choking, he stood. Ellen rose too. And touched his arm again, this time in concern.

"I'm fine." Except that he needed to step away for a few minutes to collect himself.

Before he could scrape up an excuse, Dr. Fletcher clinked his spoon against his glass. "Kiss her like you mean it. Doctor's orders for the honeymooners."

The clinking and bold words halted the conversation at the tables surrounding them. And soon the air rang with the clink of silver against crystal as the other guests joined Dr. Fletcher in the call for a kiss.

Ellen turned innocent eyes upon him. "It's okay, Harrison," she whispered.

Was she giving him an invitation? Before he could issue himself a warning to walk away, he dropped his hands to her waist, drew her body against his, and in the same movement angled in and took possession of her lips. He melded into her with all the feelings he'd kept in check for so many years.

Once unleashed, he couldn't hold his passion back and was surprised when she not only received him, but met him eagerly, almost as if she craved him.

Before he could analyze what was happening, Mrs. Fletcher's laughter penetrated and embarrassed him in the same moment. He broke away from Ellen and took a rapid step away, dizzy, rendered senseless. His pulse was galloping forward and careering unsteadily.

At the clapping around them Ellen plopped into her chair and gave a shaky laugh. Harrison attempted to lower himself with dignity even though his limbs were trembling.

Before he had the chance to catch his breath, someone at a table across the room clinked a glass, starting the chorus again. He tried to ignore it, but Ellen leaned in, her breathy laughter beckoning him.

This time, he didn't resist, was incapable of it. He turned into her, tasted her more slowly, relishing her lips, the softness of her mouth, the warmth of her breath. He didn't want to stop this time, would have kept going endlessly, shamelessly, if not for the clapping and cheering.

He broke away, and for long seconds afterward, he sat in dazed silence. Had he kissed Ellen not just once, but twice? Had he really been so bold?

His blood thrummed, and every atom sparked with extra charges.

"It's so wonderful to see a young couple like you so much in love," Mrs. Fletcher was saying.

Ellen didn't contradict the older woman but instead rested her head against his shoulder. He wasn't overly proficient in the various signals young women gave out, but he sensed this was an invitation to hold her. With as much casualness as he could muster, he draped his arm around her. Although he feigned calmness, he was sure she could hear the wild thumping of his heartbeat.

He half wished Dr. Fletcher would start clinking his spoon against his goblet again. But to Harrison's disappointment, he didn't.

A short while later, when the band started the first number, Ellen stood and held out a hand to him. "I know you've already crossed dancing off your 'Always Wanted To Do List.' But you haven't crossed dancing in a rainforest paradise off it."

He accepted her offer and and rose to his feet, struck by how happy and relaxed she was. And how healthy. Her face radiated a glow that warmed his soul. This was what he'd wanted for her—to be happy and healthy. No matter what the future held, he'd cherish this memory with her forever.

8

As Ellen began to swipe their key card, Harrison tickled her again behind her ear with the long feather they'd found on the beach.

"You're incorrigible," she whispered, unable to hold in her laughter.

She'd teased him all the way back to their room with the feather until he'd stolen it from her and began to tickle her instead. Before she could open the door, he brushed the feather up and down her neck. She spun and attempted to grab the feather, only to find him inches away.

With his own breathless laughter echoing in the hallway, he pinned her hands together then drew a tender line down her jaw to her chin with the feather. His gaze followed the trail and ended up at her lips.

He hadn't kissed her since the clinking against the water goblets. Of course, she'd thought about his kisses, but they'd been busy learning how to tango and cha-cha and rumba and dance all the dances Harrison had never been able to do before. Then after staying up all night dancing, they'd had breakfast on the beach and watched the sunrise with the other guests.

Perhaps they could share one last kiss to conclude the beautiful memory. There wouldn't be anything wrong with that, would there?

She peered beyond Harrison to a couple across the hallway. They were trading kisses with one another and wouldn't care if she and Harrison decided to share some affection too.

Harrison brushed the feather across her mouth, his eyes darkening with an intensity that made her stomach clench in anticipation. Surely, he was thinking about kissing her again. But he was too much of a gentleman to steal another kiss, no matter how much he might want to. If she wanted one, she would have to initiate it. But should she?

Before she could rationalize further, she wrapped her arms around his neck and stretched up until her mouth hovered next to his. At her boldness, surprise flashed in his eyes.

What was she doing? She wasn't experienced with men. What if she'd read him wrong? She needed to pull away. It was one thing to pretend at dinner and another to carry on now.

She began to lower herself, but he let go of the feather and gripped her arms, as though to prevent her from leaving.

Did he want another kiss too?

She hesitated but a moment before brushing her mouth across his. For several heartbeats, he remained motionless, letting her dust his lips in an enticing flutter. Then in one swift movement, he pressed her back against the door. His mouth claimed hers, bringing an end to the teasing and instead plunging her into an oblivion of pleasure.

His lips moved against hers powerfully, as though he couldn't get enough. And she responded the same way, digging her fingers into his hair and letting herself get swept into the deep current.

One thing was certain, his kisses weren't sating her. Rather, they had the opposite effect of making her want more.

"Hey, you two," came a laughing voice from the other couple. "Take it inside."

Mortification rippled across Harrison's face. He released her and fumbled with his key card and the handle, unable to open the door quickly enough. Once they were inside, Ellen pushed the door closed, leaned back against it, and gave a shaky laugh.

Raking a hand through his hair, Harrison was already stalking toward the small table lamp by the cluster of sofas. He flipped on the switch, casting soft light around the room and making the infinity pool glimmer an enticing aqua.

He walked to its edge, thrust his hands into his pockets, and stared down into the water. His back was stiff and straight, the sure sign his mind was fast at work trying to process something.

"We did a good job pretending for everyone tonight, didn't we?" She held on to the doorknob, her knees still too weak from his kiss to trust herself to walk.

"Did we?" Harrison didn't turn.

"Yes. As a matter of fact, I think we deserve an Oscar for our acting." She tried to make her voice lighthearted, sensing Harrison's mood had somehow shifted the moment they'd walked into their suite.

"Is that all it was to you?" His tone was decidedly different too, almost ominous. "Acting?"

Was he upset at her? She couldn't blame him. He'd been upfront about not wanting to act like a couple, and she'd gone ahead with it. "I'm sorry, Harrison. I wasn't expecting the Fletchers to pressure us into kissing. Maybe I got carried away, caught up in the moment."

At her words, Harrison pivoted to face her. Still attired in his tuxedo but having discarded his tie, he was just as gorgeous now as he had been when they'd left their suite hours ago. Even though his expression was shadowed, there was no hiding the pain and hurt there. "No one forced me to kiss you."

"That's not what I meant." No one had forced her either. She wasn't sure why she'd done it, maybe because deep down she'd wanted to see what it was like to be treated like a newlywed, to finally be the one with the hope for a bright future.

"What exactly did everything mean to you?" His hands were still stuffed in his pockets.

She offered him a smile, hoping to regain the playfulness they'd shared in the hallway, hoping they could avoid a difficult conversation. "Everything has been fun. And I can't thank you enough for bringing me here."

He didn't answer, and somehow she knew he expected more from her than glib platitudes. He wanted the truth. He wanted to know how she felt about their kisses, about the feelings those kisses aroused, and about how to proceed from here.

She couldn't deny that an attraction was growing between them. And this trip and their time together made her adore him even more than she already had.

But surely he understood she was petrified of making plans, had always been too scared to think of her future, and she didn't want to think about where their kisses might lead or how to move forward with their relationship.

Maybe she was healthy now, but what if the next PET scan showed that she still had cancer? And even if the cancer was gone now, what if it came back? It likely would, if the VHL was still a part of her genes.

"You've supported me through everything," she whispered, "going with me even to the brink of death. But how do I know I still won't get sick again?"

"You won't." His voice was hoarse.

How could he know? How could anyone know? It wouldn't be fair to lead him to believe there could be something between them, not when her life was so uncertain, not when there were still so many unanswered questions.

But if she didn't explore the changes in their feelings, if she didn't give him more, would he cut her out of his life? She didn't know if she could bear that. It was best if things stayed the same between them, wasn't it?

"You're my best friend, Harrison. I don't want that to change."

He shifted to face the pool again, and this time his shoulders slumped. He'd read into her words what she couldn't voice aloud—all she was capable of giving him was the present, not when she didn't know if she had a future.

She hung her head. What had she done? Despair crashed through her, and she wished she could go back and change things. She should have been more careful, should have thought more about how the kissing would affect him. Just because she lived every moment like it might be her last didn't mean everyone else did.

She'd been foolish for hurting him, for jeopardizing their friendship. She could only pray that eventually Harrison would realize she was a ticking time bomb and that they were better off remaining friends and nothing more. She didn't want him to stay upset at her, didn't want him to push her away.

A text dinged. In the next moment her phone started ringing. Now wasn't the time to worry about interruptions, but at another ding, she glanced at her phone only to discover the text was from Josie's parents.

As she read their words, her blood turned cold. Josie's vitals had crashed. She was in cardiac arrest and had been taken to the hospital's accident and emergency wing. They didn't think she'd live much longer.

* ❀ *

The jet rolled to a stop on the tarmac. Harrison glanced out the window. The lights of Biggin Hill Airport glowed through the darkness of the late hour, welcoming them home.

If only he wanted to be back.

He stifled a sigh and released his seat belt. Across from him, Ellen unbuckled hers. In her chic skirt and silk top, she looked tremendous, so young and pretty, even though she was tired and worried.

After the tragic news about Josie, Ellen had been frantic to return to Canterbury and to somehow get in touch with Marian so she could try to get holy water for Josie. Harrison had done everything he could to arrange a change in the flight plans. But it had taken a few hours before they got clearance to leave by late morning.

They'd slept during the flight back. And now wordlessly they prepared to deplane.

Before leaving Saint Lucia, he'd phoned Drake and informed him to meet them with the car and his wheelchair, and he'd texted a short while ago with an update on the time. He wasn't keen on disturbing his butler and driver at this late hour. But he couldn't take chances on anyone else seeing him walking yet and draw the attention of Lionel Inc. or some other pharmaceutical company that had been attempting to get Arthur's ultimate cure.

Once news was out that he was no longer paralyzed, he suspected Lionel would send their thugs after him and attempt to beat the truth out of him. He shuddered at the remembrance of his abduction last year when he'd been helping Marian.

He'd concluded the best thing to do was make a statement to the press. And his only course of action was to fabricate something about his recovery. He'd tell them that he'd been gradually regaining movement over the past few years but hadn't wanted to broadcast the news until he knew for sure he was progressing. It was an outright lie. And he absolutely hated to lie. Look where lying to the Fletchers about his relationship with Ellen had gotten him.

Harrison slid a glance at Ellen.

She was still reclining in her seat, her head back and eyes closed. She hadn't smiled once all day.

He knew her heart was heavy over Josie's dire prognosis. Ellen had been in communication with Serenity House staff and Josie's parents periodically. While the little girl was still hanging on to life, her connection was tenuous, and the doctors wanted to move her to palliative care.

Yet, the gulf existing between him and Ellen stemmed from more than just her worry and grief. He returned his attention to the darkness of the runway out the window and loathed the awkwardness.

It was his fault. He'd read more into their kisses and their time together than he should have. She'd only been swept up in the moment and had never made him any promises.

Even so, he couldn't understand how she could walk away from their kisses unscathed. Every time he'd touched or kissed her, he'd been seared all the way to his soul. His passion for her had moved from sparks to a blazing fire, and there was no turning back now. He couldn't extinguish the flames—didn't want to.

But she clearly didn't feel the same way. And he supposed that's what hurt most of all. Although he hadn't realized his desire when planning the trip, he could see now that he'd been hoping during their time together she'd see him in a new light, that her feelings for him might awaken, and maybe she'd even fall a little bit in love with him.

Yet, she'd lived for so many years in death's grip, she wouldn't be able to shake off her fears in one weekend.

The plane door began to open, sweeping in the chill of the night, so different from the balmy warmth of the Caribbean.

Ellen sat forward and shuddered, hugging her arms across her chest.

"Here." Harrison shrugged out of his suit coat and draped it over her shoulders. He should have thought about her need sooner. After the tropical temperatures, the UK in May no longer seemed quite as warm as it had when they'd left.

She didn't resist but instead wrapped his coat tighter. "Thank you."

With a nod, he sat back, once again hating the stilted conversation and long stretches of silence. Maybe this morning after that kiss in the hallway, he should have played along with her just as he always had. Maybe he shouldn't have confronted her and demanded answers. Maybe he should have kept his true feelings securely locked away.

Was it too late to go back before that discussion and attempt to restore their relationship to what it had been previously? He'd rather have something with her than nothing at all. If he couldn't have the feast, he'd settle for crumbs, even though such an attitude was completely pathetic.

The stairs would be down in a few minutes, and the pilot would be out to help them with their luggage. He had to have a quick word or do something soon. If he didn't, he suspected Ellen would leave Chesterfield Park just as rapidly as she could make the arrangements. Then when would he see her again? Especially now that she didn't need him?

Swallowing his dignity, he shifted forward on the seat. She was looking out the window, and her profile was as lovely as always and reminded him of that morning and the way she'd lifted her face to his, wrapped her arms around his neck, and brushed her lips across his. He hadn't mistaken the desire in her eyes, had he?

"Ellen?"

She turned her gaze away from the window and faced him with worried eyes.

With everything going on with Josie, now probably wasn't the best time to talk about their relationship. But he had to say something. "Look, love. Can we forget about what happened and go back to being friends?"

"I don't know. Can we?" Even though she included them both, her raised brow meant the question was for him. Could he be satisfied with only being friends?

The same lump of protest that had arisen earlier formed again. During all the so-called playacting around the other guests, she may have pretended. But he'd done the opposite. He'd dropped his pretenses. For the first time, he'd been real about how he felt. Could he go back? Could he pretend again that what he felt about her didn't matter? Pretend he was indifferent? Pretend he didn't want more?

He nodded. Yes, he could. And yes, he would.

He'd had the plane ride to think on it. In fact, thoughts had plagued him while he'd been sleeping. Even if he could wait and give her more time to overcome her fears, he suspected she would be better off with a younger man, someone closer in age who could give her a family to replace the one she'd lost.

Obviously, now that he was no longer paralyzed, he had a higher likelihood of being able to have children. But he wasn't keen on being an older dad. His mother had been forty-two when she'd gotten pregnant with him. His father had been fifty. While he'd never doubted their love, he'd hated that they'd been more like grandparents than parents. And he'd had so little time with them before they'd passed away.

He didn't want to do that to any children, put them through the anguish he'd experienced, and abandon them when they most needed him. The best way to avoid that was not to have children.

On the other hand, Ellen deserved to have many of them. She was young enough to enjoy them for years to come. And she needed to have a husband young enough to enjoy them with her.

The stark reality was that he wasn't suited for her—beyond friendship, that is. He'd do best to remember it, or he'd only end up alienating her altogether, if he hadn't already.

He reached across the span of seat separating them and circled her hand with his. The contact sparked desire inside him, but he rapidly doused it with the reality that he could lose her if he didn't close off that part of him. He'd had plenty of practice holding it at bay before. He could surely do it again.

"Look, we've no need to change the previous nature of our relationship." He forced out the words he knew she wanted to hear. "After much time thinking about it today, I've come to the conclusion that friendship is in our best interest."

She nodded and expelled what could only be described as a relieved breath. Had she been worried about losing him too? Or was she happy to discover he wasn't planning to demand more from their relationship?

The same frustration he'd felt that morning surfaced again, but he rapidly stuffed it down.

"Thank you, Harrison." She squeezed his hand.

He released his hold and retracted his hand to his lap. "I want you to know that even though I massively bumbled the end of our trip, I had a spectacular time."

"You didn't bumble it. I blame myself for letting things go on as I did. You didn't want to pretend to be a couple, and I convinced you to go against your principles."

"I had a choice too, you know."

A smile finally lit her face and eased the pain in his chest a little. This was what he wanted—her happiness. That's all he'd ever wanted. And if making her happy meant he had to let go of his far-fetched dream of being with her, then so be it.

He leaned forward, and before he could stop himself, he brushed a wisp of hair from her face.

Her breath hitched, and her gaze met his. The message in her wide blue eyes was anything but platonic. It was filled with longing, a longing that reached out and tugged him closer. Did she want him to kiss her?

Her lips parted slightly as if in expectation. And she drew in another shaky breath.

They weren't performing for an audience now. What reason could she have for wanting a kiss except that she'd liked kissing him every bit as much as he had her? Maybe the changing nature of their relationship was confusing her too.

"Looks like your driver is here, Lord Burlington." The pilot's call came from the open door of the cockpit.

Ellen stood abruptly, putting an end to his speculation. She spun away and reached for her bag underneath the seat. As she straightened, she fidgeted with getting the straps over her shoulder. "I'll meet you at the car, okay?"

"Right."

She hurried to the door and ducked through, her high-heel sandals clicking in her haste to get away.

Once she disappeared, he expelled his frustration, a cold chill wrapping around his heart. She was going to leave him. As fast as she could. And he would be helpless to prevent it. He sat forward and bowed his head.

The words of the Serenity Prayer whispered through him: *God, grant me the serenity to accept the things I cannot change; the courage to change the things I can; and wisdom to know the difference. Living one day at a time; enjoying one moment at a time; accepting hardships as the pathway to peace.*

He'd heard Ellen whisper the prayer often enough that it was embedded within his memory. But until now, he hadn't truly thought about accepting hardships as the pathway to peace. He'd only thought about having the courage to change Ellen's sickness.

Now that he'd done his part in helping her get well, could he accept the hardship of letting her go? Was that his next step?

He blew out another breath. He didn't know how in doing so he'd ever find the pathway to peace. At the moment, it seemed like the pathway to despair. But if he wanted what was best for her, could he do it?

"Lord Burlington?" The pilot's voice from the cockpit contained a note of alarm. "Looks like your driver is leaving without you."

Harrison jumped to his feet, the ease of the movement still taking him by surprise. He'd intended to wait for his wheelchair but strode to the door regardless. Had Ellen told Bojing to leave? She was anxious to get back to Chesterfield Park and attempt to get more holy water. But she wouldn't rush off without him, would she?

His heart pounded a protest at the thought. As he ducked through the door and started down the stairs, he caught sight of red taillights speeding away. He leapt down the steps and then stopped at the bottom. He might have gained his legs back, but he wasn't a superhero and wouldn't be able to run fast enough to stop Bojing.

He pulled out his mobile and rang Drake's contact.

Drake answered on the second ring. "Almost there, my lord."

"Almost?" Harrison watched the taillights round one of the private terminals and disappear from sight.

"Airport security was holding us up. Telling us they'd already given us clearance." His tone was loaded with exasperation.

"I don't understand." The light of something a dozen paces away on the tarmac snagged his attention. He jogged toward it.

As he retrieved it, his pulse crashed to a halt. Ellen's mobile. The screen was shattered, but the picture underneath was unmistakably hers—her last picture with Marian the previous May, before Marian had died. The two stood together in the garden of Chesterfield Park under the archway of wisteria. Both smiling brightly, arms around one another.

At the flash of lights from an oncoming car, he shielded his eyes to see his Bentley angling toward the jet. Bojing's head barely reached above the steering wheel, and Drake sat in the front passenger seat beside him.

As they pulled up, Harrison's pulse stuttered. Ellen was in the back. Surely she was. They'd simply driven away without him and now had returned. The moment the car stopped, he jerked open the rear door.

The seat was empty. She was nowhere in sight.

"Where is she?" He straightened and stared in the direction the other vehicle had driven.

"Where's *who*, my lord?" Drake swung his door wide and climbed out.

"Ellen." Harrison's pulse started pumping again but at double the pace. "She got into a car. We thought it was you . . ." If it wasn't Drake and Bojing, then who was it?

His mind spun with a dozen different possibilities and then landed on only one. "Oh Lord in heaven above, help me." He bent over, ill.

"What happened?" Drake placed a hand on his back.

"What's going on?" the pilot called from the jet doorway.

Harrison couldn't make himself say the words, but they clanged through him anyway with the force of an aircraft at full speed.

Ellen had been abducted.

9

"WE NEED TO CHASE DOWN the car that was just here." Harrison lurched for the rear door, his muscles tensing with the need to go.

Thankfully, Drake didn't waste time and jumped back into the car.

Halfway in, Harrison halted and glanced at the pilot, who was descending the stairs. "The car that was just here, did you have a look at the make or number plate?"

"Sorry, Lord Burlington. Didn't think I needed to." At the confusion in the man's expression, Harrison reckoned he was innocent of any part in the kidnapping. As a long-trusted friend, he wouldn't have given away their landing time or sent Ellen outside if he'd suspected any danger.

Harrison finished climbing in. As he slammed the door closed, Bojing took off, squealing the tires in his haste.

"That way." Harrison pointed past Bojing toward the private terminal. "I think they're headed toward the motorway."

There weren't many vehicles out at so late an hour. Hopefully, they'd be able to catch up to any other cars in the area. Regardless, Harrison brought up the number for Sybil Huxham, the local investigator he'd worked with after his abduction. She was the best in all of Kent.

"Drake, you phone the police while I get ahold of Ms. Huxham."

When Harrison had been captured at the Canterbury Cathedral crypt, his kidnappers had blindfolded him and taken him to a remote location where he'd been bullied and beaten and questioned about Arthur Creighton's research into the ultimate cure. He hadn't known much at that point and hadn't been able to give them the information they'd wanted, so they'd released him.

In the weeks following the incident, Ms. Huxham had traced one of the kidnappers to Lionel Inc., Mercer Pharmaceutical's biggest competitor. The brute had been arrested and jailed but had denied any connection with Lionel. And of course, Lionel had refuted every claim made against them.

While the abduction experience had been terrifying, other than dehydration and a few broken ribs, Harrison had been all right.

But now . . . If they had Ellen, what did they intend to do with her? They wouldn't mistreat a woman the same way they'd mistreated him, would they?

Bile welled up into his throat.

Why her?

He'd assumed Lionel had given up their close surveillance of his activities after the accusations against them and also after realizing he'd stopped searching for the ultimate cure. He hadn't seen anyone following him in recent months. Nevertheless, he'd taken precautions to keep his life and doings as private as possible. He'd been extra careful with the trip abroad not to give away their destination.

Had the news of Ellen's miraculous healing somehow gotten

out while they'd been gone? He'd requested secrecy. Besides, the medical staff were obligated to keep the results of Ellen's tests confidential. But he supposed all it took was one doctor telling a colleague for rumors to spread. He should have guessed the news was simply too incredible to remain private.

If the word of Ellen's healing had been leaked, then it was very likely Lionel had gotten wind of it. There was no telling what they might do to her now, especially if they discovered she'd ingested the holy water.

Harrison's heart banged against his chest. "Can you go faster, Bojing? We have to catch up to that car."

As Drake informed the police of the kidnapping and as Harrison did the same with Ms. Huxham, Bojing sped onto the motorway. But no matter how fast they went, they didn't come upon any suspects on the nearly deserted road. The longer they drove, the more Harrison realized the futility of the chase. Without a number plate, vehicle make, or any other identifying markers, they had no idea what to look for. And they didn't have a clue if they were going in the right direction.

Even so, how could he give up searching?

He hadn't saved her life only to lose her.

* ● *

Ellen struggled against the bindings around her wrists. She didn't know why she was trying to free her hands, not when the car was going too fast for her to make an escape. Especially not when the man on the seat next to her held a gun on his lap.

Through the darkness, she could see the glint of moonlight on the barrel. And she could still feel the imprint of that cold barrel against her neck the moment she'd opened the car door and leaned inside.

With a fresh burst of frustration mingled with fear, she closed her eyes. She'd been such a fool to run off the plane without Harrison. She'd been an even bigger fool not to pay better attention to the car waiting for them. In the darkness it had the same sleek, black look as the Bentley. But after opening the door, she'd realized it wasn't—a moment too late.

A divider between the front and back seats began to motor down, revealing two people, the driver and a passenger.

The passenger shifted and glanced at her. "Ellen Creighton. It's a pleasure to see you again, especially looking so strong and healthy."

While the night hid the man's face, Ellen had no trouble distinguishing the voice with its American accent. "Jasper Boyle."

Jasper had been Marian's coworker at the Mercer Research facility in Groton, Connecticut, had acted the part of a friend and would-be suitor. But in the end, they discovered he was working all along for Lionel and had been planted at Mercer to spy on Arthur Creighton through Marian. Unfortunately, Ellen and Harrison hadn't learned of his duplicity until after they'd disclosed critical information regarding Arthur's theory.

"You're back a day early." Jasper's tone was pleasant, as if he was simply making conversation.

But the fact that he was aware of her trip and the duration sent fresh fear skittering along her nerves. If Jasper and Lionel knew about the trip to Saint Lucia, what else had they discovered? "Turn the car around and take me to Chesterfield Park. You can't hold me against my will, Jasper."

"You got in the car of your own accord."

"No, I didn't."

"Everyone who was watching would have witnessed you opening the door and entering without anyone forcing you to do so."

She glared at him but guessed the effect was useless in the dark. "What do you want?"

"How was your trip?" His voice was again nonchalant. "I'm surprised you had the energy for it, considering your primary care physician suggested hospice."

Did Jasper's question mean Lionel hadn't yet heard about her cancer-free diagnosis? Should she try to keep it from them? "Just because I have VHL and cancer doesn't mean I can't travel and enjoy life. You know my philosophy is live my life to the fullest. I've never held back."

"Seems odd to me that someone on the verge of dying, someone who could hardly walk around on her own a few days ago, would suddenly take a vacation."

"It's not odd at all—"

"In fact, it was so odd that we followed up with your doctor's office . . ."

Ellen's racing heart came to a halt.

"It's always amazing what underpaid staff are willing to share with the offer of a bonus."

So, Jasper had bribed someone in her doctor's office to give them her records?

"Imagine our—my—delight when I learned your tests show the cancer is completely gone from your system."

"Your delight?" Ellen couldn't keep the sarcasm from her tone. "Yes, I'm sure you were ecstatic for me."

"Now, Ellen." Jasper tsked. "Of course I'm delighted. Who wouldn't be at such good news? News that's too good to be true. News that's almost *miraculous*."

"You know as well as I do that remission can happen even in the worst cases."

"True. In very rare cases. For cancer." He paused. "But how can you explain the disappearance of the VHL gene anomaly? Nothing like that has ever occurred in the records of modern medicine."

"And who says it's gone?" The genetic test results hadn't been available before they left for Saint Lucia. Had Lionel somehow expedited the test?

Even if Lionel had gotten ahold of the results showing the absence of VHL, that didn't mean the abnormal gene wasn't lurking somewhere in her body, waiting to come out again. Tests weren't always foolproof.

Jasper studied her a moment before turning around. "Since it appears you're as curious as we are to discover what happened, then I guess you won't mind having a few more tests, will you?"

Did he know she'd taken the holy water? And if he knew about her drinking it, did he also know about Harrison? She could only pray Lionel hadn't yet discovered Harrison's recovery from his paralysis. If they did, would they try to kidnap him just as they had her?

Her muscles tensed. She couldn't let them harm Harrison. For now, she'd have to stay silent about his healing and cooperate with Lionel so they'd focus on her. It was the best way to keep Harrison safe.

As the divider rolled up, the car slowed. She glanced out the window and attempted to gauge where they were taking her. Unfortunately, with the twists and turns of the roads, she'd lost track of the direction and couldn't regain it. Besides, she wasn't familiar with the Kent countryside. For all she knew, they'd gone north past London.

Regardless, if she could find a way to escape, she had to take advantage of it. Josie's life was at stake. Already Ellen felt like she'd wasted an entire day with traveling, and she was anxious to return to Chesterfield Park. Ellen had to find a way to connect with Marian and communicate the need for holy water.

The car turned onto a winding gravel driveway. As branches brushed against the car, Ellen gathered that the driveway was overgrown and seldom used. The thumping of tires over planks told her they were crossing a bridge.

They drove a short distance farther into a garage or outbuilding of some kind. Then the car slowed to a halt, and the motor was silenced.

She didn't resist when her captor forced her from the car and guided her across a grassy yard to a side entrance of a dilapidated castle. She racked her brain for information on all the castles in and around Canterbury and Kent. The area was home to many beautiful old structures—Chesterfield Park among them. And while she'd visited several other historic places over the years, she couldn't identify this particular fortress.

As they worked their way through the ground floor, she could tell from the few dark corridors they passed through that the castle wasn't currently lived in. The chairs and couches were covered in sheets. Beautifully carved mahogany side tables and bookshelves were layered with cobwebs. Large oriental rugs and the wood floors were coated with dust.

Not a single light seemed to work, and they used flashlights. Even so, she could tell the estate had once been elegant. Knightly armor stood near an embroidered wall tapestry. They passed by paintings, sculptures, and other artifacts, even a medieval-looking curio cabinet with a collection of old glass bottles.

As they started down a steep stairway, she shivered from the cold, musty dampness rising to meet them. The stone walls were wet in places with trickles of water forming thin veins. Jasper led the way, and her other abductor formed the rear, his gun a constant reminder that this wasn't a voluntary expedition, no matter what Jasper might claim.

At the landing, she stumbled over a dip in the floor but caught herself. Darkness pressed in even more. They had to be in the underbelly of the castle where the dungeons had once existed. Were they planning to lock her up down here?

She clutched Harrison's suit coat tighter around her shoulders, his sandalwood aroma still lingering in every fiber. Oh Harrison. What must he be thinking now that she was gone? He would be frantic with worry, wondering what had happened.

Ahead, Jasper reached an arched door made of slabs of thick oak with an ancient lock. He pounded against the door, and they waited long seconds before he pounded again.

Finally, the door creaked open and light spilled out, illuminating the stone passageway. They were ushered inside a chamber, and she was temporarily blinded by fluorescent bulbs. Voices and the beeping of monitors surrounded her.

"She was easier to get than I expected," Jasper was explaining to someone. "The ruse with airport security bought us the time we needed to get to the plane first."

Ellen's vision adjusted to the sight of what appeared to be a laboratory, with computers and screens along with medical equipment of all sorts—syringes, needles, beakers, flasks, and chemicals with detailed labels.

An older, balding scientist in a white lab coat and wearing rubber gloves approached. His thin face was placid, his expression almost pleasant, but his gray eyes regarded her like she was a specimen under a microscope rather than a human being. He glanced at Jasper and waited. For an introduction?

Jasper nodded. "Oh yes. Dr. Lionel, this is Ellen Creighton. Ellen, this is Dr. Lionel."

Ellen examined the scientist again more carefully. This was Dr. Lionel? The CEO of Lionel Inc.?

"Miss Creighton, I'm pleased to meet you." Dr. Lionel spoke softly with a slight accent. She'd once heard her father and Marian discussing that he was Austrian, that his family had started the business long ago, before Mercer. "After so miraculous a healing, you must know we could do nothing less than study what has taken place in your body."

"Jasper mentioned doing tests."

In the bright light of the laboratory, she could see that Jasper was still as handsome as always. He was fair-haired with a Captain America–like appeal. She should have suspected last May when he'd flown into Canterbury to be with Marian in her coma that he was a weasel, especially when he'd started flirting with her. Of course, she wouldn't have been interested in him, even if he wasn't Marian's almost-boyfriend. But at the time she'd been so distraught that she'd trusted him more than she should have.

"Yes. Tests." The detached coldness in Dr. Lionel's eyes was frightening, and she suspected this man was capable of doing anything to further his own interests, that he wouldn't hesitate to hurt either Harrison or her if it benefited him.

All the more reason to keep the news of Harrison's healing a secret. She lifted her chin, hoping she appeared braver than she felt.

10

HARRISON WANTED TO POUND SOMETHING. Anything. But he forced himself to sit in his wheelchair at the table in the library without moving.

With her back facing the wall of floor-to-ceiling bookshelves, Sybil Huxham stood in the center of the room and had positioned herself so she could see all entrance points, including the door and windows. Whenever he was with her, he noticed she was savvy like that, tuned in to her surroundings, her keen eyes seeing every detail.

In black jeans, black leather jacket, and black combat boots, she had an aura of toughness. While she wasn't Harrison's type—because she wasn't Ellen—she was beautiful with straight brown hair, porcelain features, and stunning green eyes. She was young—twenty-seven—and had served four years as a police constable for the Kent Police before being hired on as a private investigator for ABI, the Association of British Investigators.

She crossed her arms and leveled an intense look at him. "What aren't you telling me?"

He was tempted to squirm but remembered he was still pretending he was paralyzed. "I've told you everything I can."

"You haven't said enough." She spread her feet slightly, her gaze darting to the long windows that overlooked the gardens behind Chesterfield Park. She locked in on something and seemed to catalog the information before turning her sharp eyes back on him.

Midmorning sunlight spilled into the room across the glossy table, his coffee cup the only item on the pristine surface. He fiddled with the handle of the mug, the liquid inside now tepid after the past half hour of going over every detail with Ms. Huxham.

"If you want my help," she stated matter-of-factly, "you have to be honest."

"I have been."

"About *everything*."

He picked up his mug and lifted it to his lips but then remembered he had no taste for the coffee. He hadn't had an appetite for anything since he'd arrived home before dawn. All he could think about was Ellen, that she was probably suffering the same abuse he had. The thought of someone hurting her made him sick to his stomach.

"Ms. Huxham—"

"Sybil."

She'd asked him to call her by her first name on many occasions, but for whatever reason, he always lapsed to her professional title. "Sybil." He cleared his throat. "I've given you enough information to go on. No doubt she's been kidnapped by Lionel and has been hidden in the same holding place they took me. I've described it as best I can. Now it's up to you to find it."

She pressed her lips together.

"Please. I need you to find her."

She was silent for a long moment before she uncrossed her arms and started toward the door. "Can't help you, Harrison. Hire someone else."

Her boots thudded across the large area rug.

"I'll double the amount I'm paying you."

Her stride didn't waver. "It's not about the money."

Desperation welled up and crashed through him. He needed Ms. Huxham's expertise. And he didn't have the time to hire someone else, especially since she was already familiar with the complexities of the case from last year—or at least as much as he could reveal.

"Please, Ms. Hux—Sybil."

"Sorry. Can't."

As she exited into the hallway, he almost jumped up from the wheelchair. The truth propelled him, nonetheless, and the words rushed out. "She ingested holy water, and it healed her."

Sybil halted but didn't turn.

"I vow it's the truth."

Finally, she pivoted and fisted her hands on her hips, regarding him with a cocked head. "Tell me more."

"Do you believe me?"

"I saw her tests."

"How?"

"I tracked them down before coming here."

"The tests were supposed to be confidential. I made my physician swear he wouldn't tell a soul."

"It took me less than a minute to deduce which of his office clerks was selling information."

Harrison sat back in the wheelchair. Clearly, the same person had sold the information to Lionel. "If you already knew about her healing, then why didn't you say so?"

She returned and stood just inside the door, poised to leave. "I can't work with you if you won't level with me about every detail. There's no point."

"All right. I'm sorry I didn't tell you, but you must understand my hesitation in revealing the specifics about her recovery. I don't want you thinking I'm crazy."

"You either trust me or you don't."

"I'm trying."

"Then tell me the rest."

"The rest?"

"Yes. About you."

He swallowed hard. Had someone figured out his healing too? Perhaps recognized him in Saint Lucia?

Sybil would learn of it eventually. He may as well tell her now. "I'm walking again."

"I realize that. But how?"

He pushed back from the table. "How could you have any idea? None of the offices have my medical information. And I haven't told anyone, not even my private physician."

She nodded curtly toward the garden. "You left your mug on the bench so that Drake had to bring you a fresh one. And there are no wheelchair marks in the grass."

He followed her gaze to a distant bench and the mug he'd left there, identical to the one on the table in front of him. "What if the mug belonged to the gardener?"

"Your soles are caked with mud." She nodded to his feet resting on the footrests of his wheelchair. "Too much mud for a paralyzed man."

She was good.

He held her gaze. Could he trust her?

Her track record from last year told him he could, as did the sincerity in her eyes.

He dropped his feet to the floor, then stood. He strode toward the door, closed it, and faced her again.

She watched him, her expression remaining unchanged except for a slight rounding of her eyes.

"I found two ampullae in the vault here at Chesterfield."

She was already well aware of the ampullae and holy water

from the previous investigation. She knew about the holy water contributing to Arthur's and Marian's comas. But he hadn't shared anything beyond the fact that the holy water contained a powerful, valuable drug of some kind since Lionel was going to such great lengths to acquire it.

Now she had proof of just how powerful and valuable it truly was. It was a miracle-working drug. The ultimate cure.

"You and Ellen each drank a flask?" She took him in from his head down to his shoes. Upon arriving home, he'd changed into his usual suit, vest, and bow tie. But after the freedom he'd had at Saint Lucia, somehow the attire felt too constricting.

"I drank the water in the first ampulla. And once I showed Ellen I was healed, she drank the second one."

"So Lionel realized she drank holy water and wants to run tests on her in order to replicate the healing process."

His blood turned suddenly cold. Was that what they planned to do? Test her? He should have guessed as much. Of course, they'd want to replicate what had happened— or at least try to. "I'll turn myself over to them and let them test me instead."

"No." Her single command was low and level. "For now, you need to stay out of the spotlight and continue to act like you're paralyzed. If word gets out about your healing along with Ellen's, the entire world will converge on Chesterfield Park. With that kind of attention, Lionel will secure a new hiding place for Ellen we might never find."

"Not if I hand myself over to Lionel quietly and privately."

One of Sybil's brows shot up. "If you hand yourself over, you'll be signing your death sentence right alongside Ellen."

"Death sentence?"

"They'll never release her."

"They released me."

"This is different. They had no reason to keep you. In fact, they needed you alive in order to gain more information."

"Right."

"But now that you're healed, you're a valuable commodity, just like her. They'll test you both until they discover what they want, and they won't let either of you live to tell about it."

The words spread over the room like a mantle of doom. "I'll make sure that she's safely returned before I hand myself over." Panic was slowly clawing at his insides. He couldn't allow her to become Lionel's lab rat.

"Look, Harrison. Even if you happen to broker an exchange successfully—which is doubtful—they'll just go after her again at some point."

Was Sybil right? Was an exchange futile? He fought against the desperation, trying to stay calm and rational. "How much time do you think you'll need to locate her?"

"One week."

"That's too long."

"We have some time. She's too valuable for them to dispose of right away."

"How about three days?"

"Five."

"Fine, five days. After that I'll arrange a deal. My life for hers. And I'll add in an enormous sum of money if I need to."

Even five was too long to expose Ellen to whatever Lionel had planned for her. But he prayed they wouldn't harm her, not as long as they needed her alive.

●　◉　●

Ellen fought the grogginess. Her mind was filled with images of Harrison and the hurt in his eyes after that early morning kiss in Saint Lucia.

I'm sorry, Harrison. I should have been more sensitive to you. She wanted to speak the words, but they were trapped in her throat. In their last hours before leaving Saint Lucia, she hadn't handled the situation well. Instead, she'd withdrawn, something she'd gotten pretty good at doing over the years whenever relationships become too serious.

Her fingers brushed against the cold metal of an examination table beneath her. The movement awoke her to the pinch of the PICC line in her arm along with the restraints at her wrists and ankles tying her down. The steady pulse of a nearby monitor greeted her.

Where was she? Was she at the hospital again, having more tests? She tried to tune in to the talking across the room.

"So far the lab work doesn't reveal a trace of anything in her system." The voice belonged to Jasper Boyle.

"None of the tests revealed anything in Arthur's or Marian's systems either." At the foreign accent in the second voice, Ellen tried to decipher who was speaking.

"This is different." Jasper again.

Ellen opened her eyes to fluorescent lights, and the memory of the kidnapping came rushing back. She wasn't at the hospital. She was in a secret laboratory beneath a castle somewhere in the countryside.

"We knew this would likely be the case," came the accented voice again. Dr. Lionel?

She shifted her head enough to see the older man seated in front of a nearby computer screen, studying the data there. Jasper stood near him, wearing a white lab coat and holding a steaming coffee cup.

The windowless room made gauging the time of day difficult. How many hours had elapsed while she'd been drugged?

"In comparing her old labs to those we drew," Jasper continued, "we should be able to break down how the holy water interacted and bonded with the tissue receptors in cell membranes and intracellular fluid. At the very least, we should see the extent of the receptor activation."

"Yes, but that is not the case."

"If we can't find evidence of absorption or distribution in the plasma, then we should find something in the renal excretion."

Jasper, like Marian and her dad, was a pharmacokinetics specialist. His lifework revolved around testing and studying the effects of drugs in the body. But he hadn't been able to find the holy water in her system. Would they release her now that the initial testing had failed to produce results?

"We have absolutely nothing. Nothing." Dr. Lionel's tone contained an inevitability that sent a chill up Ellen's spine.

"Perhaps we're too late. The testing would have been much more effective if we'd conducted it immediately after the ingestion."

Dr. Lionel clicked away at the keyboard, typing something before pausing. "We have no choice but to proceed with the next phase of our plan."

"Do we really want to use our one flask on her?"

One flask. Of holy water? Had Lionel found an ampulla? If so, where?

"It may be our only chance to secure more of the water."

"But if we test the curative properties on my dad"—Jasper's voice contained a note of frustration—"we can study the effects immediately this time."

Jasper's dad had Lou Gehrig's disease. Last year when she'd spoken with him about the illness, his dad was holding steady. Had the older man deteriorated over the past months just like she had? Maybe Jasper was as frantic to find a cure for his dad as Marian and her dad had been to find one for her. The same way she was now anxious to find one for Josie.

127

"Even if we give your father the flask and study the effects right away, my guess is that we will still find nothing."

"But it's worth a try—"

"Must I remind you? Arthur's bloodwork showed nothing. Marian's showed nothing. And now Ellen's shows nothing. What makes you think your father's will be different?"

"I don't know—"

"Precisely why we must now seek the source."

The source? As in the source of the holy water? That's what Dad and Marian had tried to do. And they'd failed.

"It's much too risky," Jasper said.

"Someone supplied Ellen with more holy water." Dr. Lionel's tone was clipped. "We must assume that was either Arthur or Marian doing so from the past."

Ellen tried not to start at Dr. Lionel's assumption that time crossing was possible. More people were aware of the powers of the holy water than she'd realized.

Jasper sipped his coffee and then spoke. "Or perhaps Harrison's antiquarians stumbled upon the last ampullae finally."

"As closely as we've been monitoring them, we would have known if they did."

Harrison had antiquarians searching for another ampulla? She should be surprised. But she wasn't.

Dr. Lionel rolled away from his computer, the wheels of his chair scraping across the cement floor. "With the extensive search Lord Burlington is orchestrating for her, we may not have much time before we need to move out of the country. While we have access to this location, we must inject her with the dose today and instruct her to find more."

Harrison was searching for her? An ache formed in her chest. Of course he was.

"And if she doesn't want to?"

"You said she was pliable."

So, they were planning on giving her a flask of the holy water in an attempt to send her to another era so she could locate more of the water to deliver to them?

"I won't do it." The words tumbled out before she could stop them.

Jasper spun and nearly spilled his coffee, apparently not expecting her to be awake yet. Dr. Lionel stood more slowly.

Wearing only a hospital gown and covered in a thin sheet, she shivered, frigid from her fingers to her toes. "You've gotten the tests you want from me, now let me go."

"Miss Creighton, please think seriously about the matter." Dr. Lionel approached in a calculated manner, as if every word, every step, every breath was somehow important. "Surely after benefiting from so great a cure, you'd like to help others find the same healing. Perhaps Josephine Ansley."

The protest inside her fizzled. How did they know about Josie?

"Think of the good you could do for Josie and all the children who stay at Serenity House." He stopped at the end of the examination table, but Jasper hung back.

Her nerves prickled. They knew way too much about her. Did they even know she'd returned early from her trip specifically to try to find holy water to cure Josie?

Dr. Lionel's expression remained calm, but as before the coldness of his gray eyes sent a shiver of unease up her spine. Something about him warned that he would find a way to bend her will—whether she cooperated or not.

"All you need to do," he continued, "is find the source of the holy water and give us a regular supply of it."

Dr. Lionel made it sound so simple. Even so, she couldn't—wouldn't—help him. "You have to know I can't agree to it. It would be a betrayal to my dad and sister. Not to mention the abhorrent way you treated Lord Burlington last year—"

"You have no choice but to cooperate, Miss Creighton." Dr. Lionel's mouth pinched tight. "Only you have the power to save Josephine Ansley and the other children in your program. Without the ultimate cure, they will all perish. Sooner rather than later."

Something in his words and expression caused Ellen's blood to run cold. What if Dr. Lionel and his staff were behind what had happened to Josie? Had they infiltrated Serenity House and given the little girl a drug that sent her into life-threatening cardiac arrest?

No, Dr. Lionel wouldn't have purposefully done such a thing. Would he?

Jasper dropped his attention to his coffee, refusing to meet her gaze, almost as though he was embarrassed to be part of the scheme.

"It would be a shame, Miss Creighton," Dr. Lionel said, "that the children would have their lives cut even shorter. Children like Theo and Brittany and Mila."

Those were three more who'd recently stayed at Serenity House. Yes, he was scheming to kill her children. She could see it in the depths of his soulless eyes.

"How dare you?" She jerked against her bindings, but the shackles only bit into her flesh. "They're innocent and have enough problems. How could you even think about hurting them more?"

"The staff at Serenity House would be held suspect, as evidence all points to the commonality of their deaths."

Her chest swelled with the need to scream out her frustration. But she wouldn't give him the satisfaction of seeing how much he was angering her. "You're a monster. You'll never get away with this."

"On the other hand, if you supply me with water"—he said as if he hadn't heard her—"you may still have time to save Josie."

Time to save Josie. That's why she'd returned from Saint Lucia. To save Josie by ingesting holy water residue, facilitating a brief connection with Marian, and asking for her sister to put more ampullae in the vault at Chesterfield Park. Since that didn't appear to be a possibility at the moment, then maybe she had to consider falling into a coma and going completely back.

Dr. Lionel watched her face expectantly. He'd dropped the bait and was waiting for her to nibble. How could she not? What other choice did she have?

"Why me? Why not send Jasper?" She tossed a glare at the young scientist.

Dr. Lionel didn't spare Jasper a glance. "With either your sister or father there to assist you, you'll have a much greater chance of success."

True. Marian would know where to find the holy water, which would save time and effort. And if Marian truly was alive, then Ellen would get to see her sister again. The possibility sent a shimmer of anticipation through her. "If I do this, how do I know you'll let me have some of the holy water for Josie when I'm through?"

"The more water you find, the more we'll have to go around."

"How long before you wake me up from the coma?"

"It depends on how well you're able to do."

She'd never be able to trust a man like Dr. Lionel to give Josie the holy water. But maybe she could set aside some in the vault at Chesterfield Park, reserved specifically for the Serenity House children. Dr. Lionel wouldn't have to know about it. And then Harrison could give it to Josie.

"I'll expect your full collaboration, Miss Creighton," Dr. Lionel added, as though reading her mind. "You must deliver the water to me and me alone in the spot I designate. Please don't foolishly think you can get away with hiding it elsewhere for your own purposes."

Or else. He didn't say the words, but the threat hung over her, nonetheless. If she didn't do exactly as he wanted, he'd carry through with harming the Serenity House children.

"If you resist my instructions in any way," Dr. Lionel continued, "I am not sure I can guarantee Lord Burlington's safety either."

Was Dr. Lionel threatening to kidnap Harrison again? She couldn't let him, couldn't involve Harrison.

"What are the plans?" For now, she had to go along with his scheming. But surely she'd be able to figure out how to keep Josie and the other children alive and safe without helping Dr. Lionel.

Dr. Lionel returned to the desk and began stacking spreadsheets. "After studying more about the year 1382, the year your father picked, we've concluded that is truly the best time frame for collecting holy water."

She wasn't sure how Dr. Lionel had gleaned the secret information in the clues her dad had left for Marian. The scientist apparently had eyes and ears everywhere, people spying for him and providing information he needed.

"Yes,"—Dr. Lionel spoke with his back facing her as he waited for a laptop to shut down—"1382 seems to be the year that started the resurgence of miracles in Canterbury. And it's also a time when some of Canterbury's oldest buildings and structures were in existence—like this castle. Thus, you must go to 1382, locate the original wellspring of holy water at St. Sepulchre Priory, and provide us enough to continue our studies on how to replicate it."

As the screen went dark, Dr. Lionel closed the laptop, pushed in the desk chair, and then crossed to the door.

"We'll give you the dose shortly. I'll expect your first shipment within a week." Dr. Lionel didn't wait for her response but exited, closing the door behind him with a finality that left a cold grip on her heart.

Shipment? As if she was nothing more than a FedEx truck.

Jasper stared at the closed door, his expression etched with turmoil.

It reflected the turmoil raging inside her. Were they both pawns in this dangerous game? "You wanted the final ampulla for your father, didn't you?"

"Dr. Lionel promised that if I helped him, my father would be one of the first to benefit from the ultimate cure."

"That's why you started working for Lionel in the first place and betrayed Mercer?"

"Arthur wouldn't have offered to help my dad in a million years." Jasper spat her father's name like it was a contagious illness. "He was so selfish, so focused on healing you. I knew he'd never be willing to share the cure when he found it."

She couldn't respond. As much as she loved her dad, she couldn't deny Jasper's accusation. Her dad *had* been consumed with finding the ultimate cure to heal her mom. After Mom died, his obsession with finding the cure had moved to her.

"So now you think Dr. Lionel's wasting the holy water on me when it could heal your father?"

"Exactly."

Even if she still resented Jasper for betraying her and Marian, she felt sorry for him. "There's still a chance. If I find more water."

"If."

"Then you don't think time crossing is possible?"

"It's a long shot."

"What if I told you that after I swallowed the holy water, I saw Marian living in the past? That I was in the same room as her? That I heard her voice? That I saw she was pregnant?"

Jasper's eyes narrowed. "Did it really happen?"

"Yes. She was the one who put the holy water in Chesterfield's vault. There's no other explanation for how it got there, not after Harrison searched so thoroughly for so many weeks."

Jasper held her gaze as if testing the truth of her words.

Though Ellen had tried hard to rationalize everything away over the past year, she finally had to accept that the complexities of space and time were beyond the human mind's capability of understanding.

The past, present, and future intertwined somehow. Entanglement. That's what Harrison had called the phenomenon. The infinite God saw all of eternity at once with no beginning and no end. If that was the case, surely she could view time with a different perspective too and allow for more than she'd ever thought possible.

11

"WE RESEARCHED THE FLOOR PLANS of the original Reider Castle." Jasper led Ellen through the dark passageway. "And we believe the safest place to hide the holy water is in a narrow closet at the base of the dungeon steps."

Jasper lifted the latch on a door built into the side of the stairway. The door was only about three square feet in size and led into what looked like a crawl space.

Ellen squatted next to him.

"See the missing stone?" He shined the light on a spot on the opposite wall.

She nodded.

"There's a small nook big enough for half a dozen ampullae or bottles."

"Do you know if the hiding spot was there in 1382?"

"We're fairly certain." Jasper backed out and brushed the dust and cobwebs from his shirtsleeve. "We believe the stonemason who built this castle in the early 1300s purposefully crafted the hiding place to store treasures he stole while he worked on finishing the dungeon area. The spot went undiscovered until Lionel built the lab here, so it will be the perfect place to store holy water."

Ellen peered into the deep recess and then at the nearby stairway. "I have no guarantee that I'll be able to put anything down here."

Jasper began ascending the narrow flight of steps, his footsteps slapping against stone. "Dr. Lionel wants you to make this your place of residence."

"Is that possible?" She started after him, bunching the thick train of her skirt to keep it from dragging against the damp, dirty floor.

"He suggests that first you need to make the acquaintance of the family who lives here to gain access to the hiding place."

A part of her couldn't believe she was having this kind of conversation. It was as outlandish as her attire—a medieval gown Jasper had rented from a costume shop. "Make their acquaintance? How am I to do that?"

"According to the records we located in the castle library, the Worth family resided here during the latter part of the fourteenth century. A number of knighted sons and no daughters—at least recorded."

"And exactly how is that supposed to help me?"

"Dr. Lionel recommends you taking an interest in one of the sons."

Ellen halted halfway up the stairway and stared after Jasper, her blood turning cold. She waited for him to turn around, grin, and tell her he was kidding. But he climbed the rest of the stairs, leaving her behind.

Her already-difficult mission to find holy water had just grown exponentially more difficult and dangerous.

Protest pushed for release as she hurried the last of the distance. At the top, she gathered the cumbersome skirt again with its dragging train and had to practically run to catch up to Jasper and the beam of his flashlight cutting a trail through the shuttered interior.

"Jasper, please. You can't be serious."

"You're gorgeous, Ellen. One of the sons will fall for you and any story you tell him." The tone of his voice told her he wasn't entirely convinced she would cross time and that this was simply a fairy tale.

Real or not, she had to consider all her options. "I don't want to get involved with a man. Maybe you should take me to Chesterfield Park, and I'll hide the holy water there."

"Dr. Lionel wants you to hide the supply here at Reider Castle. Then he'll be assured he's the only one who can gain access to it."

Of course, Dr. Lionel wasn't about to let her go to Chesterfield Park and risk someone seeing her, not with Harrison's search effort in progress. And the truth was, she didn't want Lionel personnel to get anywhere near Harrison, not after Dr. Lionel's threat to harm Harrison.

Jasper passed through the great hall, dust motes swirling around their feet. "If you're unable to place the holy water into the hiding place at Reider Castle, then put the supply in the cathedral's crypt. The hiding place there isn't as big, but you can fit several bottles."

"I'd have more luck putting the holy water there, don't you think?"

"You'd draw a great deal of suspicion going in and out of the crypt, especially as a woman. The better choice is to befriend the Worths and use the nook at the base of the dungeon stairs."

"Don't you think that will draw suspicion too?"

"It's less public. I'm sure you'll figure out a way."

At the very least, she could become friends with the entire family—not just one of the sons. She trailed after Jasper into the front hallway, clutching her gown and trying not to trip. "As Marian's sister coming for a visit, how will I explain why I'm here and not at Chesterfield Park?"

"Tell them you were attacked from behind, separated from your traveling companion, and knocked unconscious." Jasper halted in the doorway.

Outside, the evening sky was lavender. The glow of the setting sun added a splash of colorful lace along the edges of the forest line that stood beyond the castle wall. It was hard to believe that less than twenty-four hours ago she and Harrison were on the private jet returning from Saint Lucia.

"Do whatever you need to, Ellen." Jasper softened his tone. "If this really works and you do end up in 1382, I have confidence you'll win everyone you meet to your side. You always do."

"Thank you, Jasper." She guessed he'd given her as much of an apology as he could for his part in everything.

The inner castle grounds were overrun with weeds along the high, stone walls of the bailey as well as the castle itself. In the flower beds on either side of the portico, a few tulips had managed to push their way through the dead brush that remained from the previous summer, but otherwise the outside of the castle was as dreary as the inside.

Across the expanse of the bailey, an iron gate hung half off its hinges in a crumbling arched gateway. Beyond was a bridge spanning a shallow river. If there had once been a moat, it was long gone. In the evening light, the river was glassy with the wildflowers growing along the banks reflected in the water.

Was this it? Her last look at life? Or just her last look at this present life?

"Ready?" Jasper was examining a clear test tube and the minuscule amount of clear liquid at the bottom.

If only she could have said good-bye to Harrison. The image of him in the seat across from her in the jet when they'd landed flashed into her mind. She'd felt his gaze upon her as she walked off the plane. It had seared her with each step she'd taken. She'd been tempted to turn around, walk back to him, and tell him that she did care, but that she was scared.

An ache worked its way up her chest into her throat. What if she never had the chance to see or talk to him again? Dr. Lionel might never wake her up from the coma, might use her to deliver the holy water until her body could no longer survive a comatose state and died. Even though she'd been prepared to die and leave Harrison only a few days ago before she was healed, somehow this parting seemed harder.

Jasper stared across the deserted castle grounds as though imagining what it must have once looked like. "If this works and you really cross over to the past, don't forget about all the lives you'll be saving. Not just my dad's but many others."

"I hope you're right." Especially for Josie and the rest of the children in the Serenity House.

Jasper lifted the test tube toward her lips.

"You want me to drink it here?" She took a step back. "Right outside the front doors of the castle?"

"I'd have you drink the holy water inside the castle, but we don't want the family to accuse you of breaking in." He gave her a once-over as if making sure her costume was in order. "After thinking through all the scenarios, we decided that here outside the door is the best place."

A thousand questions rolled through Ellen's head as they had all afternoon as she'd prepared to cross time. She wished she'd paid more attention to Marian's descriptions of what life had been like in the past. But she hadn't believed time crossing was possible and had dismissed Marian's talk as crazy and coma-induced.

Jasper swished the liquid again. "According to everything I've gleaned, you should show up in 1382 on this exact day and this exact time, the evening of May 18. Since Marian crossed into May of 1381, she'll have lived in the past for almost a year. But your dad will have yet to show up, since he didn't cross until May 21, 1382."

"In other words, I'm arriving about three days before him?"

"Yes. Make sure to utilize his expertise in getting the holy water."

She didn't understand how it was possible she could meet up with a dead dad and sister in the past. It seemed too ludicrous to consider. But here she was. About to venture into the unknown.

"Arthur's speculations about time crossing indicated that people have movement through the quantum energy field to the time period they last picture in their mind. That means you'll need to silently tell yourself 1382."

"1382," she whispered, trying not to think about the fact that she was about to fall into a coma and that she'd somehow, someway find herself in a completely different time and place. Or would she?

Jasper raised the glass container to her lips again. Even though her stomach tied itself in knots, this time she didn't resist. As he tipped the flask into her mouth, she let the liquid drain onto her tongue. It was cool and tasteless. She swallowed the scant drops but felt nothing different, nothing out of the ordinary. *I want to go to 1382*, she told herself the way Jasper had instructed. *1382. 1382.*

For a few seconds she stared back at Jasper, who was watching her face intently. The holy water—if it really was that—wasn't working on her.

Then everything went black.

● ◉ ●

Ellen opened her eyes to complete silence. For a moment, she felt as though she were floating in the air, suspended above the world.

At the slam of a door, her body awoke to her surroundings, to the sagging mattress underneath her, the overpowering sourness of body odor, and thick tapestries shadowing the bed.

"I do not care if she is asleep!" an angry male voice boomed nearby. "I shall question her now!"

Ellen bolted up in a tangle of sheet only to realize she was attired in a sheer chemise with thin shoulder straps and nothing underneath. Her heartbeat sped with a rush of wild thumping, and she dragged the foul-smelling sheet around her. Just in time.

The bed curtains jerked open, and daylight poured over her.

Was she in the past? And if so, apparently she'd been asleep for hours—all night and well into the next morning.

Her mind couldn't work fast enough to make sense of the details—the antique furniture and simple sparse decorations, the plainly clad and cowering people in the room, and the imposing figure looming above her.

He grabbed her arm and dragged her from the bed. It was all she could do to keep hold of the sheet as her bare feet touched the floor, which appeared to be covered in long pieces of straw or dried grass.

She straightened and found herself standing in front of a tall man with thick arms and legs. He wasn't overweight, but neither was he slender. His face was wide and his chin covered with a short beard that narrowed into two points. His dark brows angled above equally dark eyes. Although his hair wasn't yet touched with gray, the lines in his forehead and next to his eyes showed him to be a man of some age and experience—in his forties, if she had to guess. His long black tunic had a decorative trim around the collar and cuffs and was fitted at his broad waist by a leather belt fastened shut with a silver brooch containing an intricate cross pattern.

"Who are you?" His gaze roved over her. Even though she'd attempted to hide herself behind the sheet, it was a scant covering, and the lust simmering in his eyes told her he was able to see much more than he should.

Something in the biting grip of his fingers on her arm warned her she had to respond right away with a satisfactory answer, or she would be in trouble.

"I'm Ellen Creighton." She scrambled to remember the story she'd plotted with Jasper. "My sister is Marian—Durham."

"Lord Durham's wife?" The man's hold on her upper arm didn't diminish. If anything, it tightened.

Ellen prayed she was only dreaming, that she'd soon wake up. But another part of her quavered with the realization that she was truly standing in the past, that everything was too real and vivid to be a mere dream.

She tried to hold herself as regally as a nobly born woman would, although it was a difficult task considering she was attired in a thin sheet and even thinner nightgown of some sort. If this was real, was she at Reider Castle in 1382? Had someone brought her inside?

"I am traveling to Canterbury, to Chesterfield Park to visit Lady Marian. She's expecting me any day."

"Then why are you here? Why did my servants find you unresponsive on my doorstep?" His questions were harsh, his stance unyielding. Jasper had mentioned that the family who owned Reider Castle had gone by the name Worth. This was likely Lord Worth.

"My companion and I were attacked, and I was knocked unconscious." Jasper's plan had seemed solid before, but now that she was really here, she wished she'd taken more time to think through the details.

Lord Worth's eyes narrowed. "The physician said you show no signs of physical distress."

A physician had examined her? She held in a shudder and lifted her chin higher. "We were attacked from behind, and I have no recollection of what happened after that."

"Where is your chaperone?"

"Isn't she here with me?"

"No."

"Then I don't know." She tried to maintain her confidence, but under this man's glare, her trepidation was only mounting. "Now, if you will please bring me my clothes, I would like to get dressed."

Her comment only seemed to draw his attention back to her scantily clad body, and his nostrils flared slightly. "Seems to me you have conveniently forgotten too much information. I suppose you also have no recollection of how you happened to get across my moat, through my locked gatehouse, and past my armed guard?"

"That's right." She was tempted to drop her gaze but suspected looking away would be perceived as a sign of weakness, one that would put her further into his clutches.

He scrutinized her face as if by doing so he could see past her mask to the truth. She prayed her facade would remain in place, at least until he left her alone. After several seconds, the angry slant of his brows shifted so that his expression—while still fierce—took on a decidedly dangerous quality.

"I have already questioned the guard who was on duty last night." His voice dropped, and he motioned toward the narrow glassless window, its shutters open, allowing in the daylight along with a cool breeze that sent shivers over her exposed flesh.

She tried to break loose of his grip, but he was unrelenting as he guided her to the window so that the castle grounds spread out before her.

At the differences between the present and past, she almost gasped. The bailey, which had been wide open and overrun with weeds, was now like a miniature town. Wattle-and-daub huts with thatched roofs as well as long, low buildings were attached to the inner wall. Smoke curled up from holes in the centers of the structures.

Chickens and dogs roamed about the muddy interior with several spotted cows visible in a shed. A well stood at the center of the yard, and servants were drawing water and pouring it into clay jugs. An armed man was leading a horse into a stable on the opposite wall, his shoulders slumped and head down.

Except for the cluck of the chickens, the courtyard was eerily quiet.

She started to shift her sights to the densely forested land beyond the castle walls, but her gaze snagged on something dangling from the gatehouse. At first, she wasn't sure what she was seeing. Then she gasped and took a rapid step back. A soldier, with a rope about his neck, was twisting and turning in the breeze, his head at an odd angle.

She took another backward step, but the dark lord blocked her escape from the window and the gruesome scene. "My man-at-arms had naught to explain how you were able to get past him into my fortress." His tone was low and menacing. "'Twould appear, my lady, you have no better account than he did."

Had this lord killed one of his guards? Fear pushed up into her throat, and she had to swallow hard to dislodge it. "If I was unconscious, then I'll have no explanation at all except that perhaps one of your household—a servant or relative—discovered me in my vulnerable state and brought me here intending to protect me."

"Very unlikely." He cast a glance at the handful of servants still motionless on the perimeter of the room. "My servants and family would not risk peril by admitting a stranger into my estate without first gaining my permission."

It was becoming entirely too clear that coming to Reider Castle had been a dangerous mistake. She should have convinced Jasper to drive her to someplace else to drink the holy water. All she could do now was leave as quickly as possible. "Thank you for assisting me in my time of need. But now, I'd like to be reunited with my sister, Marian. If you'd be so kind as to take me to Chesterfield Park—"

He spun her around and gripped her chin, forcing her to look upward into his eyes, which were haughty and hard. "Fie, woman. If you will not tell me how you came to be inside my fortress, then you give me no choice but to hang you for trespassing with evil intent."

Ellen's pulse stumbled. So much for Jasper's assumption that the Worth men would easily become enamored with her. She could picture herself in the gatehouse next to the dead guard, her body swaying in the wind, her neck stretched to breaking. She'd been awake no longer than five minutes in the past, and already she was about to be murdered.

If only this was nothing more than a crazy hallucination brought about by the holy water. But if this was a vision and not real, then why did she feel the pinch of Lord Worth's fingers on her chin, smell the rancidness of his breath, and hear the squawking of chickens outside the window—apparently the only creatures in the castle that did not fear their master.

Please be a dream. Please wake up now. She closed her eyes and prayed that when she opened them, she'd be anywhere else but in this bedroom with this strange man. As she lifted her lashes, the same threatening face loomed in front of her.

Her muscles tightened. This was really happening. "If you take me to my sister's home, I'm sure they will be in your debt." She didn't care about locating the hiding place down by the dungeon. All she wanted to do was escape from Reider Castle alive. If only she could send a message to Marian. Her sister would surely come to her rescue.

Lord Worth released Ellen's chin and lifted his hand as though to strike her. Instinctively, she raised her arm in self-defense and in so doing the sheet slipped down.

His attention shifted to her shoulder, bare except for the shoe-string strap of her chemise.

She groped the linen and attempted to cover herself, but before she could pull it back up, his fingers came down onto her shoulder and blocked her. He didn't move for several heartbeats. Then he stroked his thumb across her collarbone, his eyes following the trail and filling with undeniable desire.

The touch made her skin crawl. She took a step away but found herself pressed against the window ledge with nowhere to run.

"Tell me, Lady Ellen, are you wed?"

She wanted to tell him she was happily married and to leave her alone. But then he'd likely ask her all kinds of questions about who her husband was—questions she was unprepared to answer. "No, I'm not wed." She was better off sticking to as much of the truth as she could. "I've been ill in recent years and didn't expect to live long enough to be married."

His gaze lifted to meet hers, his irises still wide and dark with wanting. "You do not appear to be ill."

What if he decided to violate her? No one would stop him. She needed to tread carefully, or she'd only make things worse for herself—if that were possible. "Thankfully, I've been healed in recent weeks and am feeling much better."

"Healed?" He assessed her with new interest. "By holy water?"

Ellen hesitated, sensing her answer was important but not sure how much to divulge.

He gave her a rough shake. "Speak the truth, Lady Ellen, and save my captain of the guard the trouble of forcing the truth from you with methods that may offend your delicate sensibilities."

What difference did it make whether he knew? At this point, self-preservation was more important than keeping secrets. "Yes. I drank holy water."

He studied her again, and his lips turned up into a thin, calculating smile. "I heard rumors this past year of healings wrought by the holy water. One such rumor has to do with your brother-in-law, Lord Durham, that he was healed of life-threatening injuries."

Marian had told tales of her husband, William, receiving mortal wounds while defending the king. Marian claimed she'd given William holy water to save his life. At the time, Ellen hadn't believed any of Marian's stories about the past, but now after all that had happened to her and Harrison, she had no doubt William had been healed. It was no wonder Lord Worth was curious to know more.

"Heretofore, Lord Durham has been unwilling to open the wellspring at St. Sepulchre, has indeed prevented us from taking even a drop." Lord Worth continued with his tight smile. "Mayhap, I have discovered a means to gain his cooperation."

She wanted to pretend she didn't know what he was referring to, but this had to be the wellspring Dr. Lionel had mentioned. She started to shake her head, but his grip returned to her chin with bruising force and was followed by his mouth coming down upon hers, crushing her lips and suffocating her.

She attempted to wrestle free and slap his face. Before she could manage, he broke away, spun around, and stalked across the room.

She wiped her hand across her mouth, disgusted and angry all at once.

When he reached the door, he stopped.

She couldn't keep from glaring at him.

His demeanor was calm, almost casual. "I shall not tolerate insolence or lack of submission. The sooner you learn that, the better you will get along."

What did he mean? Was he expecting her to submit to his kisses or more? "If you misuse me, my sister and brother-in-law will learn of it."

"They will also learn I may do as I please to my wife."

"Wife?"

"My children have need of a new mother, and I have need of a new wife. I shall enjoy one as comely as you."

"I'm not interested—"

He waved a hand, cutting her off. "I shall use the marriage to ally with Lord Durham. Such a union will surely be beneficial for both families."

"I haven't come here for marriage."

"You came to me, to my home. If not for the purpose of forming a union, what other reason would a young woman have for being here?"

The question baited her to divulge the truth, to spill everything—the fact that she didn't really belong in this era, that she'd fallen into a coma and woken up here. But he would think she was telling wild tales, might, in fact, think she was a lunatic. Her only hope was to get word to Marian.

"If you won't allow me to visit my sister, then at least let me send her news of my safe arrival."

He turned to go. "You will see her erelong. We shall visit Chesterfield Park as soon as we are wed. I believe Lord Durham will have more incentive to give me access to the holy water if he knows doing so will protect his family."

When the door closed behind Lord Worth, her knees gave way, and she slid against the wall to the floor. She shuddered and drew the sheet around her. None of the servants moved. None came to her aid. None even dared look at her.

Were they as trapped as she was in a life they hadn't chosen? Were they prisoners in this nightmare too?

Suddenly all she could think about was Harrison and his kisses and how tender he'd been with her. The last night in Saint Lucia, he'd been debonair with his hair slicked back, his clean shave, and his crisp white dress shirt contrasting with the dark suit. When the

Fletchers had started teasing him about kissing her, she'd sensed he was growing agitated and hadn't wanted to take advantage of her.

Why had she kept him from leaving the table? Why had she initiated a kiss?

She hadn't wanted to think about her motives, had wanted to believe she was influenced by the Fletchers' talk of kissing, was stirred by the romantic setting.

But had she only been denying the attraction to Harrison that had been building all through the weekend? Perhaps had even been growing long before that?

No matter what excuses she came up with, the kisses that last evening together had shaken her, had stirred in her something she wanted again. With him.

She didn't know what it was exactly, but after facing Lord Worth and his ugly threats, her desire for Harrison was sweet and keen. If only she'd made the time and effort to explore what had been happening between them instead of running from it.

Now she'd never know.

~ 12 ~

ELLEN COULDN'T EAT a bite of the roasted sparrow with baked quince on the pewter plate before her. Even if the fare had been remotely appealing, she wasn't hungry. She hadn't been all day.

Unfortunately, the dinner consisted of three courses, each having several dishes, mostly boiled or baked meats covered in rich sauces and accompanied by leeks, fennel, and other vegetables she wasn't accustomed to eating. She felt as though she'd been served three entirely different meals, the last one having a dessert of spiced baked apples and plum compote.

The candles in silver settings cast a haunted ocher over the now-empty platters, ewers, and basins. The enameled silver-gilt goblets contained a warm red wine that one of the other women had called hippocras.

Around her, the great hall's plastered walls were draped with embroidered panels—most of which seemed to depict gruesome war scenes: swords thrust through bloody bodies, severed heads, injured warhorses, and arrows flying through the air as well as protruding from wounded warriors.

The floor was covered with patterned tiles with a fire in the middle raised on flagstones. Simple but sturdy trestle tables and benches formed two lines along the length of the room. At the far end, she was surprised to see the same curio cabinet that had been in the present-day Reider Castle, except this one was void of glass doors and instead had wooden panels that closed off the contents inside.

"Nicholas has come at last." The woman sitting next to Ellen spoke in a breathy whisper that resembled a grateful prayer. Lady Theresa. Ellen knew nothing but the woman's name. And the fact that she liked the honey-crusted almonds and hazelnuts in the bowl placed between them. Sweetmeats, Lady Theresa had called them.

Lady Theresa eagerly watched a newcomer who had paused at the table nearest the double doors of the great hall, a young man attired in chain mail, his dark hair tousled but pulled back in a ponytail, and his profile strong and regal. Two wolflike, long-legged dogs had come out from beneath tables to greet the knight, who affectionately patted each of the dogs' heads.

For the first time, Lady Theresa smiled, giving a glimpse of the once-beautiful woman she'd likely been, now hidden behind a sallow complexion, too-thin cheeks, and a jaundiced hollowness around her eyes.

Lord Worth's loud conversation came to a halt. He was seated at a prominent table at the head of the room, his attention arrested upon the newcomer as well. His countenance, however, was much less welcoming than Lady Theresa's.

As Ellen had done at least a hundred times since arriving, she pinched herself through her gown in an attempt to wake herself from the coma. *This is only a dream*, she silently chanted.

Except in dreams, she didn't feel the coarse scratchiness of a heavy wool skirt against her legs or the snugness of the bodice. The maidservant had tied the side laces tightly, forcing her bosom upward and revealing far too much cleavage. In addition, the sleeves coiled against her arm, restricting her movement so that she couldn't even lift a hand to scratch her head, which was crowned with a tight circlet woven with dangling ribbons.

If dreaming, then surely she wouldn't hear the minstrel plucking at the pear-shaped lute, the soft tones similar to those of a guitar. Every time she glanced at the minstrel's fingers flying across the strings on the neck, she pictured Harrison's long fingers on his violin when she'd watched him standing and playing with joyous abandon the morning after his healing.

No, everything and everyone were much too real, including Lord Worth. In the dim lighting of the spacious room, his eyes and hair were obsidian. He was attired in a bold-patterned, tight-fitting coat that buttoned up the front. It fell to his midthighs, thankfully, since his pants consisted of hose sculpted to his thick legs, showing every bulge.

Although he hadn't spoken to her since the encounter earlier in the day, he had been watching her throughout the various courses. In fact, his chair at the table on the raised dais was angled so that he could see her every move. Had he planned it that way? So he could discover more about her? Lust over her exposed flesh? Or both?

She tried to pretend she didn't care, but the more he watched, the more caged she felt, as if she were a rare animal on display at a zoo, needing to be tamed and trained. The other ladies around her had made small talk, but they, too, held themselves rigidly, as though their behavior was being graded and that any offense would be disciplined later.

The truth pulsed harder with every passing moment, the truth that she wouldn't be able to awaken herself to escape from this strange reality and get away from Lord Worth. She would have to find another way.

But how? She couldn't just walk out. Not even under cover of darkness. The gatehouse was locked tight, and guards were posted around the walls.

Lady Theresa sat up straighter as the newcomer started down the great hall. The man's stride was purposeful and confident, the sheathed sword at his side bumping against the metal rings of his long chain mail shirt.

Ellen expected him to approach the head table and Lord Worth first, but he veered toward the women and stopped in front of Lady Theresa. The woman rose, and as she extended a hand toward him, her eyes took on a tender glow.

"Mother." He bowed before her, bending his head low and placing a kiss on her fingers. When he straightened, Ellen could see that up close, his features were striking, even handsome beneath the scruff covering his jaw.

"How do you fare?" He searched her face. "I pray well."

"Well enough." Lady Theresa smiled. "And you, Nicholas? I pray for you every day."

He bowed and kissed her fingers again, but not before Ellen caught sight of the sadness in his eyes. As though sensing her scrutiny, he shifted his attention to her, his dark eyes catching hers like a hunter snagging its prey in a trap.

For several heartbeats, silence hung between them. Ellen felt as though she ought to say something but wasn't sure what the protocol was for introductions. In Jane Austen novels, the gentleman had to be introduced to the lady first and not the other way around. Were the customs the same in the Middle Ages?

At the very least, she ought to stand. She pushed to her feet and waited, sensing all eyes upon her.

"This is Lady Ellen Creighton." Lady Theresa spoke hesitantly, as though she was doing something she shouldn't. "Lady Marian Durham's sister."

"And my betrothed." Lord Worth's chair scraped across the

floor as he stood. His hand went to his belt and the hilt of his sword.

Nicholas ignored Lord Worth and bowed toward her. "My lady."

When he raised his head, his eyes seemed to hold a hundred questions, including what had led her to a man like Lord Worth. Ellen sensed a warning lurking beneath the surface.

She willed him to see her distress, that she was in no way considering marrying Lord Worth, that she needed help escaping him. "I am pleased to meet you . . ."

"Sir Nicholas."

Lord Worth stepped around his table. "Why are you here, brother?"

Brother? This man was related to Lord Worth? Jasper had mentioned that multiple sons lived during this era. And some family resemblance existed in their dark hair and eyes and the shape of their noses.

While she sensed a gentler and kinder nature in Nicholas, would he be a better ally? Someone she could befriend? Or was he as dangerous as Lord Worth?

With a last bow toward her and Lady Theresa, Nicholas crossed to the head table. "I bear tidings from London."

As Lady Theresa sat back down on the bench, Ellen took that as her cue to do the same.

Lord Worth folded his bulky arms over his chest and glowered at Nicholas. "What tidings?"

"An outbreak of the plague."

Gasps filled the air. Lady Theresa fumbled for Ellen with trembling fingers. Ellen reached for the lady's hand and squeezed, all the while trying to remember everything she could about the plague.

Was Nicholas referring to the Black Death? During her nurse's training, when she'd studied communicable diseases, she'd learned that the pathogen responsible for the highly contagious disease had been carried by fleas living on rats. The biggest wave of the plague had occurred during the mid-1300s, killing millions throughout Asia and Europe. Sometimes whole families, even whole villages, had succumbed to the disease often within hours, with no one to bury bodies, bring in the harvest, or care for the livestock.

At least she was fairly certain the Black Death had struck England thirty years ago. If so, that would account for the terrified reaction from many in the room. Most of the adults had probably lived through the outbreak or at least heard the horror stories from survivors.

Lord Worth took a step back, as though Nicholas was already contagious. "Has the disease spread outside London yet?"

"Alas, 'tis only a matter of weeks." Nicholas's expression was grim.

"How do we know you are not bringing it with you?"

"Have no fear. I have kept away from those who are plagued. Now I have come to warn the people of Kent of the danger. Other king's guards are doing likewise in other shires."

Nicholas was a king's guard? What exactly did that mean? From her time attending Sevenoaks—and from Shakespeare's *Richard II*—she'd learned some English history and knew that King Richard II was currently king. The boy had ascended to the throne when he'd been only ten. He wasn't more than fourteen or fifteen years old in 1382, and certainly didn't end up a strong man like his father before him. Even so, from what she'd read, Richard hadn't been a horrible king. He'd even attempted eventually to put an end to the Hundred Years' War.

Nicholas appeared noble and strong enough to be in service to the king. Every step he took exuded strength and purpose.

"If what you say is true," Lord Worth said with furrowed brows, "we shall have to take measures to stock our supplies and regulate more carefully who may come and go from Reider."

Nicholas nodded. "Do so quickly, my lord."

Lord Worth rubbed his beard, as though in serious contemplation of the matter. "What about Lady Ellen? We must isolate her until we know she is not carrying the plague."

"Has she experienced any symptoms since her arrival?" Nicholas directed the question to his brother but looked at her.

Ellen shook her head. "None—"

"She was unconscious when we found her." Lord Worth scowled at Ellen. "What if she is already ill?"

Nicholas took her in more carefully this time. "It seems unlikely."

"I'm fine." Ellen released Lady Theresa and straightened her shoulders. "Really. I don't have the plague."

Lord Worth snapped his fingers toward the guards standing near the double doors. "Take her to the dungeons."

The other women began to rise and back away from Ellen. She wished she could convince them they had no need for alarm, but she suspected their superstitions went too deep.

Nicholas lifted a hand to halt the guards. "Isolate her in her chamber another day or two."

"She must be kept as far from the rest of the household as possible." Lord Worth motioned impatiently for his guards to continue. "Take her below anon."

"Not the dungeons, brother—"

"Who is the lord of this manor?" Lord Worth's question echoed against the stone walls, and fury rolled in to darken his features.

Every voice silenced. Every creature held its breath. Even the dogs tucked their tails and slinked under the tables. Only the lone clang of a pot in the kitchen echoed in a nearby passageway.

"My word is law," Lord Worth continued. "If you do not wish to submit to it, then begone with you."

Nicholas bowed his head in acquiescence. "Very well, my lord. I shall take my leave in the morn after breaking fast."

Lady Theresa released a murmur of protest, which rose no further than the ladies clustered around her.

Even so, Nicholas glanced at his mother, his expression apologetic. "As much as I would relish visiting longer, I must make haste to deliver warnings regarding the plague from here to the coast."

Nicholas's calm response seemed to alleviate Lord Worth's rage. He gave a curt nod to the younger man before turning again to the guards who'd taken uncertain steps forward. He motioned to them irritably. "Fie upon you. Make haste and escort Lady Ellen to the dungeons."

Ellen shivered but didn't resist as the guards approached. She imagined the cells would be much less hygienic than a modern prison. But at the very least, she'd gained more time to concoct an escape plan since with the threat of the plague, Lord Worth wouldn't be as eager to wed her.

One of the guards carried a torch and led the way through a series of passageways until he guided her down steep steps that went below ground, the same steps she'd used with Jasper. While less cracked and aged, the stairwell was mustier, reeking of damp earth.

When she reached the bottom, she glimpsed the simple wooden arched door built underneath the stairwell. Was the hiding place there in the wall where Jasper had revealed? She doubted she'd have the chance to find out since she wasn't planning to stick around a moment longer than she had to.

If she delivered holy water to Dr. Lionel, she'd have to do so via the crypt at the cathedral. He wouldn't like it, but he wasn't the one dealing with a brute like Lord Worth.

The guard turned into a low-ceilinged and stone-walled corridor. The torchlight glistened off the trickles of water that had apparently always dampened the walls. And the same oaken door stood in place with a lock.

After a jangle of keys, the guard pulled the oaken door open. As he stepped through, he lifted his torch to reveal stone arches marking the spot of each cell.

Was this where Dr. Lionel had his lab? How eerie that hundreds of years in the future, she was lying in this area in a coma. Where had Jasper and Dr. Lionel placed her comatose body? Back on the examining table or perhaps on a more comfortable hospital bed?

The guard passed several of the cells before unlocking one and opening the door. A draft of cold and damp air greeted her, reminding her that medieval dungeons weren't heated. And certainly didn't have running water or modern plumbing. They were likely infested with rats and fleas.

The guard waved her inside.

As she passed by and stepped down to the deeper dungeon floor, he held the torch inside so that she could get her bearings. The chamber was cave-like, seemingly carved from rock. The windowless walls were curved and the floor scattered with straw. A thin pallet lay on one side and a low wooden stool and chamber pot stood on the other.

"My lady." The guard pressed a bundle into her arms.

She was surprised to find he'd given her a woolen cloak and a blanket.

"From Sir Nicholas," the guard whispered.

"Thank you." She tried to catch his gaze, but he kept it trained on the ground, both fear and determination etched in the severe lines of his face. She guessed he was afraid of the repercussions from Lord Worth. But apparently he had retained enough compassion to pass along the items regardless of the consequences.

As he closed the door, the cavern grew dark much too quickly. A glow came in through the small, barred window on the door. But as the footsteps of the guards retreated, so did the light.

When the dungeon's main oak door shut a moment later, darkness fell upon her with such thoroughness that she couldn't see a single part of her cell, not even her hand, which she wiggled inches from her face.

For a moment, she stood frozen in place, disoriented, not knowing which way to go to reach her pallet or the stool. She squeezed her eyes shut.

"Wake up, Ellen." Praying she truly would wake up from her coma, she opened her eyes, only to be confronted with the blackness of the dungeon. She was still in the past. Helpless. And alone.

The fact was, being helpless was nothing new. And neither was being alone. With her VHL and the reoccurring cancer, she'd been helpless to fight the disease. Helpless to control her body. Helpless about having a future. And she'd always felt alone. Dad and Marian had spent every waking moment of their lives hoping to give her a cure. What she'd really wanted was for them to give her their time and love.

Not only had she felt abandoned by Marian and Dad, but she'd also felt abandoned by God, like he'd decided her life wasn't worth much and had given up on her.

But Harrison? He'd been there for her. He always picked up her calls, always offered to help, always spent time with her whenever she traveled back to England for a visit—which hadn't been as often in recent years.

He was the one stability in her uncertain life. Was it possible she'd been hesitant to let their relationship change because she was afraid of losing that stability? What would happen if things didn't work out between them? If he eventually decided he didn't want to take a risk with her? Or if their attraction fizzled out?

She shuffled forward, putting out her hand to keep from bumping the wall. Her head grazed the sloping ceiling at the same time her foot connected with the pallet. Carefully she lowered herself, catching a whiff of mold and the stench of the chamber pot left from previous occupants of the cell.

Once she was sitting cross-legged, she fumbled with her cloak and wrapped it about her body before shrouding herself with the blanket. While she wouldn't be entirely warm, she wouldn't freeze—thanks to Nicholas.

What kind of man was Nicholas that he would think of her, a mere stranger? Not only had he defended her to Lord Worth, but he'd gone behind his brother's back to offer her a measure of comfort. The cruel master of Reider Castle wouldn't hang Nicholas for helping her, would he?

Her mind returned to the image of the soldier dangling lifelessly from the gatehouse, his body circling in the breeze. He was dead because of her.

Guilt choked the air from her lungs as it had every time she'd glanced out her chamber window to the gruesome sight. "Oh God, forgive me." Her whispered plea rose into the dank air.

How many more people would have to die because of her? *Please, God, no more.* Especially not Josie or any of the other Serenity House children. She'd only wanted to help them, bring them some happiness in their short lives. Instead, she'd unwittingly dragged them into grave danger.

She slapped the pallet in frustration. She didn't have time to sit in a dungeon. She had to find a way to save Josie and keep the other children safe from Dr. Lionel.

If only she could somehow communicate with Harrison and let him know of Lionel's threats so that he could alert the families and police as well as be prepared for any endangerment to himself. She wasn't sure how the time overlap worked or exactly how to initiate it. All she knew was that she had to try it.

But first, she had to get free from Lord Worth's clutches. And to do so, she had to send a note to Marian and let her know she was trapped. None of the servants earlier had been willing to earn their master's wrath by bringing her writing material. Perhaps the guard who'd given her the blanket would be willing to help her again.

She closed her eyes and leaned her head against the stone wall, fighting off an overwhelming feeling of helplessness at being stuck in an alternate life and already having made a mess of things.

"God, grant me the serenity to accept the things I cannot change," she whispered. Although she'd experienced a tiny bit of hope for the future during those few blissful days on Saint Lucia, was she simply destined to die one way or another? If not from VHL, then from the coma or maybe even the danger of 1382?

"Please, God, give me the courage to change the things I can. Please." Yes, she'd learned long ago to resign herself to her own fate. She wouldn't fight it. But she couldn't leave without first trying to change all that she still could.

~ 13 ~

A GENTLE PROD AWOKE ELLEN.

She shifted on the uncomfortable pallet, her limbs stiff from the cold. Even though she was accustomed to less-than-ideal conditions from her years of working at the orphanage in Haiti, she'd always had a cot or bed.

At the distinct pressure against her arm again, Ellen's eyes flew open. A faint glow lit her cell, revealing a cloaked figure crouched next to her. A scream welled up in her throat. Before it could find release, a gloved hand clamped over her mouth.

A dozen horrible scenarios raced through her mind. Had one of the guards returned to accost her? Was someone intending to harm her?

"Lady Ellen." The hand over her mouth gentled. "It is I, Sir Nicholas."

Sir Nicholas?

She blinked, and the events at dinner in the great hall rushed back. Sir Nicholas was Lord Worth's brother and had come to Reider Castle to warn them of an outbreak of the plague.

What was he doing in the dungeon?

"Have no fear. I mean you no harm." His face was shrouded by the raised hood of his cloak, but the tallow candle on the ground beside him provided enough light for her to see kind eyes observing her.

She allowed herself to relax just a little. He hadn't struck her as a cruel man like Lord Worth, especially with the affection he'd shown toward his mother. But since he was related to Lord Worth, she had no way of knowing if he was truly trustworthy.

"Dawn draws nigh," he whispered with a glance over his shoulder to the open door of her cell. "I must be on my way."

Her pulse gave a leap. "Will you take a message to my sister, Marian?"

"I sensed you are not eager to be a guest in my brother's home. If I am wrong, I beg your forgiveness. But if I am correct, I offer you my aid in escaping Simon and shall take you to your sister's home so that you might deliver a message for yourself."

"I would be grateful. But I don't wish to endanger you in the process."

"My life is in danger every time I visit." Nicholas's voice contained a bitter edge. He didn't leave her time to think about what may have happened to cause such bitterness. Instead, he shot a look over his shoulder again and then put out a hand. "Come. We must be gone before the household awakens."

She pushed up from the pallet but then hesitated. "Why would you do this for me?" Would he expect something in return? If so, what?

"Simon has wedded three wives. All of them are now dead." Nicholas pressed his hand toward her, urging her to accept it. "I offer you my assistance because I do not wish to have a fourth dead wife on my conscience."

A chill slithered up Ellen's spine, and she placed her hand in his, allowing him to help her to her feet. Before falling asleep, she'd prayed for the opportunity to change what she could. Now here was her chance.

She had to find Marian and enlist her sister's help. Surely together they could come up with a plan to outsmart Dr. Lionel, a plan for keeping Harrison and all the Serenity House children out of danger.

Holding the candle stub out ahead, Nicholas guided the way down the corridor away from the cell. Instead of leading her up the stairway to the main level of the keep, Nicholas turned and wound through another damp passageway that gradually grew narrower and lower until they couldn't traverse it without bending low. Even then Ellen's head brushed the ceiling.

"As you can see, the tunnel connecting the garrison to the dungeons is rarely used anymore." Nicholas kicked the bones of a long-dead creature out of their path. "Simon expects the locks to be a sufficient deterrent and has not posted a guard below ground."

"The locks won't deter you?"

"No, my lady. Nothing deters me. I can make my way in and out of this castle with no one the wiser."

The corridor ended at a hatch. Nicholas proved himself right by easily picking the lock. He hoisted himself out and then reached down to assist her. Once they were through, the dim light of the candle displayed a storage room with weapons of all shapes and sizes hanging from walls along with armor and shields and other equipment she couldn't begin to name.

He led her outside of the garrison—one of the thatched buildings attached to the castle wall. Under the moonless and starless night, only the barest outline of the keep was visible across the bailey, and she prayed Lord Worth wasn't awake to see her leaving. What would he do if he caught her?

She glanced in the direction of the gatehouse, half expecting to see the guard's body still swaying from a rope. Thankfully, it was no longer there. Hastily, she followed on Nicholas's heels as he headed to a horse tethered in the shadows of the stables.

"I beg your forgiveness, my lady," he whispered as he boosted her into the saddle. "But I am afraid you will need to straddle the mount."

She was already slinging her leg over the opposite side, not sure why he would apologize, until her skirt rose to her thighs, exposing her legs. She adjusted the folds of the velvety gown, not sure why she should be so embarrassed, especially in the dark, except that she sensed Nicholas's discomfort.

He wasted no time in climbing behind her into the saddle, which was definitely not big enough for the two of them. She was wedged so tightly she had no fear of toppling off, at least she believed so until he urged the horse forward. The trot set her off balance, and she grabbed the pommel with both hands to steady herself.

How did women in the movies ride horses so elegantly and effortlessly? She'd taken equestrian lessons at Sevenoaks but had been too busy adjusting to living in a boarding school as well as a new country to take much interest in the activity. Her short time at Sevenoaks had been more about survival than anything else.

Wasn't that the story of her life? Survival? And here she was trying to survive again.

Nicholas steered the horse straight for the gatehouse. He certainly wouldn't attempt to leave through the front gate, would he? Not with her—Lord Worth's prisoner—in plain sight?

"Shouldn't we try to find a more secretive way to exit the castle?" she asked.

"No." Nicholas slowed the mount as the guard came down the steps from the tower room above the gate. "Leaving openly is for the best."

"Won't the guard try to stop me?"

"He will try but will not prevail." Nicholas reined the horse in front of the closed steel grate and then nodded at the guard. "I must be on my way. Open the gate."

The guard hesitated, holding his torch high so that the firelight fell across Ellen. His eyes widened with first surprise and then fear. Was he afraid he might catch the plague from her? Or of what Lord Worth would do to him if she left?

Nicholas's fingers slid to his sword. The guard must have noticed the movement because he retreated a step. "Wish I could let you pass with the lady, sire, that I do. But milord will hang me by the neck from the gatehouse if I let the lady go."

Nicholas dismounted and withdrew his sword. "And I wish I did not need to do this, lad." In one easy bound, he knocked the guard across the head with the hilt.

The man crumpled to the ground, unconscious.

Nicholas wasted no time in dragging him up the stairs and disappearing into the tower house. Several moments later, the gate began its upward climb, the linked chains groaning and straining in protest of being raised. When it was open and the bridge lowered across the moat, Nicholas mounted behind her and kicked the horse to a gallop.

Her heart pounded along with the horse hooves. Surely Lord Worth and his guards would hear them leaving and begin chasing them. But within moments, Nicholas directed the steed into the forest, so that the thick foliage along with the darkness of night swallowed them up.

As they charged forward, the only sound was the crackling of the brush and branches. Without the moon or stars overhead to guide them, Ellen wasn't sure how Nicholas knew where to go. She felt as though they were flying blindly along, twigs and leaves slapping them.

When they finally broke through into a clearing, the faint light of dawn had begun to soften the sky. Nicholas veered into a nearby river, likely to hide the hoofprints.

"Are you warm enough, my lady?" He spoke for the first time since they'd charged away from the castle.

"After the dungeons, I can't complain." The morning air was cool and nipped her nose and cheeks and fingers. Otherwise, she was warm, probably because she was shielded by his body and arms. "By the way, thank you for giving me the cloak and the blanket. You were very kind to think of me."

"I abhor the way Simon treats women and relish the chance to defy him every chance I have." His voice rumbled close to her ear.

She should have been conscious of Nicholas's presence surrounding her and attuned to his nearness. He was, after all, a handsome man and had proven himself to be very gallant. But she gave his attractiveness no more than a passing thought, the minuscule amount she'd given to any man she'd ever met. Any man except Harrison.

He'd been in her thoughts all throughout the long night, the first person on her mind every time she'd awoken. He would be frantic with worry over her. All the more reason to find a way to leave him a message or facilitate a time overlap to let him know what she was doing.

She'd been away from him for close to two days, the longest stretch she'd gone without seeing him in almost a year. And the simple truth was that she missed him. Missed his smile, their conversations, the time spent together doing everything from reading books to playing cards to sitting in the garden. Had she taken him and his steady presence too much for granted?

She bit back a sigh. Now that she was in the past, she had to push aside her feelings for him—whatever those might be. She wasn't holding out much hope that she'd make it out of her coma alive—not after Marian and Dad had both died while comatose.

"Will Lord Worth search for me?" Since Nicholas had broken the silence, she guessed they must be out of imminent danger.

"'Tis possible. But he will not search long nor will he go far since he fears the plague."

If Lord Worth caught her, no doubt he would hang her. And what would happen to the guard Nicholas had knocked out? Her heart gave a sickening lurch. "I hope Lord Worth won't harm the gatehouse guard because of me."

"I pray so too, lady." Nicholas's voice was low and grave. "My overpowering and binding him may earn him my brother's mercy rather than his wrath."

"So that's why you chose to leave by the main gate instead of sneaking away." The guard would have an excuse, and Lord Worth wouldn't be able to blame him for her escape. At least she hoped so. Nicholas's consideration for the guard's well-being spoke highly of his character.

"I am hoping my brother will see the error of his ways and thank me for giving you your freedom. Lord Durham is favored by the king, and Simon would be a fool to make a foe of so powerful a knight."

"Are you sure you're related to Lord Worth?" She tried to make her question mirthful. "You're not like him at all."

"We are brothers of the same father but not of the same mother." His answer in return was serious, lacking even a trace of humor. "Simon is my father's firstborn son from his first wife. My mother was his fourth wife, and I his thirdborn son."

"Your father had four wives?"

"Women were as disposable to my father as rushes. After he stomped the life from them, he wedded someone young and fresh."

"But your mother survived?"

"Bless the Holy Mother, my father died when I was but a suckling babe."

"She never remarried?"

"Simon was one and twenty when my father died and my mother only nineteen. He considered taking her as his wife since she was a beautiful woman. Praise the saints that the archbishop forbade the union. And Simon was easily appeased by a marriage to someone else."

The riverbank rose steeply on either side, hemmed in by trees with new and thick growth. The winding roots dangled where the water had worn away the soil, the tangles reaching out like snakes as though to strike them. So much like Lord Worth.

"Why does your mother still live at Reider Castle?" One day had been long enough for Ellen to get a taste of the tension and terror of living with Lord Worth. She could only imagine how stressful it was year after year.

Nicholas didn't respond to her question. But the frustration that radiated from him spoke his answer well enough. He wasn't happy about the living situation for his mother but was apparently helpless to change it.

He urged the horse up the steep riverbank, slowing as a white-tailed deer bounded away. He guided the horse past craggy boulders until they reached an open area where the moorland spread out rugged and rounded with hill after hill. The wildness of it was so unlike anything she'd seen in the countryside of modern England.

The sky had grown decidedly lighter although the cloud cover prevented spring sunshine from warming her. Away from the protective enclosure of forests and riverbanks, a chilly breeze tugged at her skirt and cloak.

Nicholas directed the horse along a deserted dirt path and nodded to the vast countryside. "Someday I shall have land and a home of my own. Then I shall bring my mother to reside with me." His voice contained a quiet desperation.

"How much longer will you have to wait?"

"Until the king rewards me for my good deeds, or until I make an advantageous match."

"And which do you think will come first?"

As the horse stepped into a puddle, Nicholas's body connected with hers. He steadied her with a hand on her waist, and his touch brought back memories of Harrison's hold when they'd been in Saint Lucia, when his fingers had caressed her, sliding over her as though he couldn't get enough of her. Keen longing for him welled up within her. What was he doing today? At this very moment?

Nicholas released her. "I would that the king recognize my unfailing service to him. Then I need not worry about making a match."

"I can tell you're a good and kind man. Surely you have women eager to marry you."

He stiffened. "I have loved once, and that is enough for me."

To pry further would only open wounds that apparently had yet to heal. Instead, she gently squeezed his hand upon the reins and remained quiet.

After another moment of silence, he nodded ahead. "We are almost there."

In the distance through the trees, a familiar stately manor came into view. A thrill wound through her. Chesterfield Park in 1382 was smaller than Harrison's home in the present, but the main three-story structure was much the same, just as regal and imposing. Some of the windows contained glazed glass; others were shuttered. The high tower on the east end was exactly where it was when she'd gone up to watch the sunrise with Harrison.

The outer stone wall surrounding the estate was larger, and the parapets and crenellations along the wall looked as though they could be used to defend against attack. The central entrance consisted of a black iron gate that opened to a gravel path leading to the house before winding off to stables and various outbuildings.

Servants scampered about the premises, carrying food from the storerooms to the kitchen, hauling firewood, and drawing water from a well into brass pots.

She smiled. "Even though it is different, I would recognize it anywhere."

"Then you have visited before?"

"Not here, not like this."

He slowed the horse as they approached the front gate. "With your unusual accent and your sister coming from the Low Countries, I assume you likewise came from thence."

Low Countries? Was that a medieval term for the Netherlands? Or Belgium? "I must sound strange to you."

"I do admit, I am confused."

"I'm sorry." She couldn't keep from laughing lightly, her relief at seeing Chesterfield making her almost giddy. "My being here is a really long story. And it's a story you won't believe even if I did tell it to you." She could still hardly believe it herself.

"I have heard some details, namely that you were attacked and abandoned."

"I had a difficult journey here." It was the truth, even if it was incomplete. "And now I'm astounded that I'm really going to see my sister. I thought she was dead, that I'd never get to talk with her again. And look, here I am." Her blood thrummed with growing excitement. "Thank you, Nicholas."

"I'm happy to help, lady."

He reined in a dozen paces from the gate as several armed men showed themselves along the perimeter. "Open the gate and let us in. I bring Lady Ellen, the sister of Lady Marian."

"We got no word of Lady Marian having family a-comin'." The young guard standing by the gate glowered at them through the iron grill. "The master's gone after the physician and doesn't want anyone disturbing the lady while she's in labor."

Labor? That meant Marian *had* been pregnant in the vision. Was she due already? If so, Ellen needed to get to her right away.

Ellen's pulse picked up pace. "I'm a midwife." While she wasn't certified as such, she'd delivered enough babies in Haiti that surely she qualified.

The guard eyed her suspiciously. "But you said you were the Lady Marian's sister—"

"And I'm a nurse."

"Nurse?" The guard and Nicholas questioned her at the same time and eyed her as though she'd grown a pregnant belly herself. She guessed a noblewoman in the Middle Ages most likely did not have training in midwifery, much less any nursing skills.

"So which are you?" The guard's brow wrinkled in confusion. "A midwife or wet nurse for the babe?"

Wet nurse? She almost laughed but then caught herself. Is that what the term *nurse* meant to them? That she was planning to breastfeed her sister's newborn?

She shook her head. "No, by *nurse* I simply mean I intend to— well, I intend to take care of Marian. As the midwife. And if you don't allow me inside, Marian will be very upset."

The guard rubbed at the few whiskers on his chin before shaking his head. "'Tis Lord Durham's anger I fear most, lady. And he said no one in."

"He wouldn't object to a midwife." She turned pleading eyes upon Nicholas, praying he would support her.

Nicholas pinned a glare upon the guard. "You would be wise not to turn away the midwife, especially at a time like this."

"The lady of the manor already has midwives attending her. How many durst she need?"

"I am needed. I assure you."

After another moment of hesitation, the guard began to unlock the gate. "Aye, then. The lady can come in, but not you, sire."

Ellen started to protest the rude dismissal. But Nicholas gave a curt nod. "Very well. I must be on my way. I have many other places to visit and shall delay no longer."

She didn't resist as he dismounted and assisted her down. When her feet were planted on the ground, she took a deep breath, more relieved than she'd realized to be away from Lord Worth and safe at Chesterfield Park. "I can't thank you enough for all you've done for me."

He gave a slight bow. "Tell Lord Durham the news of the plague and fare well."

She slipped through the gate. "You've been a godsend."

The iron clanked closed and separated them. She was anxious to be off and see Marian, but she waited until he mounted before offering him a smile and waving. "Thank you again."

He didn't smile in return, but his gaze swept over her appreciatively with the kind of bold appraisal she'd received often in her life. He offered her a nod, then wordlessly nudged his steed onward.

Once he was on his way, she picked up her skirt and began to run as fast as her legs could carry her toward the house.

14

Marian lived here and was having a baby.

Ellen wanted to push past the maid leading her through the manor. The old Chesterfield Park was simpler and plainer, but the layout was similar, enough so that she could have found her way around unaided.

Nevertheless, she slowed her steps and tried to catch her breath and take in her surroundings. From the simple homespun garments the servants wore to the scuffed wood floors to the darkly elegant furnishings, she took in every detail with wonder coursing through her. For the first time since arriving in 1382, she was truly stunned. She was in the past, walking through Harrison's home and seeing the home as it had once been.

"Oh Harrison," she whispered as she stepped from a narrow stairway into the second-floor hallway. "If only you could see this. You'd be utterly amazed."

"Do you need something, my lady?" The maidservant paused and raised a brow at Ellen.

At a faint scream echoing from one of the chambers, urgency prodded Ellen. "Let's hurry."

The maidservant nodded and then continued down the passage-way until reaching the guest room Marian had stayed in last spring when she'd been in her coma at Chesterfield Park. More cries sounded from behind the closed door.

Although the voice was hoarse, it was Marian's. And it contained a note of despair.

Ellen's pulse sped into an erratic, panicked race, and she elbowed the servant aside, flung open the door, and barged into the room. Several women near the bed paused, clearly startled at her intrusion. But Ellen didn't care. Her practiced eye captured the scene: the bloody towels, a washbasin, an assortment of herbs, a chalice of wine.

As she strode across the room, she took in Marian's writhing form on the canopied bed, her distended abdomen covered by a thin sheet. Her red hair had been plaited into a thick braid, but strands were loose and plastered to her sweat-slickened and flushed face. Her eyes were closed tight, and her lips pinched together as she attempted to fight through another contraction.

"Who are you?" A maidservant stepped into Ellen's path. With a fully rounded stomach, the servant was expecting a baby soon too. The young woman pressed a fist into her lower back to ease her discomfort. Although her expression was stern, her eyes were rounded with anxiety.

"I'm a midwife." Ellen sidestepped the woman and approached the basin on the bedside table, intending to wash her hands, only to realize the water was murky with blood. "I want boiled water, clean towels, soap, and oil. Immediately."

At her command, Marian's eyes flew open. "Ellen?" Her beautiful brown eyes were frantic.

Ellen reached for Marian's hand at the same time that she tenderly cupped her sister's cheek. "I'm here, Marian. Everything is going to be okay now."

"What are you doing here?" Marian's voice took on a note of panic. "Are you real or am I dreaming?"

"I'm real."

Before Ellen could explain anything, another contraction seized Marian, and her face contorted with pain.

"Take deep breaths." Ellen smoothed a hand over Marian's forehead and demonstrated the kind of breaths her sister should take. Marian tried to imitate her, but agonized cries slipped out instead. Her eyes clouded with tears that spilled over and ran down her cheeks. "I'm so scared, Ellen." She spoke in a gasp. "The baby is not coming, and I fear he won't make it."

"Don't lose hope yet."

As the contraction ebbed, Marian fell back into the pillows, pale and spent. "I gave them step-by-step instructions for doing a C-section, and they refuse to do it. So I sent Will for the physician. Maybe I can convince him to cut me open and save the baby."

A cesarean in the Middle Ages without painkillers or antibiotics? Ellen shook her head and began to roll up her tight sleeves. Time to get to work.

She rubbed her hand over Marian's taut belly, circling and probing and attempting to identify the baby's position. How ironic that for once Marian wasn't trying to save her, that she was the one scrambling to keep her sister alive.

Marian released a groan and arched upward again. Her grip on Ellen's hand tightened at the same moment that her abdomen contracted. The veins in Marian's arms and neck pulsed outward, the strain on her body more than she could handle.

Fear shimmied up Ellen's backbone, but she shook herself to dislodge it. She had to stay calm and retain a clear mind. It was the only way she would be able to help Marian.

"How long has she been laboring?" Ellen continued to press

against Marian's abdomen. From the upward hard bulge, Ellen suspected the baby was breech.

"Since last eve." The pregnant maidservant's tone dropped with both dread and defeat.

"And what have you attempted so far?"

Two of the women were local midwives and explained the efforts they'd already made while Ellen set to work washing her hands thoroughly with the clean water a servant had delivered and then oiling them. From what Ellen gathered, not only was the baby breech, but Marian was failing to progress. Something was holding the baby back.

Thankfully the presenting part was the baby's bottom. The bottom was better than feet, but still so much could go wrong, especially without medical technology to aid them. Ellen did a quick internal examination too, and wasn't surprised to find that Marian was fully dilated.

She prayed the cord wasn't trapped or tangled, cutting off oxygen and blood to the baby. Without a stethoscope or monitors, she had no way of knowing if the baby was still alive. Either way, they needed to get the baby out before Marian lost any more blood.

The midwives had already tried every trick they knew to turn the baby and help the delivery along. But after the hours of labor, Marian was simply too weak and tired to do more.

Squaring her shoulders, Ellen forced herself to remember everything she'd ever read or learned about childbirth. "Let's change her position, have her stand up a little. We'll have two of you support her from the back. Then one of you can palm the baby's head through the abdomen and gently push down."

With everyone helping, they hoisted Marian so she was squatting at the edge of the bed. Then Ellen knelt on the floor and rotated the baby. "Don't push yet."

Was the baby's bottom stuck under the pubic bone?

As another contraction tightened Marian's abdomen, Ellen swiveled the baby again, freeing it, and then let the pull of gravity do its work. In the next moment, the baby's buttocks slid down and out. She hooked her fingers over the flexed legs and tugged them out as well.

"The legs are born, and the cord is pulsing." Ellen's voice rose with her growing excitement. "That means the baby is still alive."

Marian released a sob.

"You have a girl." Ellen gently cradled the baby's bottom half in her hands. "Let's wrap the baby so she doesn't get cold and gasp. We don't want her inhaling amniotic fluid."

One of the other women quickly folded a towel around the infant. As the next contraction came, Ellen guided the body, turning it a little clockwise until both shoulders were delivered and the arms out.

"On the next contraction, I want you to begin pushing the head out." Ellen released the baby for a few seconds, letting the weight of the baby's body add to the momentum.

Only seconds later, another contraction tightened Marian's stomach, and she pushed until her face was red.

"Breathe, Marian. You can do this." Ellen guided the baby, even as Marian screamed with pain. The other pregnant woman held Marian up, gripping her and keeping her in place while the midwives put pressure on Marian's abdomen.

Ellen prayed the head wouldn't become stuck in the birth canal. Without forceps to help the head along, Marian would have to do the work now without her.

Exhaustion drew lines across Marian's face, and she closed her eyes. The pregnant servant had her eyes shut now too, and her lips were moving in prayer.

Ellen lifted a short prayer of her own then positioned her hands on the baby's bottom half. "This is it, Marian. You've always worked hard to get what you want, and you can't stop now."

Once again Marian's screams filled the room. The sound would have driven the sturdiest soul to weep, but Ellen couldn't. Not yet. She had to finish the job first.

"Come on. Almost there."

Marian gave a final heave. It was just enough that Ellen could help guide the baby the rest of the way, and in the next second the baby slipped into Ellen's waiting hands.

The red, wrinkled infant didn't make a sound or move.

Ellen's pulse tripped apace with the need to call out in frustration, but she gave herself a mental shake. Quickly, she began to clear the baby's nose and mouth, then thumped the baby's back to dislodge anything farther back in the baby's mouth and throat. A gurgle, then a choking cough followed by a soft cry brought swift tears to Ellen's eyes.

The baby was all right.

She worked for several more moments, until the infant gave a hearty wail. She held the baby up for Marian to see, the umbilical cord still attached. "Meet your daughter."

Ellen handed the child off to the midwife so that she could focus on delivering the placenta. She didn't have an oxytocic to help cause immediate contractions. But one of the midwives was already preparing a tincture from among an array of bottles meticulously labeled in Marian's handwriting. Ellen hoped it was one that would help stop the bleeding.

Marian had dropped back against the bed, disheveled, her face pale, with exhaustion causing dark circles under her eyes. She was focused on the baby, who was flailing her arms and legs and crying in short but strong bursts. Tears trailed down Marian's cheeks. Then her gaze shifted to Ellen, and their eyes connected.

Gratefulness, love, and admiration radiated in the depths of those brown eyes—eyes Ellen hadn't thought she'd see ever again.

Ellen's throat tightened with the need to sob. As much as she wanted to throw herself on Marian and hug her and hold her, their reunion would have to wait. She still had work to do making sure her sister and new niece were both safe.

· ● ·

"I bid you to drink the holy water." A man spoke in low, urgent tones.

The voice woke Ellen. She'd positioned herself in the chair next to Marian's bed, intending to watch over her sister. But she'd dozed and somehow missed the entrance of the newcomer.

Marian would be very sore for days ahead. But with the help of the midwives, Ellen had compressed the uterus, prevented hemorrhaging, and then cleaned out the clots. The pregnant servant woman had taken care of bathing and swaddling the baby. Once she'd placed the squalling bundle in Marian's arms, the baby had nursed for a few moments, quieted, and fallen asleep.

Not long after Ellen finished stitching a small tear, Marian succumbed to fatigue and pain. While the servants cleaned up the bedchamber, Ellen perused Marian's array of medicines in an assortment of small, colorful bottles. Ellen hadn't been sure what some of them were or the necessary doses, but she'd suspected Marian had replicated a few important modern medicines to the best of her ability. Hopefully, one of them was an antibiotic that would help Marian through the healing process.

"I do not need the water." Marian's response was hushed. "I shall heal on my own in due time."

Ellen opened her eyes to the sight of Marian reclining in the feather-stuffed mattress and propped up with pillows, the baby cradled in her arms. The room glowed with candlelight, revealing a fierce-looking but strikingly handsome man perched on the wooden bed frame on the opposite side of the bed. He was dust-covered and disheveled, strands of his dark hair loose from the leather thong tying it back. While his eyes were intense and his face grooved with worry, he stroked Marian's cheek with a tenderness and intimacy that meant only one thing. He was her husband. Will.

"A few drops." Will held a small, colored bottle.

"We cannot use up the last of what we have. We must save it for when we truly have need."

Ellen marveled at the change in the way Marian spoke. She sounded formal, more like someone from the Middle Ages than from modern times.

At a sudden yawn that crowded for release, Ellen lifted her hand to stifle it. At the movement, both Marian and her husband startled and looked at her.

"Ellen." Marian's tone held a soft rebuke.

Ellen sat up and smiled at her sister and then at the sleeeping baby, who was still wrapped as tightly as the swaddling cloths could be wound. "I see that one of you is awake."

Marian held out an arm in an invitation for a hug.

Ellen leaned forward and embraced her sister, breathing her in and trying to convince herself she wasn't dreaming, that she really was hugging Marian.

"Thank you for saving me and my babe." Marian pulled back and examined Ellen's face, cupping her cheek and studying her as though she couldn't get enough of her.

Will had risen, and now stood above the bed, the strength of his presence nearly overwhelming. "I am indebted to you, my lady."

"I'm just glad I arrived when I did."

Will nodded, weariness forming crevices in his brow. "You are most welcome in my home."

"Thank you. I'm still trying to convince myself I'm really here."

"And I am trying to figure out why you are here," Marian said softly.

Ellen didn't have to ask to know what Marian was referring to. Marian wanted an explanation for why Ellen had crossed to the past.

How could she explain? It was too complicated. "It's nice to see you too. I've missed you."

Marian reclined and managed a weak smile. "I am glad to see you, sister. Truly I am. But . . ."

Ellen reached for Marian's hand, the fingers thin and cold and trembling.

Marian's eyes filled with tears. "But I would be happier to know you are healed and safe where you belong."

"I'm afraid it's not safer."

Marian's lashes dropped, and her face constricted with pain.

"Fetch more wine for my wife." Will motioned toward a servant hovering in the shadows. The woman nodded and hurried out of the room.

The window was shuttered from the inside, giving the room a dark aura. A small fire burned in the fireplace, putting off a low glow, and a candle on the bedside table flickered with black smoke and smelled of animal fat.

Will adjusted his sword at his belt. "Now that your sister is here, I shall do everything I can to keep you both safe."

"I know you will try," Marian said. "But in this case, there may be nothing you can do."

Will leveled a serious look at Ellen. "I bid you to tell us of your peril. Then I shall know how better to strategize against our foe."

Ellen settled into her chair but hesitated. How much about the time crossing did Will really know? She lifted a brow at Marian.

"You can tell us everything," Marian said. "Will accepts me

for my strange tales of other places and times, and he will do so with you as well."

The baby made a soft noise, her eyes scrunching amidst her perfectly pink face. Marian adjusted the baby in her arms, and Will reached down and stroked his finger across the infant's cheek. The sight of the new family together—with Will gazing at both his wife and daughter with such wide-eyed adoration—was beyond precious and something Ellen would never forget.

He was obviously a kind man and a devoted husband. Was it possible Marian was happier here in the past than she ever would have been in the present? He and Marian had apparently come to an understanding about her origins and the power of the holy water. But how could he fathom their crossing time? It was difficult for her to understand, and she'd been in both eras. Nevertheless, he was supportive of Marian, and Ellen liked him for it.

Marian and Will listened attentively as she relayed the events that had transpired: Harrison discovering the symbolism in the coat of arms, finding the ampullae in the vault, both of them being healed, and then taking the celebration trip to Saint Lucia.

She left out the parts about kissing Harrison. But she spared no detail in explaining how upon their return, Jasper and Dr. Lionel had abducted and taken her to an underground lab not only to study her healed body but also to send her into the past to supply Lionel with holy water. She told of waking up in 1832 at Reider Castle in a nightgown, Lord Worth's plans to marry her, his locking her in the dungeon, and then Nicholas coming to her rescue.

"Dr. Lionel gave me a week." Ellen sat stiffly, gripping her folded hands together. "He wants me to supply him with holy water, otherwise he's threatened to harm the children in the Serenity House."

Will and Marian hadn't spoken as she relayed her story. And

now Will stared at her gravely while Marian began nursing the baby.

"My hope is that I don't need to cooperate with Lionel. I'd prefer to send a message to Harrison so that he can warn all the families as well as be on guard for himself against Dr. Lionel trying to kidnap him again. But I don't know if that's possible."

Marian shook her head. "It's much riskier to send him a note. We don't know if it would withstand the passing of time. And we have no guarantee Harrison will find a message, especially on such short notice. He might overlook it, just as he did mine in the coat of arms."

"What about causing a time overlap, similar to what I experienced when I saw you earlier in the week? Maybe using a tiny amount of holy water?"

"I tried for months to cause one with you or Harrison so that I could tell you about the ampullae I placed in the vault. But nothing worked."

"Oh." Disappointment rose swiftly within Ellen.

"I'm sorry, Ellen." Marian's expression remained somber. "You could attempt it, but I believe such a phenomenon is difficult to initiate when you're already under the influence of the holy water and in the past."

Ellen exhaled a tense breath. "If we can't find a way to reach Harrison, then I'll be left with no choice but to supply Dr. Lionel with holy water. And none of us want to help him."

"Absolutely not," Marian replied.

"But I can't let the children suffer at Lionel's hands. I may need to give him a few flasks to buy myself more time. If we get word to Nicholas, we might be able to convince him to put them into the secret nook at Reider Castle."

Will and Marian exchanged a glance.

Something in their look pricked her with unease. "What? You don't think Nicholas would be willing?"

Will met her gaze. "Sir Nicholas is an honorable and good man. Nevertheless, in defying his brother and liberating you, he has made a deadly enemy of Lord Worth and will surely no longer be welcome at Reider Hall."

"Then I'll put the holy water in the crypt of the cathedral. Jasper and I agreed it would be a backup delivery option."

"Even then," Marian said, "we would still have a problem."

Ellen's frayed nerves pushed her to the edge of her chair. "I know you don't like Lionel. I don't either, but—"

"Ellen." The foreboding in Marian's tone silenced Ellen's racing pulse and thoughts.

Will shook the glass bottle he still held. "After giving you two ampullae of holy water, we have only a scant amount remaining."

"That's all?" Ellen couldn't see anything in the colorful glass container, and guessed only drops were left. "That can't be correct. Not if you have the wellspring. Unless it has already gone dry?"

Marian absently stroked one of her daughter's tiny hands as she continued to nurse. "The wellspring is inside the St. Sepulchre Priory. But when people heard of Will's healing from mortal wounds and then of my recuperation shortly after, we could not contain the news regarding the holy water."

Will's countenance darkened. "The new bailiff of Canterbury, a miscreant by the name of Thomas Ickham, has taken possession of St. Sepulchre and the well. He will sell the water to increase his own coffers. But he cannot do so until I relinquish the keys for the barrier that covers the wellspring, which I will not do."

"Then we don't have access to the holy water?"

"No one does." Will's tone was firm and brought back the memory of Lord Worth's declaration that Lord Durham had been unwilling to open the wellspring and had prevented anyone else from having even a drop. Now she understood what he'd meant.

"Why keep those who truly need it from having it?" Like Josie. The little girl needed a dose as soon as possible. If Ellen placed an ampulla in the vault at Chesterfield Park and carved Josie's name onto the flask, surely Harrison would understand he was to give it to the girl. Even if Dr. Lionel had warned her against any secret deliveries elsewhere, she had to do something for Josie before it was too late. "We must find a way to come to an agreement with this Ickham to dole out the holy water to the most needful."

"And who would that be?" Will asked. "Who is most needful? The one who can pay a sufficient fee? Or the one who displays a righteous life? Or is it only the ones we love?"

Ellen's response stalled. She hadn't thought of such questions. With a finite amount of holy water, how could they determine who was most worthy of it among the many, many sick people both in 1382 and in the present time?

For a long moment, silence settled over the chamber, broken only by the crackle of a log in the fireplace.

Finally, Marian spoke. "I think we can all agree that we face many uncertainties with how to handle the holy water. But there is one thing that is certain. If we do not draw up more from the well, Ellen will never return to her home."

"Then she will live here with us." Will bent and kissed Marian's head.

Marian pushed up from her throne of pillows, burping the baby against her shoulder. "She needs to go back home. She'll be safer there."

"We shall take care of her." Will rounded the bed and began to cross the room with long strides. "She must learn to be content here."

Ellen bridled at his command, and she wanted to contradict him. But from her experience at Reider Castle, she was learning that as a woman in the Middle Ages she had considerably less power than men. In addition, she had no money, no transportation, and no way to take care of herself. She couldn't afford to alienate Will.

Marian's eyes flashed as she watched Will's retreating form. "You have wanted to take the well away from Ickham's control and evil intents. Perhaps Ellen's appearance is God's confirmation that now is the time to do so."

Will stopped at the door, his hand on the door handle.

Ellen was relieved to see that even though Marian was changing, she hadn't lost her fire or her ability to stand up for herself and what she believed. "Did you not say you wanted me to have a drop or two of the water this day to aid my healing? If you are master of the well, then you will be able to refill our flasks."

Will stiffened and then turned, his brows furrowed above his dark, brooding eyes. "Do not try to manipulate me, wife." Without waiting for her response, he exited the room.

Once the door closed behind him, Marian lowered herself into the pillows and pulled the baby close. "He's a stubborn man. But he always does the right thing, no matter how hard or dangerous."

"Don't worry over me." Ellen helped to situate the pillows behind Marian more comfortably. "You must rest for now."

Marian nodded.

"Everything will work out."

Marian reached for her hand. "I pray you are right, sister. I really do."

A soft rap on the chamber door was followed by the entry of a maidservant, the same pregnant woman who'd helped with the labor and delivery. She carried a platter of food along with a flask of wine Will had ordered. As the servant neared the bed, she acknowledged Ellen with an almost reverent bow.

Ellen hadn't eaten much since arriving in the Middle Ages, and her stomach gurgled at the sight of the simple fare of oatcakes, cheese, and dried fruit. "You're so very kind." She smiled at the servant, who flushed and bowed again.

After the maidservant took her leave, Marian shook her head with a smile. "How do you always do it?"

"Do what?" Ellen nibbled on a piece of cheese.

"Get everyone to love and admire you."

"She's simply grateful I saved you and the baby and admires my nursing skills. That's all. Not everyone loves me."

"At the very least, every man you meet falls head over heels in love with you."

"No. That's not true."

"Then you have not yet figured out that Harrison adores you?"

Ellen shook her head in denial even as a flush stole through her at the memory of their kisses.

Marian paused in chewing a dried plum and narrowed her eyes. Marian seemed to have a way of looking deep into her heart and seeing the things she left unsaid, perhaps even the things she couldn't understand herself. "What transpired between you and Harrison over this past year?"

Ellen dropped her focus to her simple pewter plate. "We're friends as always."

"And?"

"And maybe we've grown closer. But that's to be expected after both of us being miraculously healed within hours of each other."

"Last time we were together, I noticed his feelings for you, and I suspected he might be in love with you."

Ellen's gaze shot up. "Of course he's not in love with me." He couldn't be. It wasn't possible. Was it? Yes, he cared about her. And the trip had facilitated an attraction to one another. But that didn't mean he loved her. Not as in love-love. She swallowed hard. "He loves us both. He always has."

"His love for you is different than what he has for me."

Ellen shook her head. "No—"

Even as she voiced denial, she sensed Marian was right. Harrison cared about her in a way he never had for Marian. But that didn't mean he loved her, did it? If so, why hadn't he told her?

Marian's eyes widened. "You love him too."

"No. Don't be ridiculous."

"It's not ridiculous. Harrison is perfect for you."

Ellen broke off a piece of the oatcake and fiddled with it. Harrison was perfect. If she was honest, she'd always held him as a standard for the few men she'd gone out with—chivalrous, compassionate, considerate, giving. The list was endless.

Yes, he might be perfect for her, but she wasn't perfect for him. She was a liability. She'd only bring him heartache. And she couldn't do that to a man as wonderful as Harrison.

Marian reached for her hand. "We'll find a way for you to get back to him, Ellen."

She'd already given up hope of survival for herself. But she had to keep him out of Lionel's clutches. "As long as he stays safe, that's all that matters." If only she didn't miss him so desperately.

_15_

"It's been three days." Harrison couldn't keep his voice from rising. "Find her!"

He ended his call with Ms. Huxham—Sybil—and tossed his mobile onto his bed. The device bounced several hard hops before landing against the pillows. He shoved his fingers into his hair and blew out a tense breath.

Immediately, regret hit him. He shouldn't have taken out his frustration on Sybil. She was actually doing well considering the odds stacked against her. She was close to figuring out the place his abductors had taken him last year. Harrison had already tried to piece together the site, but he'd been blindfolded the entire time. For all he knew, they could have held him anywhere around Kent, even a London suburb.

Sybil had met with the kidnapper in prison. Since she wasn't able to get any information with intimidation, she went the route of involving an attorney and trying to work out a deal—information on Lionel for a reduction in jail time. She'd called to let Harrison know the meeting was scheduled for tomorrow.

Of course, she had numerous other leads. She'd interviewed enough people at the airport to work out the kind of car that had been used in Ellen's abduction. She'd narrowed down owners of all such cars within a hundred-mile radius. And she'd ruled out all but two of the cars, which she'd yet to locate.

No question. Sybil was brilliant. She was doing a fabulous job and working around the clock without much sleep—if the late hour was any indication. The problem was, Ellen was still missing. And Harrison was going absolutely mad with each passing day, especially when he considered what Lionel might be doing to her.

Roughing her up. Starving her. Poking needles into her. Drawing out vials of blood.

He pressed his hands against his temples. If only doing so would help push away his tortured thoughts. With a shake of his head, he stalked to his music room and grabbed his violin where he'd left it to answer Sybil's call. The one thing that could calm him—even if just a little—was his music.

He'd stayed out of the spotlight, hiding away behind closed curtains at Chesterfield Park as Sybil had requested. Even if he'd given Sybil five days to find Ellen, he couldn't stand back and do nothing one second longer.

"I can't. Can't. Can't." His words echoed in the room filled with amps, speakers, effects pedals, mix table, cable jacks, and more. He stared, feeling as helpless—perhaps even more so—as when Ellen had been racked with VHL and dying of cancer.

Why did he always seem to fail her?

With a groan, he cradled his violin in the crook of his neck and let his fingers graze the strings. Then he touched the bow to the instrument only to feel as though someone was watching him from the bedroom. At a creak in the old wooden floor, he spun.

Had someone broken in?

He stepped into the doorway and swept his gaze over the bedroom lit only by his bedside lamp. No one was there. Nothing was changed from the way the maid had left it when she'd tidied there earlier in the day. Even so, he felt something was different.

Without taking his gaze from the room, he lifted his violin and bow again. He started Vivaldi's *Four Seasons* "Summer," his fingers moving with a life of their own, the piece so ingrained in his memory he could play it in his sleep. As the waft of the notes increased in tempo, he caught the faint sound of humming. A woman's voice.

His fingers froze, but his pulse raced at a crazy speed. "Marian?"

The humming faded to silence.

Had she heard him? Was it possible they could communicate with each other? Maybe because of drinking the holy water, they had some kind of quantum particle connection?

"Marian, are you there?"

He strained to hear something—anything. But silence met him, this time so complete, he sensed that whatever was linking them was no longer present. Even so, his pulse continued its wild racing and his thoughts followed suit.

Could he regain the connection? He could let Marian know about Ellen's kidnapping and ask her to put more holy water in the vault just in case Ellen needed it. Once they found her, there was no telling what kind of condition she'd be in.

And he could ask Marian for holy water for Josie. The little girl was still alive, but the prognosis was grim.

How could he create a time overlap with Marian? What if he ingested some of the residue left in the ampullae? Would that help him communicate with her?

He set down his violin and stalked to the bedside table, where he'd stowed both ampullae after they'd emptied them. He pulled out one, wet his finger, then rubbed it inside the container. He couldn't feel any grit or dried remnant, but Marian had taken in only a few grains when she'd had her brief crossovers. Maybe he wouldn't need much.

He stuck his finger in his mouth, closed his eyes, and pictured the year 1382 since Marian would have been alive in the past for a year, would have had the best access to holy water at that point.

For a moment, nothing happened, then a soft warmth began to make a trail down his neck, torso, arms, and legs. It was not unlike the sensation he'd experienced when he drank the first ampulla in the vault, except the sensation was gentler, like a sprinkling of rain instead of a downpour.

The creak of the floor came again, this time more distinct. His eyes flew open, and he stumbled back a step at the sight that met him. It was his room, but everything was completely different—simpler, darker, plainer, and a strange mustiness filled the air along with an earthy scent.

He didn't take the time to examine everything; instead, his gaze rested on his music room, which had disappeared altogether and looked to be a dark closet.

He took one step forward only to stop abruptly at the sight of a woman emerging from the closet. Not Marian.

Ellen.

Her hair was unbound and flowing over her shoulders, and she was wearing a long, white nightgown. The soft glow of lighting from somewhere in the room illuminated her beauty, leaving no doubt it was her.

"Ellen?"

With a gasp, she halted and laid a hand over her heart. Her eyes widened upon him. Then she released a soft cry before racing to him and throwing herself against him.

As her body pressed into his, he lifted his arms around her in a tight embrace. He could feel every curve of her lithe body against his, feel the tickle of her hair against his chin, and feel the warmth of her breath near his neck. She wasn't an apparition. He really was holding her.

"I don't understand what's happening." He glanced around the barren room again. He was most definitely in the past. And Ellen was too. "What are you doing here?"

"Oh Harrison." She pulled back just enough that he could see her face, her beautiful blue eyes framed by long lashes, her slender cheeks, her delicate nose. She lifted a hand and cupped his cheek. "Are you real?"

His pulse began to beat with new urgency. "Do you have any idea where Lionel is keeping you?"

The ringing of his mobile broke the moment. He blinked and she was gone. He found himself in his room again, the music closet where it had always been, his bedside lamp lighting up his chamber, and his mobile on the bed. It lit up with the number and picture of one of the antiquarians he'd hired to track down the last of the ancient St. Thomas ampullae.

His sights zeroed in on the ampulla on the bed even as a wave of exhaustion threatened to topple him. The granules had taken him back in time. He could think of no other explanation.

He shook his head, trying to stave off another wave of fatigue. Ellen had been so real, so alive. He'd touched her, heard her, seen her. How could he have done that if she was only a vision?

"Ellen?" She'd been right there.

He swept his gaze over the room. But he sensed nothing. Her presence was gone. Every trace of her was outside his reach.

His knees began to give way, and he lowered himself to the bed, too tired to stand. Marian had experienced the same weariness after her crossings. He surmised that the vibration and expenditure of energy and heat during the time overlap depleted the body. Blinking, he fought against the haze.

Somehow, Ellen had gone into the past. Not only was she lost to him in the present, but now she was lost in the past too.

With a groan, he fell back onto the mattress. He needed to ingest more of the residue, go back, and talk to her again. He fumbled for the ampulla, but his eyes closed and sleep overtook him, so that he could do nothing else but give way to the exhaustion.

* ● *

Ellen stood motionless in the middle of the room and waited.

"Harrison?" She called for him again, but as with the other times, she heard nothing in response.

Earlier in the day after she'd left Marian, a servant had ushered her down the hall. When she'd passed by the room that belonged to Harrison, she hadn't been able to resist asking to stay there.

Of course, it didn't look like his modern room, had none of the sleekness or masculine accents and was devoid of anything that might remind her of Harrison. But just being in the same location, picturing his room, standing where she guessed he would be—somehow it had soothed her.

That evening, she'd joined Will and the rest of the household for supper in the great hall. Even though Marian was confined to her chambers, they'd celebrated the birth of another Durham. Then after spending time with Marian and the baby again, she'd retired late.

Even so, she hadn't been sleepy. And after the maidservant had helped her out of her gown and into a nightdress, she'd dismissed the woman, wanting some time to herself, to think about her predicament and plot her next move.

As she'd walked around the room and examined everything more closely, she'd sensed Harrison's presence more than ever, so much that she'd even thought she heard him playing his violin. She'd guessed it was only her imagination tricking her and reminding her of that night together in Chesterfield Park when she'd watched him play with such power and passion.

But the music had been so vivid that she'd stepped into the boudoir, half expecting him to be there. And when she'd stepped out, she'd seen him.

Hadn't she?

"Harrison? Are you still there?"

She strained to hear him, but complete silence surrounded her.

"Harrison?" She practically shouted his name this time. "Please answer me!" She needed to talk to him, tell him more about Dr. Lionel's threats to the Serenity House children and to him.

Once again, she heard nothing but her rapid breathing and racing heartbeat.

"Where are you?" She groped in the direction he'd stood, hoping she'd feel him. But only the air brushed her skin.

With a shiver, she crossed back to the boudoir. It contained an assortment of clothing, furniture, and toys that had once belonged to Phillip, Will's nine-year-old son who lived as a page with a neighboring knight. She'd met Robert, Will's younger son of seven, and learned he would also eventually be fostered out to a neighboring knight, that it was the custom for boys to conduct their training in other important homes but that Will didn't want to send away his boys too young. Marian had spoken of both children with such fondness that it was clear she thought of them as her own.

Ellen stood in the middle of the closet and tried to hear Harrison's music, but the only sound was a lonely distant bark of a hound.

She popped out into the room, straining to glimpse him, but he was nowhere in sight.

"Harrison?" She scanned the far shadowed corners, but nothing stirred.

Disappointment coursed through her.

Somehow their two eras had overlapped just briefly. Was this the same thing that had happened when she'd seen Marian? A molecular connection based on the holy water? She'd had the perfect opportunity to warn Harrison about Lionel's threats, and she'd blown it.

If only the moment hadn't passed so quickly. If only she could have had a few seconds longer, even a minute.

"I miss you," she whispered, falling back onto her bed. She hugged her arms to her chest, praying he would stay safe.

~ 16 ~

ELLEN POKED HER HEAD into Marian's bedchamber but then retreated into the hallway, her cheeks heating. Will was sitting in the bedside chair but had bent in and was kissing Marian with a thoroughness that made Ellen's insides flip with longing. For Harrison.

Harrison might be a reserved gentleman, but his kisses had been anything but reserved. They'd been hot and passionate, making her forget all reason.

Her stomach tightened with need for him—need she didn't want to feel. But it was there regardless.

Surely her encounter from last night was only making her miss him all the more. Although with the passing of the night into the early hours of the morning, doubts had crept in. Had she really seen him? Or had she become so needy for him that she'd imagined the whole experience?

Whatever the case, she was more ready than ever to begin the day and make plans for how to get ahold of more holy water.

She cleared her throat extra loud and knocked on the doorframe. Then she counted silently to three before stepping into the room.

This time Marian laughed softly, almost seductively, as she worked to extricate herself from Will, who clearly didn't care who saw him kissing his wife. "Later, Will."

Instead of stopping, Will leaned in and kissed her neck. Marian released a soft, satisfied gasp.

Ellen turned her head to hide a smile. She was happy for Marian. Happy her sister had found a man who loved her. Happy she was experiencing contentment with her new life. Happy things were working out so well for her.

Ellen hesitated. "I can come back in a little bit."

"No, now's fine. Will was just leaving." Marian's voice was weak and breathless.

Will growled something against her cheek, something that made Marian smile.

Ellen headed for the cradle near the foot of the bed. "I'm sorry for disturbing you, but the baby needs her morning assessment." She peered down at the infant, still swaddled and sleeping contentedly. "Don't you, sweet one?"

She wanted to do another APGAR test to be certain the baby was thriving after the stressful delivery. And she needed to clean the umbilical cord stump.

Thankfully, the baby hadn't had any trouble learning to nurse. The servants had been surprised a noblewoman like Marian would consider nursing her own infant instead of handing the child over to a wet nurse. Ellen had assured them that Marian feeding her own baby was the best option, assuring them the milk Marian provided was more suited to the baby than that of a wet nurse.

Her words had put an end to the naysaying, as the staff now regarded her as something akin to a saint for her quick-thinking actions that had brought an end to the delivery and saved Marian and the baby. Of course, Marian's supply of herbal remedies among the many flasks in her special medicinal box had helped too.

Ellen wasn't surprised that Marian had been busy over the past year developing drugs. One resembled aspirin using the salicylic acid from willow bark. The other was like laudanum and made from opium. Marian had described how Will's sister Christina had found opium in an old container in St. Sepulchre's apothecary. Used in ancient times, the drug had become taboo, associated with the devil and witchcraft, so that according to Marian very few people knew of it in the Middle Ages. Although laudanum wouldn't be invented for another 150 years, Marian had done her best to imitate the opiate-based painkiller.

Ellen was only administering the analgesics sparingly so they wouldn't pass to the baby through the breast milk. But even the small doses, along with several tonics, had helped take the edge off Marian's pain. A good night's sleep seemed to have aided Marian's recovery too.

"We have decided upon a name for the baby," Marian said, pushing Will up. He finally settled back in the chair, but not before tangling his fingers with Marian's.

Ellen caressed the baby's plump cheek, smiling at the way her mouth suckled even in sleep. "I hope you've picked a beautiful name for so beautiful a baby."

"We have named her Ellen and shall call her Ellie."

Ellen's gaze shot up. Marian's eyes were glassy with tears, and Will's expression was one of gratefulness.

"You saved her life," Marian said. "And we want her to bear your name."

Emotion clogged Ellen's throat. "I'm honored."

"She will be officially christened at her baptism, and we would like you to be one of her godparents."

"Of course." Ellen had already learned that baptisms usually happened on the day of the baby's birth, that the father would take the child to the church before the priest while the mother remained at home. In baby Ellie's case, Marian had convinced Will to wait on the baptism until she had recuperated and they could attend the ceremony together.

"And . . ." Marian peered at her husband with so much love that Ellen's heart pinched with the need to experience that kind of marriage for herself.

She couldn't allow her thoughts to go there. She wasn't in a position to entertain such fantasies, especially not with being in a coma and having no idea whether she would live through her experience either in the present or in the past. She'd already accepted her fate, and to allow herself to have hope of the future would only stir discontentment.

"Will has agreed to take the wellspring at St. Sepulchre away from Ickham."

Will rose from his chair, releasing Marian's hand. "Someone must stop Ickham's evil intentions from prevailing. Since I am the one who opened the spring, I must take responsibility for it and ensure it is diligently guarded henceforth."

His motivation was honorable, just as Marian had indicated. But all Ellen cared about was being able to get more of the holy water to keep Josie, the other children, and Harrison out of danger. "Thank you."

Will regarded her more carefully. "I shall guard it not only from Ickham but also from your Dr. Lionel. Neither one must have access to such a powerful life source."

"We want to help you, Ellen. But we must think of another way other than giving the holy water to Dr. Lionel." Marian's long hair was unplaited and hung in loose waves, making her look like a fairy-tale princess. Motherhood and the Middle Ages suited her well.

"Of course. We'll come up with something." Although Ellen couldn't think of what that might be. Unless she found another way to connect with Harrison and talk to him. If she knew everyone would remain safe from Dr. Lionel, she could deliver the holy water through the vault directly to Harrison.

How many days were left before Dr. Lionel followed through on his threats? Mentally she calculated the date. The time in the past was going by much too fast. Today was May 21, which meant she had three days to figure out a new plan before Dr. Lionel's one week deadline arrived.

"May 21." Her mind replayed the information Jasper had told her before she'd taken the holy water. "Isn't that the date Dad arrives?"

"Yes! Today is the day." Marian sat up, her eyes turning bright. "We must locate him as quickly as possible."

"Do you know what time he drinks the water and where we might find him?"

"I am not entirely sure what time." Marian swung her legs over the edge of the bed opposite from where Will stood. She pushed up and started across the room. "If we search midafternoon, we might be able to intercept him as he arrives."

Will scowled. "We?"

"Yes, we." Marian could hardly make it to the cushioned stool at her dressing table before collapsing onto it. She picked up a brush and dragged it through her thick, wavy hair. "I must find my father and save him from dying."

Will stalked across the room, his features turning as hard as the stone walls surrounding the manor. He bent and scooped up Marian. "The only place you will go this day is back into the bed."

"I fare well enough and shall ride out—"

"No, Marian," Ellen cut in. "Riding a horse will only cause more damage."

Marian winced, as if imagining herself upon a horse and the pain that would bring.

"I shall go in your stead." Will returned to the bed and lowered her gently.

"If you approach my father, you may frighten him. What if he will not come with you? Refuses to trust you? After all, he does not know I am here."

Ellen paused in unwrapping the baby. "He'll recognize me, and I can explain everything that's happened."

"Then it is settled." Will crossed his arms as though daring Marian to defy him. "I shall accompany Lady Ellen."

Marian offered no further protests. Instead, they discussed where to go first. Since Dad had apparently ingested his flask of holy water in the lobby of the modern-day Kent and Canterbury Hospital, they needed to visit that location, which was outside the old city walls on the opposite side of Canterbury on Old Dover Road. In the present day, the hospital was in a suburban area near Simon Langton Grammar School for Girls and the Kent County Cricket Club.

However, in 1382, the land surrounding Canterbury consisted of rural farms and moorland, which meant Dad would arrive in a field. When he awoke, he would make his way into Canterbury via the Old Dover Road. Ellen planned to be there.

Later, as she stepped outside through the front portico, she shivered against the chill and wrapped her cloak tighter, grateful Marian had thought to provide riding gloves. The sky was overcast, and the dark clouds to the west were heavy with rain. Several of Will's squires were mounted as though they intended to ride along. And a groomsman held the reins of two saddled horses, one a large beast and the other slightly more docile-looking.

At Ellen's approach, the horse tossed its head and snorted as though it had decided it didn't want to deal with an inexperienced rider like her. At least she had more familiarity than Marian, who hadn't known how to ride at all when she'd first crossed to the Middle Ages. They'd had the morning to talk and catch up, and Marian had spoken fondly of her past year even though it had been full of adjustments, and she still missed many things from her old life.

In just a few short days, Ellen already had a long list of the many items she wished she had—a stethoscope, antiseptic, sterile pads, cotton balls, and all the other medical supplies she'd had at hand, even in Haiti. She couldn't deny she also missed things like electricity and running water. She admired Marian all the more for learning to live without modern conveniences.

Ellen had wanted to bring up her sighting of Harrison from the previous evening, but she hadn't known exactly how to do so without having Marian make more assumptions about her relationship with Harrison. So for the time being, she'd remained silent about it and had instead secretly tried to overlap with him every time she stepped into her chambers.

"Lady Ellen?" a male voice called from beyond Chesterfield Park's gates.

She peered down the long driveway to find Nicholas standing next to his horse. The guard was shaking his head at Nicholas, most likely having prevented him from entering once again.

Will's attention shifted to the newcomer, his hand on his sword hilt.

Ellen waved at the guard. "You may let Nicholas in."

The guard looked to Will for his decision as though Ellen's word didn't matter at all. Inwardly she sighed but refrained from saying more.

Will studied the road both ways in addition to the forestland beyond before motioning to the guard to allow Nicholas to pass.

As the young knight made his way inside, the groomsman assisted Ellen into her saddle.

Will had already mounted and was approaching Nicholas. "Sir

Nicholas of Reider. I owe you my gratitude for safely delivering my wife's sister yesterday morn. You saved her from an unwanted union, one that surely would have provoked me to violent measures against Lord Worth."

Leading his horse by its reins, Sir Nicholas bowed his head. "I am at your service, my lord. But I fear you may still have an encounter with him."

"So be it."

Nicholas straightened. "I bring you warning of a rumor I heard last eve. Lord Worth claims Lady Ellen as his betrothed and says you have stolen her. He intends to take the case before the arch-deaconry court."

Claims her? Ellen held back a scoffing laugh. How barbaric. The threat was like something straight out of the movies.

"I fear he will do so soon," Nicholas continued, "before the peril of the plague stops him."

"I have already heard the rumor of his intentions. And I shall be prepared for any aggression he may exert." Will's shoulders were set as though he was ready to do battle. From the fierceness of his demeanor, Ellen had no doubt he was a skilled warrior. Even so, she didn't want to be the cause of a conflict.

What if the court sided with Lord Worth? Would he come to Chesterfield Park and demand that Will hand her over?

She let her attention drift to the walls that surrounded the manor grounds. Could Chesterfield Park withstand an attack? And even if it could, did she really want to bring such danger and destruction upon Will and Marian?

She expected Will to press Nicholas for more details about his brother and the rumor, but he changed the subject and for several moments questioned Nicholas instead about the plague outbreak, where it had spread, and when they could anticipate it reaching the Canterbury area.

"Although it may be a sennight or more before it moves this direction, I would take care to provision and seclude yourselves anon."

Will nodded gravely.

Nicholas glanced at Ellen before focusing back on the gate. "I have relayed the warning to Canterbury. However, before traveling to the Weald today to do the same, I considered it my duty to see how Lady Ellen fares. I could not in good conscience depart without assuring myself she was safe and happy."

"Your duty?" Will raised his brows, a hint of humor in his tone.

Nicholas's expression remained stern. In his long chain mail hauberk split at the waist in the front and back for ease of riding, with a sword strapped to his belt, and a coif flattened against his head, he was every inch what she would have dreamed a medieval knight should be—darkly handsome, strong, and chivalrous.

Will waved a hand toward her. "I give you leave to speak with the lady and question her for yourself."

Nicholas nodded and then faced Ellen, his gaze sweeping over her appreciatively. "My lady, I pray you fare well and have had a joyous reunion with your sister."

"Very joyous. I helped her deliver her baby."

"Then you are a midwife?" Nicholas's brows shot up as though he hadn't expected it, perhaps had believed it was only an excuse to get past the guard yesterday.

"I have some experience."

"She is very knowledgeable." Will shifted in his saddle, the movement causing the weapons upon his belt to clink together ominously. "If not for Lady Ellen's skill, I fear what would have become of my wife and child. She arrived just in time."

Ellen brushed away the praise. "We have Nicholas to thank for helping me away from Reider Castle and guiding me to Chesterfield Park. I couldn't have done anything without him."

"Then 'twould seem God ordained our meeting." Nicholas watched her through lowered lashes, as though banking his attraction, not willing to allow it to fan into a flame.

She didn't want to encourage his attraction, hoped she hadn't done so.

"Perhaps you are right." Will's attention pinged back and forth between her and Nicholas. "I invite you to join us later for supper."

She wanted to tell Will not to play matchmaker, that nothing could come of it. But before she could formulate a polite rejection, Nicholas spoke as he mounted. "I thank you, my lord. But I must be away to do my duty and 'twill take me long hours to travel into the Weald and spread the warning."

"Very well." Will nudged his horse forward. "Your skills as an archer in the Weald are legendary. And your bravery in defeating the French at Dover precedes you."

The muscles in Nicholas's jaw flexed. "I have heard tales of your skills and bravery as well."

Will moved forward several paces. "If you have use of an ally, you need only send me word."

"Likewise, my lord."

They made their way out of the gate. Instead of taking the road, Nicholas veered toward the woods. Before he disappeared into the shadows of the thicket, he glanced over his shoulder at her a final time and gave a nod.

She nodded in response, though again an internal warning told her she needed to let Nicholas know she had no interest in him. She didn't want to inadvertently lead him to believe she could ever like him. Not when Marian's words about Harrison had been repeating in her head since yesterday: *"You love him too . . ."*

She might not be in love with Harrison the way Marian claimed, but it was becoming clear she'd never have feelings for any other man but him.

• ● •

In the middle of the front hall in his wheelchair, Harrison held up the ampulla gingerly, allowing the daylight coming in from the large center dome overhead to give him a better look. The raised picture of an intricate flower on the front of the ampulla was faint, almost nonexistent. But it was there, nonetheless.

"It's not the St. Thomas ampulla you wanted." Mr. Smythe, the antiquarian, peered through his reading glasses at the worn pattern. "But the W on the back is the indication this could be an original Walsingham ampulla."

Harrison turned over the flask and ran a finger over the W. Most of the Walsingham ampullae had been made during the fourteenth and fifteenth centuries and contained a scallop pattern. Such ampullae were excavated all over Norfolk in the countryside where pilgrims had once used the holy water to bless their fields. Most likely they hadn't contained healing water and therefore had been more prolific and more dispensable.

But this ampulla with a flower instead of scallop? It was different. Harrison swished it carefully, feeling the gentle sway of the water left undisturbed for hundreds of years.

After reading through more of Arthur's extensive research and many books regarding Walsingham, Harrison had hoped for the slight possibility of finding holy water there, had been desperate to explore every option.

The Shrine of Our Lady in Walsingham had remained one of the most popular pilgrimage destinations throughout the Middle Ages and still drew in religious pilgrims. The miracles as recorded in *The Pynson Ballad* had taken place early after Lady Richeldis de Faverches had her visions and built a chapel there in honor of the Virgin Mary in 1061.

In rumpled garments and his graying hair poking up on end,

Mr. Smythe stood next to Harrison. The older man held an insulated coffee mug that was at least the size of a twelve-cup coffeepot.

A twinge of remorse pricked Harrison that he'd insisted Mr. Smythe drive through the night and all morning to reach Chesterfield Park. But after hearing the news of the discovery, Harrison had been too anxious to wait.

Especially after seeing Ellen last night . . .

After tasting the residue, he'd only slept for an hour or so before waking up and returning Mr. Smythe's call. During the long hours of waiting for the antiquarian to arrive, Harrison had tried countless times to extract more grains from the two empty ampullae. But either he hadn't been able to ingest enough, or he wasn't able to cross over again. Whatever the case, he'd been desperate to connect with Ellen. He'd tried again all morning as well, until finally Mr. Smythe had arrived at Chesterfield Park.

Now, a tiny thrill raced through him. Was it possible Mr. Smyth had come across more holy water? An ampulla even Arthur Creighton hadn't known existed? "How do you know this ampulla is an original?"

Mr. Smythe gulped several mouthfuls of his coffee before repositioning his reading glasses and bending in. The scent of coffee on his breath was so strong, Harrison could almost taste it. "This flower pattern is rare." The antiquarian pulled a tiny brush out of the satchel slung crosswise over his shoulder. He used the fine tip to buff one of the flower petals. "From the few references I've uncovered, the flower pattern on the flask was used for water that came from a deeper wellspring."

"Deeper wellspring?"

"As you know, Our Lady in Walsingham had two holy wells."

"Yes, I'm aware."

"A third well is believed to have existed deeper, underneath an original priory."

"So the ampullae with the flower pattern were filled with water from the deeper well?"

"Precisely. Like the two wells above it, people believed the other wellspring had curative properties."

Harrison nodded. Of course, Mr. Smythe knew the legends surrounding the healing qualities of the water. But Harrison doubted the antiquarian had any idea it was truly the ultimate cure. Harrison was tempted to jump up and show the older man precisely what the holy water was capable of doing, but he held himself to his wheelchair.

In fact, Sybil had phoned only an hour ago before going into her meeting with the former Lionel guard and his attorney. She'd warned Harrison again not to speak of the particulars of his healing yet.

Mr. Smythe brushed at another faint flower petal. "My guess is that the deeper well fed into the larger two but dried up after a time. And so that's why there are only a limited number of the flower-patterned ampullae."

"That makes sense."

"I spoke with several archaeologists and other antiquarians about the significance of the flower. Everyone agrees that the flower represents life, which of course is symbolic of the new life found in Christ."

And the new life found after being healed.

Harrison willed his fingers not to tremble in his growing excitement. "Where exactly in the shrine did you find this gem, Mr. Smythe?"

"A rare find, indeed. The shrine gardener was the one who allowed me into an ancient cellar where he'd discovered a collection of old ampullae buried behind a wall."

Harrison didn't know for sure if the liquid in the flower-patterned ampulla held remnants from the Tree of Life. But if his speculations were correct, then the third deeper well had been the source of the life-giving water for the miracles recorded in Walsingham. It was likely someone had known the lower spring contained more potent water and had bottled it differently.

"So how many ampullae are there?" Harrison asked.

Mr. Smythe straightened and sighed, his face taking on a haggardness that the coffee's caffeine jolt couldn't hide. "Of the several dozen, most were scalloped. Only three had the flower pattern, but this was the only one with anything in it."

"And the shrine didn't mind you taking it?"

Mr. Smythe took another long swig of his coffee and then smiled. "I'm personal friends with the priest administrator. When I told him this was for Lord Burlington's rare collection and that he could expect a sizeable contribution to the shrine in exchange for it, he was more than agreeable."

"Of course. I'll be more than happy to donate to their cause." What he really wanted to do was test the water, to discover if it contained the ultimate cure or if it was just another false lead. He swished the water again and examined the stopper in the top. It was hard clay or limestone and would likely need to be cracked to break it off.

Harrison checked his mobile. No messages or texts from Sybil. He guessed she was still in her meeting with his previous kidnapper and the lawyer. Hopefully, she would learn where they'd taken Ellen. And tonight he'd have her back.

But would he really?

The same thoughts that had bothered him all night came out to taunt him again. Somehow Lionel must have acquired one of the St. Thomas ampullae and given it to Ellen, forcing her to go into the past.

He wanted to deny the likelihood she'd crossed into 1382. But from everything he'd witnessed, what other possibility was there?

That meant there was a very real chance that once Sybil located Ellen, she'd be in a coma.

He fingered the flower pattern. She would need the first flask of holy water to awaken her and a second dose to keep her alive. That meant he needed to find more. Soon.

Mr. Smythe yawned noisily.

Harrison couldn't detain the antiquarian any longer. The poor man needed a break. "Well done, Mr. Smythe. After you have a rest, I'd like you to return to Walsingham and have another look, do more digging around, see if you can find any more of the flower flasks."

"Then no more looking for the St. Thomas ampullae?"

"Crack on with that as well. Search for both. Confidentially, of course."

"Of course."

"And Mr. Smythe? Finding another original ampulla continues to be a matter of urgency. Perhaps even more so now."

"Very well, my lord. You can count on me, that you can."

After Mr. Smythe took his leave a short while later, Harrison stood from the wheelchair, carefully placing the ampulla into his waistcoat pocket. He needed to test the contents. And he knew exactly how he was going to do so.

17

ELLEN SCANNED THE FIELDS and moor, her heart pounding an anxious rhythm. She didn't want to miss finding their dad today.

Before she'd left Marian's bedchamber, Marian had gripped Ellen's hands, her eyes begging for the chance to see their dad again. "Please find him."

Ellen had read into Marian's request what she wouldn't say— that she needed the opportunity to make things right with Dad after their mother's death had created a rift between them.

Plus, Marian wanted to save him. In fact, her desire to protect Dad had been one of the reasons why she'd crossed to the year before his arrival—to warn him to be careful. Though they didn't know exactly what danger he'd faced, they believed his death in 1382 had caused his comatose body in the present to cease functioning.

Ellen directed her horse toward Will, his squires not far behind, keeping an ever-vigilant watch for any danger from Lord Worth while they hunted for Dad. They'd combed the Dover Road for the past hour, passing carts and packhorses along with groups on foot. But none of the travelers had resembled her dad.

"Do you see anyone new?" Ellen asked.

Will shook his head curtly, his gaze sweeping over the road ahead and trailing a merchant leaving Canterbury with a rumbling and creaking cart. While Will was a good-looking man, he took himself much too seriously. But he loved Marian—and that was all that really mattered.

Marian adored Will too, and the more time Ellen spent with her sister, the more she understood Marian's wish to remain in the past with her husband. Will's love had made the sacrifice worthwhile.

Was that what the love of a good man would do? Take a skeptic and transform her into a woman willing to take a chance?

Ellen pushed aside the thought and the low ache it brought. She was different than Marian. She'd never had many chances. Her future had always held an early expiration date.

A light rain had begun to fall, and Ellen pulled up her hood to shield herself. The drops soaked into her cloak and filled her nostrils with the scent of musty wool. Not only was she cold and damp, but she was sore from the unfamiliar jostling—similar to the way her backside felt after riding a bike for too long.

She wouldn't last much longer. She had to search harder.

Biting back mounting frustration, she scanned the area east of Dover Road. Fields spread out with what appeared to be individual strips, most plowed and planted but some lying fallow. A few cattle, pigs, and goats grazed on grass growing on the unplanted parcels while laborers toiled with rudimentary tools among what she guessed to be wheat, oats, and barley.

The stretch of land to the west of the road contained jagged boulders along with blooming hawthorn bushes, their white flowers bright against the grayish-green landscape. Wild buttercups clustered in the long grass that was bending under the growing wind. Sheep grazed in the commons of the grassland, the rolling hills stretching onward for miles, strangely quiet except for birdsong.

Ellen prayed for a glimpse of Dad's thick gray hair, but he was nowhere in sight. "He should be here by now. What if we missed him, and he's already made his way into town?"

Will halted his horse, and his squires did likewise. "Mayhap he is arriving later than you expected."

Ellen went over the timing of their dad's crossing that she and Marian had worked out. According to their calculations, he would have arrived in the afternoon. Although she didn't have a watch or phone to check the time, the growling of her stomach indicated the nearing of the supper hour.

She thought back to her arrival into the past, to the elapse of time. From when she'd swallowed the holy water until she'd awoken, an entire night had passed. Was it possible they were ahead of themselves, that Dad wouldn't be traveling the Dover Road on his way to Canterbury until tomorrow? That he was currently lying somewhere still unconscious?

"I think we need to begin searching the fields and glens to the west." She nudged her horse off the road.

Will issued orders to his squires and followed reluctantly, clearly ready to head home and check on the preparations his men were making to defend Chesterfield Park. Ellen sensed under any other circumstance, he wouldn't have agreed to leave his home, not with the tension with Lord Worth. But Ellen was quickly learning Will would do anything for Marian, including this dangerous—perhaps even futile—attempt to find their dad.

She tried to picture the area as it was in modern times. Where exactly would the hospital stand? The grassy hills revealed nothing of what would come hundreds of years later. Without any landmarks to guide the way, she felt more helpless with each deserted rise they crested and each empty copse they searched.

Will finally reined in his horse at the edge of an area of shrubs they'd just searched. He glanced overhead, his expression grim. "Night will fall erelong. I regret we must be on our way."

Ellen nodded and suppressed a shudder. Although twilight was settling around them, she didn't want to return to Marian without their dad. A glance at Will's frustrated expression told her he didn't want to disappoint Marian either.

With stiff fingers and chattering teeth, Ellen started to turn her horse. As she spun, a spot of white among a tangle of brush caught her eye. It wasn't the soft white of clover or hemlock. Rather it was thicker, almost gray. Was it the fur of a hare tangled in a bramble?

She urged her horse closer and then gasped. The grayish-white was attached to a head, a human head.

"Will!" she called over her shoulder. "I think I found him."

Will trailed after her. Within seconds he was dismounting and prying apart branches, one of his squires assisting him. Ellen couldn't move. She was too cold and sore. But she held her breath in anticipation.

When, a moment later, Will and his squire dragged a man out, her whole body trembled. It was her dad. He was limp and pale and unmoving.

"Is he alive?"

Will removed a glove and pressed fingers against her dad's mouth, checking for breathing. "Yes. Thank the saints."

Swift tears stung Ellen's eyes, and a tight ache formed in her throat. She took him in from his full head of gray hair that had once been red like Marian's to his matching gray beard and mustache, which were full but trimmed neatly, giving him a scholarly appearance. His face was round, almost plump, just like his stomach, the result of his sedentary lifestyle of research and study.

After she'd attended his funeral a year ago and watched his coffin being lowered into the ground, how was it possible he was here and that she was seeing him again? Was it even real?

She didn't know. Maybe she was only imagining everything in her coma-induced state. Or maybe she couldn't deny Harrison's speculations about entanglement allowing for a body to share an existence even though physically separated.

Such a concept defied her comprehension. But just because she wasn't able to understand it didn't mean it couldn't happen. After all, the people of the Middle Ages couldn't conceive of a world with cell phones, internet, or airplanes. Even though they couldn't envision modern technology didn't mean it was impossible.

Whatever the case, she was helpless to do anything but go along with this strange reality. As Will hefted her unconscious father into the saddle and secured him, she lifted a prayer they would be able to keep him safe amidst the dangers that only seemed to be increasing with each passing day.

* ● *

Harrison stood in the middle of his bedroom, holding the flower-patterned ampulla. The glow of the bedside lamp illuminated the jagged opening where he'd broken the seal. He'd meticulously poured the liquid into a test tube, sealed it, and locked it away in his safe.

But he'd made sure enough remained in the ampulla that he could test some. If he could make a brief time crossing, then he'd know the water contained residue from the Tree of Life, the ultimate cure.

He glanced at the glowing lights of his bedside table clock: 11:30 p.m. He hadn't wanted to wait until the late hour, but he'd forced himself to be patient. If Ellen was in the past, he didn't want to chance missing her by appearing in the room too early in the evening when she might not be there.

On the other hand, he couldn't wait overly long. He needed to meet with her before Sybil and a team of special forces raided an underground lab that the former Lionel employee had disclosed during the meeting.

Sybil hadn't divulged the time they planned to execute Ellen's rescue, but she'd indicated it would be sometime during the night since they hoped to utilize the darkness in aiding their efforts.

His desperate prayer was that Ellen would be back at Chesterfield Park by dawn. He'd brought in the best medical equipment in preparation for her return, and he'd informed his physician to be ready. He didn't know what state she'd be in, but he suspected she'd be comatose.

The trouble was, he needed to communicate with Ellen first and tell her to put two more ampullae of holy water into the vault. Then he'd be certain he could revive her from the coma safely. He needed two doses to keep her alive—he'd learned that lesson well enough from Marian. If the Walsingham ampulla contained real holy water, then she'd only need to find one more dose. But he wanted her to put in two—just in case.

Lifting the ancient ampulla, he closed his eyes and prayed fervently, as he had earlier, that the water was the real thing. He tipped the broken flask to his lips and let the remaining droplets fall onto his tongue.

He held himself still for several long seconds, waiting for the rush of warmth to blow through his veins. When nothing happened, he tapped the flask and shook it, trying to get out the last remnants. A final drop fell into his mouth. But still he felt nothing.

He willed himself to see into 1382. "Come on now. Take me to her."

At a startled gasp and shuffling of sheets, his eyes flew open.

Darkness enveloped him. The mustiness and dampness of the air was the same as when he'd crossed over the previous night.

His pulse kicked hard. Thank the Lord. He was in the past again.

He strained to see the bed. "Ellen?"

"Harrison?" Her response was groggy.

She was here. Urgency prodded him forward. He needed to give her instructions before he was jerked away from her. "Listen, love." He fumbled through the dark in the direction of her bed. "You need to put another flask of holy water into the vault right away. Two, if possible."

"You're back." The sleepiness fell from her voice.

He bumped into the bedstead. "Then it's true. You're in the past?"

"Yes, I'm with Marian." In an instant she was gripping his hands as though she planned to force him to stay.

"Ellen, listen to me, love. I need the two doses to wake you."

"Harrison. No. I need to warn you." Her pull was strong, and the momentum of her tug threw him off balance. Though he tried to steady himself, he toppled to the sagging mattress so that he was half on her and half on the mattress.

"It's Dr. Lionel," she was saying, holding him tight. "He's behind Josie's cardiac arrest. And he intends to harm the rest of the children unless I deliver holy water to him within the week."

With the sweet pressure of her body against his, he knew with clarity that this moment was all too real. His physical reaction to her touch was too swift and too electric to be anything but genuine.

As much as he wanted to wrap his arms around her and hold her, he knew that wouldn't keep them together. They would be ripped away from each other without any notice.

"Promise to get holy water, Ellen."

"Promise you'll warn all the families to be careful. Get them someplace safe. And then alert the police."

He didn't know what she was talking about and would sort it out later. For now, he had to make her understand the urgency of providing the holy water. "My investigator has located you in Lionel's underground lab. And now you have to get the doses of holy water into the vault as soon as possible."

She stilled, as though finally hearing him. "Will and Marian only have one bottle left. And they don't have control of the wellspring anymore. But Will's agreed to try to regain possession." Her fingers skimmed his ribs.

Another heated current sizzled through him—just as it always did when they connected.

"Be extra careful, Harrison. Dr. Lionel's threatened to come after you . . ." Her voice grew faint. An instant later, she was gone. And he found himself lying on his bed alone, the lamp casting a glow over the empty space beside him. The modern temperature control of his room and scent of his masculine soap replaced the mustiness.

Gentle fingers on his shoulder shook him. "My lord?"

He glanced up to find Drake at his bedside.

Though fatigue settled into every bone, Harrison pushed up to his feet. Something was wrong. "What is it, Drake?"

"Ms. Huxham is here, my lord."

He glanced at the clock: 11:35. His whole interaction in the past had lasted only minutes. If only he could have stayed with Ellen longer. If not for Drake's waking him, would he have had more time?

"Ms. Huxham would like to speak with you."

The gravity of Drake's expression told Harrison the matter was serious. He nodded his thanks and stumbled out of his room, fighting the exhaustion that came after the time overlaps and trying to make sense of Ellen's warning through the haze in his mind.

What had she said? That Dr. Lionel had been the one to hurt Josie and had threatened to harm the others?

Had Ellen gone into the past to try to find holy water to save the girl? Or had Dr. Lionel forced her to cross time by threatening to harm the Serenity House children?

She was obviously worried for them. And for him. He wasn't surprised to learn Lionel was threatening to come after him.

As he made his way into the entryway, Sybil stood just inside the front door. She was attired in her usual black leather jacket and jeans, and her brown hair hung in a long straight curtain. But her shoulders were uncharacteristically slumped, and she pressed her fingertips into her temples as if warding off a headache.

At his approach, she dropped her hands, straightened her shoulders, and faced him square. "Harrison. The mission was a failure."

The words fired into his chest like a bullet, stealing the air from his lungs.

"I'm sorry."

He hadn't expected them to attempt the rescue until earlier in the morning. "What happened?"

"We planned for oh three hundred as a disguise and executed the real attack at twenty-two hundred."

His muscles tensed. "And Ellen?"

"She wasn't there."

"They'd already moved her?"

"No. She'd never been there."

His legs wobbled. He groped for the edge of the nearest settee and lowered himself. He could barely hear Sybil as she explained they'd found evidence that the warehouse had once been a primary lab—likely the place they'd taken Harrison. But Lionel had moved locations since then, leaving only a small lab behind as a decoy.

All he could focus on was that Ellen hadn't been there. Now they were no closer to finding her than they were at the beginning.

He groaned and buried his face in his hands. "She didn't deny being held in a lab. But I should have pressed her for more information. Even if she didn't know exactly where, she could've given me more details."

Sybil fell silent.

He sounded like a raving madman. But he was too distraught to care.

She cleared her throat. "You've seen her?"

Sybil had accepted his explanation about his healing from the holy water without any scoffing. Now that she'd seen its power, would she be more open to the fact that the holy water could cause time crossings? "I'm not sure if you'll believe me if I tell you what's going on."

She spread her feet as though bracing herself. "You should know by now that I don't rule out any evidence until I've proven it wrong."

"True."

"I can't do my job if you're withholding information from me."

He finally met her gaze. Her green eyes were as keen and honest as always. And devoid of any mockery. He sat up and leaned back. He nodded to the spot opposite his. "Have a seat. I think you'll need to be sitting while I inform you of everything else."

She lowered herself and poised to listen as openly as always.

Even as he tried to formulate an explanation, one thought rose above all others. He had to communicate with Ellen again.

~ 18 ~

"HARRISON IS ON THE VERGE OF LOCATING ME," Ellen said. "Once he rescues me, he wants the two flasks, one to bring me out of the coma and another to keep my body alive in the present."

"He is now aware that you have crossed into the past and are here at Chesterfield." Marian reclined against a mound of pillows and patted the baby's back after nursing. Sunlight filtered in through the open shutters, highlighting the baby's fuzzy red hair.

After seeing Harrison for a second time last night, Ellen had finally confessed Harrison's visits this morning to Marian.

"I just wish there was a way to overlap longer so we can communicate better." But once he disappeared, Ellen hadn't been able to reconnect like the first night she'd briefly seen him.

"My first overlaps with Will were so short, we hardly had time to exchange but a few words."

A soft knock sounded on the door. A maidservant poked her head into the room. "Your father has awakened, my lady."

Ellen stood quickly. She'd checked on their dad only an hour ago in the room where they'd taken him last night and had begun to wonder if he'd ever awaken. She shuddered to think what would have happened if she and Will hadn't found him when they did. How would he have survived if he'd been exposed all night to the cold and rain?

Cradling her baby, Marian climbed out of bed, her eyes alight with excitement. "How is he?"

Before the maid could answer, their dad stepped through the door into the room. He was attired in dark hose and a long gray tunic that stretched tight across his wide girth. He looked almost comical in the ill-fitting garments, except that his expression was entirely too serious.

"Marian? Ellen?" His brown eyes were wide, almost frightened. "What are you doing here?" He still spoke with his British accent, which had never diminished, even after living in the States for most of his married life.

Ellen started to explain, but he rushed forward. "I'd hoped the servants were wrong when they told me that Lady Marian was my daughter."

Marian stiffened, and her welcoming smile faded. "I am sorry to disappoint you. But it is I."

Their dad crossed the room, his tight shoes and garments making his movements stilted. "You shouldn't be here. This was never part of the equation."

"Whether or not it was part of your equation, we are here."

Stopping at the bedside, he reached out and grazed Marian's face as if to make sure she was real. "What happened?"

Marian softened just a little against his touch. "I crossed back in time a year ago."

His fingers visibly trembled against her cheek, and his eyes turned glassy. "You've been in the past for a year?"

She nodded. "My body in the present is dead."

He brought his shaking fingers to his mouth. "No."

"This is where I want to be. With my husband. And now my babe." She peered down at Ellie swaddled and sated.

Dad dropped his gaze to the baby, and his eyes widened. "God in heaven. What have I done?"

"I wanted to stay. With Will, my husband. Because I love him."

Dad shook his head in disbelief or despair or perhaps both. Then he turned to Ellen. "And you? Are you dead in the present too? How long have you been here? Do you have a husband and child too?"

Ellen smiled. "No. I've only been here for a few days. And as far as I know, my body is still comatose in the present."

He didn't return the smile but instead grabbed on to the bedside chair and sank into it as though he couldn't bear his weight a moment longer. He looked from Ellen to Marian and back. "I never intended to drag you two into the past. Never."

"It's all right, Dad." Ellen reached for his hand, marveling that she was doing so, especially since she'd been the one to close his coffin. Of course, Harrison had been there for her, helping her with each step of the funeral preparations, and holding her up through her grief.

"I'm being held captive by Dr. Lionel," she blurted. "And he's threatened to harm many people, including Harrison, if I don't deliver a supply of holy water to him."

Her dad's mouth dropped open, and his hand tightened around hers. So much had happened. How could she expect him to understand unless she started at the beginning?

"It's a long story." She sat on the bed and tugged Marian down beside her. "Let's start at the beginning."

Although Ellen hadn't wanted to divulge the news to their dad about his death, there was no other way to explain what had led

Marian into the past. They had to be honest with him about everything, even if the news wasn't pleasant.

By the time they'd each explained the sequence of events that had led first Marian and then Ellen to the past, Dad was wiping tears from his eyes. Was he disturbed to know he'd died in the present and could possibly still die in the past? At least now that he was aware of the danger, he could be more careful, and they could all work together to keep him safe.

He sat forward in the chair and held his head in his hands. "I've made such a mess of things, haven't I?"

"Things might be a mess, but this isn't your fault." Marian reclined against her pillows again. "We all made our own choices, and now we have to live with the consequences."

"I agree." Ellen rubbed his arm.

Her dad sighed loudly. "What good did the cure do you, now that you're Dr. Lionel's prisoner? He'll have no regard for your life or the damaging experiments he's performing on your body."

"During my overlap with Harrison last night, he said he was close to rescuing me from the lab where Dr. Lionel is keeping me."

"I pray the rescue attempt is successful, although against Dr. Lionel, it won't be easy," Dad said. "Lionel and Mercer have been in competition for decades. From what I've heard, his family has always been corrupt, even having ties with the Nazis as far back as World War II. They're as brutal and unethical now as they were then."

Ellen wasn't surprised by the news. But it certainly made Dr. Lionel's threats more dangerous.

"From the very first time Dr. Lionel realized I had started searching for the ultimate cure years ago, he's been racing against me to find it. But only because he cares about himself and the profit he stands to gain. He has black market ties with radical terrorist groups and will auction the holy water to the highest bidders, likely making billions in the process."

If that was true, then all the more reason not to give Dr. Lionel the holy water. "He told me he was planning to continue studying the water to attempt to replicate it."

"Oh, he'll do that too," Dad said. "He won't ever give up trying to create it for himself."

Marian nodded gravely. "After the efforts you undertook to hide your research, I realized you didn't want it to fall into the wrong hands. Even so, I didn't know the extent of the danger."

"The danger is immense." Her dad combed his fingers through his hair, making it stick up on end. "In fact, I considered abandoning the search for the ultimate cure altogether. But every time I looked at your mother's picture, I knew I couldn't stop. Not when so many people—like Ellen—needed help."

Marian brushed a hand over her baby's head, earning a soft, sweet baby noise in response. "Then you believe the benefit is greater than the risk?"

"I was holding out hope that was so. My plan was to locate the source of the water, the original wellspring on St. Sepulchre, so that Mercer could drill for it. At the very least, I hoped to provide Marian and Harrison with a steady supply for as long as I could, a supply we could eventually add to the current trial medicine for VHL."

"So you'd planned to use it only in the drug for VHL?" Marian asked, her brow rising with surprise.

"We would never have enough holy water for every illness of every kind. And if very ill people started experiencing miraculous healings, that would draw too much notice, as well as unwanted attention from the worst kinds of criminals who would stop at nothing to steal whatever supply we have, just like Lionel is doing now."

Was that also happening with Ickham and the wellspring? Causing coveting and conflict? What would happen if Josie and the other Serenity House children were miraculously healed? Ellen could only imagine the terrible fighting—possibly even wars—people would wage to gain control over the holy water.

Her dad's plan to pair the holy water with a specific drug would still create a sensation, but perhaps doing so would be more plausible and lead to less strife.

"But now," her dad continued, "seeing you both here in the past, I'm not so sure my efforts were worthwhile. I've caused irreparable damage."

"Not with Ellen," Marian replied. "We still have a chance to save Ellen if we can regain the control over the wellspring and provide Harrison with the holy water to wake her from her coma."

At that moment, a servant knocked lightly on the door and entered with a platter of almonds, dates, and raisins along with a glazed ceramic jug containing ale. The brew, made from malted barley without hops, was a slightly sweet but weak beer. Ellen would have preferred water but had learned that since the water was untreated and could contain dirt and disease, most people drank ale instead.

Once Marian thanked and dismissed the servant, Dad began eating with gusto. Ellen dragged a stool over to the bed but only nibbled from the tray on the edge of the bed, her appetite rebelling no matter how much Marian prodded her to eat the food.

"It's possible to save Dad too," Ellen said, absently picking at an almond. "If we keep him alive this week, maybe we can change his death in the future."

At the reminder of his impending death, her dad swallowed hard. "No, I'm afraid the future is fixed."

"So, we can't change anything?" Ellen asked.

"God's providence always prevails. In his state unbound by the constraints of time, he sees what happens from beginning to end and has the details arranged before we even come to be."

"Yes, only God knows each of our timelines," Marian quickly interjected. "Some are shorter than others. But shouldn't we do all we can to live and endure to the best of our ability?"

"Very true, Marian." Dad wiped his mouth and hands. "Since none of us know when our timeline ends, we should take care to do our part by living wisely, being healthy, and seeking medical advances."

"Then, there is still the chance we could save your life here," Marian insisted. "We know you're in danger somehow, and we shall be on guard, look for ways to protect you."

Ellen nodded. "What if bringing you here last night out of the cold and rain saved your life? Maybe the first time you came you caught pneumonia."

Dad picked up a date, chewed it, and stared above the bed canopy, clearly lost in thought, his brilliant mind working as hard as it always had. After long moments, he dug for a handful of nuts from the platter. "But that's just it. There wasn't a first time. This is my only time. Whatever happens to me is yet to come. We cannot escape the fact that I'll experience a trauma that causes my body to languish and die in both eras."

Marian's eyes flashed with familiar determination. "I died in the present, but I am still alive in the past. If I lived, we must hold out hope for you that your timeline is not yet coming to an end."

"I don't know—"

"Maybe you died in the earthquake aftershock," Marian persisted. "If we are more careful of your whereabouts and what you are doing, we can try to keep you safe."

"Earthquake." Dad jumped to his feet and peered at his watch, tapping it before pressing it to his ear. Had it stopped working?

"The earthquake was supposed to strike yesterday in the early afternoon."

Dad wavered, and Ellen stood, steadying him. "We didn't experience any earthquakes here in Canterbury yesterday."

Again, Dad stared off into the distance, his mind clearly searching through the mountains of information he had stored there.

"Do you think the date of the earthquake was off?" Marian glanced to the open shutter and the sunlight streaming inside as though gauging the hour.

That was another thing Ellen missed. Not having a digital clock to easily access the time.

Dad muttered several calculations under his breath. Then his eyes widened. "It's possible the Julian calendar being used at the time overcompensated for the length of the solar year. If my recollections are correct, they added an extra day."

Marian scooted toward the edge of the bed. "Do you think the earthquake happens today?"

"Yes. It's very likely."

"Will it cause much damage?" Ellen took the baby as Marian rose and donned a robe.

"Yes. Quite a lot, actually." Dad caressed the baby's head. "Since the British Isles sit in the middle of a tectonic plate, small tremors occur a dozen times a year and cause only slight movement of objects. But the earthquake that hits in 1382 is one of the rare larger quakes. It's a 5.8 on the Richter scale."

Marian cringed as if the ceiling was already about to collapse on them. "'Tis after midday already." Marian's voice took on a note of urgency. "We need to warn everyone."

As they made their way out of Marian's chamber and through the passageways of old Chesterfield Park, Dad continued with his nearly photographic relay of information about the 1382 earthquake that he'd researched before traveling back in time. The belfry of Canterbury Cathedral would sustain severe damage, the bells would dislodge and fall to the earth, and the cloister would suffer structural stress. Other churches, manors, and castles would experience damage too. He assured them the safest place for all of them during the earthquake was outside away from any objects that could come tumbling down.

Ellen helped Marian to spread the news throughout the household, informing the staff to remove themselves from the manor as swiftly as possible. Marian explained that normally Will's mother, Lady Felice, also lived at the manor but had gone to stay with an ailing sister in London. In her absence, Marian had more control over the servants, and they did her bidding, clearly respecting and liking her.

As the servants poured from the house, Will ducked out of the blacksmith building near the stables, shielding his eyes from the sun, his youngest son Robert on his heels. With more rumors regarding Lord Worth's aggression, Will had been busy standing guard with his knights as well as making sure weapons and provisions were ready to withstand an assault.

As Will homed in on Marian and the baby standing near the raised garden beds, he strode down the dirt wagon path that connected the outbuildings to the main house. He wore a long colorless padded jacket Marian had referred to as a gambeson, which would provide cushioning for his plate armor when he needed to don it.

"What is this about, Marian?" His brows furrowed together above eyes containing concern.

She tugged her cloak about her more fully to shield her nightgown and robe underneath. "I wanted everyone to be safe from the coming earthquake."

The servants, who were clustering nearby, paused at Marian's declaration.

How could Marian possibly explain her ability to know about an earthquake before it struck? Would they consider her a seer? A heretic? A witch?

Ellen remembered reading that the outbreak of the Black Plague earlier in the century had stirred up irrational fear in the people. Of course, they hadn't known the real cause of the plague. Instead, they'd looked for scapegoats. Many innocent people had been accused of being witches for starting the plague and had been burned at the stake as a result.

If another outbreak of the plague was sweeping through the country, anyone who hinted at being different would become suspect. Should Marian have been more discreet in speaking of the earthquake? Perhaps they should have come up with another plausible reason to have everyone go outside.

"I think perhaps you are still overly tired." Will spoke in a low tone. "There is no earthquake—"

The moment he spoke the word, a rumbling, like that of a nearby passing freight train, filled the air. The rumbling turned into a loud rattling. Ellen's body wobbled, with a sense of vertigo she'd never had before.

The ground shook and then shifted, and she felt as though she were standing in a boat that was being rocked by waves.

Screams and cries erupted around them. The servants clutched at one another or knelt on the ground, crossing themselves and praying aloud.

As her dad swayed, flailing his arms to keep his balance, she grabbed on to him. "We need to get down."

Together they knelt, the ground still shaking. She looked up in time to see the chimney at one end of the manor crack and the stones fall like a stack of blocks that had been knocked over. They hit the roof and rained off in a shower of debris.

After less than thirty seconds, the destruction tapered to a halt, and Ellen sat in stunned silence. Whimpers and the soft cries from the others drifted around her. A glance in Marian's direction told her that Will had covered both Marian and the baby within the arch of his body and draped an arm over his son. They were all safe.

Ellen surveyed the others. No one was bleeding or injured—at least that she could outwardly see. She shifted to Dad, anxiously taking him in from his disheveled hair down to his shoes. "Are you all right?"

"I'm just fine." He sat back on his heels, examining the destruction of the house, the stables, and the other outbuildings. "Looks like we got outside without much time to spare."

"How did you know about the earthquake?" Will pulled away from Marian and assessed her and the baby.

At Will's question, a strange silence descended upon the servants. Instead of gratitude and appreciation, their faces filled with both fright and wariness.

Their reaction was as Ellen had suspected. Hundreds of years away from the discoveries that would explain natural disasters and diseases, the people still relied mostly upon superstition.

Marian didn't immediately answer Will but clutched her baby closer as though already feeling the ache of having her child ripped from her arms under the accusations that she was unworthy.

"I told Marian about the earthquake." Dad's voice rang out clear and calm amidst the eerie silence.

Ellen turned startled eyes upon her dad. His brown gaze locked with hers for just an instant, but it was long enough to see the gravity there, to know that he'd recognized the truth of the situation just as she and Marian had. Marian was in danger for predicting the earthquake, but instead of letting her come under suspicion, he was shifting the blame to himself.

Dad pushed off the ground with a grunt. "I have studied the pattern of earthquakes in Kent. It would appear that a quake of this magnitude happens about one time every century. My careful calculations proved to be true for a quake today."

Will stood and assisted Marian to her feet, watching Dad's face, his intense gaze unrelenting in its pursuit of honesty. Dad didn't back down or look away, and a message seemed to pass between the two men.

"I am grateful for your warning." Will spoke in a measured voice. "You may have saved lives. At the very least, you have saved many from injury."

Dad bowed his head slightly. "I'm glad to be of service."

As the servants began to disperse, they now shot furtive glances toward Dad instead of Marian. Ellen prayed they believed his explanation, that it would suffice to dampen their suspicions. Because the last thing any of them needed was more trouble.

* ● *

Harrison paced the length of his property behind the greenhouse near the rear gate. "Check the vault multiple times every day. And once a flask of holy water appears, you need to inject it into my body."

Sybil had propped one boot on a stone bench, her gaze following his every move back and forth. She hadn't said he was insane, and her expression didn't betray any emotions. But he sensed that even though she'd witnessed his healing, the possibility of crossing time went beyond the scope of her imagination.

Whatever the case, as long as she was willing to have a go at his plan, that's all that mattered. "After the holy water is in my system, I should awaken within a few hours. It might take longer. Maybe a day."

Drake stood in the shade of the building, out of the afternoon sun. His furrowed forehead spoke louder than words. The older man didn't want Harrison taking so great a risk.

But what other choice was there? Harrison had attempted to communicate again with Ellen off and on during the remainder of the night as well as throughout the morning. But he hadn't had the slightest overlap. All he was doing was using up precious droplets.

During the long hours, he'd come to the conclusion that the only way he could truly save Ellen was by drinking the holy water and going into the past with her. Then he could talk with her for an unlimited amount of time, sort out what was really going on, and learn the location of where Lionel was keeping her.

He assumed the wellspring Ellen mentioned was the one Marian had told him about before she died. From what he gathered, it was open but no longer in Will and Marian's possession. Apparently, Will intended to regain control of it. And now Harrison needed to convey the urgency of the mission and offer to help.

If for some reason they couldn't gain access to the wellspring, he'd convince Will and Marian to give him their final flask of holy water, and he would put it into the vault so Drake and Sybil could awaken him.

The minute he was conscious, he'd share all the particulars about Ellen's location with Sybil, and then she could commence another rescue straightaway, hopefully this time in the right place.

Of course, then he'd need at least three more flasks of holy water—one to keep himself alive and two for Ellen. And there was the possibility that they might not find one for him in time to save his life, but at least he'd free Ellen from Lionel's clutches and buy her more time until Marian and Will could retake the wellspring or uncover more holy water elsewhere.

"You don't need to do this, Harrison." Sybil straightened and crossed her arms. "I've got other investigators casting around every warehouse in Kent. It won't be long before we get another lead."

"We don't have time to play a game of hide-and-seek with

Lionel." He was sick to death with worry over Ellen and couldn't sit around waiting any longer. Not when he needed to speak to Will and Marian. Surely once they knew of his plans to save Ellen, they'd do whatever they could to help him.

"Chesterfield Park is under tight surveillance."

He'd shared Ellen's warning about Lionel threatening to harm him and the Serenity House children. Sybil had immediately phoned a private security company and enlisted guards to protect him. She'd also alerted all the Serenity House families to the possible threat as well as arranging for security outside of Josie's hospital room.

"I'm not worried about me. All I want is to find Ellen. That's all that matters." He was surprised at how desperate his voice sounded.

When one of Sybil's delicate brows arched, he ducked his head.

"You love her." Sybil's statement contained certainty.

He'd tried hiding his feelings from everyone, including Ellen. Why keep his love a secret any longer? "Yes, I love her."

Sybil nodded curtly.

Harrison reached into his waistcoat pocket for the test tube and pulled it out. He popped off the lid. Then he nodded at Drake. "Keep on Mr. Smythe. With any luck, he'll find more of the flower-patterned ampullae."

Drake's frown deepened. "You're certain you cannot wait another day or two, my lord?"

"I've waited long enough."

The older man sighed, his shoulders stooping even more than usual.

He'd explained to Drake that he needed to drink the holy water outside, that he couldn't take a risk of suddenly appearing in a room in Chesterfield Park. And this spot near the edge of the property would hopefully allow him to arrive unnoticed and give him the time he needed to awaken. Then he'd be able to approach the house without arousing too much suspicion—although some might wonder how he made it past the gates.

Harrison turned toward Sybil. "I'll find out where Ellen has got to. I promise."

She straightened, putting both feet on the ground. "You sure about this, Harrison?"

His answer was to tip the glass container to his lips and drain the liquid. In an instant, the world turned black.

~ 19 ~

"LORD WORTH INTENDS TO CLAIM Ellen as his bride on the morrow."

Sir Nicholas's announcement from the doorway brought silence to the great hall so that Ellen could hear the sudden racing of her heart. The clanging of pots and the clatter of utensils echoed in a corridor connecting the hall to the kitchen, where servants had been running back and forth, bringing their supper.

Will's chair scraped through the fresh rushes against the floor as he stood from the long, broad table covered in a white linen cloth and graced with polished brass candlesticks.

"He has gained the support of the Archbishop of Canterbury for his betrothal to Lady Ellen," Nicholas announced. "They will be riding to Chesterfield Park in the morn to force you to hand her over."

Ellen stiffened on the bench where she sat across the table from Will and her dad.

Will's hand immediately went to the hilt of his sword, which she'd learned was a permanent fixture at his belt. "'Twould appear

Lord Worth has availed himself of not only Ickham but now also the archbishop. I have no doubt they are colluding to gain access to the wellspring and will sorely use Lady Ellen in an attempt to wrest the keys from me."

The very thought of being *sorely used* made Ellen's skin crawl. "If they come, I'll refuse to go with him."

"If the archbishop demands it," Will said, "we shall have little choice in the matter."

"The church cannot force me to marry someone I don't want to."

"The archbishop's authority comes from the pope himself. To defy him will bring great censure and difficulty to all those in my household."

Ellen didn't want that to happen. But she wouldn't willingly go with Lord Worth and marry him, even if the archbishop demanded it. What could she do? Run away and hide?

Will stared into the distance, his silence stretching taut, until at last he motioned to the empty place next to Ellen. "Sir Nicholas, I pray you will join us for supper."

Nicholas hesitated. His leather boots and chain mail were dusty, and his face was etched with weariness. No doubt he'd run himself ragged riding throughout the countryside spreading the news of the plague, which made his warning regarding Lord Worth all the kinder.

"There may yet be a way to avoid conflict," Will said. "But I shall need your assistance."

Nicholas nodded and started across the room. The inside of the hall had sustained damage from the earthquake—cracked ceilings and walls, broken dishes and decorations, overturned shelves and cabinets. But thankfully, no one had been injured.

As Nicholas took a place beside her, a waft of forest and earth emanated from him. The conversations around the hall resumed.

For a short while, Will questioned Nicholas about the extent of the devastation from the earthquake throughout the countryside.

Finally, as Nicholas pushed back his empty plate and wiped his mouth, Will narrowed his eyes upon the man. "I have spoken to several of my trusted knights about you, Sir Nicholas. They all agree you are a man of honor, fortitude, and integrity. You have not only won the favor of the king, but you have proven to be a man of valor in battle."

Nicholas bowed his head in acknowledgment of Will's compliments but remained silent.

"Thus, I shall offer you my wife's sister as a bride this night."

"What?" Ellen stiffened and sat up at the same time as both Nicholas and her dad.

"I cannot—" Nicholas started.

"No." Her dad protested at the same moment Ellen did.

"Hear me out." Will's steely tone silenced them. "If Lady Ellen is wed to Sir Nicholas then Lord Worth must forfeit his right to have her. He will have no recourse for claiming her."

"My brother will not be so easily swayed."

"If you are wed in the sight of God and man and consummate your union, there will be naught he nor the archbishop can do to change the circumstances."

Nicholas cast a glance at her from beneath his long lashes. His eyes were dark and unreadable.

Would he really consider Will's offer?

She absolutely couldn't. She'd never considered marriage before and wouldn't start now. Besides, her heart yearned for only one man. Harrison. Even though she couldn't have him, she had no desire for anyone else.

Adamantly she shook her head, but Will cut her off. "You are my responsibility now. And I shall have the final say in the matter." He spoke as if the decision was already made.

Ellen opened her mouth to contradict him, but her dad spoke first. "You know Marian and I both desire for Ellen to return to her country. We don't want her to stay here indefinitely."

If only Marian were present to speak up too. Though she'd wanted to join them for supper, Will hadn't succumbed to her pleading and had insisted she remain in her chambers for the duration of her post-birthing confinement, which for noblewomen in the Middle Ages could last up to a month.

"If she belongs to Sir Nicholas," Will said, "then she will spare us this conflict with Lord Worth and the censure from the archbishop."

Ellen's ready retort stalled. Did she really have the power to spare Will and his household additional problems? Would a marriage with Nicholas prevent needless difficulties—difficulties brought about because of her arrival at Reider Castle in the first place?

Her dad shook his head. "Ellen belongs with Harrison. And she must go home to him."

Belongs with Harrison? What was her dad saying?

"She is stuck here without a way home." Will's tone was like granite. "She must learn to make a new life with a new man."

Nicholas pushed back on the bench. "I thank you for so generous an offer. I am honored you would consider me as a husband for Lady Ellen. But this is hasty."

"I shall give you land as Lady Ellen's dowry."

In the process of rising, Nicholas froze.

Ellen could only guess how tempting the offer was to a man like Nicholas, who wanted a place of his own in order to provide a home for his mother.

"The land will be adjacent to Chesterfield Park so that my wife may have her sister living close by, as I know such an arrangement would bring her great joy."

Nicholas sat back down and clenched his fingers into fists on his lap.

Harrison had indicated he was close to rescuing her from Lionel's lab. Perhaps he already had and she was back in her modern room at Chesterfield Park. It might be some time yet before they could deliver holy water to the vault to awaken her, but in the meantime, she couldn't marry Nicholas, no matter how much Will wanted it.

"She can't." Thankfully Dad spoke again, this time more firmly.

Will glowered, clearly accustomed to having his word obeyed without question. "If Lord Worth forms an alliance with the archbishop, we will need to abandon our plans to retake the well."

Will and Dad had been plotting how to take back the wellspring at St. Sepulchre tomorrow. With the destruction wrought by the earthquake, everyone would be distracted and busy. It would be the perfect time to sneak into the priory.

Dad expelled a sigh. "Your hasty marriage with Marian may have worked out for the best, Lord Durham. But Ellen is different. She belongs with Harrison."

How could her dad know that when she hadn't said anything to him about her relationship with Harrison? She met his gaze. His eyes radiated with sincerity. "Harrison loves you. I guessed it several years ago."

"You did?"

"He never said anything. But I could see it."

If Dad and Marian had both seen Harrison's love for her, how had she been so blind to it?

This time Nicholas rose to his feet and away from the bench. "If Lady Ellen is betrothed, then I shall not interfere."

Will pushed up from the table too. "She has little hope of being reunited with her betrothed and must make alternate arrangements."

"Even so, I would that Lady Ellen be in agreement to the plan. I am not my brother and will not force an unwanted union."

"I am not a brute and shall not force an unwanted union either. But she is my charge and must see the wisdom in such a marriage."

"I see the wisdom in it but cannot do it." Ellen shifted on the cushion beneath her, not accustomed to men talking as though she didn't exist.

Will's muscles radiated tension, and he looked first at her and then at her dad. "If Harrison loves Lady Ellen, why has he not already claimed her?"

"He tried, but I didn't allow it." The words were out before Ellen could stop them. Harrison had made an attempt that last morning in Saint Lucia to *claim* her—or at the very least to take their relationship to a new level. And she'd been the one to shut him down.

"A worthy man would not give up so easily," Will insisted, "not if he truly values you—"

The hall door slammed open. Thad, Will's steward, stumbled in, half-dragging a man with him. Blood slickened the man's dark hair and ran down his temple.

She stood, attempting to assess the injury. "What's happened?"

With what appeared to be great effort, the man lifted his head, revealing a handsome, smoothly shaven face and green eyes.

Her heart stopped.

Harrison? Were they having an overlap? Here? Now? Would he suddenly disappear from sight as he'd done the other two times?

"Harrison?" Her dad's surprised voice told her she wasn't imagining things. Harrison really was there.

She glanced around at the other tables. Closest to the head table sat the most important members of the household including the armed men, the chaplain, the chief of household servants, and the marshal of the stables. The lesser servants dined at the far table, including the gardener, baker, brewer, blacksmith, and others she couldn't name.

After Dad's prediction of the earthquake earlier, what would they say about her or Dad if Harrison vanished before their eyes?

Her heart resumed beating but at a frantic pace. She had to get Harrison out of the room. "He's injured. Take him to one of the bedchambers, immediately."

* ● *

"No need to fret, love." Harrison allowed Ellen to guide him on one side while the ruddy-faced servant held him up on the other. Dizziness plagued Harrison with every step, but he fought against it.

Ellen kept glancing over her shoulders down the stairs, anxiety creasing her forehead.

As they reached the landing, he extricated himself from the servant. "I've got a bump. That's all."

Ellen kept her arm around Harrison's waist and attempted to hurry him down the hallway. "I've got him from here, Thad. If you'll be so kind as to get me some warm water, soap, and clean towels, I'll tend to Harrison's injury."

Thad hesitated at the top of the steps, obviously uncertain about leaving Ellen alone with a strange man. In that one move, Harrison liked the man. Immensely.

"Don't worry," she called to the servant, tugging Harrison along unrelentingly. "I know Harrison well. And he won't harm me in any way."

Even with the assurance, the servant lingered.

"Hurry, now," Ellen whispered. "Hopefully Dad will distract everyone from coming after us, at least for a few minutes."

Ellen guided Harrison into the closest room and then shut the door behind them. Once they were alone, she expelled a breath and let her shoulders sag. "We've already given the servants reason to think we're witches. I can't have you vanishing into thin air. They'd likely take us right out and burn us at the stake."

Before he could formulate a reply, she pushed him down into a chair beside the door.

"What happened to your head?" She gingerly began to comb through his hair.

"I think I may have landed on a rock after I made the time crossing."

Her fingers came to a standstill.

He was agog with everything he'd seen since the moment he'd awakened half an hour ago and found himself lying in the long grass behind the greenhouse—which was a barn in 1382. In the waning evening light, he'd almost felt as if he were dreaming. As he'd made his way around the barn, the scent and sounds of the livestock told him it was all too real.

He'd wanted to stop and explore each of the buildings that belonged to industries a manor like Chesterfield Park needed to survive—a forge, brewery, barracks, mill, bakehouse, and a storehouse with a staff dormitory above. A grove of fruit trees filled part of the walled acreage as did raised beds with what appeared to be both herb and vegetable gardens. Even a bee colony stood along the far end of the property.

Except for chickens and geese, the yard was deserted. As he made his way toward the house, he knew he was lucky no one was around to question him. He guessed they were at supper. And the guards on the walls were too busy watching the outside of the manor to pay attention to a lone man inside. It gave him a little time to gawk, everything appearing the way Marian had described after her time crossings.

The front yard was overgrown with trees instead of the artfully arranged flower beds. The house was still three stories high with the tower on the east end, but everything was simpler and basic with areas that appeared to have recently sustained destruction.

He'd wanted to run his hands along the cold stone, touch the thick opaque windows, graze the grainy timber frames. But he forced himself to keep going toward the front entrance.

It wasn't until he'd reached the portico that he realized he was injured. And as the ruddy-faced servant opened the door, Harrison swayed on his feet and almost fell. He introduced himself as Lord Burlington, which got no reaction. When he mentioned his name was Harrison, the man's eyes widened, and he ushered him inside.

Now Harrison was sitting inside the historic home—Ellen's room in the past and his in the present. He recognized it from the previous times he'd crossed. Only now, he took stock of it more carefully. The double-sized bed was comprised of a rope-slung frame and fitted with a feather-stuffed mattress. The tapestries were thick and tasseled, the chair cushioned with the same rich damask, and the wood furniture a dark mahogany, the detailed carvings on each piece exquisite.

"What do you mean, time crossing?" Ellen stepped back from him and regarded him warily. "Are you here to stay this time?"

"Yes—and no."

"Harrison, please tell me you didn't get captured by Lionel and forced into the past."

"No. They don't have me. I'm safe."

"Then why are you here?" Her voice rang with distress.

"I came to find out where Lionel is holding you. Then I intend to awaken, tell my investigator, and rescue you."

"And how will you awaken?"

"I'll need to place holy water into the vault. If we don't get more, then we'll use the bottle that Will and Marian have saved. Drake and Sybil—my private investigator—are staying vigilant for my delivery."

"Then you'll go back just as soon as we get the holy water?"

"Right."

"What about Josie? Is she still alive?"

"Yes. We've placed extra security outside her hospital room."

"And the other Serenity House children?"

"They've all been contacted and alerted to the threat."

Ellen released a breath and stalked toward the open window, the shutters thrown back to allow in the fading evening light. For the first time, he noticed what she was wearing—a long blue gown with laces crisscrossing her rib cage and showing a linen shift beneath. Ribbons wound through her hair, which hung in silky waves down her back. In the light of the fading sun, she was as breathtaking as always.

Before he could summon the words to express himself, the door swung open and a brawny man with dark hair walked into the room. His features contained a fierceness that was matched by the intensity in his eyes.

Will. Harrison didn't need introductions to know this was Marian's husband.

Harrison stood and straightened, attempting to school his bearing into that of a lord. "I am Lord Burlington, and I'm truly sorry for barging into your home this way."

"This is Harrison." Ellen stepped away from the window.

Will didn't spare Ellen a glance. Instead, his attention remained riveted on Harrison. "You came for Lady Ellen?"

"Yes, I did."

"Then you have proven yourself worthy. You will wed her anon. This night."

"Wed Ellen? Tonight? I couldn't—"

"You are betrothed, are you not?"

"Of course we are." Ellen's voice cut through Harrison's confusion.

His gaze shot to Ellen. What was she talking about?

She nodded at him, and her gaze beseeched him, as though attempting to send him a message to pretend with her. Again.

"Yes." Even though he knew he shouldn't play along with another ruse, he couldn't deny her.

Ellen began to cross toward him, and his mind filled with remembrances of her innocent touches in Saint Lucia and how they had affected him. She might be able to play with fire and not get burned. But he couldn't. In fact, he was still nursing his burns from before and had to maintain some distance from her.

"We cannot get married tonight." His statement came out in a rush, one he hoped would prevent Ellen from coming too near.

As if hearing a warning in his tone, she halted in the center of the room.

"You must." Will's tone left no room for arguing. "The matter is settled."

Before he could figure out how to respond, several servants entered the chamber carrying the items Ellen had requested. Arthur followed on their heels. Amidst the reunion with his friend and Ellen's treatment of his head wound, Harrison was relieved when Will slipped from the room.

Harrison's gash didn't require any stitches, and as soon as Ellen finished tending it, they went to Marian's chamber for another happy reunion. He hugged Marian, held her baby, and listened to the tales of Ellen's arrival at Chesterfield Park in time to help with the delivery.

As Marian's attention shifted to the door, everyone grew quiet. Harrison gently passed the baby back to Marian and looked up to find Will striding toward him, a robed man scurrying on his heels.

"I have the chaplain." Will's expression radiated determination. "Time for the wedding."

248

"No. Ellen isn't ready for marriage." Harrison crossed his arms. It was one thing to pretend they were betrothed. It was another thing altogether to actually get married. He had to put a stop to Will's insistence before Ellen ran off.

Neither Arthur nor Marian spoke against it, were, in fact, overly occupied with the baby. Beside him, Ellen was too quiet.

"Come. Let us begin." Will motioned the priest forward.

Harrison lifted his chin, unwilling to back down. "It will only be time when Ellen says so."

Ellen slipped her hand into the crook of his arm. "It's time."

The protest building within him stalled. He shifted to study her face. What was going on? Was she finally ready to embrace the attraction that existed between them?

"I have to get married tonight to protect Will and Marian and their household from conflict and censure from the Church." Her soft response doused the last embers of hope he'd been unable to stamp out. She still had no desire to be with him. The marriage was another charade. A noble charade, apparently. Something she was only willing to consider because she had to.

Her eyes radiated with an apology, almost as if she knew his thoughts and his hurt. For an instant, he had the urge to tell her that this time he couldn't pretend with her, that she couldn't expect him to.

But he swallowed the urge and forced a smile. "We can do whatever you want, love." He had no reason to be hurt when she'd never made him any promises. Besides, he couldn't forget the resolution he'd made after returning from Saint Lucia—the one to keep his relationship with her purely platonic.

Ellen's brows furrowed, but before she could respond, Arthur stood from the bedside chair. "Lord Worth is coming tomorrow with the archbishop to claim Ellen as his bride."

Lord Worth? Harrison's mind spun with all he'd ever heard

about the Worths. The last he'd read in the *Daily Express*, George Worth had been arrested for black-market ties with radical terrorist groups, particularly in illegally purchasing Mesopotamian antiquities which helped to provide an enormous source of income for the terrorists. The Worth estate in Kent, Reider Castle, had been closed up with only a servant or two left behind.

How in the world had Ellen gotten mixed up with Lord Worth? Presumably one of the ancestors who had lived there in 1382?

"Lord Worth of Reider Castle is claiming you as his bride?" Harrison stared at Ellen, trying to make sense of what had happened. "Why? What makes him think he has a right to you?"

Everyone started to speak at the same time. But suddenly Harrison knew. "You ended up in Reider Castle because that's where Lionel is holding you."

Reider Castle, like Chesterfield Park, had been in existence in 1382. It was the perfect place for Dr. Lionel to hold Ellen.

Arthur's voice rose above the others. "Once Ellen is in Lord Worth's possession, we have reason to believe he'll harm her if Will doesn't give up the keys to the wellspring."

The pronouncement caused Harrison's blood to run cold.

For several minutes, Ellen explained in more detail the situation with Lord Worth. The more she divulged, the more he understood Will's urgency. It was clear that not only did Will desire to protect his family, but he wanted to keep Ellen from being forced into a union with a brute like Simon Worth.

"Will is right." Harrison nodded at the imposing lord. "If Ellen is married, then Lord Worth won't be able to have her."

The rigidness in Will's shoulders seemed to ease just a little. "He will have no choice but to relinquish his right to her when he learns that you, her betrothed, have come and married her."

"He wouldn't dare try to take another man's wife, would he?"

"Not without earning for himself great shame."

"Then it's time." Harrison echoed the words Ellen had spoken a few moments ago. He tucked her hand more securely into the crook of his arm and then pivoted so that they were facing the priest. "Let the wedding begin."

~*20*~

ELLEN PRESSED A HAND against her stomach to calm the war within. The tenderness in Harrison's voice as he spoke his vow stirred one side of the battle. The other was her own selfishness, telling her how awful she was for using him once again.

"To have and to hold from this day forward, for better, for worse, for richer, for poorer, in sickness and in health"—Harrison squeezed her hand—"to love and to cherish, 'til death do us part. According to God's holy ordinance, I plight thee my troth."

The priest peered at Harrison expectantly. "The ring?"

"At such short notice, I regret I do not have a ring."

"Ellen should use mine." From the bed beside them, Marian slipped off a band and held it out to Harrison.

He regarded it skeptically.

Ellen shook her head. "No. I can't—"

"You can give it back to me once Harrison is able to commission one just for you."

Will took the ring and forced it into Harrison's hand. "We must give Lord Worth no reason to question the authenticity of your vows."

That was all the prodding Harrison needed. He took the ring and placed it on the open prayer book the priest was holding.

As the priest blessed the ring, the delicate gold band with the intricate vines and flowers twined together mocked Ellen. Harrison wouldn't commission a ring for her. Not when their marriage wasn't real. Because it wasn't, was it?

After all, Harrison had assured her he was only staying as long as it took to get the holy water into the vault. Of course, now with their attempt to thwart Lord Worth, Harrison would have to remain at least until he could show himself publicly and prove he was here.

But after that, Ellen would do everything she could to convince Marian and Will to let Harrison have their last flask of holy water. She didn't want him to be in the past in the middle of the danger. She wanted him as far from it as possible.

Harrison reached for her third finger and began to slip on the ring, repeating after the priest. "With this ring I thee wed. With my body, I thee worship. And with all my worldly goods, I thee endow. In the name of the Father, and of the Son, and of the Holy Ghost. Amen."

As he finished, his gaze dropped to hers. For an instant, it was as if the curtains had been thrown back. Raw emotion—dare she say love?— emanated in the beautiful green depths of his eyes. Both Marian's and Dad's declarations about Harrison loving her rang in her mind. Were they right? Did he love her?

As if sensing her question, he shifted his attention to her hand and the ring. And in the next instant as he glanced up, it was as if he'd yanked the curtains closed. Only his usual friendly warmth remained.

Was that how she'd missed his love? Because he'd become adept at hiding it from her? Even as she examined his face again for any hint of his feelings, she knew she wasn't being fair to blame him.

If he'd gotten good at hiding his emotions, he'd done so because he'd known she would get scared—just like she had the last morning in Saint Lucia.

The priest linked their right hands together. "Those whom God hath joined together, let no man put asunder."

Let no man put asunder. The words reverberated through Ellen along with the reality of what she was doing. She'd just made sacred vows to Harrison. And if by some miracle they both returned to the present, she couldn't disregard them, could she?

She and Harrison needed to have a talk later. This was all thrust upon them so hastily that they hadn't had time to discuss the ramifications of their decision.

". . . have witnessed the same before God and this company, and thereto have given and pledged their troth either to other, and have declared the same by giving and receiving of a ring, and by joining of hands. I pronounce that they be man and wife together."

They were man and wife. A strange thrill whispered through her, one mingled with fear. She'd never believed she'd get married. And here she was. A married woman.

The priest closed the holy book and smiled at them benevolently.

Would he make the declaration of kissing the bride? Or was that not yet a part of wedding ceremonies of 1382?

Will slapped Harrison on the back. "Come. Bring your bride. And we shall drink in celebration."

Harrison nodded. "First we must dispatch a messenger to Lord Worth, letting him know of the marriage."

Will offered one of his rare smiles. "I have seen it already done. Erelong, word will spread throughout the countryside of the nuptials."

As they returned to the great hall to celebrate, the minstrels struck up a tune, the servants poured the wine freely, and the conversation was festive. As Ellen sat next to Harrison, her thoughts turned again to Saint Lucia, their dancing all night and watching the sunrise on the beach. She'd loved every moment of their time together . . . because even though they'd been with everyone else, she'd felt like they were in their own world together.

But tonight, though they were sitting side by side, she felt far away from him. Harrison was distracted by how different everything in the Middle Ages was—the food, clothing, furniture, and customs. And then, when he wasn't exclaiming over something or another, he was speaking to Will or Dad.

As the conversation shifted to planning for the takeover of the wellspring at St. Sepulchre, she was sure Harrison had forgotten she still sat beside him.

Harrison bent over a parchment map her dad had sketched of old Canterbury—an attempt to replicate a large map he'd once displayed in his terraced home on St. Peter's Street. "I believe the tunnel is here. And it crosses here into St. Sepulchre." He dragged his finger to another location.

Will sipped wine from his goblet and followed the path. "You are certain a passageway leads into the priory?"

Dad gave a small shrug. "The Romans dug underground passageways during their occupation of the British Isles. While I believe this one leads into St. Sepulchre, I can't know for certain it does until we get down there. But I have memorized numerous routes and can hopefully guide us there one way or another."

Harrison traced the path her father planned to use. "The question is whether the tunnels will be damaged now as a result of the earthquake."

"We can clear it out as we go, can't we?" Dad asked.

"Let us pray so." Will focused on the map. "Where does the tunnel emerge within the grounds of St. Sepulchre Priory?"

Her dad reached for a handful of honey-glazed almonds from

the bowl at the center of the table. He popped them in his mouth, and while he chewed, he studied the small area on the map that appeared to be St. Sepulchre.

Will sat back in his chair. "I own freely to being in the grounds many times and have never seen any indication of a hatch."

"I would venture the hatch has been covered in order to conceal it." Dad dusted the sugar from his hands. "We'll need a plan for removing the impediments."

"I shall send a message to my sister, Christina, who is a nun at St. Sepulchre and shall ask her to locate the tunnel entrance and make certain the way is free of obstructions."

Dad nodded, shocks of his thick gray hair standing on end. Ellen wanted to reach over and smooth down the hair along with smoothing the worried lines from his forehead. He wore the same harried, busy look he always had whenever she'd visited him in recent years. Apparently, traveling to the past hadn't changed his perspective or his method of handling things. He was as distracted as always.

Was Marian disappointed she hadn't been able to speak more privately with Dad and work at rebuilding their relationship? Time was running out for being with him. He had only two days left to live—unless they could somehow find a way to make sure he survived whatever calamity was yet to come.

"Right, then." Dad patted the table and the map as if the matter was settled. "Tell your sister to be prepared tomorrow night. We'll enter the nunnery under cover of darkness. Once inside, we'll take Ickham's guards by surprise. If they're expecting an attack from the outside walls and gates, then they won't be looking for us to infiltrate the priory from within."

Dad believed the earthquake had opened up the wellspring— which was why he'd chosen to cross time in 1382 on May 21. He was surprised to learn that Will and two of his servants had dug at the site of the old wellspring and already reopened it. Apparently there hadn't been much water. Will had sealed and locked the well, otherwise there wouldn't be any water left.

"And the well?" Harrison pushed his empty goblet away. "Where exactly is it located within the grounds?"

Will pointed to a spot on the map. "Ickham has several guards posted around the well at all times. But he cannot open it, as I have the keys."

Harrison leaned over the map again, studying it carefully. "Does Ickham know of the tunnel?"

"'Tis likely no one knows." Will shot her dad a narrowed look, as though he was trying to understand how Dad knew so much not only about the earthquake but also about the tunnels underneath Canterbury.

Harrison smothered a yawn. His head wound had turned out to be superficial. She guessed his dizziness and weakness had more to do with waking up in 1382 than it had from banging his head.

Even so, the hour was late, and Harrison was likely exhausted just as she had been after her first day in the past. She tugged on his arm. "I prescribe rest for my patient. Time for bed."

He cast her a brief smile. "I didn't realize I was your patient."

"Of course you are." She smiled in return, but his attention immediately returned to the map.

Will pushed away from the table, eyeing her and Harrison. "There will be no slumber until your marriage is consummated."

At Will's bold words, Ellen bolted up from the bench. "Harrison is injured and tired—"

"You must consummate this night." Will spoke the words matter-of-factly, as if discussion of the marriage bed was in the same category as the attack on St. Sepulchre. "We cannot give Lord Worth any reason to question the validity of your union."

"You're quite right." Harrison didn't look up from the map.

Her dad just cleared his throat before shoveling in another handful of sweetmeats.

Heat climbed into Ellen's cheeks. She wanted to protest further but doing so would cast suspicion upon their hasty marriage. Instead, she stood awkwardly, uncertain what to say or do next.

Harrison picked up his empty goblet and twisted it as though examining its fine details. "You go ahead, love. I'll be up shortly."

She managed a nod before spinning and starting across the great hall. The train of her gown dragged through the rushes and her feet ached in her poor-fitting, slipper-like shoes. Even so, she tried to exit the room as gracefully as she could, especially with so many stares following her.

By the time she ascended the stairs, she felt as though she would melt from the heat of her embarrassment. Even within the confines of her chamber, as the maidservants helped her from her gown into a shift of lightweight linen, their knowing smiles made her want to duck under the covers and disappear.

She allowed one to brush her hair until it had the sheen of spun gold while the other scattered juniper and flowers across the floor and turned down the bedcovers. Finally, they led her to the bed and situated her against a mound of pillows, leaving one candle aglow on the bedside table.

After they left the room, her stomach twisted into knots. Surely Harrison didn't intend to go through with consummating their marriage, did he? The question had been plaguing her since leaving the great hall, and now it arose with a clamor.

And if he did? Would it be so bad? After all, the attraction between them was undeniable—or at least it had been in Saint Lucia. She didn't want to make their marriage official, did she?

For so long she'd closed herself off to men and relationships that she wasn't sure she could set herself free to embrace the possibility. There were still too many unknowns.

But what about Harrison's needs and desires? She wanted him to be happy and fulfilled. The question was—did he truly love her and want this marriage for real? Or was he only going along with her once again because he was so accommodating and sweet?

"The priest will validate that the deed is done." Will's voice came from the corridor outside the chamber.

"That won't be necessary." Harrison's reply was smooth. Will started to protest, but Harrison cut him off. "I'm sure you would agree that Marian wouldn't consent to such an arrangement."

Several beats of silence prevailed before Will spoke. "Your circumstances are different."

"Rest assured, I won't let Lord Worth take Ellen away from me." Harrison's voice was low—and possessive?

Her stomach fluttered.

"Very well," Will said after a moment. "The priest will pray over you once you are in the marriage bed with your wife, then he shall leave you to have your wife in private."

They exchanged no further words. She could picture Harrison dipping his head, easily fitting into this era with his practiced nobility. A second later, the door opened and Harrison entered, followed by the priest.

She caught a glimpse of Will standing in the hallway, torch in hand. Upon seeing her waiting in bed like a proper bride, he nodded and spun on his heels, satisfied she and Harrison would seal their marriage and leave no room for Lord Worth to claim her.

* ● *

All it took was one glimpse of Ellen in bed for Harrison's pulse to speed and his mouth to go dry. He turned around and faced the window, wishing the shutters weren't closed so that the air could cool his rapidly heating skin.

As the door clicked shut behind the priest, Harrison drew in a breath and tried to bring his thoughts into order. But all he could think about was Ellen, only a dozen paces away waiting for him in their marriage bed.

Marriage bed.

He shoved a hand into his hair and closed his eyes—as if that could somehow block out the image of her reclining against the pillows, her hair cascading all around her, the scooped neckline of her nightshift much too revealing.

For the love of all that was holy, he absolutely had to get ahold of himself. He gave himself a mental shake, straightened his shoulders, and shed his suit coat and shoes, then started on the buttons of his waistcoat.

He half expected Ellen to question why the priest was in the room with them, but she didn't make a sound. Was she as nervous as he was about how far this charade had gone?

It was sheer madness, but now that they were in this mess, they had to play along just a little longer.

He pulled off his waistcoat, let it fall to the floor with his coat, then proceeded with his shirt. He could feel Ellen watching his every move. And a flare of heat seared his insides as it had done often throughout the so-called celebration in the great hall. The duration of the evening had been pure torture, sitting next to her, realizing that his dreams had finally come true, that she was his wife, but that it was only a charade.

Now, here he was, continuing the game and needing to convince everyone he was going to bed with her.

He paused, swallowed hard, then forced himself to keep undressing. As his shirt hit the floor, he hesitated at his belt. Ellen had seen him on the beach in his trunks. Surely, his boxers were no different.

Dragging in a fortifying breath, he let his trousers slide down. As he kicked them aside, he turned to find her wide eyes upon him as he'd expected . . . Were they filled with admiration? Did she like how he looked?

He started toward the bed and didn't dare let himself gaze upon her. Not if he hoped to retain the self-control he would need to get through the night. He sat down on the bed frame, hoping that would suffice for the priest. But the older man kept his head bowed so that his tonsured silver hair ring and the encircled bald spot was all Harrison could see.

Behind him, Ellen shifted. Was she nervous about what to expect? Surely she knew he wouldn't pressure her, that he was too much of a gentleman to take advantage of the situation. What she didn't know was that he loved her too much to ever push her into anything. He'd hold himself back even if he killed himself in the process.

He took a deep breath and remained perched on the edge of the bed. "Are you ready to pray your blessing, Father?"

"As soon as you are ready, my lord." The priest glanced at the bed and the spot next to Ellen.

The priest wasn't going to let him get away with merely sitting there. He would have to climb in beside Ellen and face temptation head-on.

Carefully, he slid backward into the sagging mattress. The dip of the ropes underneath propelled him against Ellen until he found his bare shoulder pressed against hers. He casually slipped his arm around her and pretended to gather her nearer. With the other hand, he jerked the cover over his body, and in the process caught sight of Ellen's long legs where her nightshift had crept up.

After he was situated, the priest approached the bed, closed his eyes, and spoke a prayer that involved words like "womb," "fruit of loins," and "be fruitful and multiply." With every passing moment, he could feel Ellen grow stiffer, until at last he was afraid she might crack at the least pressure.

When the priest finished, he made the sign of the cross above them. Then with a final blessing, he retreated from the room and closed the door softly behind him.

For long seconds, Harrison sat unmoving next to Ellen, waiting for the priest to pop back inside, like a school headmaster, making sure his pupil was obeying when he was supposed to be. Ellen didn't move either.

Would the priest wait outside the door and listen to them?

Harrison leaned his head back, trying to breathe normally and bring sanity into this preposterous situation. Maybe a couple of noisy kisses would give the priest a tale to tell everyone.

But at Ellen's rigid posture, Harrison's heart stuttered a protest and reminded him of how sensitive she was. He'd learned his lesson the last time he'd kissed her, that pushing for more would scare her away, and he couldn't frighten her tonight of all nights.

"Look, love," he whispered, "when we returned from Saint Lucia, I promised you friendship. And that's what we'll have. We've just got to get through tonight."

"You're a good man, Harrison—"

"Maybe I once entertained the possibility of having more than friendship, but I've come to my senses." He wasn't interested in listening to her platitudes about him again, how he was a good man, her best friend, and how much she cared about him. He couldn't stomach it. Not anymore. "The truth is, when I was paralyzed, I became somewhat of a confirmed bachelor. I don't think I've ever really seen myself with a wife, and especially not with children, not when I'd be such an old dad . . . like my parents."

She blew out a breath. "Oh . . ."

"I know you only want friendship too. And I promise I'll fix this somehow." He motioned between them.

She remained tense. "So is this marriage binding? I mean, if we somehow make it back to the present, will we be married there too?"

JODY HEDLUND

"No. We won't have a marriage certificate or any record of it. So it's just for tonight."

"Really?" Did her voice contain a note of disappointment?

He wanted to adjust his position and look into her eyes and read her expression. But he didn't trust himself to move.

"I thought our vows were sacred. No matter where we are—whether past or present—we are man and wife. We're married."

He shook his head. "I think it's the intent behind the vows. And since neither of us meant the vows and are only pretending, like we have previously, we needn't worry."

The door handle jiggled, and he guessed the priest was planning to peek inside to make sure they were indeed doing their marital duty so that he could report truthfully to Will or the bishop.

Quickly, Harrison shifted and pressed more fully against Ellen. "We have to playact again for the priest, love." Resisting the urge to kiss her full on the mouth, he bent in and nuzzled his nose into her neck and her hair. As the door scraped open a crack, he let his hand skim along her arm.

He had to give the priest a convincing enough performance that he'd leave them alone. He let his lips connect with the soft spot beneath her ear with a breathy kiss. At the contact, she gasped, letting her arms slide around him and glide over his back.

Her touch lit a blaze within him as it always did, making him need her more than he wanted to admit, even to himself.

He dropped another kiss to her jaw, then another. Each time he made contact, she drew in a short, sharp breath, the sound beckoning him nearer to her lips.

When his mouth finally brushed hers, she arched into him and released a murmur of pleasure, meeting his kiss eagerly, her fingers digging into his hair.

He lost himself and was helpless to do anything but deepen the kiss. He forgot about time and space and everything and everyone except her. All he wanted was her. Forever.

At the click of the door closing, he paused and pulled back, trying to bring coherency to his passion-laden conscience. What was he doing? He couldn't lose control now. He'd only hurt her again. And that's the last thing he wanted to do.

Her gasping breaths bathed his lips. Lord in heaven above, he wanted to keep kissing her. But he sensed that if he gave his passion any more leeway, he wouldn't be able to stop, especially because her arms were tightly wound around him and her fingers curled against the bare flesh of his back, almost as though she was giving him permission to keep going.

He closed his eyes so he wouldn't be tempted to look at her mouth again. "Well done, you."

She released a pent-up breath. "What?"

"We're becoming first-rate actors, you and I."

"Actors?" She released him.

He wanted to gather her close and hold her just this one night, all night. But he couldn't. He wouldn't make it another five minutes beside her without wanting more than he should take. "This time we really should win an Oscar for our performance."

She rolled away.

"It's almost as good, if not better, than the performance we gave in Saint Lucia." Once the words were out, he could hear the bitter edge to his voice and wished he could take them back.

She faced the opposite wall and didn't turn to look at him.

He sat up and buried his face in his hands.

"I'm sorry I hurt you there, Harrison." Her statement was low and sincere. "I realize now that I was very selfish and didn't think about what was best for you."

Her apology made him feel worse. "You've nothing to fret about, love. You're an angel and always have been."

"That's not true. I was selfish then, and now I've selfishly dragged you into my life once more." Her voice wobbled.

He reached out to comfort her but then pulled his hand back, afraid of touching her again while together in the bed. Instead, he pushed himself up, walked to the closet, and stared into the darkness.

"We're best friends." He forced the words he knew she'd want to hear. "And friends do hard things for each other."

She was silent for several heartbeats before whispering again. "If we get out of 1382, I promise I'll never put myself into a situation where we have to pretend to be a couple again. It's not fair to you."

Her promise should have brought him comfort. She was finally recognizing how difficult the innocent pretending was on him. But somehow, he was only filled with a deep sadness that an unbridgeable gap still existed between them and was perhaps even wider than ever.

～ 21 ～

HER WEDDING NIGHT. It wasn't anything like Ellen had imagined it would be. Not that she'd ever imagined it. At least not often.

With a sigh, she tried to expel the desire pulsing through her veins. But she couldn't, not with the imprint of Harrison's lips still upon her skin.

His lecture about friendship had put her swiftly in her place, reminding her of what she wanted from their relationship. Only she wasn't so sure that's what she wanted anymore. But like everything else she'd done, asking him for more would have been selfish. Especially considering his revelation that he was content with being a bachelor and hadn't ever seen himself having a wife or children.

She'd wanted to tell him that she appreciated his maturity and argue that age didn't have to be a factor in a relationship. But where could such a conversation go?

From across the room, he released a tense breath. It reminded her of the way his labored breathing had caressed her skin and mouth just moments ago. It would be easy to invite him back, to tell him she wasn't pretending any more, that she wanted to kiss him because she cared.

Pinching her eyes closed, she dug her fingers into the flimsy mattress to keep herself from turning over and holding out her arms to him. She couldn't. He'd made it clear this wasn't a real marriage to him, that he hadn't meant the vows.

At the sound of voices in the hallway, Harrison quickly crossed back to the bed. She tensed, her nerves tightening with anticipation of him climbing in beside her again. If he so much as grazed her, she doubted she'd be able to hold back from rolling against him and kissing him again.

His breathing was soft but labored above her. But he didn't lower himself. Instead, when the voices went away, she could hear him situating himself into the chair next to the bed.

Her grip against the mattress tightened, and she lay awkwardly, her heart pounding a demanding rhythm, one she needed to ignore.

He remained quiet.

"You should have the bed," she whispered. "I'll sleep in the chair."

"No." His answer came quickly and was low and hoarse. "Let's stay where we're at and try to sleep."

She wanted to roll over and take him in, study his features, let herself ogle him in his half-clad state. But she couldn't. She had to think of what he wanted and needed instead of giving way to her own impulsive and selfish desires.

Long minutes passed, and as her breathing evened, she let her clutch on the mattress loosen. And as drowsiness began to settle, she told herself she'd done the right thing in keeping their relationship from progressing down a road neither of them were ready for.

Finally, she dozed, and by the time she awoke, Harrison was

gone. She called her maidservant and inquired after him, only to find that Will, Harrison, and a small group of witnesses to the wedding—including the priest—had ridden out at daybreak to Canterbury to meet with the archbishop and assure him of the legitimacy of Ellen's marriage to Harrison.

They returned at midday with news that though Lord Worth was contesting Lady Ellen's marriage, there wasn't much more he could do, especially since the archbishop had no choice but to accept the union. With the threat of conflict abated for the time being, the men closeted themselves in Will's antechamber and plotted the takeover of the wellspring at St. Sepulchre.

Ellen spent much of the day with Marian and baby Ellie. When both succumbed to sleep, she wandered from the room and found her dad leaving the planning meeting. She offered to catch a breath of fresh air with him at the top of the hall tower on the east side of the manor.

With the afternoon sunshine warming them, they stood side by side, peering through the crenels and taking in the rolling countryside covered in woodland intermingled with a patchwork of meadows. Sheep grazed on a distant hill with a winding brook in the valley. The profusion of May wildflowers turned portions of the bright green into a calico dotted with white and yellow.

The view took her breath away, so different from the urban development of modern times, especially the thick Weald. Will had explained that the forestland stretched for one hundred and twenty miles long and thirty miles wide through portions of Kent, Sussex, and Surrey with all manner of hardwoods. Surprisingly absent were most varieties of pine and fir, which apparently had yet to be introduced to England.

"It's beautiful, isn't it?" Dad's voice contained reverence.

"Sometimes it's difficult to believe this is Kent."

"It certainly has changed . . . like all things must."

She had the feeling he wasn't talking about the landscape. She slanted a look at him, but he was still staring out.

He was quiet for a few moments. "I admit. I'm happy you're with Harrison. Even if your marriage came about in the most unusual of circumstances, I can accept my fate—whatever that may be—knowing you and Marian both have fine men to spend your lives with."

Strange disappointment prodded Ellen, the same that had settled inside during her tense night with Harrison. "Our marriage is temporary. Harrison doesn't want to spend his life with me."

"Nonsense. Harrison wants nothing more than to be with you."

If only that were true . . . She sighed and turned from the view, leaning against the cool stone parapet. "I admit, I've had a fear of commitment for a very long time, never saw myself having a future—with my VHL and cancer and everything."

Dad winced, as if the very mention of VHL was still painful for him.

"But even if I could overcome my fear to form a permanent arrangement with Harrison, he made it clear last night that he doesn't want anything."

"Harrison said that?" Her dad's bushy brows rose.

"He thinks he's too old to get married and start a family."

"You're never too old to start anything."

Of course she agreed with her dad's optimistic outlook, but this was different. "He doesn't want to be like his parents."

"He doesn't have to be."

She sighed. If only it was that simple.

"He loves you, my dear. And though perhaps it's taken some time, I think you've grown to care about him too."

"Yes, I have." After last night's rejection, her longing for Harrison was even keener.

"Then grasp the love you're given while it lasts, for you never know when it will slip away from you."

She'd embraced living in the moment but hadn't made room for loving. Was it possible to do both? To love someone for as little or long as they both lived?

"In spite of the pain of losing your mother, I wouldn't give up a single second of what we had together." Dad studied her face, his expression gentling. "You're as beautiful as her, you know."

Ellen smoothed down a strand of hair that the wind was teasing. She'd never liked being compared to Mom. Yes, her mom had been beautiful, even in the last year of her life when cancer had ravaged her body and left her a shell of what she'd once been. But aside from the beauty, the real reason Ellen hadn't liked being linked with her mom was because she'd hoped emphasizing their differences would spare her from going through the same trauma. Maybe even in her heart of hearts, she resented her mom for giving her VHL.

"I'm sorry for not being there with you more in recent years." Her dad's tone was edged with regret. "I realized too late that you're not your mother and that I don't have to see her every time I see you."

Was that what had happened? Why he'd become so distant? "It's okay, Dad. I'm just glad we got one more chance to be together."

"Me too." He reached for her hand and squeezed it.

One more chance. Mrs. Fletcher's words from Saint Lucia echoed in the corners of her mind. *"When second chances come, you have to grab them up while you can."* She wasn't squandering this second chance with her dad. Maybe she needed to try harder not to squander the time with Harrison too.

"Don't fear telling Harrison how you really feel," Dad said, as though reading her thoughts.

"I'm afraid of being selfish again."

"You'll work it out. You'll see."

She wasn't so sure they would work it out, especially since Harrison hadn't spoken to her since last night.

Dad released her hand and then gazed around again at the battlement. "There aren't many places that lasted from 1382 until the present. But this tower is one of them. If all else fails, I would consider hiding holy water somewhere up here."

"First we need to recapture the wellspring."

"Methinks we shall have it before day's end."

"Methinks?" She grinned. "You're already sounding right at home in the Middle Ages."

He grinned in return. "Methinks I am."

She could only pray they would find a way to keep him alive.

* ● *

Harrison crept behind the other men in the low and narrow tunnel. The dankness of the soil and roots filled his nostrils. The grit of dust coated him so that he could taste it on his lips and tongue.

"Take heed!" The urgent call came from someone nearby as the ground rumbled and a shower of dirt cascaded over their heads.

Harrison ducked and covered his head with his arms as the debris rained down.

The tunnel was a death trap.

The walls were supported by rafters, many of which were rotted and crumbling and aged with time. Those that hadn't decayed had likely cracked in the recent earthquake. Every step they took, every bump of a head against a rafter, every clink of a sword against the wall could cause an avalanche that would either bury or trap them.

The clattering tapered to silence. Harrison rose tentatively to see Will, at the front of their group, start forward again carrying his torch. Arthur followed close behind, directing Will. A half dozen of Will's armed men trailed, and Harrison followed at the rear.

Harrison stepped over a pile of wreckage, then ducked underneath a loose beam. They'd already had to stop three times to dig away rubble that had blocked their path. The digging had set them back by hours. If they had any hope of infiltrating the priory before daylight, they couldn't encounter any more obstacles.

Even with the danger at every turn, a thrill of excitement pulsed through him. He'd recognized the tunnel almost from the moment they'd started through it at Canterbury Cathedral. It was the same one he'd used last year to journey into the crypt to retrieve the ampulla Marian had left there. Of course, the tunnel had been enlarged and strengthened with cement walls and ceilings during World War II. And of course, it was shorter, only extending to St. Thomas's Catholic Church since St. Sepulchre had been torn down ages ago.

As the squire ahead came to a standstill, Harrison almost bumped into him. With his body hunched, Harrison tried to see past the others to discover the holdup. But he had to wait, as he had before, for word to filter back.

"We've arrived at the priory, my lord," the man in front of him whispered.

After several more long moments, the line of men began to move again until Harrison reached a thickly corded rope. The squire was already shimmying up one hand over the other, using the knot holds for his feet. Once he neared the top, Harrison started up. He didn't want to admit to anyone he'd never climbed a rope before. If Arthur could manage—even with a little assistance from those ahead and behind—surely he could too.

The rope was secured tightly at the top, probably by Will's sister. Though Harrison was slower, he finally reached the hatch, and gloved hands reached out to drag him through.

Once standing, Harrison took stock of his surroundings illuminated by Will's torch.

"We're in a cellarium, Harrison." Arthur's whisper came from beside him. "Isn't this absolutely astounding?"

"Quite." Barrels that smelled of ale and salted fish stood along one stone wall. Crocks were neatly arranged on a shelf. Baskets of dried, withered apples and seeded onions emanated a sweet but pungent odor.

"Who would have guessed the two of us together like this." Arthur's eyes gleamed with the same thrill Harrison was experiencing.

"It's sheer madness, Arthur, old chap. That's what it is."

Through the crowded room, Harrison caught sight of Will speaking in hushed tones with a nun, no doubt his sister. She wore a white habit and black scapular along with a white wimple that covered most of her face and neck. Even with so little of her showing, Harrison could see the family resemblance between brother and sister. Sister Christina was a brave woman to risk so much to help her brother in his quest to regain control over the wellspring.

After a moment, Will turned to them, his expression grim. "We shall need to eliminate two guards at each entrance and two standing guard at the wellspring."

Harrison fingered the hilt of the sword his manservant had given him. He'd mostly adjusted to wearing the chain mail and carrying the heavy sword.

But *eliminate*? His stomach turned queasy at the prospect of eliminating anyone. Six to their seven—excluding Arthur, who was wearing chain mail but hadn't brought a weapon. Harrison wasn't sure if he should include himself either. He'd learned some fencing in uni and had met other men who took to wheelchair fencing. But it hadn't held his interest for long.

Nevertheless, he'd told himself during all the planning that he was doing this for Ellen. They had to take back the well and get access to the holy water. For her. So she could return safely to the present.

"Let's go." Will motioned for them to follow after Sister Christina. "Stealth shall be our greatest asset this night."

They ascended up a short flight of steps into a long passageway. Apparently the nuns had already returned to the dormitory after reciting Matins, and now the hallways were deserted, at least until they awoke for Lauds.

Even though the men crept silently through the cloister, there was no way to muffle their footsteps or the rattle of their weapons against their chain mail. For a place where silence was the rule, any noise was sure to be heard. And any of the nuns loyal to Ickham had probably already sent a message regarding their arrival.

When a rush of cool air slithered around him, Harrison realized a door had been opened. His mind conjured the images he'd committed to memory after studying the map Will had drawn of St. Sepulchre. They would leave from a side door that led into the large, enclosed yard of the priory.

"Godspeed," Will whispered as the men began to break into their prearranged groups. Will planned to take two squires and lead the charge to overcome the guards at the wellspring. He'd instructed Arthur to stay close behind him.

Harrison had agreed to go with Will's manservant, Thad, and restrain the guards at the back gate. Two others would do the same for the guards in front. Harrison was well aware of all the particulars for accomplishing their mission, but he followed the young man along the building with trepidation nonetheless. They skirted the cloister wall until they entered the forested area at the back of the priory, a section that had once likely contained cultivated fruit trees but was now growing wild.

Thad darted through the brush and twigs with minimal noise.

But Harrison was neither as young nor as lithe as the manservant and was soon breathing hard in his effort to keep up.

"Now!" Thad whispered, lunging forward. In the next instant, the clank of clashing swords filled the predawn air. Adrenaline rushed into Harrison along with the realization that he had to participate in this battle. If he didn't, he might jeopardize the mission.

As he tripped over a loose tree limb, he bent and swooped it up. He swung it hard, aiming for the second guard whose outline was visible in the faint moonlight. The man had already raised his sword to engage with Harrison and was clearly unprepared for Harrison's unorthodox fighting approach. The branch whacked the man's head and sent him tumbling backward against the convent wall. He hit it with a heavy thud before sliding down and crumpling into an unmoving heap.

Harrison froze, waiting for the man to move, to prove he was alive. But at the stillness, a sick weight cramped his gut. Had he killed the man? If only he could call for an ambulance. He started to jog toward the man, but a strangled gurgle nearby stopped him. He pivoted to the sight of Thad's knife deep in the other guard's throat.

For the love of all that was holy. What madness had he gotten himself into?

A ruckus arose close by. Thad didn't waste time. He bolted forward, this time charging through the trees without stealth. Harrison darted after him. His pulse pounded in his temples as he dodged logs and branches.

As they broke through a cleared area, Will stood in the middle of the dead and wounded, clutching a blood-coated sword, his expression as sharp and lethal as his blade. His men and Arthur remained a distance behind him.

Had he single-handedly brought down the guards around the well?

"The back gate is secured, my lord." Thad wiped the blood from his knife before sheathing it in his boot.

"And the front?" Will barked the question at another man trotting toward them from the opposite direction.

The soldier nodded. "We overtook the guards easily."

Will stomped on the hand of one of the injured soldiers who began to reach for a weapon. "Open the gates to the rest of our men then post guards at both entrances and sound the alarm when Ickham arrives." Two squires jogged away to do Will's bidding. The remainder worked at binding the prisoners and carting off the dead.

Harrison aided as best he could and forced himself to face the brutality of the situation, imprinting it into his memory as a reminder of what could happen back in the present time if the source of the holy water was uncovered. The fighting over it would lead to more wars and strife. And with modern weapons, Harrison could only imagine the violence that would erupt.

One thing was becoming clear: although the water could bring healing, it also brought death.

An iron structure rose above the well almost like a mausoleum. The scratches and dents were signs Ickham had tried his best to open the wellspring. He'd stopped short of destroying Will's protective cover since doing so would cause it to cave in and pollute the water with dirt and debris.

Without the keys, Ickham had been helpless. And now without Ellen, Lord Worth had lost his ability to bargain with Will for access to the keys.

Harrison shuddered at the thought of how close Ellen had come to ending up in Lord Worth's clutches. And how close she'd been to marrying Nicholas. Not that Nicholas seemed like a terrible fellow. After Harrison's arrival, thankfully the man hadn't persisted in Will's original proposal. Instead, he'd ridden off, offering to spread the news of Ellen's marriage.

Will produced a ring of keys, knelt in the dirt, and began the process of unlocking a dozen keyholes with a dozen different keys. Harrison had to hand it to him. He'd done an astounding job of securing the holy water and keeping it out of the wrong hands.

After working for long minutes, Will stood and grasped one corner of the covering. "Heave now."

It took several men to lift away the iron covering. As soon as they dropped it to the ground, Harrison, like Arthur, peered over the edge of the well to the water below. The scent of moist earth filled his nostrils. And the chill of dawn brushed at his perspiring face.

This was real. He wasn't dreaming. He was here in a place he'd never thought he'd be. Gazing at miraculous water that was related to the Tree of Life in the garden of Eden. From the look of wonder on Arthur's face, he knew his friend was reveling in the moment too.

The thick iron wall Will had built to surround the well only came to Harrison's waist, and the inside wasn't more than the length of a tall man, with a wooden bucket tied to a piece of hemp dangling inside. In the dark chasm, Harrison guessed less than a hand's depth of water remained. Though it wasn't deep and endless, the amount was still impressive, since only a tablespoon was required for healing or crossing time to occur.

With the rising of the sun, Sister Christina and several other nuns provided a simple breakfast. A short while later, the head abbess approached them, and though she spoke calmly and softly, anger flashed from her eyes while she questioned the intrusion. As Will pulled out a pouch of coins, she stopped arguing, accepted the money, and left them in peace.

When they finished resting and eating, Will allowed one of his men to lower the bucket into the well. After drawing the water, Will filled a leather drinking flask, then promptly ordered the well's closure.

When one of the locks jammed and refused to close, Will sent for a locksmith.

As they waited, Harrison remained near the well, even as Arthur wandered off with Sister Christina, who indicated she had located two more of the original St. Thomas ampullae in the convent apothecary.

Tired from the long, sleepless night, Harrison leaned against the ancient ash tree that seemed to be standing guard over the well. In their quest for the holy water, had they unearthed something God hadn't wanted them to disturb? While healing and health were incredible gifts, was healing always the best course, or did the suffering and hardship that came with disease serve a purpose too?

Harrison couldn't deny he was grateful for the miracle of using his legs again. Yet, he could look back at his life and see the many blessings that had come through his paralysis. Without it, he might have taken an entirely different course with his life, might never have met Ellen.

His mind returned to the image of her waiting in bed for his arrival last night, and a low flame fanned to life in his gut. Even though they'd spoken wedding vows, he had no right to her, not when their marriage wasn't real. Though she'd seemed slightly confused, maybe even hurt, she would thank him later for having the soundness of mind to keep them from getting carried away. Maybe some day they'd even laugh about their experience.

But at the moment, all he wanted to do was get the holy water into the vault and rescue her from Dr. Lionel. He was relieved Will had agreed to take enough to aid both him and Ellen, though it was clear he didn't quite understand why they needed the water. While he may have accepted their tales of future times and places, the reality of it was simply too difficult to grasp.

Harrison didn't realize he'd dozed until a shout awoke him. "Ickham's drawing nigh!"

The soldiers Will had assigned to guard the well straightened and drew their weapons. They would stay behind to protect the well, along with the locksmith, who seemed to be finishing his repairs. But Will was already jogging through the woods toward the priory yard.

Guessing he'd slept over an hour, if not longer, Harrison scrambled to his feet. He hastened after the others, his pulse drumming a rhythm of dread. They'd expected retaliation along with more fighting. But after the first skirmish, Harrison wasn't sure he could stomach more killing.

As Will's men congregated at the front gate, they made themselves ready for battle. Arthur was nowhere in sight, no doubt still inside with Sister Christina. As for himself, though Harrison didn't want to have another confrontation, he could do nothing less than fight alongside Will since this was his battle too. He drew up his mail hood and unsheathed his sword, wishing for another stiff tree limb instead.

Will was the first to leave the priory, his expression calm, his mouth set with determination. Even as Harrison's admiration of Will grew, he couldn't keep from feeling sorry for him—that his way of life in the Middle Ages was so full of fighting and bloodshed. Marian had only spoken briefly of Will's tortured soul, but it had been enough to realize that Will was a peace-loving man and didn't relish taking lives.

The gate swung wider, and Harrison moved with Will's men outside onto the street. When they'd sneaked into town last night, darkness had obscured all but the outline of the homes and businesses. But now by daylight, Canterbury was in full view.

The first thing Harrison noticed was the pointed roof, flying buttresses, and lofty spires of Canterbury Cathedral towering over everything else. The cathedral was a work of art unto itself in the present day, but even more so in 1382, especially in contrast to the other buildings around it.

The traders' shops lining both sides of the narrow street were crammed closely together, the projecting signs with pictures revealing the trade inside. The painted bread loaf indicated the baker, the bushel on a pole signaled the alehouse, the iron scissors depicted the tailor.

The collapsed beams of several structures attested to the destruction of the earthquake. But the damage hadn't stopped the businesses from opening their countertops and selling their wares. A fish market stood closest to the priory with racks of herring and mackerel drying in the sun. Only a short distance away was a butcher shop with carcasses and joints hanging from hooks in the shade while other slabs of red meat sat on the counter in the sun, swarms of flies hovering everywhere.

The scent of dung and sewage lingered in the morning air. And the clang of a blacksmith's hammer was the only sound in the eerily silent street. Ponies and packhorses were halted. A rural laborer steering a cart laden with eggs, milk, and cheese had frozen still. A boy shoveling up droppings from the street didn't budge.

Most traders had moved away from their displays and now stood within the confines of their doorways, wariness on their faces as they stared between Will and another imposing man waiting a short distance down the street, several armed men on either side of him. He wore a black surcoat and long matching cap, contrasting his pale, almost translucent, skin.

"Lord Durham," the newcomer said, "I have to say, you took us quite by surprise. I must compliment you on your successful infiltration even if it is short-lived."

Will spread his feet, his arms stiff, his grip tight around his sword. "I intend to protect the holy water from abuse by those who wish to profit from it."

This had to be Ickham. The bailiff's smile was brittle. "The king has appointed me the guardian of his lands in Kent. St. Sepulchre falls under my jurisdiction."

"The well belongs to my jurisdiction since I am the one who made the discovery."

Ickham motioned at one of his soldiers, who pushed a man out from behind them. A big-boned fellow with thick gray hair standing on end stumbled and fell to his knees. His mouth was gagged with a rag, his hands bound behind him.

Harrison's heart slammed into his ribs. Arthur.

22

How had Ickham captured Arthur?

With a racing pulse, Harrison strode forward, only one thought pounding through him. He had to get Arthur back. If he didn't, Ellen and Marian would be devastated.

Will stepped into his path and nodded at his men, somehow communicating to them so that they lunged forward, grabbing Harrison and restraining him.

His panic mounted, and he struggled in vain to free himself. "Let Arthur go!"

Ickham gave Harrison a once-over, his lip curling up disdainfully. "My men located this man sneaking around the crypt of the cathedral."

In the crypt? Across the distance, Harrison met Arthur's gaze. Had Arthur backtracked through the tunnel without them? Why?

"Unhand my wife's father at once." Will's tone was low and dangerous.

The guards surrounding Ickham unsheathed their swords as though preparing for a battle. But Ickham didn't move, not even to blink.

Will repositioned his sword. "You have no reason to keep him, as he has nothing to do with our rivalry over the well."

The bailiff tossed a glance toward a nearby business. A burly man cloaked in chain mail exited with several armed knights close on his heels. Of course it was Lord Worth with his swarthy skin, black brows, and forked black beard.

As he stepped onto the street, he glared first at Will, then Harrison, his dark eyes filled with malice.

Harrison hadn't spoken with Lord Worth yesterday during the meeting with the archbishop. Will had requested that Harrison stay back with his squires while he attended to matters. Nevertheless, Lord Worth's anger had been as visible then as it was today.

"I have heard rumors regarding this man." Ickham inclined his head toward Arthur. "Rumors he is in league with the devil."

"That's not true." Harrison jerked again to loosen the grip of Will's men, needing to aid Arthur somehow.

Ickham's brow rose, and he took in Harrison's beardless face. Harrison had already been mistaken on several occasions as a clergyman and had quickly learned that most noblemen had beards. "Lord Burlington, I presume?"

Will positioned himself more directly in front of Harrison. "Leave him out of this."

"I have it on word from Lord Worth that Lady Ellen is also a witch."

Harrison's blood turned suddenly cold. "Neither my wife nor her father are witches."

"Lord Worth has gathered evidence to the contrary."

Will didn't responded with the denial Harrison would have preferred.

Marian's husband had proven he would fight for many things. But would he fight for a father-in-law condemned to be a witch? Doing so would put a target on him and his entire family.

The desperation inside Harrison spiked. "Look, Arthur Creighton is the kindest, gentlest soul you'll ever meet."

"Then how was he able to predict the earthquake?" Ickham asked. "And how did he locate a secret tunnel?"

"He is a learned man."

"There are those who say his arrival and that of your wife into our country coincides with the outbreak of the plague."

"That's ludicrous." Harrison tried to keep the panic from his voice. "From what I understand, the disease broke out in London over a week ago. Arthur and Ellen arrived after that. Neither are connected to the plague in any way."

"Everyone knows the previous outbreak of the plague was caused by witches in league with the devil." The bailiff's eyes contained a calculated glint. "If we burn the witches as soon as we catch them, perhaps we shall prevent the plague from spreading. Lord Worth has graciously offered to hold the witch in his dungeon and oversee the deed on the morrow at midday."

Graciously? Harrison's gaze pinged back and forth between Ickham and Lord Worth. Could they proceed without a trial? Surely they had to follow legal protocols even in the Middle Ages.

"We do not need to resort to such measures." Will drew himself up. "You will hand my father-in-law over to me, and I shall contain him until the plague has passed."

Ickham took several steps, his black coat swirling like a phantom about his legs. If anyone was in league with the devil, it was this man. "'Tis possible you may yet take custody of your father-in-law and attempt to subdue his sinful nature." He glanced at Lord Worth.

The burly man braced his feet apart. "If that is your wish, you must abandon your efforts to oversee the wellspring and devote your attention to your wayward family."

So that was it. This had nothing to do with Arthur being a

witch. The accusation was merely their twisted method of gaining back the wellspring. Since Lord Worth couldn't use Ellen as a bargaining tool, he'd decided to use Arthur's life instead. And now they planned to kill Arthur if Will didn't hand over the well and keys.

As if recognizing the same, Will started forward, raising his sword. Harrison had no doubt Will would battle Ickham and Lord Worth single-handedly if need be.

Lord Worth grabbed Arthur and pressed a knife to his throat. Arthur released a muted cry through the gag, and an instant later, blood trickled from beneath the blade. "Perhaps I shall eliminate him here at this very moment."

Will halted.

Arthur's eyes were wide as though he expected this was his end. Was this, then, how Arthur died? In a battle for the holy water over a well that had been dug up because of his research and quest to find the ultimate cure?

Harrison's heart protested the thought. But even as he tried to make sense of everything and come up with a plan, Will shook his head. "And what is it exactly that you want in exchange for vowing in the presence of these witnesses that you will drop these charges against my wife's family and nevermore pursue them?"

Ickham nodded to the leather drinking flask at Will's side. "You will hand over all the water and take none for yourself."

"No!" Harrison couldn't contain the word. "We must have at least the drinking flask."

"We want it all." Lord Worth's tone brokered no room for negotiation.

Will glanced at Harrison, his dark eyes deferring to him.

"I need it to save Ellen," Harrison whispered through a constricted throat.

Will nodded curtly, then looked at Arthur. The older man

couldn't move or speak. But his eyes said everything—that he was willing to sacrifice his life in order to save his daughter.

Will retreated a step. "We shall deliberate the matter and give you our decision on the morrow."

"Very well, Lord Durham." Lord Worth's attention remained riveted to the drinking pouch. "But do not think you can fool us by keeping back some of the water for yourself. You will hand it all over to Ickham's control where it rightfully belongs. If we learn that you have kept any, you will force us to make widely known your connection with witches. Perhaps your wife is a witch too?"

Will visibly stiffened but didn't speak.

Harrison's chest tightened with uneasiness. Will loved Marian more than anything and would never put her in danger. He'd never risk using the water. Not for him, Ellen, or Arthur. Were they all now doomed to die in the past?

* ◉ *

Peering out the window, Ellen caught sight of the riders approaching Chesterfield's gate. "They're back."

She raced from Marian's room, through the corridor, and down the steps, her heart thudding with fear. For all the men and her dad. But it beat hardest for Harrison.

She prayed, as she had throughout the long night, that Harrison had remained safe and that he hadn't taken part in any fighting. Last night when she'd seen him in the chain mail and wearing a sword, she'd practically begged him not to go. Harrison was too tenderhearted to fight, much less kill.

But he'd insisted on being a part of the mission, apparently feeling some manly need to prove himself. Or perhaps he'd wanted to participate in order to make sure he could claim some of the holy water for his plans to return to the present and rescue her.

As she pushed through the front door and stepped outside onto the gravel path, the afternoon sunshine had disappeared behind cold, dark clouds. A chill in the air hinted at the coming of rain.

She was surprised to find Marian beside her, draped in a robe and waiting breathlessly, having left the baby behind with the servants. Her red hair was unbound, her cheeks flushed, and her eyes sparkling.

Ellen reached for Marian's hand. "I don't know how you bear doing this." In the ongoing war with the French, Will had to be away often on missions for the king, although he wasn't gone nearly as much or as long as he used to be.

"'Tis never easy." Marian squeezed her fingers. "I loathe his leaving, but the reunions are beautiful."

Ellen imagined Marian's reunions with Will entailed lots of kissing and guessed that wouldn't be the case with her and Harrison. Nevertheless, she focused anxiously on the riders making their way through the gate. Thad led the way, followed by Will and Harrison side by side. Though they were both dusty and weary, Ellen couldn't see signs of any injuries.

Had they survived intact?

"Oh please, God," she whispered.

Marian smiled gently. "He'll be fine. Will wouldn't let any harm come to him."

She'd been hoping that was the case, or at the very least hoping they hadn't faced much resistance in taking over the well. With only a few men accompanying them in their return, she guessed Will had left the remainder behind to stand guard. And from the look of things, they'd left Dad behind as well. More likely Dad had insisted on staying to study the water to his heart's content.

As they drew nearer, their haggard and somber faces sent a tremor of more fear through her. Something warned Ellen they bore news she wouldn't like. Had their mission failed after all?

Not only did she and Harrison need the water to survive, but what about Josie? Even though Harrison had assured her the little girl was alive, she was in dire need of a miracle. Maybe Ellen's idea to use the holy water for all the Serenity House children had been idealistic and not entirely plausible. But she still wanted to find a way to at least help Josie.

Marian's fingers tightened within hers as if she felt the tension too.

The men dismounted, and a stable boy ran up to assist them.

"Did you not retake the well?" Marian asked as Will approached.

He untied a leather flask from his belt and handed it to her.

"Holy water?" Marian released Ellen's hand and took the flask reverently.

He nodded and started to speak, but Harrison beat him to it. "They have Arthur as their prisoner. I'm sorry, Ellen. Marian."

"What happened?" Ellen asked.

Again, Harrison answered before Will could. "Ickham and Lord Worth are accusing Arthur of being a witch. They've demanded control of the wellspring for Arthur's life."

Marian's face turned pale. "You didn't give in, did you?"

Harrison shook his head, his eyes brimming with sadness. "They demanded all the water, including the drinking flask."

Ellen's stomach had bottomed out, and she felt as though she was scrambling to find a solution, anything. "We'll take out what we need, return it, and they'll be none the wiser."

"I wish it was that simple, love. But Ickham has threatened to accuse Marian of being a witch too if he learns of Will taking any more holy water."

"We can do it secretly," Ellen insisted.

"Nothing that happens here remains secret," Will said.

"And what is he intending to do with my father?" Marian's voice shook, and Will reached for her as though to pick her up. She held up a hand and leveled a look at Harrison.

Harrison visibly swallowed. "Lord Worth is planning to burn him at the stake tomorrow at midday."

"How can he do such a thing?" Ellen asked, her frustration mounting with each passing moment. "Surely he doesn't have the authority."

"Ickham will get approval from the archbishop," Will stated. "And there will be little we can do to stop them. Not with such serious accusations leveled against him."

"Then we must give them everything, all of the water." Marian's frantic gaze went from one face to the next.

"We shall not give up the wellspring, Marian." Will's voice was firm and yet gentle at the same time. "Harrison and I are in accord. Neither Lord Worth nor Ickham can be trusted, not with the holy water."

"Please, give it back to them." Marian pushed the holy water at Will but then swayed. This time Will hoisted her up against her protests. He handed Harrison the drinking flask before carrying Marian inside.

Harrison stared at the scuffed leather casing before lifting his gaze to Ellen's. "I'm sorry, love. I shouldn't have let Arthur out of my sight."

"It's not your fault, Harrison. If anything, I'm to blame for bringing Lord Worth into this. He wanted me, not Dad." She reached up and laid a hand on his arm. The moment she touched him, he stiffened and glanced at her hand.

She withdrew. She'd always been an affectionate person, even with Harrison. But now it was obvious it affected him and that she'd been insensitive about the touching.

Her dad had insisted Harrison loved her and that they could work through any issues standing between them. But what if it was too late for them to find love and a future together?

At least the awkwardness from their wedding night was gone and they were talking like friends again.

Harrison stared off beyond the wall surrounding Chesterfield Park. The clouds drifted low, almost seeming to bear down with their dark underbellies and touch the treetops. "Will and I talked on the way back. We're going to attempt to rescue Arthur in the morning."

"Is such a thing possible?"

"Will plans to send missives today to the knights in Kent who might be willing to come to his aid. Since he has garnered favor with the king, he believes together they may have some influence in demanding Arthur's release."

"And if the show of intimidation and the demands don't work?"

"Then Will intends to force the cooperation."

"How so?"

"He's a seasoned warrior from his time fighting in France and knows tactics that can flush people out of the castle." The grimness in Harrison's eyes told her that such tactics would be dangerous to everyone within the castle, quite possibly cause the loss of many lives.

Ellen's mind filled with images of Harrison riding off last evening, and her stomach quavered at the prospect of him doing so again into another dangerous situation. "What about your plan to drink the holy water and then tell Sybil my location?"

His hair was mussed and strands stuck to his forehead. The grit of dust coated his face. And dark stubble covered his chin and jaw. He was already beginning to look like he'd lived in the Middle Ages for years instead of mere days. "I'll do it tomorrow, after I get back."

But what if he didn't come back this time? The unspoken question hung between them. No doubt he'd concocted a plan with Will that if something happened to him, Will would place the holy water in the vault with a clue of some kind for Sybil regarding Reider Castle.

"It's just one more day. As much as I need to return, talk to Sybil, and initiate your rescue, I have to do this first."

She hesitated, wanting to convince him to change his mind.

"This is my fault, Ellen." His voice dropped with anguish. "I should have been paying better attention to where Arthur was and what he was doing."

"He shouldn't have wandered off." A drop of rain hit her in the face.

"I think he was attempting to hide doses of holy water. In the cathedral crypt, perhaps in other locations. During all our planning, he was of the mind to drain the well and disperse the water by placing it into diverse hiding spots that survived the test of time. He claimed that would keep people from fighting over it, that eventually they'd forget all about the well and the holy water discovered there. Hiding the water would also prevent it from being used so rapidly."

"So he decided to start hiding it himself?"

"Sister Christina gave him ampullae she found within the priory. He probably suspected he had little time left to hide them and wanted to do so before it was too late." Harrison rubbed a hand wearily across his eyes.

She wanted to argue with him and convince him not to join in the rescue efforts tomorrow, but now wasn't the time, not with the weary lines in his forehead testifying to his exhaustion. "You should get some sleep."

With more raindrops pelting them, he didn't resist as she led the way inside and up to her bedchamber. When he lowered himself into bed and immediately fell asleep, she gently covered him with a blanket and then stood back.

In spite of the uncharacteristic raggedness of his appearance, he was as handsome as always. And he was as kindhearted and noble as always.

An ache formed in her chest. While she understood his need to help rescue Dad, she couldn't let him go out again. The battle wasn't his to fight. And it wasn't Will's either.

She'd been the one to bring about the conflict with Lord Worth, and now she needed to be the one to solve the problem. Would Lord Worth consider trading her life for Dad's? Perhaps he would marry her after all. She could request an annulment.

Did she dare attempt the feat? Even if she failed, she'd rather try it than allow Harrison to risk his life. And she definitely didn't want all those within Reider Castle to suffer if Will and his allies resorted to dangerous warfare techniques.

The only problem was that Harrison would lock her away if he realized her intentions.

Her gaze landed on the leather pouch filled with holy water.

He wouldn't be able to stop her if he wasn't around to do so.

A light rain pattered outside the open window, and the room was dark and damp, sending a chill over her skin.

Before she could talk herself out of her idea, she swiped up the flask and slipped out of the room. She knew exactly where Marian kept a supply of small bottles made of thick glass. And she also knew from Marian where Will stored the key to the vault.

Harrison had once saved her. Now it was time for her to do the same for him.

～ 23 ～

HARRISON AWOKE WITH A START. He stared straight up, blinking and trying to remember everything that had happened since his crossover two days ago—he'd married Ellen, spent a torturous night with her, prevented Lord Worth from claiming her as his bride, helped take over the wellspring at St. Sepulchre, and then watched Arthur get captured and accused of being a witch.

During all that time, he'd rested very little, and after returning to Chesterfield Park with the holy water, he'd been drained.

How long had he slept?

"Lord Burlington?" A woman's voice came from beside the bed—a voice that didn't belong to Ellen.

He tried to focus on the bed canopy overhead. But all he saw was white.

"My lord?" This time a man spoke to him. "Are you awake?"

Harrison shifted toward the voice. He nearly recoiled at the sight. "Drake? What are you doing here?" Had his faithful servant taken holy water too? Or . . .

The canopy above the bed was gone, and the white belonged

to the ceiling. Glass replaced the shutters in the windows, and artificial lamplight cast shadows, instead of the glow of the candle.

His heart sank. He'd returned to the present.

"Lord Burlington." The female voice spoke again.

He pushed himself up to his elbows. At the same time, Sybil rose from the chair beside his bed. She'd tossed aside her black leather jacket to reveal a form-fitting white shirt, and she'd pulled her long hair into a ponytail.

"What time is it?" His throat was tight and hoarse.

"Oh three hundred hours." Sybil didn't have to look at her watch, which told Harrison she'd been keeping meticulous track of the time—likely since he'd been unconscious.

Drake held up a glass of water and pressed the straw inside Harrison's mouth. "You've been in a coma for over two days."

Harrison took a long sip. The last thing he remembered was riding home, giving Ellen and Marian the news about Arthur's capture, and then falling into bed. What time was that? Was it afternoon? If so, now that it was 3:00 a.m., he'd been asleep for twelve hours, if not more.

The bigger question was, how had he crossed back to the present? He hadn't put any holy water into the vault. Hadn't planned to until after he'd helped rescue Arthur.

He finished his drink and nodded his thanks to Drake. "How did you wake me up?"

Sybil slanted a glance to the bedside table and the small dusty green glass bottles. "We were checking the vault every hour and finally two bottles showed up."

He could sense her unasked question: How did they get there? She probably still didn't believe anyone could cross into the past and put them there. But after the bottles had appeared from seemingly out of nowhere, she wanted him to explain how it had happened.

Who had done it? Marian hadn't been keen on using the holy

water—had wanted to return it to Ickham to ensure her dad's safety. And Will was too up front to resort to deception, especially since they'd already made plans for Arthur's rescue.

That left only one person. Ellen. She must have taken the leather flask after he'd fallen asleep. But why? He'd explained his wish to wait and help Arthur. "Ellen put them there."

One of Sybil's eyebrows cocked just slightly. She was usually impeccable at hiding her reactions. But he guessed his explanation was too difficult to believe. No doubt she thought he was absolutely mad.

"So you spoke with Ellen?" Sybil's brusque, no-nonsense expression fell back into place.

"Lionel is holding her at Reider Castle. In the underground chambers, the old dungeon area. They've set up a laboratory there."

Sybil studied his face, her eyes radiating questions.

"Please believe me, Sybil. I'm not fabricating any of this."

"It's as good a lead as any I've had yet, though communicating with the dead is not something I advocate nor is it my expertise."

"I wasn't communicating with the dead . . ." Did she believe he'd had a séance, conjuring, or some other ritual where he'd spoken with Ellen—or even Marian or Arthur? "How could I? I've been in a coma."

She reached for her jacket slung over the back of the chair. "Let's not worry about how you know. Let's focus on pursuing the lead. I'll speak with the chief constable and sort out a plan to investigate Reider Castle."

Harrison struggled to sit up amidst the tubes that had helped him survive the past couple of days. "We have to keep this as private as possible. If Dr. Lionel knows he's been found out, he'll disappear and take Ellen with him."

She shrugged into her jacket. "I'll be discreet, Harrison. I'm determined to make sense of this case every bit as much as you are."

As she exited the room, Harrison reclined against his pillows, fatigue hitting him and making him dizzy. Although he wanted to rush over to Reider Castle and storm inside, he was too weak to get out of bed just yet. In an hour or two, though, hopefully, his body would be rested enough to join in the rescue attempt.

Why had Ellen sent him back to the present? He closed his eyes and attempted to remember their last conversation together. Her words, spoken in the heat of the moment, rushed back to him. *"I'm to blame for bringing Lord Worth into this. He wanted me, not Dad."*

What if she planned to offer herself to Lord Worth in place of Arthur?

He bolted up. Over the passing of the hours that he'd been asleep, she might have gone to Reider Castle and made the exchange. If so, there was no telling what Lord Worth could have done to her. What if he decided to burn her at the stake instead of Arthur? Or what if he demanded that she marry him? Once word of Harrison's coma and death spread, Simon Worth would have every right to take her.

The very thought of her being with the cruel lord made Harrison's stomach twist painfully.

"For the love of all that's holy." He swung his legs off the bed but then swayed. "Help me up, Drake."

Drake was at his side in an instant. "You're weak still, my lord, and should be abed for a while longer, eh?"

"I can't." But even as he pushed to his feet, he could only stare at his room and the door, his helplessness rendering him immobile. He wanted to rush to Ellen's aid as he usually did, propose solutions, and come up with a viable plan.

But there was nothing—absolutely nothing—he could do for the woman he loved.

* ● *

Ellen stood in the shadow of the stables holding the lead rope of the saddled horse. Dawn was several hours away, and she would have only scant moonlight to help her find her way to Reider Castle. If only she could call a minicab. And if only she had her phone with the map app.

She held back an exasperated sigh and pressed the pouch beneath her skirt, feeling the bulbous glass bottles with their long necks. In addition to the two doses she'd placed in the vault for Harrison, she hadn't taken much of the holy water, only two more tablespoons.

This day marked her dad's passing. That meant it was the day he was gravely injured in the past, an injury that had contributed to his present comatose body dying. The real question yet to be answered was whether or not he also succumbed to death in 1382. If she succeeded at rescuing him from burning at the stake, he would still be in danger from something else. But what?

Whatever might happen, he would need another dose to live, perhaps even two. She was going after him prepared to save him, somehow, someway.

The May morning was cool, and she drew the coarse cloak about her further, making sure the hood hid her hair. The stable boy had willingly given her the disguise for two half pennies. He'd also agreed to saddle and bridle a horse as well as unlock the back gate.

Ellen checked both ways, and seeing no one, she set off across the stable yard toward the rear servants' gate. Thankfully, the horse followed docilely.

Once she was outside the walls of Chesterfield Park, she found herself standing in a field of long grass and wildflowers shrouded in fog. A doe and her fawn glanced up from where they were grazing nearby at the wood's edge. The moonlight illuminated their big, frightened eyes and noses wet with dew.

As beautiful as the countryside was, she couldn't dawdle. She mounted the horse and glanced one last time at Chesterfield Park. "Good-bye, Marian."

At first, Ellen hadn't wanted to admit to Marian that she'd used some of the holy water for Harrison's return to the present. But word had spread quickly through the manor that Harrison had fallen ill. She'd reassured everyone that Harrison wasn't suffering from the plague, but the servants had stayed away nonetheless.

Ellen had instructed Marian not to revive Harrison, knowing he'd remain alive in the present time after his body in 1382 deteriorated and died. She hadn't left any holy water for herself so that no one would interfere with her plans to rescue Dad. And, as difficult as it had been, she hadn't left a bottle for Josie either for the same reason, to prevent Harrison from using it on her instead of the little girl.

She hoped she could still find a way to aid Josie, but she also knew that once she was in Lord Worth's possession, he'd never let her go. He'd hold her captive, using her as a pawn to do all he could to get the wellspring. She just prayed Will and Marian wouldn't give in to his demands so that her sacrifice would be worth it.

The truth was, she suspected she'd live out her final days with Lord Worth, however long that might be.

Blinking back tears, she started in the direction of Reider Castle, having a vague idea of the direction to go from her recent ride with Nicholas, using the woodland as her guide.

The expanse of the Weald never failed to amaze her. She'd heard the men talking about how the Weald had a life of its own. She took that to mean people also lived within the depths of the Weald and that she would be safest if she stayed along the perimeter.

Although the road was deserted in the early hour, she remained vigilant. She hadn't traveled long before she heard the pounding approach of riders. Quickly, she slid off her horse and drew it into the woodland, hoping to avoid detection, especially with the covering of her brown cloak.

As several men passed by, she suspected the party was going to Chesterfield Park, another group of knights joining up with Will. Already one neighbor and his armed men had arrived late last night. Several more had pledged to arrive in the morning. Will and his retinue of retainers along with the other knights planned to ride to Reider Castle in advance of midday and the scheduled execution. She needed to get to Lord Worth well before they did.

When the thudding of the riders faded, she straightened, but not before a hand snaked over her mouth and fingers clamped down on her arm.

Fear spurted through her chest. She jerked against the hold, trying to free herself, and bit down on the hand that cupped her mouth, but all she tasted was the bitterness of a thick leather glove.

Warm breath fanned against her cheek. "It is I, my lady. Nicholas."

The whispered words penetrated the alarms ringing inside. She ceased her struggle and sagged against him.

"'Tis much too dangerous for a beautiful woman such as yourself to wander the Weald alone."

She nodded.

"You seem to have a penchant for putting yourself into threatening situations, lady." His tone was edged with rebuke as he lifted his hand away. "One might begin to believe you have no regard for your life or your future."

Was Nicholas right? Did she give herself over easily to danger? Maybe the acceptance of her fate had made her more reckless.

"I want to live and have a future." Somehow the whispered words slipped out. And once they were out, she knew they were true, perhaps always had been. She'd simply been too afraid to say them aloud, afraid that if she allowed herself to hope, she'd only end up disappointed.

Nicholas released her and scanned the landscape. "Then you are fortunate I have many eyes and ears throughout the Weald and learned of your presence here before any peril could befall you."

A cool breeze gusted against her, making her cold outwardly. But now . . . the desire to live—truly live—burned hot in her chest. She couldn't stuff it away any longer.

Nicholas motioned to her horse. "I shall accompany you back to Chesterfield Park anon."

"No. I'm riding to Reider Castle to offer myself as a prisoner to Lord Worth in exchange for my father." Even as she straightened her shoulders and lifted her chin, a part of her hoped Nicholas would stop her.

He pinned her with a dark gaze. He wore his usual chain mail with his sword upon his belt. But this time, he also had a quiver and shouldered a bow. "You cannot expect me to believe Lord Durham approves of such an exchange."

"No, I don't expect that of you. I'm doing so without Will's knowledge." He'd been too busy making plans to pay her any heed.

"Then you leave me no choice but to return you to him." His gloved hand clasped her arm.

She yanked away, but his grip only tightened. "Your brother intends to burn my father at the stake at midday, and I am the only one who might be able to stop him."

"And if he is a witch, why should he not burn?"

"Because we all know he's not a witch and that your brother and Ickham are using my father to regain the wellspring at St. Sepulchre. They'll drop their charges against him if they have another means to the holy water." At least she hoped they would.

Nicholas paused and seemed to consider the truth of her words.

"I would make a mortal enemy of Lord Durham if I allowed you to go through with your intent. I beseech you to abandon the cause."

"I cannot." This time when she pulled away from him, he let her go. "I'll not abandon my father."

Nicholas pressed his lips together.

"We also both know your brother won't release my father unless Will sacrifices the wellspring. Rather than do so, Will and his company of knights will inflict great harm to Reider Castle and the inhabitants, including your mother."

Nicholas was silent for several heartbeats before replying, as if seeing the truth of her words. "If you give yourself over in an exchange for your father, what will stop Lord Durham from waging a rescue for you and inflicting just as much harm?"

A part of her wanted to allow herself to hope Will would come after her and set her free. But at the same time, by annulling her marriage to Harrison and offering herself to Lord Worth, she had the potential to save many lives. Perhaps she could even be the one to broker a peaceful compromise between those battling over the wellspring.

"I might not be able to stop Will, but I'll do the best I can and work toward peace." She swallowed the protest welling up within her, telling her not to sacrifice herself so readily this time. "Neither of us wants to lose any more people we love."

Nicholas stared straight ahead, his eyes tortured and filled with deep sorrow. Was he thinking about the lost love he'd mentioned once before?

After long moments with only the wind creaking in the treetops above, he expelled a sigh. "The safest course for everyone is for me to go inside and free your father."

"As in rescue him?"

Nicholas nodded.

"Is such a thing possible?"

"If anyone can get into Reider undetected, it is I."

Yes, Nicholas had mentioned his ability to come and go from the castle at will, something he'd perfected during his childhood. Was his plan worth a try?

Again, the hope inside tried to loosen from its prison. She'd always believed she was living out the Serenity Prayer by accepting that she'd been given a short life; but had she given up too easily and failed to change what she could?

She shook her head. Hope was a dangerous thing. And she wasn't sure she could allow herself the hope that things would work out for her life, not when so much was uncertain and not when she was still at such great risk.

"We'll go into Reider Castle together," she said firmly. Nicholas started to protest, but she cut him off. "You have no guarantee of being able to free my father. If something goes wrong, then I'll be there and hand myself over."

Without waiting for him to stop her, she hoisted herself into the saddle and nudged her horse forward. She only made it a dozen paces before he was upon his horse and riding next to her, situating his bow across his shoulder more securely.

"Very well, lady." His tone held resignation, and she guessed he was thinking about the safety of his mother. "If you come inside with me, you must heed my instructions exactly."

"I will."

Nicholas trotted out of the thicket ahead of her. The darkness still shrouded them, but she guessed Nicholas could find his way without any light to guide the way.

"Do you really think we can rescue him?" The question spilled out, her words edged with a longing to survive she didn't want to feel.

"We shall pray for courage." His voice was so low she almost didn't hear him above the crunching of horses' hooves in the windfall. "And then do the best we can."

Courage. Instead of always giving up or running away in fear, maybe it was time to pray that she could face the uncertainty of the future with courage.

~ 24 ~

ELLEN DANGLED FROM THE ROPE on the outer wall of Reider Castle. Her hands burned and her muscles ached from the climb. At the top, Nicholas stretched over the edge in an attempt to reach her, inching the rope up. Even so, she hadn't made the ascent as quickly as he had.

Had she made a mistake to insist on going inside with him? He would have been able to move more swiftly without her. Though dawn had yet to break, daylight would soon be upon them. With the coming of light, they would have a difficult time making their way out of the castle with Dad.

At the back of the fortress wall on the opposite side from the gatehouse, the murky moat beneath Ellen was silent and still. If she slipped and fell, she'd alert the guards on duty to their presence.

Thankfully so far, they'd had no issues. Nicholas had known exactly where to find the raft he'd built years before and hidden a distance away in the woods. He'd known exactly when to begin the two-minute row across the moat under the cover of darkness.

He'd known exactly where to hook the loop of rope that would bear their weight during the climb up the wall in the very spot he'd climbed dozens of times in his life. He'd known they'd have ten minutes to get off the wall before the guard walked past.

At the echo of boot steps coming their way, Nicholas motioned toward her to cease her efforts, then he disappeared to hide. As the boot slaps neared, Ellen held her breath and tried to flatten herself against the stone.

Nicholas had warned her that his brother would likely have more guards on duty in anticipation of Will attempting to attack and rescue her dad. All the more reason Nicholas had wanted to go in and liberate Dad by himself.

The footsteps hesitated only a few feet away. She sensed the guard was peering out over the moat and prayed he wouldn't look down. Though the moon was shrouded in a thin layer of clouds, a faint glow illuminated the castle grounds and moat, enough that the soldier would be able to see her if he looked in the right place.

As the steps continued away, she resumed her jerking motions, lifting one hand over another in her slow climb. An instant later, Nicholas leaned over again and this time made contact with her hand. Within seconds, he pulled her up the rest of the way, and once she was kneeling next to him on the ledge, she sucked in a shaky breath.

Without wasting a second, Nicholas crouched low and led the way to a stone tower. The door was unlocked as he'd predicted it would be. To prevent the door from creaking and alerting the guards, Nicholas lifted it upward, pressing the slab hard against the hinges. Once through, he did the same to close it.

They tiptoed down the spiraling stone staircase. At the bottom, he led her across the bailey, sprinting from shadow to shadow. Nicholas suspected Lord Worth had sealed the guardhouse entrance to the dungeons after Ellen's escape earlier in the week.

Instead, Nicholas had decided to use the lower-level kitchen door to enter the keep. With soft, cautious steps, they made their way inside, winding through the kitchen. As the dogs lifted their noses toward them, Nicholas commanded the creatures with a simple motion of his hands to remain where they were on the flagstone near the hearth. Without an alert from the dogs, the kitchen staff sleeping on their pallets remained undisturbed.

The passageways were lit only by the faint light emanating from a sconce here and there, so that darkness mostly concealed them. When they reached the heavy door that led to the bowels of the castle, Nicholas crept down the stairway ahead of her. The cold dampness of the walls sent chills down to her bones.

The glow coming from the bottom illuminated the veins of water on the walls and the slick spots on each step. Voices grew louder the farther down they went. At the bottom, Nicholas held up a hand, urging her to remain in the stairwell. He slipped out before she could question why, and the scuffle and grunts of fighting rose in the air.

She held her breath.

A moment later, silence descended.

She waited, her nerves tightening with every passing second. What had happened? Did she dare peek around the corner?

Nicholas stepped back into the stairwell and held up a ring of keys. His expression was grim, almost pained. As he limped away, she caught a glimpse of blood oozing from a gash in his thigh below his hauberk.

The two guards, who'd been engaged in a game of dice, were both now sprawled out on the floor in pools of their own blood. She tried not to look at them as she passed by and had to suck in several deep breaths to quell the rising nausea.

She couldn't bear the thought of any more bloodshed. She didn't want danger to come to Will and his knights. Nor did she wish danger upon anyone in Reider Castle. The best thing was to get Dad out of his cell and back to Chesterfield Park as rapidly as possible. In fact, he would likely need to go into hiding for a time so that no one could try to recapture him. If she survived today, maybe she would need to go with him.

At the archway, Nicholas inserted a key and opened a thick oak door, bringing a waft of dank, cold air. Grabbing a torch from the wall holder, he ducked through and started down another passageway, this one lined with dark cells. Following after him, she hugged her arms, the memory of her time in the dungeons all too vivid.

Nicholas stumbled, and she nearly bumped into him. Had his injury been worse than he'd let on? Should she look at it and see if he needed a tourniquet?

Before she could question him, he paused in front of one of the cell doors, inserted another key, and swung it open as soundlessly as he had hers when he'd come to set her free. Even though the circumstances were dire, and they still had to get out of the castle without being detected, gratefulness welled up nevertheless for this man and his help. She wouldn't have survived her time in the Middle Ages if not for his intervention.

He limped inside the cell and gingerly lowered himself to one knee beside her dad before shaking him. "Lady Ellen and I have come to take you away."

Her dad pushed himself up. "Ellen's here?"

At the distress in her dad's voice, Ellen stepped forward. "I'm fine, Dad. We made it in without anyone noticing us, and we'll make it out the same way." At least she prayed so.

Nicholas helped her dad up from his pallet. "We must make haste."

Her dad took a wobbly step forward, his body likely as cold and stiff as hers had been from her night in the dungeon. He was dusty and dirty but didn't show any other signs of injury. At least not yet.

Ellen tugged the pouch holding the bottles out from beneath her skirt and pressed it into her dad's hands. "Take these. If we get separated for any reason, I want you to have them."

He took the pouch, felt it, then hesitated. "You should keep them. What if something happens to you?"

She pushed the pouch more firmly into his hands and stepped back. "I brought them along for you." She met his gaze solemnly. She wouldn't speak of the tragedy he'd face today in front of Nicholas. But she hoped her dad could read in her eyes that he would need the holy water more than she would. She could only pray the same thing that had happened to Marian would also happen to her dad, that when his present-day body ceased to function, his body in 1382 could be revived so that he might continue to live in the past.

Nicholas grasped her dad's arm and began to guide him from the cell, both hunched under the low ceiling. She stepped out after them. "Nicholas, if my father is injured, promise you'll give him a bottle of holy water in the pouch?"

"As you wish, my lady."

"Thank you."

He didn't respond except to hurry her dad down the passageway.

She couldn't make her feet move to follow. Instead, she stood in the darkness with the premonition of danger heavy upon her. "If anything happens to me, promise you'll get my father out of the castle?"

"No, Ellen." Her dad paused and attempted to peer over his shoulder at her, but Nicholas continued to urge him along. "I won't leave this castle without you."

"We shall all be caught erelong if you do not cease from speaking." Nicholas moved with surprising speed despite his uneven gait as he passed through the arched door and stepped over one of the motionless guards.

"Perhaps I should take a quick look at your injury, Nicholas," she whispered. "At the very least I can tie a temporary bandage to keep you from losing too much blood."

"I have had worse injuries and am strong enough." He pressed forward without a glance backward. "I beseech you to make haste."

She'd never met men as strong and stubborn as Will and Nicholas. While their code of honor was impressive, she much preferred the subtle and yet powerful strength of Harrison's character. He won her over not with a show of authority but with tenderness.

Was it too much to hope she could ever be with him? That she could make it out of Reider Castle with Dad and Nicholas and that perhaps if she returned to Chesterfield Park she could put holy water in the vault there and make it back to Harrison?

They were over halfway done with their rescue mission. She had to push forward with courage, couldn't give up.

Her pulse pattering with renewed determination, she started forward, but at a strange beeping behind her, she paused and turned. She nearly buckled to her knees at the sight that met her—Dr. Lionel's underground lab, the whitewashed brick walls, the sterile equipment, the bright computer monitor, and a digital clock on the wall that read 4:55 a.m.

The fluorescent lights overhead suddenly blinded her. She blinked, and as she opened her eyes, only darkness remained.

What had just happened? Had she stumbled upon a time overlap? Perhaps her quantum particles were experiencing the overlap in both eras now that her bodies were both physically in the same vicinity.

She blinked again, trying to bring the present back into focus.

"Lady Ellen." Nicholas beckoned to her. "Come."

She peered through the passageway toward him. Dad had already disappeared up the steps, and Nicholas waited on the bottom one, motioning toward her to hurry.

The ground beneath her feet began to tremble. Was she somehow crossing back over?

The sense of danger pressed on her again. Had it been a week since she'd been kidnapped? She'd lost track of time. But it was possible after a week that her comatose body was dying. She strained to see the lab, but only the iron gates and dungeons filled her line of vision.

The swaying beneath her feet set her off balance. Something was happening. But what?

She braced herself against the wall.

The cavern rumbled. A second later, dirt showered down on her.

Before she could analyze the situation further, several beams across the ceiling split. The ground shook again, this time harder, and she swayed like a bridge with the spring thaw swelling against it, ready to sweep it away and submerge it.

At another loud crack, an avalanche of dust and rock fell into the tunnel ahead of her. She glimpsed Nicholas waiting for her on the step. His eyes widened, and he opened his mouth to call out to her. But the snapping overhead echoed with a violence that ricocheted around her. The thunder was followed by the roar of falling debris. Before she could duck or dive out of the way, something slammed into her head and the world went dark.

* ● *

Harrison perched on the back seat of the Bentley, his muscles stretched tight enough to snap. He stared at the deserted road leading to Reider Castle. Through the darkness of the early morning, moonlight revealed the tangle of spindly weeds growing alongside the driveway as well as poking through the cracks in the pavement.

The estate had fallen into disrepair since the previous owners had left. Now it was clear why that was so—to fool everyone into believing it was deserted.

"What time is it, Drake?" Harrison closed his eyes, still weak since awakening from his coma but unwilling to remain at Chesterfield Park while Sybil and a team of AFOs, authorised firearms officers, executed the rescue.

"Ten minutes past five, my lord." Drake sat beside Bojing in the front seat. "Perhaps another paracetamol is in order?"

Harrison crossed his arms to keep them from trembling. "The only thing that will make me feel better is knowing we have Ellen."

They'd parked slightly down the road from the castle but not close enough to see past the overgrown shrubbery to the river and beyond. Sybil hadn't wanted him to come at all, had indicated she could very well have two missing persons to look for instead of one if he wasn't careful.

But he was desperate to see Ellen. It felt like days, even weeks, had passed, although technically he'd spoken with her only hours ago when he'd returned from St. Sepulchre.

Harrison forced back the aches and tiredness that plagued him and checked his mobile again, hoping to see Sybil's number brightening the screen. But it was still as dark as the castle. "Can you see any movement, any signs they've gone in?"

"None, my lord."

Of course Drake wouldn't. Sybil had assured them that they were entering under cover of darkness and would phone once they had the lab and Ellen secured.

What was taking so long?

He wanted to drive up, race into Reider Castle, and confront Dr. Lionel for his illicit practices. But doing so would only cause more trouble.

As much as he needed to do something, he had to let Sybil handle Ellen's rescue in her way without any interference. If only the waiting wasn't killing him.

"If God gives you a second chance with her, you can't let it go this time, eh?" Drake's voice held a gentle rebuke.

If God gave him a second chance.

Had he ever really had a first chance? Not when she'd been so determined to keep him at arm's length. Or perhaps after her healing, he'd expected too much to change too soon. She might have been healed physically, but she'd still needed time to heal emotionally.

He could have been more patient. Maybe he could have even continued to pursue her. Instead, he'd let his own fears of the future make a coward of him. If he wanted her to face her fears, then shouldn't he be willing to do the same?

"Perhaps you're right, Drake. Perhaps I need to learn to fight a little harder for what I want." Was it possible he and Ellen could somehow still find a way to make a life together in spite of all the obstacles?

At the sudden buzzing of his mobile, his pulse picked up speed. The screen lit up with Sybil's name and number.

With a flick of his finger, he answered it. "Yes?"

"We found Ellen." Sybil's voice was grave amidst the chaos and noises in the background.

The air squeezed from his lungs. "And?"

"Her pulse just flatlined."

~25~

ELLEN COULDN'T DIE. Harrison's heart thudded louder than
his footsteps as he sprinted down a passageway into the underground level of Reider Castle.

Drake's pounding steps echoed behind him. "Out of the way!"
Drake shouted at an AFO coming out of an arched doorway.

Harrison didn't care that he nearly plowed the man over. All
he wanted was to get to Ellen as quickly as possible. The couple
of minutes since Sybil's call had taken an eternity even though
Bojing had raced the car to the castle entrance, and then he and
Drake had bolted as fast as they could through the castle to the
dungeon stairway.

Had Lionel killed Ellen? Perhaps injected something lethal into
her system the moment they'd known they were under attack? Or
had Ellen died in the past? If she'd attempted to rescue her dad,
it was likely she'd been captured and killed.

As he pushed into the laboratory, the fluorescent lights, monitors, security screens, and assortment of other equipment obscured
his view. But at the sight of Sybil and several officers surrounding

a body on a hospital-style bed and attempting to perform CPR, he darted forward.

Sybil glanced up and waved him forward. "They gave her epinephrine. But she's still asystole."

Harrison's long stride didn't waver. He elbowed aside those in his way until he stood over her. Ellen. Her face was deathly pale, almost pasty. The veins in her neck and arms seemed bluer. Her arms were bruised in multiple places—likely from all the needle pricks.

He shoved his hand into his suit coat pocket and retrieved the glass bottle—one of the two Ellen had placed in the vault. She'd intended for him to take it. And he needed the second dose if he hoped to live.

But at this moment, all that mattered was saving her.

He popped the plastic lid he'd already substituted for the disintegrating cork stopper and lifted the bottle to her lips.

One of the officers shot out a hand to stop him. "Hold on, now."

"Let him." Sybil's command was sharp. "The medicine will help her."

Harrison had a fleeting moment of wondering whether he should clear everyone out of the lab while he administered the holy water. After all, how would he explain what kind of medicine it was? Especially since Ellen was practically dead.

The fact was, he didn't know if the holy water could bring Ellen back. But he had to try.

Drake was already lifting Ellen. Harrison opened her lips and pressed the mouth of the bottle there. Injecting the holy water into a muscle or even into her IV port would probably be easier. But he couldn't waste the time preparing a syringe.

Carefully he dribbled a little in her mouth, then waited to make sure it didn't leak out.

Please, God. Please. He glanced at the EKG, which was still a flat line, and then studied her face, as beautiful as ever.

Two officers and Sybil remained at the bedside and watched him silently. But around them, the rest of the AFOs continued the search for Dr. Lionel, Jasper, and other personnel. From what Harrison could gather, the security cameras had picked up movement from the AFO, giving the Lionel staff time to make an escape, but only just enough, forcing them to leave Ellen behind.

He poured another scant amount of the liquid into Ellen's mouth, hoping her body would absorb it rapidly. After all, during the couple of times he'd ingested the tiny amount of holy water residue, he'd had almost immediate reactions.

He watched her again, waiting for some sign the ultimate cure was working, that he hadn't gotten to her too late.

She remained limp and lifeless.

Frustration welled up within him. This wasn't how it was supposed to end.

"Come on, love." He angled the last bit past her lips.

As the liquid settled in her mouth, the EKG monitor beeped. A wave on the screen jumped up and then receded. A moment later, the machine beeped again, and another wave crested.

"Her heart's beating!" one of the officers said.

"She's alive!" said another.

The exclamations rose around Harrison. Still, he tipped the bottle, draining every drop of holy water. This time she visibly swallowed. At the same moment, the heart monitor pulsed into a steady rhythm, drawing more comments.

Drake gently lowered Ellen back to the bed.

Harrison's gaze connected with Sybil's. Relief flooded her eyes.

"Many thanks." His throat tightened with emotion. If Sybil hadn't acted as quickly as she had, he probably wouldn't have made it down into the lab in time.

She nodded. "You good here?"

"Yes." That was an understatement. But now was neither the time nor place to make a show of his churning emotions.

Her attention shifted to her team. She spoke into her mobile and took off at a jog toward a side door that now stood open, revealing another passageway.

He studied Ellen's monitor, marveled at the steady beat of her heart, and then silently whispered a prayer of thanks. God had saved her again. Was this the second chance Drake had mentioned?

His heart hammered, the pressure hard and fast with the need to seize the second chance and not let it go.

"I'll get a transport, my lord." Drake was already punching at his mobile. "And phone your physician?"

"Yes, right away. Thanks."

Drake lifted his mobile to his ear and began speaking. As he did so, Harrison bent down and pressed a kiss against Ellen's forehead. Then he bent and whispered what he'd been wanting to say for a long time. "I love you."

* ● *

Ellen's head ached. She tried to lift her hand to massage her temple but couldn't get her limbs to work. What had happened?

In the hazy oblivion, her mind returned to the last seconds she remembered before losing consciousness. She'd been in the dungeons under Reider Castle, rescuing her dad with Nicholas. Then everything around her had started shaking and rattling and crumbling.

Almost as if another earthquake had struck . . .

Her thoughts stalled. What if it was the aftershock of the earthquake? Marian had mentioned that one took place.

What about Dad? And Nicholas? Had they been hurt?

She shoved hard, trying to work up the strength to get up, brush off the rubble, and go to them. But she couldn't open her eyes, much less stand up.

A voice nearby spoke softly. Steady beeping and whirring floated on the air. A heart monitor. After her years of working as a nurse, she'd recognize the sound anywhere.

Was she having another crossover to the present? How long would it last this time? She had to wake up and get to Dad and Nicholas.

She whispered a prayer. For so long, she'd thought God had left her when she'd gotten her VHL diagnosis. But what if she'd pushed God away the same way she had most other relationships, afraid of getting close, of being let down, of daring to have any hope? Maybe God was still there with her, just as Harrison had been, never leaving her, always wanting to help her, always loving her.

At a gentle stroke upon her cheek, she tried to open her eyes. But she was so tired. She just wanted to sink into oblivion and sleep.

"Ellen, love."

Was that Harrison? She had to be having another time overlap. But how was he in the dungeons under Reider Castle . . . unless he'd already orchestrated the rescue and had come down to be with her.

"I should have told you sooner." His voice tickled her ear. "But I was a coward."

Harrison was far from being a coward. He was one of the bravest men she knew.

"I love you." The words were an anguished whisper. "Please, never leave me."

She wanted to call out that she wouldn't leave him, but her voice wouldn't work. As much as she wanted to stay with Harrison, blackness enveloped her and threatened to pull her back to the past.

~ 26 ~

SOMEONE WAS HOLDING HER HAND.

Dad? Had he and Nicholas dug through the debris and found her?

She cracked open her eyes to find a bed canopy overhead. Somehow she'd been rescued from the rubble and was back at Chesterfield Park. But the lighting was too bright, the temperature too pleasant, and the scents too fresh to belong to 1382.

Her heart gave an extra beat. She'd returned to the present.

How had she gotten here? Had Harrison found another dose of holy water someplace?

The pressure against her hand was solid and warm.

She shifted her gaze to find Harrison sitting in the chair beside the bed, elbows resting on his knees, his head hanging, his dark hair mussed.

"Harrison?"

His head jerked up, giving her a view of his face. His cheeks and jaw were unshaven, just as they had been during their few days together in 1382. He'd tossed aside his suit coat, leaving his waistcoat unbuttoned along with the top couple of buttons of his

318

dress shirt. Though he looked harried and exhausted, he'd never been more handsome.

As his eyes locked with hers, the murky green depths only added to his appeal. "How are you feeling?" His voice was soft but contained an edge of sadness.

"Better." She pushed up and took in her surroundings again. She was in the guest room she'd occupied for the past months at Chesterfield Park. "How long have I been back?"

"It's early afternoon, so about eight hours."

"I didn't expect this."

"You almost died." He tightened his grip on her hand. "When Sybil got to you in Lionel's lab, your heart had just stopped."

"Do you think I died in 1382?"

"I venture so. What happened?"

She hesitated, knowing he wouldn't like her tale and how much danger she'd put herself in to rescue her dad. But she relayed the events anyway and ended with her last memory: "The dungeons collapsed on me."

Harrison's forehead was grooved with frustration and worry. "It must have been the aftershock from the earthquake earlier in the week."

"That's what I'm concluding."

"So you don't know if Arthur made it out alive?"

"No. I can't be certain." Her heart ached at the prospect that she may have failed her dad in his greatest hour of need.

Harrison was silent for several seconds as if recognizing and empathizing with her frustration. "Nicholas knew the place well. If anyone could get your dad out, he could."

"What if they were both killed?"

The torture in Harrison's eyes likely matched the torture in hers. "We can't go there, Ellen. We just can't. We did all we could for him, and now we have to let him go."

She'd wanted to believe that her mission into the past, the whole purpose of her going, had been to save not only Marian from dying during childbirth but also her dad from whatever calamity he faced. But apparently that hadn't been the reason. She hadn't even been able to help Josie or any of the children in the Serenity House.

She released a sigh and fell back into her pillows.

Harrison's shoulders slumped, and he hung his head again.

Something wasn't right. A sick feeling wedged in her gut. "Where did you find more holy water to bring me back?"

He didn't look up.

The unease spread. "Harrison?"

He started to release her hand, but she clung to him.

"What did you do?" She didn't need to ask. She already knew. "You gave me the second dose of the holy water meant for you."

His silence was all the answer she needed. She let go of him and sat up. "It was meant for you, Harrison." Her voice rang with anger. "For you! Not me!"

"I know. And I was planning to take it." He finally lifted his head. His eyes radiated with his own frustration. "But Ellen, you were dying. You couldn't expect me to stand back and do nothing to save the woman I love."

Woman I love. His declaration silenced her protest. The words she'd heard earlier came back to her. *"I love you. Please never leave me."*

"Yes, I love you." Each of his words was laced with grief. And now she knew why. They might have been reunited, but they had no future together any more now than they ever had. In fact, their expiration dates loomed nearer than ever.

"I've loved you for years." His admission was a whisper. "I'm just sorry I waited so long to say it. I talked myself out of telling you, came up with one excuse or another why I shouldn't. But I'm not going to do that anymore. Not even if I scare you away."

320

She swallowed the familiar rising panic, the panic that urged her to flee, to hide, and to protect herself. But after everything she'd gone through, she couldn't run. Not today. Not ever again. She had to remember to be courageous.

He cleared his throat. "You don't have to love me back." His tone was gentle, almost as if he sensed his admission had frightened her. "But I had to tell you . . . before it's too late."

Again she swallowed. She had to express how she felt about him. But could she? "Harrison . . . it doesn't have to be too late. We can find more holy water, can't we?"

He blew out a tight breath. "I've checked everywhere, and I can't find any."

"The vault?"

"Numerous times."

"The crypt?"

"Sybil's checked. Nothing's there."

If only Marian knew they needed more holy water, she'd put it into the vault for them. "We could try a time crossing to let Marian know."

"I've given it a go with the residue left in the bottles, and it didn't work."

"I'll try it."

He retrieved a bottle from a container on the bedside table.

As she took it and rubbed a finger inside, she forced herself to concentrate on Marian and the year 1382. But when she stuck her finger into her mouth, nothing happened. She attempted several more times with the other bottles and ampullae Harrison had placed into a special box. But none of the residue had any effect on her.

She handed him the last bottle to return to his collection. "Do you think the holy water stops working eventually?"

"I've been pondering the matter and trying to make sense of

it all. I can only conclude that at some point a body that has experienced the intense energy vibrations of the holy water begins to adapt to those vibrations. Like with any drug, use of the holy water results in a person's body building up a tolerance, requiring higher dosages to have the same effect."

"Then we won't cross time anymore, even a little?"

"It's probable. Particularly with the smaller ingestions. Or it's possible that once a body dies in either era, the overlaps no longer become possible."

Harrison's phone buzzed. He pulled it from his pocket, glanced at the screen, then answered the call. "Sybil. Did you catch Dr. Lionel?"

"Still only Jasper Boyle, and he's not talking."

"Then please tell me you've found another bottle somewhere in the lab."

"No. Sorry, Harrison."

Harrison's shoulders sagged, and he expelled a frustrated breath.

The investigator's voice was clear enough. And so was the message. They were doomed.

* ● *

Harrison paced the length of the bedroom. He was getting weaker. He could feel it with each passing hour. The life in his comatose body in 1382 was ebbing away. And once it was gone, his body in the present would die too.

But he couldn't go until he made sure Ellen would live.

He glanced to the bed, to her sleeping form. Though she'd lost weight from her ordeal over the past week down in Lionel's lab, thankfully the color was returning to her face.

But for how long?

The latest message from Mr. Smythe in Walsingham had been

the same as all the others: he hadn't located any other flower-patterned ampullae from the deeper wellspring. He'd scoured every original structure in Walsingham to no avail. Harrison had also checked with his other antiquarians without any luck.

Sybil was periodically looking in the cathedral. Drake continued to search inside the vault on a regular basis, but maybe they had to face the possibility that since Reider's dungeons caved in, then Chesterfield Park's vault might have filled with debris from the earthquake as well.

Harrison hoped eventually Marian and Will would consider that Ellen may have been injured, perhaps mortally so, in the aftershock, and deliver more holy water. But so far, it appeared they hadn't learned of her fate.

Harrison paced back to the bed and stopped beside Ellen as he'd done a dozen times over the past hours as she slept. Her long lashes fanned against her elegant cheekbones. Her hair was loose and tangled from her ordeal but was still a silky frame around her face. She was as exquisitely beautiful as always. And he loved her more now than he ever had.

He still couldn't believe he'd gathered the courage to tell her how he really felt. A part of him still questioned whether he'd done the right thing in making the declaration. Her eyes had filled with wariness, even fear. Maybe she would have bolted if she hadn't been so tired. Maybe she still would leave . . .

He rubbed at the growing ache in his temples and kneaded the back of his neck. Weariness nearly blinded him. Yet, he didn't want to rest and chance missing out on any phone calls—although he knew Drake would wake him with any important news.

His legs wavered, and he lowered himself to the edge of the bed. Would it hurt to lie down for a short while? Maybe the rest would even prolong his life a little longer.

At a curt rap against the door, he tried to stand but couldn't find the energy. When the door opened a crack to reveal Sybil's face, he motioned her into the room.

"Any more news?" he whispered, praying her team had found a lead on where Dr. Lionel had gone off to.

"Not much." She crossed the room, her hands in the pockets of her leather jacket. "We've learned he made his way out of the castle through a secret passageway to a car parked on the south of the property. But beyond that we have no trail."

Harrison sighed. If Dr. Lionel remained a fugitive, then it was only a matter of time before he would attempt something else, especially after witnessing the healing power in Ellen and deducing that's why Harrison had been healed too. With the mad race through Reider Castle to get to Ellen in time, he hadn't used caution, and now the word about his being able to walk—and run— was public. Although Sybil had cautioned all those who'd been present not to speak of what they'd seen, word had leaked to the media anyway.

Whatever the case, Dr. Lionel's threat wouldn't mean anything if they couldn't find more holy water to sustain his and Ellen's lives.

Sybil paused next to him, withdrew her hands, and held out a green glass bottle, just like the ones Ellen had placed in the vault for him, just like the empty two in the box on the bedside table.

Harrison stared at Sybil's discovery, a tremble starting deep inside and radiating into his limbs.

She held it out to him. "In conducting a search over every inch of the castle, I found it in an ancient cabinet located in the great hall."

Lord in heaven above. With shaking fingers, he took it cautiously and shook it. A scant amount of liquid swished within. Was it holy water? If so, it was worth more than gold, silver, or anything else in life.

Who had placed it in Reider Castle? How and why?

He shook his head. It didn't matter. At the moment, all that mattered was giving Ellen the second dose of holy water so that she could live. He had to do it now, before she woke up and protested. She wouldn't take it if she knew they only had one bottle, not when it would mean she'd live while he died.

He wiggled the cork stopper, pieces crumbling away. "Help me give this to her."

Sybil removed a pocketknife from the inside of her jacket and seconds later had cleared out the cork.

Harrison lifted it to Ellen's lips while Sybil gently propped Ellen up. As the liquid trickled into Ellen's mouth, she shifted as though she might be waking. But as soon as she swallowed the holy water, she released a deep, almost contented, sigh.

They laid her back, and Sybil straightened, stuffing her hands into her jean pockets.

"Many thanks, Sybil."

She nodded curtly. "Do you still need one more? For you?"

He shrugged. "You were lucky to find this. I doubt you'll find another."

"I can have another look."

"May as well crack on."

She was silent for a beat. "I admit I don't believe everything you claim about the holy water. But I do know it has some sort of power."

"As deluded and fabricated as everything may sound, I appreciate your commitment to finding Ellen."

"I'm just glad we got to her in time."

"You've done excellent work and labored tirelessly on this case. I plan to make sure everyone knows."

"Not necessary. I didn't do it for the recognition."

"Even so, you deserve a promotion and raise." Before she could protest, he continued. "No matter what happens to me, promise you'll do everything possible to keep Ellen safe from Dr. Lionel."

Sybil's gaze narrowed on him.

"Please?"

"I won't rest until we catch Dr. Lionel."

The tension eased from his shoulders. As much as he appreciated Arthur Creighton's brilliance in discovering the power of the holy water in curing disease, he was coming to the conclusion that the holy water was best left undisturbed.

While he couldn't deny the miracles he and Ellen had experienced, perhaps the truest miracle was that he was learning to be braver in loving. He'd been whole and healed, and he'd still held back. He couldn't do that anymore. He had to abandon caution, stop waiting for the perfect conditions, and go after love anyway.

Whatever the case, once Dr. Lionel was caught and jailed, hopefully all the talk of the ultimate cure and holy water would die away just as it had in the past. It was better that way.

After Sybil left, he watched Ellen's face, feeling suddenly tired. He started to push himself up and transfer to the bedside chair, but at a soft sigh from Ellen, he stopped. Her expression remained peaceful and unchanged. And suddenly all he wanted to do was lie down and spend his last hours on earth right by her side, so that the memory of her would be with him into eternity.

He lowered himself beside her, careful not to touch and waken her. He tried to keep his eyes open, but the moment his head hit the pillow, sleep claimed him.

~ 27 ~

ELLEN STIRRED AND STRETCHED, only to find arms tightening about her.

A strange panic coursed through her. After everything she'd experienced, what was happening now?

Her eyes flew open and connected with a solid chest clothed in a waistcoat and dress shirt.

Harrison. She released a breath. Somehow, Harrison had ended up in bed next to her.

She wasn't sure how that had happened, but she was securely buried underneath her covers, and he lay on top fully clothed. There was nothing indecent about their situation.

Her fear dissipated, and a delicious tremor wound through her.

She tilted back enough to see his face, his dear, dear face. The dark shadows under his eyes spoke of the toll the past few days had taken, and the creases in his forehead spoke of the worries that plagued him even in his rest.

Carefully, she extricated her arms from beneath the covers. A part of her urged her to get up, allow him to sleep. But another part of her protested wasting any more time. If they had so little left, she didn't want to squander a single second of being with him.

She started to lift her hand to his cheek but stopped. She was still wearing Marian's ring on the third finger of her left hand. Somehow it had stayed with her.

She stared at it, wonder expanding through her.

The slender golden band intricately engraved with leaves was proof she had seen Marian and Dad, that she hadn't just experienced a realistic, coma-induced dream. It silenced any doubts that she'd really crossed into the past.

She wiggled her finger. The smooth band was as real as any other ring she'd ever worn, the visible sign of her marriage to Harrison.

Maybe he hadn't expected their union to be permanent or their vows to carry over into the present. But the ring was all the confirmation she needed to know that their marriage had been binding throughout time, that she was his wife as much in the present as she'd been in the past.

She gently laid her hand against his cheek, the dark stubble rough and sensual. This man was her husband . . . and she didn't want to let him go.

But was it too late? They both needed another dose of holy water if they had any hope of surviving. What was the point in giving way to her feelings for him now that the end was so near? Why torture herself with what would never be?

She started to move away from him, then hesitated. No. That was the kind of thinking that had held her back before—accepting her fate too easily and denying herself the future, no matter which era she was in. Maybe it was finally time to stop letting fear hold her back in relationships and give herself freely to Harrison—even if only for a few days.

Was she brave enough to do so?

She let her fingers roam once more, tracing the strong line of his cheek to his chin. Courage. She had to have courage.

Before she could stop herself, she bent in and pressed a kiss to his jawline. One kiss was followed by two, then three, until she lost count as she left a soft trail. She stretched higher, arching into him and feeling the long length of him.

She could sense his wakening as fingers splayed at her back and as his breathing quickened.

Did she dare kiss him? Truly kiss him, not because they were pretending for someone else but to show him how much she cared about him?

She brushed her lips against his lightly, testing him. He'd admitted he loved her and had for years. But that didn't mean he felt the same way about their marriage as she did.

He rubbed his bristly cheek against hers, their chins brushing and then their noses. Maybe if she told him how she felt . . .

"Harrison—"

His mouth captured hers hungrily, putting an end to the teasing. He swept in as powerfully as he always did, the crushing intensity sending gusts of heat through her middle. The heat rushed to her limbs and to every part of her body, setting her on fire.

She slid her hands up his torso, letting her fingers dance across every ridge of his ribs until she found his heart. The pulse there was strong, hard, and steady.

"Harrison," she whispered, breaking their connection. "I'm not pretending today."

His breathing was labored against her lips.

"Actually, I don't think it ever was playacting," she whispered. "I was just too scared to admit it was real."

"It was never playacting for me either." He bent his head, and his lips made contact with her neck near her collarbone.

She dug her fingers into his shirt. His kisses were making her lose coherency. She had to say the rest of what she needed to before she lost the chance.

At the pressure of something between her hip and the bed, she reached down, and her fingers brushed against a small glass item. A bottle.

She broke away from him and discovered it was one of the green bottles she'd used for filling holy water from the leather flask. Except this one was a slightly different shape than the two she'd left in the vault for Harrison. Small enough to fit into the palm of a hand, it had a bulbous body that was somewhat misshapen with a long neck. It was one of the two she'd put into the leather pouch she'd given to her dad.

Extricating herself further, she pushed up.

Harrison didn't make a move to draw her back and instead stared at the bottle too. From the calmness of his demeanor, it was clear he wasn't surprised by the sight of it.

"Where did you find this?" She swished it. It was empty and the cork pieces sat in a pile on the bedside table.

He closed his eyes and pressed his lips together as if he didn't want to have the conversation. Then he sighed. "Sybil found the bottle in a cabinet inside Reider Castle."

"Just one?"

He nodded.

Ellen's heart sank. Had her dad or Nicholas left it behind? If so, why? A dozen scenarios raced through her mind. If Nicholas had wanted it for himself, he wouldn't have placed it in the cabinet. He would have taken it with him and hidden it someplace safer.

That meant maybe Dad had meant it for her. Somehow, he must have realized she had been injured or even died. And perhaps he'd suspected that the ancient cabinet survived the ages and hoped someone in the present would find the dose of the holy water to enable her to live.

But if he'd done so, why had he only left one when he'd known she would need two? Unless, of course, he'd only had one. Perhaps Dad had been mortally wounded, and Nicholas had used one of the bottles to revive him just as he'd vowed to do.

Regardless of her speculations, the bottle was here. And it was empty . . .

Again, she glanced from the cork pieces to the bottle and then to Harrison. He finally opened his eyes. The truth gleamed within the green depths. He'd given her the dose. And he'd left none for himself.

"We'll find more." She slipped off the other side of the bed, drawing a blanket around her nightgown. "We have to find more."

"Sybil's still looking."

Ellen's legs shook. She needed to go over to Reider Castle for herself and join in the search. Her heartbeat sped to a frantic pace, and she spun and crossed to the boudoir. Grabbing the closest sundress, she stepped back only to find Harrison blocking her way to the lavatory.

"I wanted you to have it." His voice, though gentle, was threaded with a plea that matched the one in his eyes. He wanted her to accept what he'd done and not fight it.

An ache swelled in her chest. He couldn't expect her not to do anything to save him. She ducked past him. "You shouldn't have given it to me without talking to me first."

"I knew you'd say no." He stalked after her.

"And you're right. You came out of your coma first and needed it sooner than me."

He grabbed her arm, stopping her before she could close herself away to change into her clothes. "I don't want you to race off, love."

"I won't stand back and let you die when there's a chance we could find more holy water and save you."

His dark brows furrowed with intensity. "There's a chance we won't. And then we'll have wasted the little time we have left. Someone very wise once told me she wanted to spend her final days relishing every second of every minute. And now I think I'd like to do the same."

She clutched the sundress, her throat burning with the need to weep. After all she'd gone through, the months of suffering from the effects of VHL now seemed like a distant past.

He released her suddenly and grasped at his chest.

"Harrison, what's wrong?"

He sucked in several sharp intakes. "My chest. It hurts."

As he slapped at his heart and struggled to draw in a breath, she fought not to panic. Marian had gone into cardiac arrest before she died. Was that happening to Harrison? Was she going to lose him now, just when she finally understood how much she wanted to be with him?

28

THE STEADY BEEP OF MONITORS didn't comfort Ellen the same way they normally did. Even if the aspirin and nitroglycerin had brought Harrison relief from the chest pain in the short term, the reality was that he was dying.

She perched on the edge of the bed next to him, struck by the irony that only hours earlier, she'd been the one languishing there.

Now his handsome face was pale, and even with the oxygen tube, his breathing was labored. He'd rested peacefully since the doctor had prescribed the heart medicine along with a mild sedative. But no matter how much she and the doctor worked to ease Harrison's pain with modern medicine, they couldn't prevent him from dying, not with his body deteriorating in the past.

Of course, Drake had been on the phone with all Harrison's contacts again, trying to track down another dose of the holy water. Now he paced in the corridor, and as he finished his call, he stopped in the doorway and shook his head, his face etched with frustration.

Her shoulders fell. Though everything within her urged her to get up and join the search for holy water, she grasped Harrison's hand more firmly. She didn't know how long he had left, perhaps only hours, and she wanted to be by his side.

Was this a time to accept the situation, or did she need to have the courage to change what she could? *Give me wisdom to know the difference*, she silently prayed.

She combed a strand of his hair back, taking in the familiar lines of his handsome face. She bent down and pressed a kiss against his forehead, letting her lips linger there.

She loved him.

There it was. The truth. She loved Harrison.

She'd tried to deny it, tried to run away from it. But even when she'd gone far into the past, she hadn't been able to escape her feelings for him. In fact, the truth had only become more visible when everything else had been stripped away.

She pulled back slightly only to have his hand slip up around her neck and draw her down. His eyes were open, and he was focused on her mouth.

"I'm sorry," she whispered. "I didn't mean to wake you—"

He lifted enough to silence her by capturing her lips in a kiss. It was a drowning kiss, one where she could easily sink into oblivion and never come up. But she forced herself to break away, to think about him and how fragile he was right now.

His hand at the back of her neck was surprisingly strong and didn't let her get too far. She wanted him to know she wasn't going anywhere. Not now. In fact, she had to tell him how she felt before it was too late. "Harrison, I love you."

He stilled, his breathing coming in short bursts.

"You've always been the one for me, Harrison. Always. And I should have told you so the day you brought me here to Chesterfield Park to die."

He studied her face as though testing the sincerity of her words. Didn't he believe her?

"I shouldn't have let my illness interfere, but I did. And I'm sorry. I'm sorry for pushing you away. If I could go to Saint Lucia again, I'd do it differently."

She fought back the tears at the memory of how much pain she'd caused him, but several squeezed loose anyway. She regretted she'd wasted so much time, time she could have spent loving this man. And now they had so little left.

"Don't cry, love." His voice was weak, and he used his thumb to dry her trail of tears.

"Oh Harrison. Please tell me you can forgive me."

"I can. And I do."

"That easily?"

"I'd do anything for you. Don't you know that by now?"

She nodded, more tears spilling over. He tried to brush them away and then struggled to sit.

"Rest, Harrison. Please." She pressed his shoulders, trying to force him back down.

He pushed up again and this time swung his legs over the edge of the bed. "I don't want to spend my last hours hooked up to machines." Before she could protest, he pulled out his oxygen tube.

"Harrison, you can't—" But even as she lifted the tube to reposition it, her dad's words rushed back: *In spite of the pain of losing your mother, I wouldn't give up a single second of what we had together.*

Harrison lowered himself to one knee in front of her, reached for her hand, and peered up at her, love radiating from his eyes. "When I spoke my marriage vows to you, I meant them with all my heart. Whether in the past or present, you're my wife, Ellen."

"Oh Harrison." Her heart welled with both joy and sorrow,

so much that the tears kept falling. She laid her hand against his cheek. "I meant my vows too."

"Even so, I want to do this right, since I didn't have the chance to do it before."

"Do what right?"

He reached for her hand and smiled. "Will you marry me? Today? Now?"

"In my heart, we're already married."

"I want our marriage to be official here in the present, so there's no question in anyone's mind that you're my wife."

He didn't have to say the words, but she understood what he meant. He wanted to have a certificate and witnesses so that when he died he could leave her Chesterfield Park. "I don't care about anything but you. You're all I want."

His eyes brightened, and his smile inched higher.

Somehow, her response had made him happy. Was it possible she could bring him even more joy during his last hours on earth? If making their marriage official would do that, how could she deny him?

She caressed his cheek. "Yes."

"Yes?"

"Yes, I'll marry you again, Harrison. Today. Now."

* ● *

With each winding stair up the tower, Harrison's lungs burned.

"We can have the wedding anywhere, Harrison." Ellen ascended next to him, her arm linked in his. The nurse, Drake, and the priest followed behind.

He couldn't get out a response past his breathlessness. Maybe they should have had the ceremony in the sitting room or some-place easier for him to navigate. But he couldn't think of a more romantic spot than the tower—especially since that was one of the first spots they'd stood together side by side the morning after their healings.

As they reached the top and stepped out, Ellen gasped. The sky with the setting sun was streaked with a garden of colors to rival the tulips below. "Oh Harrison, it's amazing."

He watched Ellen's face, soaking in her beauty, a sense of wonder filling him. How was it possible that this stunning woman loved and wanted him? He wouldn't let himself think about the fact that they'd waited until much too late. Instead, he was determined to live the remainder of his life with no regrets. It was how he should have lived all along. But better to recognize his failure too late than not at all.

She slipped her arm around him, and he drew her into the crook of his body. For a long moment, they stood silently as the sky put on a display that no wedding planner could ever replicate.

His breathing began to even, and he managed to drag in the damp May air filled yet with the sweetness of Chesterfield Park's gardens. "We watched the rising sun together here. And now it's only fitting we should watch it set here too."

When her blue eyes peered up at him with a keen sadness, he wished he could take back his words. "What I meant is that this is the fitting place for us to seal our vows."

"I agree." She gazed out again, blinking back tears. She smiled too brightly and then turned to face him. "I'm ready."

The priest took his place in front of them. The older gentleman had come within the hour, wearing his clerical collar as well as a silver cross on a long chain.

The nurse remained by the doorway, but Drake stood at Harrison's side. The butler was as stoic as always, his chalky skin pale in contrast to his dark suit. But his eyes were warm and approving. With Drake's help, Harrison had groomed and donned one of his best suits.

Ellen had changed into an elegant, form-fitting gown that was the same shade of sky blue as her eyes. With Marian's simple strand of pearls and her hair coiled up into a fashionable twist, she was as lovely as if she'd spent hours getting ready for their wedding rather than a mere thirty minutes.

As the priest began the wedding ceremony, Harrison held Ellen's gaze, seeing in her eyes the memory of their wedding only a few nights ago. Although he'd offered to give her another wedding ring from among his family heirlooms, she wanted to keep Marian's.

Within minutes, the priest concluded the ceremony. "In the presence of God and these witnesses, Harrison and Ellen have given their consent and made their marriage vows to each other. They have declared their marriage by the joining of hands and by the giving and receiving of a ring. I therefore proclaim that they are husband and wife."

Together they placed their hands onto the priest's Book of Common Prayer, and he joined their right hands. "Those whom God has joined, let no one put asunder."

At the final pronouncement, tension eased from Harrison's shoulders, a tension he hadn't known was there. Their marriage was legal and binding. Now upon his death, Ellen would have everything that belonged to him. Not that she needed it. She already had a fortune of her own. Even so, he could think of no one else he wanted to inherit all his earthly goods.

The priest closed his book and smiled at them. "Now Lord Burlington, you may kiss your bride."

Ellen lifted her face to him, and he was amazed all over again that she'd declared her love for him. "This was the part of our first wedding ceremony that I missed."

Surprise and delight ricocheted through him. "You did?"

She nodded with a shy smile.

"Then let's rectify that right now." He wrapped his arms around her, drew her closer, and dipped in, letting his lips fuse with hers. Even as weak as he was, the kiss kindled fire in his blood, combusting desire deep inside. Tonight might possibly be his last night on earth. And he couldn't think of a better way to spend it than with his beautiful bride.

He had half a mind to pick her up and carry her down to his bed. But his manners as a nobleman held him in good stead. He needed to thank the priest for coming on such short notice.

With a final kiss, sealing the promise of more to come, he drew back, breathless again, but with happiness spilling through him.

Her eyes reflected her joy but also a sorrow that she was trying so desperately to contain. And he loved her all the more for it.

After they completed the paperwork, Drake escorted the nurse and priest away. Once Harrison was alone with Ellen, he drew her close again. "I love you, Lady Burlington." He kissed the top of her head.

She started to meld into him but then stiffened. Her attention riveted to a section of the tower floor awash with the last light of the setting sun. She wriggled away from him and approached the spot almost reverently.

He followed. "What is it?"

She knelt and brushed her hand across one of the stones. "Has this engraving of the tree always been in this stone?"

"I rarely come up here." He had only been up a time or two when Drake had carried him as a young boy. "But as far as I know, it has been there."

Ellen traced the simple outline of the tree. "The day my dad and I were here together, he said that if all else failed, he would consider hiding holy water in the tower since it's one of the original structures of Chesterfield Park that weathered time."

Harrison bent to take a closer look at the stone and markings.

"Do you think your dad had the tree engraved to mark another hiding place?"

Ellen glanced up, her eyes alight with hope. "It's a tree. Why else would there be an engraving of a tree?"

Wariness settled over Harrison. She was desperate enough to hope in anything. And he didn't want her hopes to rise only to have them crash. But what else could he do except figure out a way to pry the stone loose?

He phoned Drake to bring tools. And as they waited, they dug at it with their fingers but to no avail. When Drake returned with a knife, chisel, hammer, and several other items, they began to chip away. Drake mentioned having seen another engraving like it in a hearth stone in one of the guest rooms that was seldom used.

Harrison was surprised when the stone began to loosen after just a few minutes. Ellen's face reflected her easy optimism. But he couldn't allow himself to anticipate anything. It would be too cruel to give way to the possibility he might get more than one night with his wife.

As the stone shifted, Ellen dug harder, until at last Drake used the chisel as a lever to lift the stone out of its place. It scraped and screeched as it came free, clearly not having been moved in hundreds of years.

Drake grunted as he hefted it aside, revealing a space underneath.

Ellen peered into the hole and then quickly covered her mouth with both hands, her eyes rounding.

Harrison's mouth went dry, and he couldn't bear to look. "What is it?"

She met his gaze. Tears spilled over and began to run down her cheeks. She reached inside and removed a bottle crafted out of the same green glass that she'd used for the other holy water.

"Dad did this." She choked the words out even as she cried

more tears and laughed at the same time. "Do you know what this means?"

Harrison sat back on his heels, suddenly so overwhelmed with relief that he couldn't speak.

"It means Dad made it out of Reider Castle back to Chesterfield Park."

Drake gently took the bottle from Ellen and began to pry at the cork.

"The rescue worked, Harrison." She smiled through glossy eyes. "Dad lived."

The cork began to crumble. Drake made quick work of clearing out the pieces and then handed the bottle to Harrison, his eyes beseeching him to drink it right away. Harrison lifted a hand to take it from the faithful servant but found he was shaking too much.

Ellen intercepted the container. "I couldn't ask for a better wedding present from my dad than this."

Had Arthur placed the holy water here as a part of his plan to divide and disperse the water? Maybe he'd hidden bottles in many places and marked the spots with the tree engraving.

Ellen's smile amidst her tears radiated joy. "Dad saved the life of the man I love."

"Come on now, my lord," Drake said more urgently. "Let's get on with it."

Harrison placed his hand over Ellen's, and together they tipped the glass bottle. Harrison drank the liquid, and the warmth of the healing water spiraled through his veins and throughout his body. The journey they'd taken hadn't been easy. But he'd learned that hardships truly were the pathway to peace. And love.

Whatever might lie ahead, they wouldn't walk around the hardships and aim only for the wellsprings. Instead, they'd walk hand in hand through the difficulties, growing stronger together.

29

"ARE YOU READY, LOVE?" Harrison held out his hand. In a crisp suit with a waistcoat and tie, he looked suave and darkly handsome and irresistible.

Ellen slipped her fingers in his and crossed the grand entryway of Chesterfield Park.

A private security guard stood by the portico door. At Harrison's nod, the guard spoke into a wireless mic to more men positioned outside. There was a staff of bodyguards on duty twenty-four hours a day, and Ellen was grateful for the extra protection. With Dr. Lionel still on the loose and as more information about his connections with terrorists surfaced, Ellen feared they hadn't seen the last of him.

Now, they had to attempt to explain to the curious public how they'd both been healed of lifelong illnesses. She and Harrison had talked at length about the approach to take, whether to tell the truth about the holy water and its curative properties or whether to attribute the cure to her dad's research in a more generic fashion, leaving out any mention of holy water.

Finally they decided the world wasn't ready—and perhaps never would be—for the truth about the Tree of Life and the holy water. Harrison was afraid people on every continent would begin searching for the ultimate cure, that more old flasks and bottles containing the water would be found, or perhaps even other unknown water sources would be tapped for remnants.

The thought of holy water in the hands of irresponsible people who didn't know the repercussions chilled Ellen just as much as it did Harrison. They knew too well the risks and had decided the best option was for people not to know anything about it.

They'd concluded that the Tree of Life needed a guardian angel, just like it had from the beginning and throughout time. Perhaps Marian and Dad had gone back to be guardians during a time when the life-giving water had surfaced. Now she and Harrison needed to be guardians in their generation of any water that might surface again.

Whatever the case, Harrison had decided to put forth a statement claiming that while they'd benefited from Arthur Creighton's research into a powerful drug, it had also contributed to Arthur's and Marian's deaths. The risks of the drug were too great, the danger too imminent, thus all research had been destroyed.

Harrison stopped several feet away from the closed door. "You know you don't need to go out there. I can handle it for us."

"As much as I've loved spending every minute of the past two days here with you, I realize we can't stay secluded forever."

He leaned into her, his long, lean torso pressing against her body and igniting her. "We might not be able to stay secluded, but our honeymoon is far from over." His breath and lips touched her ear, fanning the smoldering flame inside.

Her chest tightened with a desire for him that she was learning was insatiable. No matter how much they were together, she never tired of lying in his arms and kissing him.

"How long?" Her voice came out embarrassingly breathless.

"How long is what?" He spoke as he made a trail of kisses across her jaw.

"Is our honeymoon?"

"Forever."

She wound her arms around him until she was crushed in his arms, where she wanted to be. His lips sought hers eagerly with the kind of kiss that made her forget about all their troubles and reminded her why the pain had been worth it. If she hadn't gone through it all, she wouldn't have shed the fears holding her back from the one thing that truly mattered—a deep relationship with someone she loved.

Harrison had assured her he would have children and was willing to be an older parent for her sake. But she'd explained that she never wanted to have any children of her own and risk passing on VHL. Although they'd finally gotten the genetic tests back that showed her body was clear of the gene anomaly, she still didn't want to take any chances. She was perfectly content to continue with her charities, especially Serenity House.

At the clearing of a throat of one of the bodyguards behind them, Ellen broke away from Harrison at the same time that he released her, although reluctantly. His breath bathed her forehead, and his healthy heartbeat thudded in the space between them.

After almost losing him, she was grateful for every second of the extra time God had given them. "I'm sorry I wasted so much time."

He caressed her back. "Let's have no more regrets between us. Without our past and everything that's happened, we wouldn't be where we are today."

"Even so, I want to make up for the lost time and the hurt I caused you. I want to spend the rest of my life making you happy."

"You already make me happy."

She smiled up at him innocently. "So, are you saying there's nothing I can do to make you any happier?"

The green of his eyes darkened. "Well, there might be one thing."

Her heart quavered in anticipation of his next words.

He lifted a hand to her cheek and drew a light line from her ear to her lips. "Let me kiss you and never stop." His voice was husky.

She pressed into him, needing and wanting only him. He dropped his mouth to hers and at the same time wrapped his arms around her and swept her into his embrace, bringing her home to exactly where she belonged.

• ● •

The statement to the waiting press outside the gates of Chesterfield Park took less than a minute amidst the flurry of reporters and flashes of cameras. Harrison didn't stop to answer the dozens of shouted questions. Instead, he'd hurried her into the waiting Bentley, and they'd sped away. Bojing drove them to the hospital, with only one detour along the way to pick up a strawberry shake.

As they pulled up to the Kent and Canterbury Hospital entrance, more news media waited outside while a team of doctors and specialists greeted them. Harrison drew Ellen closer into the crook of his body, and somehow she knew that side by side, they could face anything the future might bring them.

They followed the medical professionals to the critical care unit, and Dr. Li was already waiting in the private room they'd arranged for the procedure. Mr. and Mrs. Ansley stood beside Josie's bed, holding Josie's hands, their expressions hopeful, even excited.

"There's my girl." Ellen broke away from Harrison and rushed over to Josie, frail and fragile in the hospital bed.

A smile lit up Josie's face, one that told Ellen the little girl was aware of her presence and remembered her.

"Guess what I have for you, sweetheart?" Ellen brushed her hand across the girl's forehead, combing back the silky blond curls.

"My unicorn?"

Josie's eagerness brought a round of laughter from the others in the room, and Ellen joined in.

Josie tried to sit up, and one of the nurses began to raise the head of the bed. After the past days of being near to death, Josie was weak and lethargic. But thankfully she'd lived.

"The unicorn ride will be waiting for you once you come home from the hospital." Ellen lifted the strawberry shake, the straw already inserted. "But for today, I've brought you a strawberry shake."

"Really?" Josie's eyes widened.

"Really. And even though you're not supposed to have anything right now, Dr. Li is making an exception for you. Because you're so special."

Josie smiled again. And Ellen lifted the straw to the girl's lips.

Josie's body was prepped and ready to go. And while Dr. Li hadn't necessarily wanted to wait for Josie to have a sip of her strawberry shake before administering the experimental gene therapy drug he'd worked on for the past year, he hadn't been able to deny Ellen's request, especially since she had contributed so much to the cause. In fact, she and Harrison had made numerous phone calls over the past couple of days and were instrumental in finally clearing the way through all the regulations.

"Go on and have a few sips," Ellen gently encouraged the child.

Josie nodded and then took a long draw on the straw.

"Be courageous, sweetheart," Ellen bent in and whispered. "Be courageous."

Ellen met Harrison's gaze across the room where he still stood by the door, chatting with several other doctors. His warm eyes assured her that they'd done all they could. The stone hiding place with the tree symbol in the guest room had been empty of any bottles. Even though they hadn't found holy water for Josie, they'd come to a place of understanding and acceptance. Sometimes miracles happened in ways they couldn't explain. But most of the time, miracles occurred because of the people who persevered and worked hard to make them happen.

As the pink of the shake began to snake up the straw and filled Josie's mouth, Ellen pressed a kiss against the little girl's head.

Josie swallowed, leaned back, and closed her eyes. In the next instant, she was asleep.

Ellen pulled the shake away, caressed the child's cheek, and then straightened. "Looks like all of the excitement has tired her out."

Mr. and Mrs. Ansley nodded their agreement. "We can't thank you enough for all you've done."

"It's the least I could do." Even if she couldn't bring about physical healing, she had so much more she could do for those with terminal illnesses, especially in helping them not to just accept their fate but to have courage to live out their remaining days with purpose, especially in loving the people God had placed in their lives.

As the team of medical professionals closed in to begin the procedure, Ellen passed the remaining shake to Mrs. Ansley to refrigerate for later and then crossed to Harrison.

He held out his hand, his eyes radiating with love. "Ready?"

She nodded. She was ready to spend the rest of her life, however long that might be, with the man she loved, making the most of the time God gave them.

Jody Hedlund (www.jodyhedlund.com) is the bestselling author of over 30 historical novels for both adults and teens and is the winner of numerous awards, including the Christy, Carol, and Christian Book Awards. Jody lives in Michigan with her husband, busy family, and five spoiled cats. She loves to imagine that she really can visit the past, although she's yet to accomplish the feat, except via the many books she reads.

Go Back to the Beginning of the
Waters of Time Series

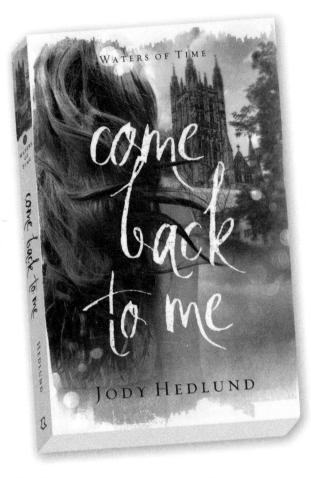

Scientist Marian Creighton was skeptical of her father's lifelong research of ancient holy water—until she ingests some of it and finds herself transported back to the Middle Ages. With the help of an emotionally wounded nobleman, can she make her way back home? Or will she be trapped in the past forever?

Connect with
JODY

Find Jody online at
JodyHedlund.com
to sign up for her newsletter and keep up
to date on book releases and events.

Follow Jody on social media at

 JodyHedlund   AuthorJodyHedlund   ⊙ JodyHedlund